SHOCK
WARNING

SHOCK WARNING

MICHAEL WALSH

PINNACLE BOOKS
Kensington Publishing Corp.
www.kensingtonbooks.com

PINNACLE BOOKS are published by

Kensington Publishing Corp.
119 West 40th Street
New York, NY 10018

All Kensington titles, imprints, and distributed lines are available at special quantity discounts for bulk purchases for sales promotions, premiums, fund-raising, educational, or institutional use.

Special book excerpts or customized printings can also be created to fit specific needs. For details, write or phone the office of the Kensington special sales manager: Kensington Publishing Corp., 119 West 40th Street, New York, NY 10018, attn: Special Sales Department; phone 1-800-221-2647.

PINNACLE BOOKS and the Pinnacle logo are Reg. U.S. Pat. & TM Off.

ISBN-13: 978-0-7860-2412-4
ISBN-10: 0-7860-2412-7

First printing: October 2011

10 9 8 7 6 5 4 3 2 1

Printed in the United States of America

For Greg Clary

Adapt yourself to the place where your lot has been cast, and show true love to the fellow mortals with whom destiny has surrounded you.

—MARCUS AURELIUS, *Meditations*

PROLOGUE

New York City

"Department of nuclear medicine," said Celina S. Gomez into the telephone. Gomez was a technician in the radiology department at Mount Sinai Medical Center on the Upper East Side of Manhattan. A technician was nowhere near as prestigious as being a doctor or a nurse, but for a girl who had worked her way across town and down eighty blocks from Little Santo Domingo on the West Side, it was good enough.

The *S* stood for Selena. Her mother had been such a fan of the late pop singer that she had, in effect, named her twice. "Just like New York, New York," *mamacita* used to tell her. "The town so nice they named it twice." Celina didn't want anybody calling her Celina Selena, so she kept her middle name a closely guarded secret, but she enjoyed using her middle initial in honor of her mother and because it was cool.

If only mama could see her now. But mama couldn't, because she had been killed six years ago, when she caught a stray bullet as she was on her way to the *supermercado* over on Broadway. Celina had still been in high school then, a senior at Mother Cabrini in Washington Heights, and was on a day trip to The Cloisters in nearby Fort Tryon Park when she heard the news. The easy thing would have been to drop out of school at that point and get pregnant, like many of the girls she knew, but she stuck with it, buried her mother, and went to King's College in Brooklyn.

She'd made the right choice, because now here she was, living on the Upper East Side, in what the gringos used to call the little girls' neighborhood—safe, boring, secure. She could walk to her apartment over on First Avenue, maybe even hit one or two of the bars on Second on the way home to her walkup, where she paid eighteen hundred dollars a month for the privilege of living with her cat.

"I would like to speak to Saleh," said a man's insistent voice at the other end of the wire. She'd heard that expression "the wire" from one of the older women on the staff, and loved its retro sound. It was a throwback to the days when phones really were connected with wires—not like today, when cell phones and smartphones could give you brain cancer if you weren't careful. Celina knew enough to stay away from as much unnecessary radiation as possible. In her line of work, she was exposed to it every day, to gamma radiation mostly, injected into heart patients to chart the blood flow through their damaged or diseased organs. She felt sorry for them, mostly middle-aged men who had suddenly realized they no longer had a shot at playing shortstop for the Yankees, or dating girls in their twenties, or a host of other fantasies that time had just disabused them of.

"I'm sorry, there's no Dr. Saleh in this department," she replied without even looking at the directory. Celina knew everybody on the staff—not just in radiology, but pretty much the entire medical staff. She didn't intend to stay a technician all her life, so she spent every spare waking moment studying the workings of the hospital, learning the names of all the doctors and nurses and even their faces whenever possible. How else was she ever going to be like them if she didn't know them?

"Are you quite sure?" said the voice. "No Saleh?"

In a city of a million accents, this one stood out. In addition to a near-photographic memory, Celina had an outstanding ear for accents and dialects. New York, Boston, Southern, standard American, Long Island, Puerto Rican, Nyurican, Spanish Harlem, Jamaican, Haitian, Central American, Mexican, Canadian, British, Scottish, Irish, Australian, New Zealand, South African, Japanese, Chinese, subcontinental Hindu/Muslim, Atlantic Avenue Arabic, and whatever. This one was "whatever." She had to find out more.

She glanced at the phone's display screen—no ID. Even when calls went through the main switchboard, the system generally preserved caller ID. Whoever had called this way, he didn't want to be known. She went on alert. "Can you hold a moment, sir?" she said. She pressed the hold button and collected her thoughts.

Since 9/11, all hospitals in New York City, and especially those in Manhattan, had instituted heightened security procedures. For hospitals were a terrorist's dream, a veritable one-stop shopping depot for all manner of deadly things. It was ironic that a place devoted to healing the sick and saving lives should also be a potential source of destruction, but there you were. Why, right here in radiology, there was probably enough radioactive waste to fuel a small dirty bomb.

She got back on the line. "I'm sorry, sir, but I can't seem to find anyone on the medical staff by that name."

"Are you sure you know how to spell it?" came the voice. "S-A-L-E-H. Aslan Saleh."

"What kind of name is that, sir?" she inquired.

"An American name." The tone had turned resentful. "What do you think?"

"Of course it is. I meant, where does it come from? Sorry if I'm being nosy, but it's kind of a hobby of mine. Names, cultures, languages . . . accents. You know the old saying: 'Nothing human is foreign to me.' "

"It's Arabic," said the man. "Yemeni, I believe. Maybe Palestinian. Lebanese. Whatever."

Whatever. "Well, I'll certainly be happy to give Dr. Saleh a message for you. Can you please give me your name and telephone number?"

A short pause. Then: "Of course. My number is . . . wait a moment. I want to make sure I have the right place."

Celina smiled. "Of course." She could hear the man rummaging through some papers.

"I'm terribly sorry," he said, coming back on the line. "I seem to have made an error."

"That's quite all right, sir. Now, if you will just give me your name and number . . ."

"I don't know how I could have been such a fool. This is the New York City Police Department, isn't it? The Counter-Terrorism Unit?"

"No, sir, this is Mount Sinai Medical Center Radiology, Department of Nuclear Medicine." This wasn't good. Nobody made a mistake like this, unless they wanted to. But what could she do about it? Mr. Wald was due to arrive in five minutes for his stress test, and the last time she saw him, he didn't look so good.

"Yes," said the voice. "It is, isn't it?" The voice was cold now, ice cold, its temperature having dropped a hundred degrees in an instant. "So listen to me carefully, Celina S. Gomez. . . ."

Her blood froze. How did he know her name?

"I want you to get a message to Detective Aslan Saleh at the NYPD. Office of Counter-Terrorism. Are you listening to me? Are you writing this down?"

"Yes, sir. I am." She was scared but excited. This was like one of those episodes of *Law & Order* she liked to watch on TV, except that she was in it. If only Mama could see her now . . .

"I've already spelt the name for you"—*spelt,* he said, not *spelled*—"so I expect you to get it right. His friends call him Lannie. So please tell Lannie that he has an appointment at Mount Sinai Hospital in three days' time in the Department of Nuclear Medicine. It is quite urgent. In fact, tell him it is a matter of life and death."

Celina scanned the appointments book for three days from now. Nothing. "Life and death," she repeated. "How am I supposed to find this Detective Saleh?"

A longer pause this time. "That," said the voice, "is your problem. Just give him the following message, please."

"And who may I say is calling?"

"You may not. Now take this down: 'We are discovered. Save yourself.' Do you have that? Repeat, please."

" 'We are discovered. Save yourself.' May I ask—"

"You may not. He'll know what it means."

"Will he?" She was listening as hard as she could, soaking in every syllable, every nuance, every breath. There was something about the voice that gave her a chill. Something she couldn't place. Something evil that this way came.

She would get it. She would get him. From now on, it was a point of pride.

"Can you repeat that for me, please? I want to make sure I have it just right."

Listen.

Listen hard.

Listen like your life depends on it.

What an idiot she was! Why hadn't she thought of this before? She switched on the recording device that came as part of the new phone system.

He was still there. She knew it. She could, just barely, hear him breathing.

He spoke, but this time the words came out in a rush and she didn't understand them at all. Some foreign language, Arabic, Hebrew . . . she couldn't tell.

"I'm sorry, sir," she said, but he was gone.

CHAPTER ONE

Echo Park, Los Angeles

Ghosts everywhere. Ghosts all around, ghosts of the past and ghosts yet to come. Ghosts looming through the fog, reaching out to him, some beseeching and pleading, some clawing and snarling. Vengeful ghosts, sorrowful ghosts. Ghosts of those whom he had once loved and ghosts whom he still hated. The ghosts of his mother, who died protecting him, and of his father, who died fighting back. The ghosts of Milverton, his back broken, and of Raymond, that boy under the Central Park Reservoir, his eye gouged out and his head blown off.

All of them dead. And all dead because of him.

Was there vengeance in the next world? "Vengeance is mine," the Lord supposedly said, but if there was no God, then vengeance belonged to the shades, souls existing along the great continuum of being and nonbeing, of something and nothing.

And, as every scientist knew, the greatest difference in the universe lay between zero and one. Everything else was commentary.

If the greatest distance between two points was not one and infinity but one and zero, then the shortest distance was between life and death. Until the lights go out, there is yet light—but in darkness there is only nothing.

He strained his eyes in the darkness. Not yet nothing; he could hear his own breath. Even if the points of light he could still see with his eyes closed were illusions, optical memories, random bits of electrical impulses shooting through his eyeballs, there was yet light. God created light with a command, and Lucifer, best-loved, was the Bringer of Light. The light was both friend and enemy; in darkness lay solace. Because something was more terrifying than nothing.

Not yet nothing: his heart was yet pounding, his new-found heart, his reborn heart, his breathing becoming shallower and more insistent. He clutched life as he dealt death.

And there she was, just beyond his grasp, as real as he was. Looking away, unable to see him or hear the sound of his voice, her gaze fixed on something distant, her dark hair cascading down her naked back, moved not by the wind but by a careless toss of her head, almost coquettish, as she gestured to one unseen.

Was she looking at him, perhaps in her own dream, her own vision, her own fantasy? Or was there another?

Close enough to touch her now, he reached for her—

—and she dissolved at his touch. Melted, not like a real woman should but as a dream woman does, filigreeing away in a shower of light, as if she had never really existed, merely a figment of his imagination, a succubus come to save him from his own private demons, not a real woman to console him in his own private hell.

"Maryam," he heard himself saying. Her name was an incantation to a god in whom he did not believe.

She could not hear him. Something was drowning him out. A sound, like the beating of the wings of a gigantic bird, the *thwack thwack thwack* of a helicopter's blades, like the roar of an approaching tornado. Like the gunning engine of an airplane, and him alone on the Midwestern plain, helpless, mystified, and alone, like George Kaplan or Roger Thornhill. Or, worse, like his namesake, T. R. Devlin, who put the woman he loved in needless, fatal peril, just to do his job, and risked everything to get her out.

He screamed—

—and sat bolt upright in his bed in the house in Echo Park. The traffic on Sunset, down the hill, was quiet at this hour, the Mexican restaurants closed, the Dodgers game at the nearby Stadium long over. Not even the sound of gang-related gunfire, which occasionally punctured the stillness of L.A. nights. The city was never this quiet, especially this close to downtown and the intersection of two great freeways, but at this moment he was all alone in the world. He could even hear the freight trains, passing through the central city like the ghosts of civilizations past.

But over everything was the beating of his hideous heart.

He rose and shook his head, trying to clear it of the ghosts who haunted him now, more than ever. But they would not go gently. . . .

He shook his head again, harder. A confidential op should never see ghosts. Seeing ghosts was a sign of weakness, or sentimentality, a sign of—if you were given to portents and runes—impending doom. Seeing ghosts was a sign of conscience. A sign of a heart. And a heart was the one thing he could not have. Not if he wanted to live.

A heart was no use in prison, especially a prison in which the lights were always turned off. In which you were not plunged into darkness, but in which you dwelled in darkness—the vast emptiness wherein the only sound was the voice of Lucifer, whispering that he could bring light that God Himself could not—would not. That he could salve the wounds, sever the irons bonds of superstition, and welcome you home.

"Maryam!" he cried.

A couple of blocks away, the spires of St. Andrew's, the Ukrainian Orthodox Church, caught the first motes of sunbeams, the gleam in the eye of God.

He was not alone.

He would save her, no matter where she was, no matter what it took.

No matter what it cost him, no matter whether it cost him his life.

For a life was a small price to pay, to banish the ghosts and see the light once more.

For, God help him, he had sent her into the monster's lair, a poisoned pawn, bearing the gift of NSA technology in the form of the secure computer he had given her. They both knew the chance she was taking, and they had both signed off on the operation. Consenting adults, and all that. It was only business.

But that didn't make him feel like less of a heel.

He stepped into the shower and let the scalding water play over him. Water was a precious commodity in Los Angeles. He didn't care. He didn't care about anything—not about the ghosts, not about himself, not about anything. He cared nothing for the whole fucking lot of them. He only cared about her.

In the distance, the secure phone. Only three people on earth had that number, all of them on a need-to-know basis. Even more important, on a need-to-call basis. Since the events in New York and their aftermath, there had been little to know, and even less to call. The last phone call, the one from his stepfather, had said it all:

Stand down, for your own safety. Branch 4 will go forward without you. Keep your head down, stay out of sight, and, whatever you do, do not try to find her.

From this moment forward, she is dead to you, dead to us. While she may yet still live, her death is merely a formality of the future, an i to be dotted, a t to eventually be crossed, and crossed off. If you're lucky, your photo and hers will go on the Wall of Shame in Fort Meade. If not . . . then you already have all the immortality you are ever going to need.

The phone, more insistent. The relays kicked in, routing the call through a series of secure servers, to determine the real number and the actual location from which the call was being made. Anybody could fake anything these days, especially the National Security Agency, but he knew them—because he *was* them. At least, he had been, for as long as he could remember.

It must be some sort of a joke. After what had happened, why would anyone call? Why would Seelye call him, or the new secretary of defense—or, even more unthinkable, the President of the United States? Skorzeny had escaped again, Maryam had defected to her native country, and everything he had done for his country, all the bodies he had left in his lethal wake, amounted to nothing.

Most likely, they had burned him, as they always said they would. It was the code of Branch 4, that once an op was burned he or she was no better than dead, and it was only a matter of time before the killer announced himself, two .22s in the back of the head, just like the mafia but more lethal.

It was always your friend, and never your enemy, because what worse enemy could a man in his line of work have than a friend?

This line was designed so that, if the incoming call passed all the security checks, the ring would continue to loop until it was answered. It didn't matter that the person on the other end of the line would have rung off; the instant he picked up the secure instrument, he would automatically be connected, via a series of secure cutouts, with the person who had called. That way, the security checks ran in both directions, and both parties could be sure they really were speaking to each other.

He picked up the line and waited. No beeps and blips, just utter silence . . . until, finally, a voice:

"Is that you?"

"Who else?"

"You're wanted."

"Bullshit. Try to kill me and you're in a world of hurt. I know where all the bodies are buried."

"You should. You put most of them there."

"And there's at least three more to go if you fuck with me."

"This is supposed to be a friendly call."

"Then start acting like it."

"Okay, I have three words for you."

"They'd better be good. Because if they're not, I have three words for you."

"Skorzeny. Maryam. Devlin."

For a moment, he had nothing to say. "Have I got your attention now?" said the voice, the voice he knew so well.

"Where?"

The answer surprised him. "The La Brea Tar Pits, tomorrow, one o'clock . . . not in them, don't worry. Look for the wooly mammoth and await your contact."

"Does he come armed or unarmed?"

"He's a she. Jacinta. Act like a gentlemen."

"And then what?"

"You'll know what to do."

"How? A miracle?"

The line went dead.

He stood there, still naked except for a towel around his waist, his hair dripping.

"Dad? Dad?"

Nothing. Emptiness, as usual.

He poured himself a short whiskey. It was a short step onto

the terrace. To the south, he had a panoramic view of down-town. Nobody cared that he wasn't wearing any clothes. This was L.A. Nobody wore clothes in L.A., not really, just cos-tumes.

The Bruckner symphony he'd been listening to was still playing. The Fourth, all horns and majesty and a slow death march and a vision of the afterlife and just enough harmonic wild cards to keep a listener on his toes as he contemplated the face of—

He raised his glass in a toast to the desert city by the ocean—water water everywhere and not a drop to drink—to Hollywood, and to the wide world beyond. The Hollywood Sign, from which poor Peg Entwhistle had thrown herself in revenge against its utter indifference, was behind him and off to his right, out of sight, which was where it belonged. Danny could see it from his house on Hobart Street in Los Feliz, could look up at it, just off to the west of the Griffith Park Observatory, the original rebel without a cause, white, gleaming, illuminated—a beacon in the L.A. darkness, reaching out to the heavens—redemption, if not quite salva-tion.

Not like the pagan Hollywood Sign, which appealed to the basest instincts of every kid who got off the bus, every hack screenwriter, every hooker-in-waiting, the waitrons of the past, present, and future: buy here, buy now, but buy, buy, buy.

If he had his way, the sign would not read HOLLYWOOD. Instead, it would read: FUCK YOU, SUCKER.

"Here's looking at you, kid," he said.

In the silence of the night he could say things like that. Because he knew that, after this drink, he had a job to do.

He was Devlin.

CHAPTER TWO

Tehran, Iran

The Grand Ayatollah paused and waited for the reaction from his subalterns. Like all great imams—and none was greater than he, certainly not those Sunni infidels in Cairo, no matter their exalted titles at Al-Azhar University. Unbelievers, all of them. As they—and the world—would soon discover.

He paused for a moment, collecting his thoughts, making sure they were in accordance with the sacred word of Allah, divinely revealed through his Prophet, Mohammed. He took a deep breath. How wonderful to have been freed of Western superstition—the blasphemy they called "science"—by revelation. Those years spent in England, at the London School of Economics—what a waste. How foolish had been his country and his countrymen, still in thrall to the throne of England, upon which, in just a few decades or, Allah (PBUH) willing, a few years, the new caliph would sit, resplendent in his glory and beckoning to the twelfth Imam, the Mahdi, the expected one, to deliver the world from iniquity and unbelief.

How close it all was.

"O Muslims," he began, his intonation stentorian, as befit his station. Another pause. He looked out upon the sea of humanity—all male—that faced him expectantly. Hanging on his every word. Watching him for signs and wonders. Never was he more conscious of his station, or of his sacred duty.

The Grand Ayatollah Ali Ahmed Hussein Mustafa Mohammed Fadlallah al-Sadiq said a silent prayer to Mohammed ibn al-Hasan al-Mahdi, still occulted at the bottom of his well in Qom. *Soon, my lord, soon will you come again, accompanied by Issa to unite the world of holy Muslims and benighted Christians against the Jews and infidels, ushering in the final era of peace and submission to Allah's holy will. Soon.*

"O Muslims," he began again. "For thirteen hundred years have we, the Faithful, awaited this holy day. For thirteen centuries, O my brothers, have we patiently and faithfully observed the strictures and commandments of the one true faith. Triumphant have we been, and oppressed by the lies of the Jews and infidels, who have taken from us the holy cities of al-Quds, of al-Andalus. We have patiently awaited the day of deliverance, the day on which even the rocks and the trees cry out to alert us to the presence of the Jew, and reveal to our holy warriors his infernal hiding place, that we might kill him, his women, and his children."

The crowd rose and cheered its approval. The Faithful could always be counted upon.

"Signs and portents were we promised by the Prophet and his holy Imams. And today I stand before you, Ali Ahmed Hussein Mustafa Mohammed Fadlallah al-Sadiq, to bring you the joyous news of fulfillment. O Muslims, I bring you the news of our Brother Arash Kohanloo, a glorious martyr to the sacred cause, who has struck a great blow against the Great Satan, the United States—such a blow as not even the

Great Atta and his fellow martyrs on that happy day of September 11, 2001, could have dreamed."

An enormous roar rumbled up from the crowd of the Faithful, here in Azadi Square, beneath the great tower of Freedom. Let the infidels of New York call their blasphemous tower, still rising after more than a decade, a sign of their surpassing impotence and of the immanence of the Twelfth Imam, call their pitiful attempt at reconstruction the Freedom Tower. Here was the heart of true freedom, brought by the Arabs a millennium and a half ago but since purged and purified of their desert savagery. The destruction of the Sassanid Empire and the abolition of the Zoroastrian religion was a small price to pay for enlightenment.

Thus spake Zarathustra? Only in the infidel lands. Here, only Allah spoke, and always spoke the truth, immutable and eternal and preserved forever in the Holy Qu'ran.

From here he could see the Alborz Mountains to the north, from what used to be called the Square of the Shahs, Shahyad, before the Revolution. How inspiring they were— almost as inspiring as the Holy City of Qom and the holy mosque of Jamkaran.

Soon.

"O Muslims," he began again. "Of signs and portents and wonders have we long spoken. Of the Occultation. Of the Expected One. For centuries have we endured and suffered under the false promises of men such as Mohammed Ahmad, who slew the infidel Gordon at Khartoum but left us with nothing but blood and desolation and disappointment while the Crusaders took our lands, even unto the blessed city of al-Quds, where the Jew sits, plotting against us.

"O Muslims—the time has come, for I bring you joyous news." He paused once again, for effect but more—for divine inspiration. He breathed the air in deeply, letting the breath of Allah wash over him, purging and cleansing him, revealing holy Truth to him as had been vouchsafed to only a handful of great men in the centuries since al-Hasan secluded his holy person in the sacred well.

Greatness. It felt good. It felt holy. It felt right.

"O Muslims. The Day of Deliverance is at hand."

He stopped and waited. Part of being a holy man was the sacred caesura, the final dramatic pause that signified to the Believers that Truth had been revealed, the sacred Promises had been made—Promises that must and would be kept. Because a holy man also knew that Promises unrealized, Promises unkept would be turned back on him with the force of a thousand suns—with the force of the infidel Jew Oppenheimer, who said "Now I am become Death, the destroyer of worlds," at the birth of Trinity.

So far away and yet so near. Deep in the heart of the Jew city of New York, at one of the Jew holy places for a people who had lost their faith. No longer would the Brothers bomb their so-called holy places, for not even the Jew believed in them anymore.

No, this time they would strike at the heart. Their great financial center the Believers had already destroyed. But that was not enough. Not enough for the Jew, who could always find money. Money could be lost and found again—they had been doing that for centuries, frustrating the Believers, who had forced them into *dhimmitude* in al-Andalus and made both them and the Christian dogs like it.

But health—life—was something else. They might die for money, but unlike the Believers, they would not die for Death.

The infidel West no longer believed in the afterlife. It was too cowardly, too solicitous of its own misery. But a Believer would willingly give up his life and the lives of his women and children, in furtherance of the Truth.

Which was, at last, in the person of Ali Ahmed Hussein Mustafa Mohammed Fadlallah al-Sadiq, so near to hand.

* * *

"O Muslims," he shouted. "The Messiah will not rise unless fear, great earthquakes, and sedition take place. The worst kind of humans will become leaders. Women will rid themselves of the hijab. Men will dress like women. Adultery will become common."

They responded with a roar. The signs and portents were all around. They knew that the time of the Coming was near. They were shaking their fists at the heavens, their ranks a sea of signs proclaiming DEATH TO THE GREAT SATAN, DEATH TO ISRAEL, DEATH TO AMERICA.

"O Muslims, on all sides we are afflicted with oppression and injustice, just as the holy Prophet, blessings and peace be upon him, so long ago predicted. And what did he say? That a nation from the east will rise . . ."

He was working the crowd now, letting their anger and their faith swell and build like a mighty wave.

". . . and prepare the way . . ."

"*Allahu akbar!*" shouted the crowd.

". . . prepare the way—for *the Coming of the Imam Mahdi!*"

He threw out his arms as if to embrace all of creation, slowly raising them upward.

As that moment, a blinding flash of light tore through the sky. It was like a lightning bolt hurtled from the hand of Allah, propelled to earth, there to form and coalesce into . . .

"O Muslims," shouted al-Sadiq, "so it is written, so shall it be done. After a thousand years—behold the Face!"

For a moment, as the vision became manifest, nobody said or did anything. And then, as one, the men prostrated themselves upon their prayer rugs in homage, and let out a deafening cry that shook the heavens:

"*Allahu akbar!*"
"*Allahu akbar!*"
"*Allahu akbar!*"

And then, once more as one, they rose, their faces purple with rage and yet suffused with a divine fire. Truly had they become holy warriors, *mujahideen*, ready for the final battle, which was now at hand.

The Face hung in the sky, the Face that none had ever looked upon, the Face that only blasphemers and infidels had ever imagined in their degenerate art . . . the Face now revealed at last to the Believers, the Face that would lead them to the final confrontation and to ultimate victory.

The Face of the Prophet, as he had been in life, and so was in life eternal.

"Allahu akbar!" he cried, and then dared to gaze once more upon its magnificence, forbidden no longer.

He glanced in the direction of the sacred well of Qom, the holy well in which dwelt Ali, the occulted Twelfth Imam, in hiding from the infidels and the crusaders all the Unbelievers since the year 941 in the Christian dog calendar. Deep within, he could already sense the stirrings. . . .

"Allahu akbar!!"

He heard the sound. And it was good.

At last, after more than a thousand years, He was coming.

And he, the Grand Ayatollah Ali Ahmed Hussein Mustafa Mohammed Fadlallah al-Sadiq, was the instrument of his holy wrath.

CHAPTER THREE

Central California—the San Joaquin Valley
near Coalinga

"Get ready for stinky!" shouted Danny Impellatieri as they drove north on the Golden State Freeway toward San Francisco. The Five, people called it now, just as they now called the Santa Monica Freeway the Ten. It was a sign of the decline, he decided. The end of the world, for all real Californians. In the old days, when he was growing up in Los Angeles, people knew the difference between the Santa Monica Freeway, heading west, and the San Bernardino Freeway, heading east. Between Highway 101, heading north through the Cahuenga Pass, and the Hollywood Freeway, after it split off in Valley Village and became Highway 170. Between the 110 that was the Pasadena Freeway and the 110 that was Harbor Freeway.

Between the days when California had names and today, when it had numbers. Between romance and quantification. The poetry had fled, to be replaced by the accountant's green eyeshades. And yet the state was broke, diminished, destroyed.

Progress.

Hope, Emma, and Rory had never been to San Francisco, and they were more than a little trepidatious. To all too many Americans, especially those in the Midwest, the City by the Bay was a combination of Sodom and Gomorrah without Lot's saving grace—as Herb Caen used to call it, Baghdad by the Bay, back in the day when Baghdad meant Sin City, not Saddam City. But to Danny, it was the city of DiMaggio and Lefty O'Doul; the city of Geary Street, not O'Farrell Street. The city of white-gloved women on their way to take in *Lucia di Lammermoor* at the Opera, of foghorns, and the military might of America, over in Oakland, or Vallejo, or on Treasure Island. To Danny, it was a city of what America used to be, not what America had become.

All of which made him today the bad guy. When the thought police, the PC Nazis, came, he would be one of the first to go—maybe to Alcatraz, maybe straight to the needle at San Q. How fast the country had changed. But somebody had to be the bad guy, and it might as well be him. After all, his wife, Diane, was dead. And with her had died so much, more than a year ago. . . .

He reached over and laid his hand, ever so gently, on the thigh of the woman sitting next him in the passenger seat. Not his dead wife but soon enough his new wife—the woman for whom he had released the past and embraced a new future that he had never envisioned, had never prepared or planned for, but which he joyously welcomed.

Was it wrong? Could you stay married to a ghost, or did the ghosts of the past demand that we, the living, go on living? Why wouldn't they? Didn't they want to go on living themselves? Had they died willingly? Didn't all God's creatures want to live? Wasn't that the first principle of life, of the life force? To go on living, even after death? If you fought against the dying of the light, if you fought against death, did not that bring you closer go God? Or was He just another myth, a fairy tale told to children by their elders to explain away the terrors of the night? Those things that exploded in the midst of the safest environments, that robbed you of your certainty just before they stole your life and the lives of others, randomly, capriciously, in the way of the Greek gods, or the Fates, or, God help us, the meaningless lares and penates.

Her name was Hope. Hope Gardner—and soon enough, if she accepted him, Impellatieri. And then where once there were two families with four parents and three children, there would now be one family with three children.

He was going to propose to her in San Francisco.

"I know this place on Clement Street." He pronounced it right, with the accent on the second syllable. In every city, there were test words, the ones that separated the natives from the locals. Cle-MENT Street was one of them. Like HOUSE-ton Street in New York. Not only was all politics local, so was pronunciation. And it was precisely in these interstices that spies and illegals and confidential ops got killed.

It was never the big things. It was never the cover stories. It was the little things, the details, that tripped you up, like DiMaggio's batting average. The Great DiMaggio, who accompanied Hemingway's Old Man on his fateful journey to the Sea, in spirit, if not in person. Simplicity, not complexity. The best cover story was 99.9 percent true. Everything important must be true except for the sliver of a lie that you told. Even to the ones you loved most.

And this was your life; to lie to everybody important to you, to everybody you loved, and to tell the truth, the whole truth and almost the entire truth, to those whom you despised, to those whom you loathed, to those whom you were about to kill.

After all they'd been through in the past year, it was a vacation well-deserved, and in his favorite city. No matter how nutty it was, San Francisco was still the best town in the country, a place devoted to wine, food, natural beauty, and the pursuit of sybaritic happiness. If Thomas Jefferson were alive, thought Danny, he'd live in San Francisco. Although maybe not George Washington . . .

"How stinky, Dad?" asked Jade, his daughter, from the back of the BMW. He could almost hear her mother's voice. Diane's voice. Diane, whom he'd loved so much that they had conceived the most wonderful daughter together. But she was gone now. And no matter how much you loved a woman, you could not make love to a ghost. You could not even love a ghost. All you could do was honor her memory and love the creature that allowed her to live on. . . .

"Real stinky, I hope!" shouted Rory, Hope's son and younger child. "Gross-out stinky! Barf-in-your-socks stinky! Girl gross-out stinky!"

Rory was sitting in the backseat, between his sister and Jade, still getting used to the idea that, horrors, he might have yet another sister in his future. Two against one was by his standards a fair fight on the playground, but the backseat of a car was an entirely different proposition. You couldn't hit a girl, not if you were a real man. Not if you were like his dead father, or like Danny, who had lost his wife in that terrorist attack in Los Angeles, or like the weird guy who had saved him from the bomb back in Edwardsville, Illinois, where they used to live before his dad got killed and his mom met Danny and . . .

"Okay, hold your noses, kids!" shouted Danny. "Here comes Cowschwitz."

Hope bit her tongue even as she held her nose. Everybody knew the term "Cowschwitz" was incredibly un-PC, even as most Californians who drove up and down I-5 between L.A. to San Francisco used it.

There would be cows as far as the eye could see on both sides of the freeway, that Rory knew. Cows for miles. Nothing but cows, mooing, lowing, farting, sending vast plumes of methane into the atmosphere, killing the ozone, destroying the climate, and alerting the aliens on Mars, or the Mother Ship or the planets orbiting Alpha Centauri or Betelgeuse to our malevolent presence. Nothing good could come out of Cowschwitz, thought Rory, except maybe some milk and some really good steaks.

The girls squealed. Rory expected shrieks from Emma, his real sister, but Jade, Danny's daughter and only child, was an altogether mysterious creature. She was four years younger than Emma, but she seemed older, wiser, more mature. Maybe that was because she had lost her mother and she was an only, whereas he and Emma had lost their dad, but at least they had each other. And their mom . . .

"Here we go!" said Danny, gunning it.

Instinctively, Rory threw his arms around his sister, Emma.

"Any moment now," said Hope, getting into the spirit of things. Rory glanced at his mother just as she tossed a smile at Danny. There was definitely something going on with those two. . . .

Jade clutched his hand. "Ready, Rory?" she asked. He nodded, then made like a deep-sea diver and held his nose as he went under.

"Pee-you!" shouted the kids, almost in unison.

Emma was the first to see it. She said nothing, but only let out a small gasp, as if the gap between expectation and reality were something that might be papered over in the next quarter mile. Rory, however, had long ago learned to interpret his sister's gasps—

"What is it?" he asked.

"Look," she said, pointing. And whispering.

At first, Rory only saw the vast expanse of the Central Valley in all its uncinematic nonsplendor. Miles and miles of nothing, flatlands, with invisible mountains to the east of them and to the west of them, and a vast ocean not far away.

Then Rory saw it—

A dead cow.

One, at first. And then two. And then ten. And then at least a hundred.

Dead, all dead.

"Mommy!" screamed Emma. "Make it stop. Make them go away!!"

The car hurtled northward at more than seventy-five miles an hour. The CHP never stopped anybody on this stretch of I-5. But still the dead cows would not stop. They kept on coming, in serried ranks collapsed in homage to a bovine Morpheus, lying on their sides as if sleeping, but their bellies already bloated with death, some of them already burst open, their guts spilling out, the stench rising. . . .

"Oh, my God," said Hope. "What . . . ?"

"I don't know," said Danny, already punching the keys of his secure iPhone. As per the agreed-upon code with Fort Meade, he hit a pound key in the middle of his home phone number, then a series of rotating digits depending on the day of the week minus four, which he knew would send the message directly over a secure channel to the one man who could possibly answer his question. To the one man whom he needed to alert, right now, before the situation got even further out of hand. To a man he'd never met, but whom he trusted beyond all others.

There was an overpass, just ahead. As they approached—

"Look!" shouted Rory. "Over there—people!"

Danny slammed on the brakes, screeching and skidding. A small group of people was clustered to one side of the overpass. He could see candles flickering as they huddled around something, looked at something—something that, to judge from their gazes, was on the concrete wall of one of the bridge's struts.

The car slowed and rolled to a stop. "Stay inside," Danny commanded, but it was Hope who relayed the order and gave it parental authority.

"Nobody move," she said. "Let Danny handle it."

He got out of the car, ready for anything.

A group of Mexicans, farmworkers, was huddled together, their faces illuminated, flickering in the light of scores of candles, all eyes turned toward an object on the wall . . . muttering to themselves in Spanish. No, not muttering— praying.

Dios te salve, María, llena eres de gracia, el Señor es contigo. Bendita tú eres entre todas las mujeres, y bendito es el fruto de tu vientre, Jesús. Santa María, Madre de Dios, ruega por nosotros, pecadores, ahora y en la hora de nuestra muerte. Amen

And then he saw it. "*Jesús, Maria,*" he gasped

CHAPTER FOUR

Los Angeles—the La Brea Tar Pits

The woolly mammoth's eyes were wide with fear, pleading with him to stretch out and pluck the ten-thousand-pound animal from the muck.

Fat chance: The great beast stood twelve feet tall at the shoulder, with a pair of enormous tusks that could shish-kebab an elephant. But, trapped in the seductive, bubbling asphalt, the dumb thing had no place to go but down. Look where ignorance, greed, and hunger got you.

"You're in the soup now, buddy," muttered the man known as Devlin. "Guess that makes two of us."

He wiped the sweat from his eyes and glanced around the grounds of what was technically called Hancock Park, although no Angeleno ever called it that. To everybody but foreign tourists reading a map, it was the La Brea Tar Pits, and always would be.

"Where are you?"

He was trying to spot the woman—Jacinta, she called herself, like the flower. Hyacinth. No Last Name. Nobody had a last name anymore. Or if they did, they never used it.

Just him. Devlin. Even though that wasn't his real name, it was good enough. It would have to be. It had been good enough most of his life.

It was always fun trying to match a voice with a face. The pretty ones always turned out to be ugly, and once in a while vice versa. The young, old. The hot, not.

As he scanned the crowd, Devlin could see the towers of Park La Brea across Sixth Street, feel the eternal traffic of Wilshire Boulevard at his back as his gaze roamed across the reeking expanse of major urban America's only open oil field. "Miracle Mile" if you wanted to go retro-civic-boosterish. He dabbed his brow with a pocket square and replaced his hat on his head. No place like the tar pits in October, if you liked heat. Good thing his suit could breathe, even if he couldn't.

It was the usual collection of tourists in shorts, baseball caps, and flip-flops. Devlin shuddered, as he often did in the presence of *boobus Americanus* in his colorful native costume. You could chart the decline of America strictly by the togs. Beachwear for all occasions. Earringed men and tattooed women. Ten-year-old girls tarted up like hookers and twelve-year-old boys duded out as gangstas. And more butt cracks than a plumbers' convention.

In this muck, the mammoth had plenty of company.

Devlin looked at the time on his cell phone display: one-ten in the pyem. In the old days he would have looked at his watch, but who needed watches anymore when you had instant, time-zone-sensitive, satellite-calibrated time on demand?

For the tenth time he read the signage in front of the sculpted monster: MAMMUTHUS COLUMBI. That was the dying creature's scientific name. It sounded like the kind of thing any kid with a halfway-decent command of pig latin could make up. Any kid in his day, that was; how many kids today spoke pig latin? Mammuthus my utt-bus . . .

One-eleven.

Should he light a cigarette? Only social renegades, rich people, undocumented aliens, and teenage girls smoked in L.A. anymore. Would a carelessly tossed match, caught just so by a breeze, ignite not only the tar pits but the entire latent Wilshire Boulevard oil fields, setting off a chain reaction from the still-functioning oil derrick on the grounds of Beverly Hills High School to La Cienega and Stocker Street, blowing all of central Los Angeles to kingdom come? It might be fun to find out.

One-twelve.

He never used to smoke until . . . until.

He lit up.

One-thirteen.

"Señor Harris?" Harris was the name he was using for this assignment. Like all his aliases, it was a name of a Jimmy Cagney character from one of his old movies, in this case, *Blonde Crazy*.

It was nice to be right, for a change. Skin: light brown. Age: somewhere between thirty and ninety. Height: five feet in heels on a footstool. Weight: don't ask, don't tell. Ethnicity: illegal-American.

Devlin turned his attention from the doomed behemoth to the small, supplicant woman. She was dressed all in black and wore an Angels baseball cap to ward off the broiling sun. "Jacinta?"

Jacinta thrust a dog-eared manila folder at him, as if that were reply enough.

"We have to know the truth."

A girl in low-rider jeans crossed his field of vision, her lower-back tattoo as visible as a circling buzzard in the desert. Wings of some kind, splayed across her small. No doubt her boyfriend enjoyed the view. Devlin wondered how the lad's replacement, a decade down the line, was going to feel about the anonymous Venice Boardwalk artist's handiwork when it was three times life size and fading even faster than the lady's desirability.

Pay attention. "We?"

"About what's happening. The padre—"

His secure PDA buzzed. In a time of iPhones, Androids, BlackBerrys, and everything else, he still reflexively called whichever device he was using at the moment his PDA. Personal digital assistant. It made him feel like he had a friend in this world, even if he didn't. "Excuse me for a moment, sister," he said, glancing down at the display.

Danny, although he never would call him that. His most trusted personal nondigital assistant, and yet they had never met face-to-face and had never exchanged any personal details. And yet he was, at this moment, the man whom Devlin felt closest to in the world. Still, it was not a secure location to answer.

He pressed the IGNORE button, although with this particular caller, the call would be sent to a special voice mail that would be turned immediately into a text message and displayed. "You were saying?"

"Padre Gonsalves. He wants to see you. About this." She opened the folder and out tumbled a set of Polaroids, caked with powdery debris.

"*Mira,*" she said. A command. He *mira*-ed.

The blazing midday L.A. sun wasn't helping. It glinted off the folder right back into his eyes; that was the downside of no clouds, ever, except when there were plenty of them. Living in Los Angeles for the past few months, Devlin more easily understood the parable of Paradise from the book of Genesis: feast or famine, my way or the highway. It never rained in California, but man did it ever pour.

He shifted position to catch the tentative shade of a palm tree. As he did, he came once again face-to-face with the statue of the dying *Mammuthus,* perpetually frozen in the awful realization that its next bite was also going to be its last meal. If it could think that far ahead.

The first picture: not as expected—

A smudge of white light. A starburst against the backdrop of an infinite, threatening darkness. His mind raced, free-associating as it always did when absorbing new information. Talk about Genesis: Let there be light. But was this the beginning, or the final flameout?

He caught himself. It was the overexposure of an aperture, the misfire of an amateur accidentally aiming a camera at the noonday California sun, although for what reason he couldn't guess. He was Rorschaching even before he had to.

"The door? You see it?"

He saw no such thing. Tijuana in a fair-weather cumulus; Megan Fox in a rain-threatening cumulonimbus. You saw what you wanted to see. And what you almost always saw was yourself. He moved on.

Variations on the Theme of the Smudge: blurs, splotches, gradually clearing. Moving from solar apogee toward the horizon. Dusty mountains, dustier deserts. Lancaster. Or worse, Barstow. Or worst, Needles. Middle of the Mojave. The most forlorn, desolate place on God's sometimes-green earth.

He kept leafing. More sky, more mountains. Some people. Then more people: huge crowds. Mostly Hispanic, by the look of them. A prizefight, a cockfight, a bullfight?

Ten pictures down so far nothing to see. It reminded him of television.

Then something—flowers. Desert plants, two feet high, with dull green stems and brilliant hungry yellow flowers that soaked up the sun as if it belonged exclusively to them alone.

"Marigolds," said Jacinta.

"So?"

"Her flowers." She motioned for him to keep looking.

The next one was a little different. Fairly well-registered, it showed the desert sky, the distant mountain range, and the desert floor.

"*Mira*." Jacinta, urging him, pointing at something. Her expectant expression was irresistible.

Devlin took a deep breath. In New York or Washington, you never had to be alone if you didn't want to, because there were always plenty of intimate strangers around. But in L.A., alone was the default mode; the whole town was one big party you weren't invited to. It was the only city in America, Devlin thought, where you could be truly, blissfully all by yourself.

If he hurried he could still catch lunch at Tom Bergin's over on Fairfax and bang back a couple of cold Smithwicks while he pondered how he was going to kill his evening before heading back to his place in Echo Park alone. He hadn't had anyone there since she was there, hadn't had anyone period. Because while she might have betrayed him, he would never betray her.

What was the first rule of a confidential op? Keep your cover story 99.9 percent true. And what was the second? Never trust anybody, never fall in love with anybody. He had broken all those rules, and now he was paying the price—in heartache and career ruination. Whether he would pay the ultimate price remained to be seen.

Maryam . . . where are you?

"Excuse me, señor?" asked Jacinta.

"Nothing," he said. "Please continue."

Who sent her? It might have been Seelye, trying to steer him some business since his disgrace. It might have been President Tyler, torturing him, or playing him; he used to think Tyler, running desperately for reelection now against a formidable female candidate who was leading him by double digits in the polls, was a blithering idiot, but the way he had played them all over the past two years had revealed the hand of the master.

Or it could be Emanuel Skorzeny. For his money, Door Number 3 was always where pure evil dwelled, and at this point he saw no reason to reassess his experience.

"*Mira*," insisted Jacinta, shaking the Polaroid photo at him.

What looked like a rainbow was circling the sun. A rainbow in the desert, where the temperature was at least one hundred and twenty degrees, and the humidity near zero. A place where there hadn't been any rain since the dinosaurs.

"You don't believe." A pudgy finger punched the Polaroid. "Look again. Closely."

And then he saw what she was talking about: a white, vertical rectangle blazing against the darkness. It might have been Kubrick's famous black monolith from *2001*, bleached out. A reverse image, like the Shroud of Turin, unnoticed until somebody had the bright idea to take a photo of it.

This is what she was looking at. This is what she wanted him to see.

"The doorway. You see now."

One more photo to go. As he looked, he shot a last glance at the condemned mammoth, still beseeching him to do something. But sometimes you just had to embrace the suck.

Lucky thirteen:

At first glance, it was nothing but a big white splotch, vaguely pear-shaped. It could be anything, including what it no doubt was, a photographic irregularity. Involuntarily, he looked up at the sky, but even through the polarized sunglasses, the only thing he could see was the endless Los Angeles blue. Not a cloud, not a shadow.

All right, embrace the suck:

If you half-closed your eyes, you could barely, just barely, convince yourself you were looking at—

"You see?"

He squinted and looked again.

Devlin took off his shades, blew on them, wiped them off with a handkerchief. This was beyond crazy, the kind of thing Mexican women saw in moldy tortillas or on the side of freeway overpasses. Crudely faked by a gangbanger with Photoshop and fobbed off on a bunch of superstitious *campesinos*.

He could see it. "When?" he asked.

"On the thirteenth of every month."

"Where?"

"In the desert. Near California City."

He didn't want to have to ask his next question, but as long as he was taking the job, it was his job to ask. "What do you want me to do?"

She shook her head. "Not me. *El padre* . . ."

"What does the padre want me to do?"

She looked at him as if he were simple: "He wants you to follow her."

"*Her?*"

Jacinta slipped the pictures back into the folder without answering. As she did, Devlin got a look at what he had assumed was simply schmutz inside the folder. Pale, pink . . .

She caught him looking. "Rose petals," she said, reaching inside and handing him one. "From the desert."

She pointed across Curson Street, toward a black Escalade with tinted windows, idling amid the fleet of yellow school buses. "Hurry," she said, rising. "We have so little time."

Devlin stopped. "Why? What is coming?"

She looked at him with fear in her eyes. "The Great Chastisement, scñor. Now, come!"

CHAPTER FIVE

The Central Valley, near Coalinga

Danny moved closer, to make sure that he was actually seeing what he thought he was seeing.

At first glance, it looked like a water stain on the concrete. The freeway underpasses were a riot of abstract designs caused by the rush of occasional rainwater from the road above to the constantly thirsty land below. With a little imagination, you could always make out something—the World Trade Center here, a rutabaga there. Not that, under normal circumstances, anybody ever stopped under an overpass in order to discover some *l'art trouvé,* but these were hardly normal circumstances.

The Mexicans were deep into the rosary now, praying with renewed fervor. These were the good, religious, hard-working people from an ancient culture, family people, descendents both of the conquistadors and the Indians, of Cortés and Juan Diego. Coming to America, thought Danny, may have improved them financially, but it had diminished them culturally, with what unknown consequences the next generations of both Mexicans and Americans would have to discover.

Dios te salve, María, llena eres de gracia . . .

Gently, he moved forward, toward the object of their veneration. Some of the candles had guttered out already, but fresh votives had already replaced them, flickering in the breeze.

He thought he knew what he saw, but he had to make sure. . . .

Closer now and closer still . . .

A large woman blocked his way. The crowd, which was growing in size by the minute, pressed forward, knocking him into her. "Excuse me, señora," he said, but it was no use apologizing because the press of humanity was too strong and he found himself propelled ever forward until, like water bursting through a dam, he went sprawling into a small clearing.

Behind him was the crowd, a mixture of awe and wonder on their faces. Before him were the candles, their hot melted wax running down the pavement. And above him was . . .

A Face. The face of a woman. The most beautiful face he had ever seen.

Her eyes were half-closed, her gaze downward, a look of ineffable sadness and suffering—and yet of peace and even joy—upon her visage. She was wearing what the kids today called a hoodie, which concealed most of her hair, revealing only her face and a bit of her throat.

"Who is it?" he found himself whispering, prone, worshipful.

"Nuestra Señora de Guadalupe, señor," someone said.

"Who?" He should have known. Every Angeleno, whether Latino or Anglo, knew the Virgin of Guadalupe, the miraculous image impressed by the Lady upon the cloak of the Indian, Juan Diego, in 1531. It was one of the first recorded apparitions of the Virgin in the New World. It ensured the conquest of Latin America by Catholicism, and it turned Juan Diego into the first native American saint. And the cloak remained to this day in the *Basilica de Nuestra Señora de Guadalupe* in Mexico City.

Powerful voodoo, if you believed. Powerful even if you didn't.

As one look at the Face would tell you.

He looked at Her, right in the eyes—

Miracles were curious things. Like pornography, you could not define them, but you knew one when you saw it. It wasn't as if she looked directly at him—great images, like the Mona Lisa, did that all the time, the eyes following you around the room, out the door and across the street—but she may as well have, for the effect it had on him. Not just at him, but *in* him and *through* him and *with* him, just like in the doxology, the one he had had learned so many years ago, before reality had intervened, and the world had taken his breath away.

Suddenly, unbidden, the words of the Eucharistic prayer came back to him, half-remembered, as in a dream, but tantalizing and near . . .

Per ipsum, et cum ipso, et in ipso . . .

What was the rest of it? He couldn't remember

He took a deep breath. The fetid smell of the bovine corpses lying just over the freeway was already wafting over. Something terrible had happened, and he needed to know what it was. He glanced back to his car, to see if Hope and the kids were all right, but the crowd was too large, and getting larger every moment.

There was no way out: he was penned in on all sides by the locals, mostly Mexicans now, he could see, who had been joined by a few Anglos, landowners most likely. The primitive illumination of the candles had given way to the

powerful flashlights of the farmers, who had augmented
their torches with shotguns. Whatever had happened, it required firearms to deal with.

"What the hell is going on here?" barked a big man. He
was at the head of a group of white men, the only one unarmed, and he moved through the crowd of Latinos as if he
owned them, which he probably did.

The crowd parted like the Red Sea, and soon enough
Danny found himself looking up at the big man, who prod-
ded him with his boot.

"Don't do that," said Danny softly. He was still process-
ing what he had seen just now, and was in no mood for a reality intervention just yet.

"I said," repeated the man, "what the hell is going here?
There are dead cows from here to Stockton, and I want to
know why."

The Mexicans were backing away, their candles flickering out. Struggling, Danny forced himself into a sitting position, from which he could get a view of the car. Damn! Rory
was getting out, a young man coming to the aid of an older
man, a man not his father but who soon would be, at least in
the eyes of the law and perhaps even, if he played his cards
right, of the Lord. . . .

"Rory, stay in the car!" shouted Danny.

"I asked you a question," said the big man, which inter-
rogatory was followed by another prod, this one closer to a
kick—

Big mistake.

In a flash, Danny flipped to his feet, whirled, and dropped
the man with a high kick to the Adam's apple. Two throwing
knives shot from his sleeves, pinioning the trigger hands of
two of the armed men. Quick, vicious punches brought
down the others. It was all over in less than a minute, just the
way he had been trained so long ago, in the special forces
and the 160th SOAR.

In another time, in another life, Danny might have made sure his opponents were down for the count, unable to rise and hurt him. But now he didn't care. It was not that he had lost his edge, but that he had found a new one—a higher power than the ones he formerly had answered to. He didn't know what it meant, wasn't sure what he would do with this newfound clarity, but it didn't matter. He still had more to learn, and that was what some power had brought him here, at this moment, to do.

The past sloughed off—all of it. The military operations, the night flights into Iraq and other places in the world he never talked about, never admitted, the contract with Blackwater, now called Xe—none of that mattered anymore. It was past, gone, and yet . . . and yet the past was always prologue to whatever new life was coming your way. *Embrace the suck*, was the old motto in Iraq. Well, he was embracing it now.

In the distance, he could hear car doors opening and shutting. His car. He knew it was his car. Rory was already out, and so now it was the women, the women he was suddenly responsible for, not just his daughter Jade, wounded in the terrorist bombing of the Grove but now by the grace of God healthy and well, but Hope and her daughter Emma, poor kidnapped Emma, for whose rescue he had flown into the heart of that bastard Skorzeny's prison in France.

Mission accomplished. Emma was restored to her mother and her brother, and Jade restored to life. Both he and Hope had lost their spouses—she in the siege of Edwardsville, he in Los Angeles—but somehow she had found him and together they were becoming stronger than they had ever been in the past.

It had never been personal before—not even during the darkest days in Iraq. He had a job to do, and he did it. The body count was not his concern. He was a warrior, trained and sent into action by his country; if he had had to live with one of those JAG monkeys on his back, he never would have made it out of country alive. But now, after all that had happened—to him, his family, to Hope, her family, and to their country—it very much was personal. He could only hope—and, now, pray—that he would be the divine instrument of infinite justice.

The Mexicans had pulled away from the crazy gringo. The white men were down. And now he found himself swarmed by the people in his life whom he most loved. Hope and Rory and Emma. And Jade. Always brave Jade.

Who was staring at the image on the wall. If Danny thought he was empathetic, Jade was positively telepathic. She got it from her mother, Diane. . . .

For a long time Jade said nothing, just took in the image of the woman, the mother, the Blessed Mother, her sorrow, her tears.

"What is it, Jade?" asked Danny softly. "What is she saying?"

Still, Jade said nothing. Danny knew better than to press her. Teenage girls were never to be rushed. They could see things others could not, hear things audible only to a special few. As they bloomed and blossomed, they not only transformed themselves, they transformed the world—sacred vessels, receptive, the gateway to the unknown, the promise, and the future.

"What does she want?" whispered Danny to his daughter. He had to learn her secret.

What was she trying to tell him? What was she trying to tell all of them? Not just those present, but everyone in the Central Valley, everyone in California, the country, the world? Had she witnessed whatever calamity lay just outside the sacred circle of candle fire?

She had something to say—but what?

Jade shuddered a little, then stepped back, coming out of

a kind of trance. She nodded to the image, then turned to her father.

"What did you say, Daddy?" she asked.

Danny waited a moment. "What?" he hissed. "What did she say?"

Hope moved toward them. "Danny," she said softly. "Let Jade—"

"No," said Danny. Then, to Jade: "You heard something?"

In the distance now, sirens. Lots of them. Sirens coming from both the north and the south, their wails building in harmony with the scope of the disaster. The stench was becoming overpowering. They had to get out of here, go on north, on to San Francisco, toward their hotel, the restaurant, the moonlight walk near Fort Point.

"Hear something," replied Jade. "I *hear* something. She's talking to me. To you. To all of us."

Rory looked at the image on the wall. "Awesome!" he exclaimed.

Protectively, Hope threw her arms around the children. Neither Jade nor Danny moved.

"What is she saying, darling?" asked Danny. The sirens were very near now.

Jade moved toward the wall, on which the miraculous image had been projected, and started to put her ear to it.

The force of the shotgun blast would have taken her head off, but the shot was high and to the right, chipping the concrete and sending it flying. Danny had hardly heard the blast when he jumped on his daughter, the memory of the Grove explosion still vivid in his memory.

In one smooth motion, he scooped Jade up in his arms while signaling for the others to run. The Mexicans scattered as another blast came—this one hitting the Virgin right in the face. The miracle was over.

They hit the car running and hopped in. It wasn't a chopper, but Danny could still make it fly, and they peeled out long before the inevitable third blast—the one directed at them—came. But they were already far away, and the force of the shot dispersed itself into the fetid air.

"What's happening, Danny?" asked Hope, but at this moment, he only had ears for his daughter. "What did she say, Jade?" he asked again.

"Awesome!" exclaimed Rory, as Emma began to cry.

They were traveling through a nightmare landscape. On both sides of the Golden State Freeway were acres of dead cows, cows stretching as far away as they could see, an endless silent horizontal parade of dead cows. *Poison*, he thought, *but what kind?* And how delivered? Was it in the water supply, or just in the troughs and trenches? He wanted to turn on the radio, but he needed to hear what Jade was saying first:

"Repent," she said.

"What else?" whispered Hope.

Jade turned to the woman who would soon enough be her stepmother, even if neither of them knew that for a fact quite yet. "Nothing else," she said.

"Repent?" asked Danny. "That's all?"

"Repent," she repeated. "Over and over."

The flashing lights of the oncoming CHP cruisers rushing south gave a ghastly ambience to the scene. The sirens were deafening.

"What's going on, Danny?" cried Hope.

"I don't know, honey," he said. "I don't know. But I'm going to find out."

He reached in his pocket and pulled out his iPhone.

Under the rules, there was no way he could know if his earlier alert had gone through. He was not supposed to follow up.

Time to break the rules.

You weren't supposed to text while driving, but this was another rule just begging to be broken under the circumstances. Quickly, he typed in a single word, a word he'd been told would immediately summon him.

DORABELLA

He punched a single key and the word shot into the cloud, was instantly erased from the phone and all the civilian networks. A word that had never existed, but a word that meant so much.

It would find him, and it would bring him. It had to.

CHAPTER SIX

Los Angeles

Devlin got into the backseat alongside Jacinta, who slid over as far away from him as possible—which, given the size of the Cadillac tank, was saying something. The doors locked automatically as the driver slipped the SUV into gear and turned east on Sixth Street. He checked out the driver: an ambulatory refrigerator in a formfitting chauffeur's uniform. Native American? Samoan? Aleutian Islander? Los Angeles made New York look positively monochrome.

Riding several feet above the traffic was not his idea of a good time. Most SUV drivers, in Devlin's experience, fell into three categories: small blond women, small Asian women, and small Persian women. All of them rich.

"Where are we going?" he asked. If either of his compadres knew, they weren't talking. *No habla ingles.* The all-purpose excuse. Gardeners, Major League Baseball players, even California politicians could conveniently forget the English language whenever it suited their purposes; hell, some California politicians never bothered to learn English at all. There sure weren't any votes in it.

East on Sixth. Unless you were going to Hancock Park—
not the La Brea Tar Pits park, but the tony residential neighborhood of the same name, Beverly Hills before there was a
Beverly Hills—nobody went east on Sixth. Because nobody
knew anybody who lived there. Los Angeles was not only
one of America's biggest cities, it was one of America's most
segregated cities, with ethnic neighborhoods as clearly de-
lineated as though Chief William Parker had drawn them up
on a blackboard. Which, in a way, he had. And though Parker
had been dead for decades, his vision of Los Angeles, en-
forced by the LAPD and by consenting patterns of residential segregation, lived on. Nobody went east on Sixth.

They flew past Western, heading for Vermont, riding in
silence across the endless urban landscape of strip malls and
three-story buildings, the dead end of the American Dream.
California ugly.

Los Angeles had leapfrogged this part of town, bounding
from Bunker Hill, hopscotching up from West Adams,
pogo-sticking past Hancock Park and its front-row-center
view of the Hollywood Sign, and finally landing west of
Robertson, where Beverly Hills began. And from there it
was "the west side," all the way to Pacific Palisades and the
ocean. The only place to go from here was back home or in
the drink. Defeat in both directions.

Supermarquetas, check-cashing places, bail bondsmen.
Korean beauty shops, Korean barbecue. Wary white and
black cops, locked inside their black-and-whites, obliquely
eyeing brazen street people in the only part of town it wasn't
a crime to be a pedestrian.

He glanced over at Jacinta, who was fingering some
wooden rosary beads. Just for fun, he tried to remember the
Mysteries: Sorrowful, Joyful, Glorious, and the new one,
whatchamacallit, each with five subdivisions. No wonder the
Protestants thought of Catholics as idolaters. Mary worshippers. Heathens.

"Why me?" It was worth a try.

The Escalade humped over one of L.A.'s innumerable unnoticed hills. San Francisco fetishized its humps, turned them into tourist attractions. L.A. pretended they weren't there.

"Because you don't believe." Although her eyes were invisible beneath her visor, Devlin knew they were trained on him.

"I don't believe in Santa Claus, either."

"But you did, once. So there's still hope."

The mute driver wheeled left on Rossmore, then took a hard right on Third.

Which is where the trailing car handed them off to the next pursuer.

He hadn't wanted to say anything, because officially this assignment didn't exist and officially he didn't exist, and thanks to Maryam he already was in enough trouble. This gig most likely had been a mercy fuck from Seelye, something to keep him active while Tyler and that hard-ass new secretary of defense, Shalika Johnson, decided what to do with him.

Maybe *this* was what they'd decided to do with him. Maybe he was going for a ride.

Better than anybody, Devlin knew the code of Branch 4 ops—the minute your cover was blown, or you were otherwise compromised, you were a dead man. You were Ishmael, with your hand against every man's and every man's hand against yours. And that included fellow Branch 4 ops, people whose names and faces he didn't know, but who would have complete access to his dossier, for the sole purpose of killing him.

And here he'd trusted his stepfather, the man who had raised him—General Armond "Army" Seelye, now the head of the National Security Agency/Central Security Service, and thus his direct superior.

For him, Devlin was lightly armed. Leaving his house in Echo Park, he'd selected a pair of H&Ks Mark 23 .45s with twelve-round magazines, and a throwing knife from his underground armory. The Heckler & Koch sidearms had been developed for the Navy SEALs and the Army's Special Forces; at a couple of thousand bucks apiece they were expensive but as reliable as the old Colt 1911 .45 that they had replaced. They ought to be able to handle a single—

No, make that two trailing vehicles. Whoever was tailing them was good. And they weren't just tailing anymore. They were getting ready to box the big Caddy and probably flip it. Auto accidents happened every day in the City of the Angels, and even on the surface streets you could get up enough speed to kill yourself if you tried; Third Street in this part of town was one of them. If some other car was forcing you to that speed . . .

Devlin looked over at Jacinta, but she was too wrapped up in miracle pictures of marigolds to have noticed anything. The driver's shaded eyes remained on the road.

One of the trailing cars, a Mercedes with tinted windows, suddenly sped up and pulled even with the backseat. It drove nearly parallel with them for a bit, then dropped back, as if the driver had decided not to try and pass the Caddy after all. Just as it dropped back, Devlin pointed what looked like an Android at them and pressed the button.

He glanced down at the screen: a complete image of the inside of the vehicle, courtesy of advanced backscatter X-ray technology that Homeland Security had been developing for a couple of years now. The otherwise-useless DHS was using a less sophisticated version in the roving anonymous vans it had deployed on the streets of major American cities; they could scan both vehicles and pedestrians for weapons and explosives involuntarily, Fourth Amendment or no Fourth Amendment. The CSS had simply "borrowed" the technology and, as the liaison with the cryptology divisions of the armed services, had improved and weaponized it based on a prototype he'd developed for use in the field.

A third car had joined the pursuit, just up ahead at the intersection with Western. He knew it would pull out in front of them and drive them toward the gas station on the southeast corner, and probably right into the pumps. It would make for a hell of an explosion and a great lede for the evening news, unless he did something about it.

His Android had also taken an electronic reading of the Benz's vital systems and had hacked into the onboard computer, which meant he could control the vehicle. Down in New Orleans, he'd taken out that poor snoopy reporter's car on a race down St. Charles by freezing the engine block, which flipped the car; he'd had to go back and risk his life and his identity saving the guy's sorry ass.

No worries about that this time. This was enemy action.

The car up ahead, a new Jag, was making its move, getting ready to turn left into Third Street.

The Mercedes was pulling up again in the left lane.

The other car, a Honda, was inching up behind them, getting ready to give them a push from the rear.

Seconds now.

A quick glance at the driver—still impassive. He was in on it. He had to be—

A hidden partition suddenly appeared between front and back, slowly rising.

They were almost at the intersection. . . .

For the first time, the driver turned his head to the right, a little smile playing across his lips.

NOW.

In practically a single motion, Devlin thwacked the driver behind his right ear, while at the same time pressing a button on the Android. Its steering disabled and its accelerator torqued, the Mercedes spun out to the left, a guided missile headed straight for the Jag.

The unconscious driver's foot slipped off the Escalade's gas pedal, causing the trailing Honda to smash into the much larger vehicle from the read. The sudden jolt knocked the Escalade forward and into the intersection, just as—

—the Mercedes broadsided the Jaguar—

—Devlin fired a single shot into the Escalade's dashboard control panel, stopping the partition—

—the Honda rammed them again—

—the Mercedes caromed off the Jag and back into the intersection—

—and Devlin swung himself feetfirst into the front seat.

The driver had slumped over to the right, blocking the steering wheel. Devlin went over him, his right foot landing on the accelerator, his left foot on the brake.

He hit them both simultaneously. The big car jerked and tailed off to the right, sliding aside as the damaged Mercedes spun past them.

From behind, the Honda rammed them again, but this time it wasn't a clean ram, more a glancing blow, which caused the Honda to spin out to the left, rear first, whipping the front end of the car around and around as it sailed, rudderless, to the northeast, finally colliding with the hulk of the Jag.

Both cars exploded into flames.

The Mercedes continued south on Western, past the gas station pumps, running up on the sidewalk and then crashing headfirst into the retaining wall on the other side of the alley.

And then they were through the intersection and speeding east on Third, as if nothing had happened.

It would be only a few minutes, Devlin knew, before the sirens would start and the cops and the fire trucks got there. He needed to be far away. He turned at the next side street and dropped down to Sixth again. It was slow going through the side streets, but a zigzag course was the best idea under the circumstances, since the LAPD hardly ever ventured off the main arteries in this part of town. Whatever minor damage had been done to the Escalade would go unnoticed.

At a safe distance, he stopped the car.

"Help me, Jacinta," he said, but there was no response from the backseat. Had something happened to her? Was she dead? No time to worry about that.

He reached into one of the man's ears and pulled out an earbud. No wonder he couldn't hear him.

Devlin took out the other earbud and held them both up to his ears. There was some kind of music playing, more chanting really. He brought the earbuds closer.

Music *and* chanting. The music he recognized. It was Schubert's "Ave Maria," sung in Spanish, and the chanting was the voices of a congregation reciting the "Hail Mary" in Spanish.

Not dispositive. He could have been religious and still one of the bad guys. And he wasn't blind—he should have seen those tail cars, should have responded.

Devlin was strong, but the man was big and out cold. He rolled him over the front seats and practically into Jacinta's lap. She showed no emotion, didn't move. "Sister," said Devlin, "you have to help me. At least get out of the way."

She did neither. She looked up from her photographs and stared at him, her lips moving.

"Okay, have it your way." He managed to fold down half of the backseat and roll the body into the Escalade's capacious rear compartment. The rear windows were tinted, which was legal in California. With any luck, they'd be downtown shortly. And then he could sort out the problem of the driver.

He slipped back into the driver's seat and swung east. They were in the twilight zone between Latino Broadway, Little Tokyo, and Chinatown. The old L.A. downtown, ten times farther from Beverly Hills than New York City.

At Main Street he turned left. At Second, he turned right and continued down the street, almost to Los Angeles Street and, beyond it, Little Tokyo, until he could duck in behind the old church.

Not just any church: the Cathedral of St. Vibiana. Second and Main streets. Crippled since the Northridge earthquake of 1994, condemned since 1996. Restored now—not as a church but a community arts center, called, simply, Vibiana. Saints need not apply around here anymore. Especially third-century virgin martyrs. Come to think of it, virgins need no longer apply, either.

Devlin got out of the car, catching the blast furnace right in the face, stepping over the flopped homeless in their cardboard boxes, their shopping carts parked neatly outside. Everybody had wheels in Los Angeles.

He turned. Jacinta was nowhere to be seen. It was as if she had never existed.

And then the doors of the dead basilica swung open and Devlin stepped inside a piece of vanished Los Angeles.

He knew just how the mammoth felt.

CHAPTER SEVEN

Los Angeles

The cool interior was a welcome relief from the heat. The Spanish knew what they were doing when they invented California architecture. Space, air, breezeways, and let nature do the rest. Or God. Whichever.

Earthquakes—well, they were the work of the devil, which is why this particular cathedral had been abandoned in favor of the modern monstrosity up the hill, across from the Music Center.

God had moved. The new Cathedral of Our Lady of the Angels sat up on what was left of Bunker Hill, looming over the Hollywood Freeway. There it was, the sacred and profane, back to back and belly to belly: That was Los Angeles in a nutshell, no contradiction noted or accepted. Take it or leave it, all or nothing. Mammon Found, Paradise Lost.

There was no God here. Except for the old altar, everything ecclesiastical had been stripped away, leaving only the cracked walls and rocked foundations of a building that had finally met the California earthquake code it couldn't survive or finesse.

No pews, no confessionals. Even the stained-glass windows had been removed; from the side; the cathedral looked like the gap-toothed mouth of one of the bums out on Second Street, who drank Ripple and screamed obscenities at the few civil-service souls who passed by on their way to and from their cubicles and the taqueria.

The empty church was as eerie as an AA meeting with no drunks. Funny, he'd thought the conversion to the arts center was long-since complete.

"Mr. Harris? Mr. Bert Harris?" Male, Hispanic, early thirties—this much he knew without even turning around. "I'm Father Gonsalves."

Looking back on it, that should have been the tip-off right there. Father Last Name in a world that had lost both its faith and its surnames. Not Father Tom, or Father Mike or Father Ed. Priests hadn't used their last names since the Primate was a pup.

The guy looked straight enough. Black cassock, white dog collar, the usual outfit. Good, firm handshake. Devlin liked that.

"I don't know how much Jacinta has told you," Father Gonsalves began, his words echoing in the vaulted space.

"Just this," replied Devlin. He opened his left hand and displayed the rose petal. "Which is, I guess, all I need to know."

Father Gonsalves moved toward the altar, the only flat surface other than the floor. Its marble top was pebbled from years, decades, of use. Instead of a chalice, there was a small pile of folders and documents lying atop it.

"I don't know how much you know about miracles—"

"I believe them when I see them, and that's not very often. As in never."

"Good. May I ask if you're a Catholic?" said the padre.

"You may. I'm not."

"Not anymore, you mean."

"Guesstimation or revelation?"

"Have a look at this, please."

It was a computer printout, tens of pages in length. Dates, locations, number of people. Starting in 1900 and running up to the present. Devlin scanned it quickly, his eyes picking out various incidents:

DATE	PLACE	# PEOPLE	DISPOSITION
1900	Tung Lu (China)	many	None
1914	Hrushiv (Ukraine)	22	None
1931	Stenbergen (Holland)	1 woman	None
1939	Kerrytown (Ireland)	crowd	None
1945	Amsterdam	1 woman	YES
1953	Cossirano (Italy)	young girl	NEGATIVE
1961	Garabandal (Spain)	4 girls	NEGATIVE
1981	Kibeho (Rwanda)	teenagers	YES

He handed the pages back to the padre. "Looks like an epidemiological study for some sort of disease. An outbreak of some kind. What was it? Hemorrhagic fever? Smallpox?"

Father Gonsalves indicated something on one of the pages. "Note particularly the concatenation in Spain in 1931. Ezquioga, Izurdiaga—"

"Basque country. Just before the civil war. People see things when they're crazy."

The priest shot him an impressed look. "Very good. Zumarraga, Ormaiztegui, Albiztur, Barcelona, Iraneta. All in Spain, within the same year."

"A mental illness of some kind? Mass psychosis, brought on by the proximity of war? If you look at the dates—"

"You're a data miner, Mr. Harris. You figure it out."

Interesting choice of words. "Data mining" was not a term in common parlance. Most people had no idea what it meant. Seelye must have put him up to this.

He shook his head. "Too small a sample. No way to create an association algorithm. Probably need to use an API . . ."

"Let me help you." Father Gonsalves leafed through the pages, found what he was looking for, pointed—

1917	Fatima (Portugal)	3 children	YES
1968	Zeitoun (Egypt)	crowd	YES
1981	Medjugorje (Bosnia)	several	Pending

"Are you familiar with California City?"

"North of Lancaster, in the Mojave." Hell on earth.

"It will take you a couple of hours to get there. Although at that time of day, the traffic will mostly be coming the other way."

Was he for real? Traffic in L.A. ran in all directions pretty much twenty-four hours a day, six days a week. The myth of a "rush hour" that flowed one way in the morning and the other way in the evening was strictly an East Coast import, one of the things displaced people from the wrong side of the Mississippi clung to, like faith, to help them rationalize the irrational world that was God's country. He'd seen the Sepulveda Pass clogged at 4 A.M., and once sped west on the Santa Monica Freeway on a fine spring day without braking once between downtown and the beach. Miracles sometimes did happen. Just often enough to keep the suckers in the tent.

"I haven't agreed to anything yet," Devlin objected.

"Sure you have," replied the priest. "You're here, aren't you?"

They stood there staring at each other. Jacinta was still nowhere to be seen. Father Gonsalves gestured at the floor as he reached for the stack of papers. "I'm sorry, the rectory's . . . closed to visitors."

Devlin sat on the floor; the seat of his trousers would have to like it or lump it. The padre squatted like a Southeast Asian, rocking back on his haunches. That was a position Devlin had never quite mastered, couldn't have even had he wanted to. It made him feel like the last refugee not to make it out of Saigon, and he had not yet fallen that low. Not quite.

"There's more pictures. Do you want to see them?"

"Not unless you tell me what this is all about."

"Listen to this." Father Gonsalves closed his eyes and recited from memory. " 'Dear children! This is a time of great graces, but also a time of great trials for all those who desire to follow the way of peace. Again I call on you to pray, pray, pray—not with words, but with your heart. I desire to give you peace, and that you carry it in your hearts and give it to others, until God's peace begins to rule the world.' She said that. Here—"

More pictures. Not the desert: green hills, snowy mountains. A church with twin spires. "That was in 2002. Keep looking—"

A rocky, treeless hillside. Euro-hovels. A million Arabs in mufti, looking up at the sky. Skyscraper windows, sunlight glinting. A saltwater stain on a highway underpass, before which stood a makeshift altar, adorned with candles. And icons.

"You see? We need—"

"We?"

"—to know whether she's real. Jacinta showed you the pictures from California City." The pictures in the desert. "Have you ever heard of Juan Diego?"

He thought for a moment; even though he wasn't originally from California, he remembered something about a baptized Indian, hundreds of years ago, somewhere in Mexico, who had an encounter—probably peyote-fueled—with a beautiful woman.

"She gave him roses and told him to go to the bishop in what is now Mexico City. And when he opened his *tilma*— her image was imprinted on his cloak. We call her Our Lady of Guadalupe. But it's not that Juan Diego I'm talking about."

Instinctively, Devlin looked at the rose petal he was still carrying in his hand as the priest fished a photo out of his stack. A dour *bracero*, by the look of him, Zapata mustache, floppy hat, holding a rosary. A group of people were kneeling beside him, praying, in the desert. In the background, he could make out a fenced-off area of white rocks with a sign in front of them.

The floor was even less comfortable than it looked. Devlin rose, brushing off his rump. "Sorry, padre, but I don't believe in fairy tales, Bible stories, global warming, or the Dodgers' chances this year."

His answer seemed to please the priest. "That's why we picked you." He waved the pages as if fanning himself. "A string of negatives and no decisions—exactly the way the church prefers it. As a person of Mexican descent it embarrasses me to say this, but there is no limit to the imagination of superstitious peasants." He handed Devlin a couple of folders. "The data's all in here. Mine it"

Devlin got the picture. "Devil's Advocate, huh? Debunk and demolish. Scrape the holy mold off the taco, so to speak."

"More like Serpent's Advocate."

"Or the Great Red Dragon's."

"You read the Bible."

"Only in hotel rooms. Scripture's for Protestants."

"I thought you said you weren't Catholic."

"You don't have to be Catholic not to read the Bible."

"Armando can drive you, if you'd like."

So that was his name. "Armando's sleeping."

"Twenty thousand dollars ought to cover it. Half now, half upon receipt of your . . . thoroughly mined . . . report."

The padre sprang up from his squatting position and extended his hand. It had a stuffed envelope in it.

Footfalls echoing, they walked toward the front doors. "One last question," said the priest, yanking at the heavy wooden portal.

"Shoot." The western sunlight hit him right in the eyes.

"Isn't it rather hot for that suit?"

Not a question he hadn't heard before. Nobody wore suits in Los Angeles anymore, except lawyers and agents, and even the lawyers took off their ties once they made partner, or on Fridays, whichever came first.

"Since when does hell have a dress code?"

The doors closed behind him. The bums were still homeless. The Escalade was waiting outside, a passenger door open. He stepped over a couple of prone winos, and wondered how long it would be before he joined them.

His secure smartphone buzzed. He looked at the screen. A single word:

DORABELLA

Oh, Jesus.

He switched off voice contact and the browser, but left messaging on. Might as well give eternity and redemption his best shot, and yet still stay in touch with the outside world. It was the least he could do. After all, he was on his way to meet the Blessed Virgin Mary.

There was a map on the front seat, with a location in the

desert outside California City circled in red. There was a Polaroid camera, loaded and ready to shoot—extra film, too.

And one other thing. Actually, many other things: rose
petals and hyacinths, all over the seats.

A voice from the backseat. He looked in the rearview
mirror to make sure he was not seeing a ghost. But it was
only Jacinta.

No time for questions. No time for thinking. Only time
for believing. He wasn't sure he had that in him, but he
would have to try.

What was the Hollywood motto? *Fake it 'til you make it.*

Or was it, *Fuck you, sucker*?

No matter. He hit the gas and the car sped off, toward the
desert.

He glanced in the rearview mirror. Nothing was following him, at least nothing corporeal.

Ghosts, he couldn't do anything about.

CHAPTER EIGHT

California City, California

The procession was taking forever and the cell phone service was terrible. But what did you expect out here?

Dorabella could mean only one thing. Skorzeny. And Maryam.

It was the last communication the Central Security Service, his agency, had received from her, the unbreakable code that Major Atwater over at NSA had finally cracked by understanding that the series of squiggles, all variations on the Greek letter *e*, was not a conventional cipher at all, not a substitute for clear text but a substitute for musical notation. The unseen, unheard mystery of a melody that only Elgar could notate.

He looked around for Jacinta, but she had disappeared. How could he have lost her? She must be here somewhere, commingled with the mostly Hispanic crowd.

California City was probably the unlikeliest place to be named after the Golden State. Flat, dry, dusty, a collection of desert cinder-block architecture married to macadam and concrete, it was the kind of place old priests with dark secrets went to die, just like in *True Confessions*. Out here in the Mojave, there was nothing between you and God except your faith or lack of it, and his lack of it was manifest, even to himself and the God he didn't believe in.

Make that, no longer believed in. It was hard to believe in a merciful and compassionate and just God when your mother died in your arms, instead of the other way around, like He did.

Why "Juan Diego" had picked this spot over all the others eluded him. The same desolate desert landscape stretched in all directions. The Mojave wasn't like the Sahara or the Gobi—it was not a limitless expanse of sand and camel dung. On the contrary, the California desert was the same only different in each direction you looked: mountainous here, rolling hills there, flat over there, with cactus and desert flowers and Gila monsters and horned toads and dry dirt and drier gullies that miraculously filled with water a few times each year.

There was a clump of rocks and near it a tent. Vendors hawked sacred bullshit, mostly images of Our Lady of Guadalupe. Euro-tourists, big blond Swedish women hoping for a walk on the wild side with Geronimo, strolled around in short shorts and cameras. Polaroids. Everybody had Polaroids.

Finally, the procession was approaching the tent. Was that Jacinta among them? It certainly looked like her, but then half the women in this crowd looked like her.

Devlin had spent plenty of time in Mexico, and his admiration for the Mexican people knew . . . well, it knew one bound. Drugs had destroyed these good, religious, hardworking, faithful people—demolished their families and turned the entire country into a sewer of hopelessness and despair. They were beheading people in Mexico now. Every day, the pathologies of the Middle East were drawing nearer—the clash of civilizations was no longer at Tours, or Seville or Vienna, but on the Tijuana border.

A dry wind blew across his face, snapping him out of his reverie—and propelling him headlong into another. Not all deserts looked, felt, or smelled alike. The California desert reminded him of another desert altogether, the one surrounding the Iranian city of Tabas, hemmed in by high mountains. The place where Jimmy Carter's feckless Desert One mission, Operation Eagle Claw, came a cropper in 1980. At that moment, the Iranians lost their fear of the Great Satan.

Was Maryam there?

No time to dwell on that now. They were both in need of redemption, but the only soul he could save at the moment was his own.

He kept respectfully silent as "Juan Diego" passed by, an imitation priest surrounded by imitation acolytes. The voodoo pull of the Whore of Rome still exerted a powerful attraction; had Vatican II never happened, had the reforms instituted by Pope John XXIII never happened, odds were that the world would be a better place. Faith might be crap, but it was better than nothing, and it was obviously a terrible thing to lose.

The crowd of worshippers and tourists fell to its knees as "Juan Diego" began to pray. Devlin's Mexican Spanish was long since up to snuff and he heard the man's words directly, in his head and in his heart:

"O brothers and sisters," began the charismatic preacher. "O beloved of Jesus and of His holy mother, Mary." Devlin could hear the rosary beads clicking as the old ladies told the prayers, ripping through the Our Fathers and Hail Marys at lightning speed.

"We are gathered here today, as we gather on the thirteenth of each holy month, to honor our Blessed Mother, and to hear her. For she is angry, my brothers and sisters. Angry at the way God's people have turned their backs on her Son. Angry at the indolence and corruption of the people, who lack only a Golden Calf to make their degradation complete.

"She comes, bringing us the Word. It is not a happy Word, not the Word of joy, but the Word of warning—there are trials and tribulations ahead, O my brothers and sisters. Days of great sorry, of misery and despair. And we are here to witness her warning.

"But do not abandon Hope. For so it must be, for so it is written and so shall it be done. Behold—she comes, roses strewn in her path!"

Somehow, a stray cell signal got through. His phone buzzed. Still kneeling, he glanced down at the display:

LOVE = HATE.

Quickly, he tried to retrace the call, but no luck: the signal had evaporated like moisture in the desert.

". . . believe, my brothers and sisters. Point your cameras toward the heavens, and witness the miracle of love."

The "priest" pointed up at the blazing sun. Five hundred Polaroids pointed in its direction.

He looked up, trying at once to avert his gaze and yet stare directly into the sun. Then he remembered the camera he was carrying. The Polaroid Jacinta had left for him.

"Behold—the Door of Heaven!"

He aimed and fired.

The camera whirred, then spit out its picture. It would take a minute or so for it to develop.

He shielded his eyes from the sun and looked back up, but his hand had been just slightly too late and the rays caught him with full force. For a moment, he couldn't see a thing.

In his blinded state, he suddenly felt something brush

against his forehead. He swatted it away as respectfully as he could. The cell phone messages could only have come from one man, and he knew that that one man would only contact him in the midst of a dire emergency.

Slowly his sight was returning. He blinked, the reverse images—like X-rays—still flashing in his brain. There was something there, at the edge of his vision, but he couldn't quite see it.

He was moving back toward normal polarity now. Gradually, he became aware of a murmuring in the crowd, a swell turning into a shout of hope and radiant glory.

He didn't want to, but he had to—the thing he sought was still there, at the edge of his vision, but fading quickly. Try as he might, he couldn't grasp it as it slipped away.

Gone.

He opened his eyes.

Rose petals everywhere. People were picking them up, pressing them into devotionals, putting them into their pockets, even eating them in the hopes of absorbing some of their miraculous patrimony.

His eyes fell upon the Polaroid picture, now fully developed. It was the shot he had taken of the sun. There it was:

A rectangle of light, created by the aperture in reverse. And, at its center, darkness where there should be have been light. Darkness . . . and something else.

A figure? The image of a woman? Once you were blinded, whether by the sun or by superstition, anything could look like anything.

Then he saw the word. Anything could look like anything, but nothing could look like this. It was what it was.

A single word: *Repent*.

Time to go.

He found the car, just where he had left it. No sign of Jacinta.

Just a single rose on the passenger seat—fresh, glistening as if plucked from a spring shower.

About ten miles south of California City, his phone buzzed again. Devlin hit the scramble button. President Tyler himself didn't have access to the encoding technology that his smartphone did. As soon as he hit the TALK button, the entire conversation would be encrypted, uplinked to a secure tech satellite, voice-scrambled, digitally unsequenced, retransmitted, and then unscrambled at the point of reception.

"Who am I talking to?" He waited for the operation code. There was only one right answer; otherwise he would assume the relationship had been compromised and would act accordingly. That would be too bad. He liked Danny, the man had always been there for him. But rules were rules.

"Don Barker."

"Speak."

A brief pause. Something was wrong. "What do you know about poisons?"

"Get to the point." Secure wireless conversations didn't stay secure forever.

"V-series nerve agent, Novichoks, QNB—I can't tell yet."

"Where are you?"

"Coalinga, heading north to San Francisco. Every cow within fifty miles is dead."

"People?"

"Not yet."

"Then it's probably not poison. What's the news say?"

He could hear "Don Barker" fiddling with the radio. He could hear other voices. Devlin's keen ears picked them up—three females, one boy.

"Reports just coming in now."

"Get over to Lemoore and stand by." Lemoore was a

naval air station between Coalinga and Visalia. "Hope and the kids will be safe there."

"Roger that."

"Anything else?"

"Do you believe in miracles?"

Until an hour ago, the answer would have been no. "Yes," he said, and rang off.

CHAPTER NINE

Washington, D.C.

President John Edward Bilodeau Tyler looked at the latest poll numbers on his computer screen, then turned and reached for the fresh whiskey that Manuel Concepcion, his personal steward, always had ready for him. Especially these days.

"This fucking bitch."

That would be Angela Hassett, the other party's nominee. She'd been crowned in Kansas City, at their convention, her candidacy covered by the cable news networks as breathlessly as the Second Coming. The First Woman Major Party Candidate! The greatest orator since . . . since, well, the last one. Surprisingly feminine—hot, even—and yet as ruthless as any man. A ball breaker, as a matter of fact, and wasn't that great? About time the boys got a taste of their own. Served them right for hundreds of years of male chauvinist piggery-pokery, to coin a word.

As for him, let him so much as take a swing at her and the enemedia immediately went into its protective crouch, deploying its legions of sycophants and feuilletonistas in her defense. A fixed fight would have been one thing, but a fixed fight in which the designated tomato can wasn't even allowed to throw a fig-leaf punch was another. Now he knew what Robert Ryan must have felt like in *The Set-Up*, except at least he fought back. And look what happened to him. Reflexively, he glanced down at his right hand, to make sure it was still working.

There were just weeks to go before the election, he was behind by double digits, he couldn't seem to lay a glove on her, and the country hated him even more today than it did in the aftermath of the Times Square disaster. He used to think his doofus predecessor was a moron, but now he was acquiring a strange new respect, as the media hacks liked to say. It was a match between a puncher and a boxer, and the boxer was kicking his ass. Still, all he needed was one punch, something to put the bitch on her butt, to teach the women that more than a century after the Nineteenth Amendment, if they wanted to play with the big boys, they had to be prepared for some broken bones and bloody noses.

He didn't even have to ask Manuel for a refill, because, as always, it was always there. If he had to go into premature retirement, he had to figure out a way to take Manuel with him.

"Anything else, Mr. President?" asked Manuel.

"Better poll numbers?"

"I don't think we have that, sir," replied Manuel.

"A decent movie in the White House theater tonight?"

"You'll have to ask Hollywood for that, sir," said Manuel. "It's above my pay grade."

"Mine too," mused Tyler.

In one smooth motion, Manuel slipped him a new glass and whisked away the empty. "Besides," he said, "they're all going to vote for her."

Tyler grabbed the glass and downed the whole thing. "Don't I know it," he said. "And after all I've done for them.

"No justice," said Manuel.

"No peace," finished Tyler. "Now, what do you want, besides getting me drunk?"

"General Seelye is here to see you, sir."

Tyler sighed. "Hasn't he caused me enough trouble? After what's happened, he's lucky I haven't fired his ass."

"Maybe you should have, sir."

"And look like an ungrateful sonofabitch who can't or won't defend his own people? What happened in New York wasn't his fault. It wasn't the NYPD's fault. Hell, it wasn't even the fault of those useless wankers at the Langley Home for Lost Boys. It was the Iranians' fault—that bastard Kohanloo and that woman I let . . ." He caught himself. "Never mind. That's classified."

"Above my pay grade."

"Correct. Now show General Seelye in. And bring me another drink. This one will be gone before you know it."

Concepcion turned to leave. Tyler followed him to the door and opened it to admit Seelye. Then he noticed the refill was already on the *Resolute* desk. Good man, Concepcion.

"What is it, General?" he said.

"It's important, Mr. President," said the head of the National Security Agency.

"It had better be. Can't you see there's a war on and I'm losing it?"

"Yes, sir," said Seelye. "May I sit down?"

Tyler waved him to a chair. "Give it to me straight."

Seelye tossed a manila folder on Tyler's coffee table. "These were taken by one of our operatives in Iran yesterday. Qom, to be exact."

"We have operatives in Iran?" said the president, sarcastically. "Who knew?"

"Please look at the pictures, Mr. President."

Gingerly, Tyler picked up the folder. He didn't like it

when Seelye called him "Mr. President." It was too formal. It meant trouble.

A bunch of mustachioed men with their asses in the air. A big mosque. Clouds. Sky. "What am I looking at?" He had been handed pictures like these for years; in the middle of the eternal War on Terror, Muslim men at prayer or in rage were a staple of the morning intelligence briefing, just as they had been for his predecessor and would be for his successor. Make that, successors. For it would never be over until either the West brought down the hammer in most brutal, final way possible, or Islam submitted. And that, he knew, would never happen. Not until the Last Trump. This was a fight to the finish, even if only one side had figured that out.

Well, as the old saying went, better to die on your feet than to live on your knees. For months now, his political advisers had been advocating a bold stroke—something so dramatic that it changed the game overnight. The nuclear option, so to speak.

Except this time, it really was the nuclear option.

The October Surprise, for which Angela Hassett would have no answer, no reply, no comeback. Two days before the election, he had already decided, he would use the bomb on the Iranian nuclear facilities, as payback for the 1979 hostage crisis and for every other sin the Muslim world had visited upon the West and Israel since then. There was nothing to lose except the good opinion of the Europeans, and they couldn't vote, and a world of rich Iranian votes in Los Angeles to gain.

Whatever jack-in-the-box Angela Hassett and her minions were planning on springing on him in October, it would be no match for his little gift to the American people.

After all, wasn't freedom just another word for nothing left to lose?

"The sky," sir," General Seelye was saying. "Look at the sky."

Maybe he should have fired Seelye after New York. Sure, his boy Devlin had cleaned up that mess, salvaged what was left of the city, taken down Kohanloo, and dealt with some other putz with a peripheral involvement—a kid about whom there had been repeated inquiries by that broad on the People's News Network, who'd apparently had a run-in with him near the Metropolitan Museum. For Tyler's money, she looked better in a wig, after that scalping she took, but what did he know? In any case, it had been a good career move, since Ms. Stanley was now anchoring the evening news on the highest-rated news network in the world.

"The sky, Mr. President."

Very well, then, the sky. Tyler looked. Nothing. "What am I looking for?" he asked.

"Can't you see it?"

What was this? Twenty Questions?

"See what?"

"The image, sir. The image."

Tyler was still struggling.

"The face."

Seelye's right index finger landed on the photograph, pressing hard. "This face."

Gently, Tyler moved Seelye's finger, then his whole hand, aside. Looked hard . . . harder . . .

And then he saw it.

His first thought was that it was one of those Danish cartoons, the ones that had caused such consternation and mayhem among the Believers when they were published in some newspaper or other. The ones that had set off riots across the Muslim world, had caused the deaths of thousands and rained down a host of threats upon the West for the simple act of putting pen to paper.

Naturally, there was a host of fellow travelers who decried the cartoonists' effrontery—their blasphemy—and more or less gave tacit, if not actual vocal, approval to the various assassination attempts that ensued. Always eager to be on the right side—that is to say, the anti-Western, anti-Judeo-Christian side—of any issue, the international loonies had howled like werewolves at the moon, a suicide cult eager for the dropping of the blade, preferably accompanied by shouts of "*Allahu akbar*." God is the greatest.

Well, as far as Jeb Tyler was concerned, Dire Straits was the greatest, followed closely by Elvis, BeauSoleil, and his mother. And he'd be good and goddamned if a bunch of ragheads were going to tell him different. He was the fucking President of the United States, which meant that he was the last man on earth who had to adhere to the intellectual fascism known as political correctness.

And if it cost him the presidency, so be it.

"This?" he said. "Mohammed?"

"Mohammed, yes, sir," replied Seelye. "Or somebody who looks very much like him."

"A projection—like a searchlight. Hollywood does this sort of thing all the time. Look—up in the sky. It's a bird. It's a plane. It's Batman. Or whatever."

"It's not Batman, sir. It's Mohammed."

"Call Spielberg and ask him how they did it."

Seelye took a respectful step back. "They didn't do it, sir," he said.

"How do you know?"

"Because it's not a projection, Mr. President. At least not from earth."

Tyler reached for his scotch and saw that the glass was empty, with no Manuel in sight. "What do you mean, it's not a projection from earth? What the hell is it?"

"We don't know. It appears to be some sort of holographic image, generated from space, creating the impression you can see here."

Tyler took a closer look. Once you got past the denial your Western brain imposed upon the image, it was pretty clear: The image, floating in the clouds, was that of a bearded Arab man, his eyes blazing. . . .

"We've compared the images to all known images of the Prophet—"

"I thought Islam brooked no representations of their so-called 'prophet,' " said Tyler.

"Not a hard-and-fast rule, sir," said Seelye. "In the first few hundred years of Islam, pictures of Mohammed abounded, especially in Iran. Remember, sir, Iran has a rich cultural history that antedates the Arab conquest. . . ."

"Worst thing that ever happened to them," mused Tyler. "Why couldn't they be more like the Indians? Why didn't they fight back?"

Seelye was in no mood for a history lesson, but the timely application of one never hurt. "Because the Indians had Hindusim," he explained. "Some of them converted, mostly by the sword, which is where Pakistan comes from. But Persian Zoroastrianism could not withstand the onslaught. And here we are."

"With Islam."

"Yes, sir. No, sir. With Shiite Islam. With a kind of imitation of Jewish and Christian eschatology."

"What?" Tyler didn't like big words. Big numbers, that was different.

"Eschatology, sir. The end times. Jews and Christians, as you know, believe in the Messiah. The *Moshiach*. For the Christians, He has already come; the Jews are still waiting, having had many false messiahs along the way. In fact, there was one in Brooklyn a few years ago. . . ."

"Forget Brooklyn," snapped Tyler. "Get to the point. What about the Shiites?"

Seelye thought for a moment, wondering how best to proceed. "That would be the Twelfth Imam, sir," he said.

"Whose current residence is down a well in Qom. Where these pictures just happen to have been taken. The city, I mean. Not the well."

Seelye tossed another manila envelope to the president. "Go ahead, take a look."

This time the pictures were clearer. Color, not black and white. Clearly of the sky, although the sky was seen in reverse-image, deep-night black when it should have been blindingly blue, the sun a gaping black hole surrounded by a corona. Inside the hole was an illuminated rectangle, in which he could just make out—

"What the hell is this?" barked Tyler.

"I don't know, Mr. President," admitted Seelye.

"Then who does? Who took these pictures?" As Tyler stared more closely, he could see the outline of a figure—female, it seemed to him, beckoning. . . .

The head of the National Security Agency took a deep breath. A very deep breath. "Devlin, sir," he admitted.

That was all Tyler needed to hear. "I thought you fired his ass," he said. "In lieu of killing him, I mean. After all, the man is a traitor."

"We don't know that for sure, Mr. President," said Seelye.

"Terrific," said Tyler, rising to signal that the meeting was over. "And where is he now?"

"In Los Angeles, sir," replied Seelye, also rising and gathering up the folders. "On administrative leave, as you ordered once we intercepted—"

Wrong thing to say. The famous Jeb Tyler volcano was just about the spew molten lava. "Where is she? I want her found or dead, and preferably both."

"We're not sure, Mr. President," said Seelye, backing away like a bonze in the Forbidden City circa 1800. "Working on it."

Tyler took a final swig of the dregs of his empty glass. "Where in Los Angeles?"

Seelye took a last look at the final picture in the L.A. series before shoving it into the folder. "From the looks of things," he said, "communing with the Virgin Mary."

His secure communicator buzzed. Normally, he shut everything off and down before entering the Oval Office, but the old norms no longer applied. Everyone who mattered was available 25-7, to distinguish from the peons who were only available 24-7. It was a world in which privacy had died and the First Amendment had been repealed and nobody knew it and nobody had voted on it and nobody cared. The NSA had gone from No Such Agency to the nation's snooping nanny, reading everybody's private e-mails in the name of national security, seeing every teenage girl's Sweet Sixteen topless party pictures in the name of national security, every psycho's threats, every nutsack's nocturnal emissions.

In the future, everybody will be notorious for fifteen seconds. And fucked for life.

Did somebody say fucked?

"Mr. President," began Seelye, "I think you'd better have a look at this. Sending to you now, sir. . . ."

It was against protocol, sending something from a wireless device to an Oval Office computer, but under the circumstances it didn't matter. Not only was this a matter of national security, it was a matter of presidential reelection: an October Surprise that this president would want to know about.

Something chimed softly on the President's computer screen, incoming.

"On your screen, Mr. President," said Seelye. "Highest security level and FYEO."

For Your Eyes Only. No fucking around with mere SCI—Sensitive Compartmented Information. This had to go right to the top. Who, as it happened, was sitting right across from him.

Tyler was already punching buttons. For a president, Seelye had to admit, he wasn't quite a complete idiot.

"Do you have it?"

"I think so, yes . . ." More button-punching. "Cows."

"Dead."

"All of them."

"A vegan's wet dream, yes sir. Fruit-bat paradise: no more meat."

"Your words, sir, not mine."

Tyler slide-showed the photos. Rows upon rows, ranks upon ranks of dead cows. "Who sent these?"

"One of Devlin's ops, sir."

"Name?"

"We don't know. He's Devlin's man. You know the drill."

Mount Tyler seethed for a moment, then subsided. "I can't have a possible traitor operating a private army, General Seelye. I simply can't have it."

"Devlin's in California, sir. In exile. As per your wishes." A pause. "Perhaps you'd like to recall him, send him up north. What have we got to lose?"

Tyler shot Seelye a glance. "The presidency?"

"Paris is worth a Mass, Mr. President."

"Go to hell."

"I'd rather go to Paris, if it's all the same to you, sir. After all, if you're going to fire me . . ."

The volcano finally exploded. Tyler picked up the monitor and hurled it across the room. In the old days of computer monitors, it might have exploded in a shower of sparks; today's monitors simply guttered like dead candles and went out. Everything was a metaphor these days.

Seelye waited a decent interval. ". . . if you're going to fire me, it ought to be over something important. Human life or death—the kind of thing that wins elections. Dead cows—we can handle that."

Tyler was settling down. "But what do they mean? What do those pictures mean? What the hell is going on?"

It was time to leave and get to back to work. "Three

choices, sir," said Seelye. "One, happenstance. Two, coincidence. Three, enemy action. Me, I'm for number three."

Tyler smiled. "You know your James Bond, Director Seelye." At last, his real title; he'd never advance as a general again, so DIRNSA was as far as he was ever going to go. "So . . . Devlin?"

"Only you can bring him back. But let me tell you something, sir—if you don't you won't be sitting in this office for very much longer. You and I both know there's a link between whatever the Iranians are up to and what's happening in Central California."

"What do you recommend?"

"Have Secretary Colangelo order immediate DHS lockdown on the reservoirs, Hetch Hetchy, L.A. Water and Power, everything. In case it's poison."

The idea of getting Homeland Security involved did not thrill him. He had zero confidence in the cumbersome, useless bureaucracy's ability to get anything done and wished to God he had the political capital to get rid of the whole damn thing. Maybe after he won the next election . . . *If* he won the next election. "Then what?"

"Get Devlin. And pray."

Tyler looked at Seelye for a long moment, then nodded his head: dismissed. The general said nothing as he left the room, leaving the president deep in thought. After a decent interval, Tyler pressed the buzzer under the *Resolute.*

After an indecent interval, Manuel Concepcion appeared in the doorway. "You rang, Mr. President?"

The scotch was already on the silver tray.

"Am I as dumb as I look? Wait—don't answer that."

Too late—the words were already out of Manuel's mouth. "No, sir."

Tyler thought for a moment, then smiled. "Good answer," he said, reaching for the fresh drink.

His private phone line buzzed—that would be Millie

Dhouri, his secretary. "What is it?" he barked, a little more loudly than necessary. Better slow down on the scotch.

"Major Atwater to see you, sir," she said. "He says it's extremely urgent."

President Tyler had the drink halfway to his mouth, then set it back down. If anybody knew what the hell was going on, it was Atwater. The man was dutiful and smart; if he'd decided to buck the chain of command by coming directly to the White House, it must be pretty damned important. Otherwise, it was Atwater's ass, but he knew that already.

Tyler liked moxie. And when you were as fucked as he was, what harm could it do? He glanced over at Manuel, who had gone into statue mode. No help there. He was on his own.

"Send him in, Millie," he said.

The door opened. The major stood in the doorway, holding a salute.

"At ease, Major," said Tyler. "Come in."

The President rose to greet the analyst. The man had done good work, that he knew, cracking one of the famous unbreakable codes—something to do with classical music, which Tyler couldn't even pretend to understand. He gestured to an empty chair. "Sit down, Major. Drink?"

"Yes, sir. No thank you, sir."

"Sure about that?" asked Tyler. "You've come in here, elided your chain of command, barely just missed seeing your boss, so what you have to tell me is obviously pretty damn important and for my eyes only, so if I were you I'd have me a stiff one because I know I only got one chance to make my case and if I don't I've just kissed my career goodbye."

Atwater eyed the president's whiskey. "No, thank you, Mr. President," he replied.

Tyler grabbed the drink and handed it to him. "Drink this. And that's an order from your commander in chief."

Atwater picked up the drink. "Down the hatch," ordered Tyler. And down the hatch it went. "Feel better now, son?"

"Yes, sir. Thank you, sir."

"Now get to it."

Atwater took a deep breath. The fellow had balls, Tyler had to give him that.

"The codes," he began. "The ones Director Seelye asked me to interpret."

"And so you did, especially that, whattyacallit one, the Elgar thing."

"The *Dorabella* cipher, yes sir. Not a code at all but a blueprint. That was the clue that gave the whole thing away. I'm sorry that I didn't see that until just now, Mr. President."

Tyler had no idea what the man was talking about, or why, if this was some inside-baseball code discussion, he didn't take it up with Seelye or some other NSA geek. Before he could say anything, Atwater was banging away again.

"Here they are, sir—notes that came in via e-mail directly to the DIRNSA's classified inbox. Each one alludes to a famous code, either in literature or reality. The first one reads, 'DIRNSA Seelye—What are the Thirty-Nine Steps?' "

" 'The Thirty-Nine Steps is an organization of spies,' " quoted Tyler from memory.

"Right, sir, the Hitchcock movie. But that line's not in the book—in Buchan's book, the steps are just that: steps. They have nothing to do with an organization of spies. It's a clue—not to the code but to the sender's intent. You see what I'm getting at?"

Tyler's expression told him he didn't.

"It's a signal from the sender that we're not to take the codes literally, but figuratively. Steps. In other words, taken together, they are sending us one big message. So let's look at the next one. 'To Lt. General Armond Seelye or To Whom It May Concern, Edgar Allan POE. (signed) the Magician.' "

Tyler decided he might as well play along. "What the hell does that one mean?"

Atwater looked the President right in the eye. "Well, this one tells us that the overall message is really for you, sir—which is why I took the liberty of coming directly to you about it. You see, back in 1839, Poe published a couple of cryptograms as a challenge to his readers. The first was deciphered fairly quickly—it was a basic substitution cipher—but the second had to wait for nearly one hundred fifty years and the advent of computer technology. It was a doozy; the letter *e* alone had fourteen variants. . . ."

"Get to the point, Major."

"Right. So the point is, the cipher was eventually cracked and it turned out to be just crummy poetry, but it's not so much the codes as the name under which Poe published them: W. B. Tyler. We think Poe did that to annoy President John Tyler, who had ignored his entreaties for a government job."

"What's 'the Magician' got to do with it?" asked the President.

"Ah, that—that comes from a line this 'Tyler' wrote in submitting the ciphers, in which he said that the art of concealment by cryptography gave him 'a history of mental existence, to which I may turn, and in imagination, retrace former pleasures, and again live through bygone scenes—secure in the conviction that the magic scroll has a tale for my eye alone.' "

"So it's a threat?"

"Yes, sir. I believe it is, sir. . . . Shall I continue?

Tyler nodded.

"The third one everybody knows: 'UG RMK CSXH-MUFMKB TOXG CMVATLUIV.' That's the substitution cipher from Dorothy L. Sayers's book *Have His Carcase*, and it means 'We are discovered. Save yourself.' Has to do with lovers, I believe. You see where we're headed?"

It was clear that the President was still evaluating the veiled threat, so Atwater plunged ahead:

"The numbers—317, 8, 92, 73, 112, 79, 67, 318, 28, 96, 107, 41, 631, 78, 146, 397, 118, 98, 114—well, they're the Beale cipher, the one that was deciphered. This one's a double whammy—the Beale Cipher refers to a still-unlocated buried treasure somewhere in Virginia, which picks up the Poe theme, since Poe's most famous exercise in cryptography, "The Gold-Bug," also has to do with buried treasure. But the key to deciphering Beale Cipher No. 2 turned out to be the Declaration of Independence."

"Which brings the whole plot right back to this office," said Tyler.

"Not quite. Because while the sender is obviously obsessed with exacting some sort of revenge upon you and the United States government, he's also consumed with sexual jealousy. We see that in the Sayers quote and even more transparently in the *Dorabella* cipher, which as you know I may modestly say that—"

"You broke it."

"Not by breaking it, but understanding what its true nature was: a blueprint for something else."

"Let me see that damn thing again," said Tyler.

Eighty-seven characters, squiggles based on the letter *E,* arranged in three rows:

"So that's what love looks like," he muttered. "And the last one?"

Atwater brightened. He may have been discussing matters of crucial national importance, but he was still a code breaker, and this was his finest hour. " 'Masterman. XX.' The overt reference is to the British practice of doubling captured German spies during World War Two and using them for disinformational purposes. The Roman numerals stand for the Committee of Twenty, which was run by Cecil Masterman. But, sir, I think as you can now see, they have a more sinister significance. . . ."

"Death," said Tyler. "Twin Xs, negating everything that has gone before. A double cross . . ."

Atwater was impressed—Tyler really was as quick a study as his reputation suggested. Maybe that was why he was president, and Atwater was not.

"Very good, Mr. President, and not only that . . . look, it's really quite ingenious. The final clue refers back to the first one, to *The Thirty-Nine Steps*, both wartime references to German spies. Our correspondent is a creative artist in his own right, a man of immense wealth—that's what the double image of buried treasure signifies—and one with a tremendous animus toward our country and to you, and also one who is severely suffering in love. This is a very angry man, Mr. President, and an extremely dangerous one."

Tyler had never been more ready for another drink in his life. "So he's closing the circle. Wrapping things up. You missed that, Major Atwater, didn't you? There's a ticking clock here, the sands on the hourglass are running out. That's also what the two Xs mean—time's up, show's over, the end. All he needs is one more X. Oh Jesus—that's it!"

"What's 'it,' Mr. President?"

Tyler threw an arm around Atwater's shoulder as he walked him to the door. "Son," he said, "have you ever heard of an October Surprise? Well, unless you boys do your job, we're in for a hell of a big one."

Manuel appeared. Tyler took the libation, but not before he had shouted to Ms. Dhouri, "Get General Seelye and Secretary of Defense Johnson in here, on the double."

Then he had his drink.

Chapter Ten

Baku, Azerbaijan

Emanuel Skorzeny settled back onto the plush sofa, his feet up on an ottoman, feeling every inch a prince. They had been here for a while now and he was both at ease and at home.

For a Muslim-majority country, the Republic of Azerbaijan could have been a lot worse. Officially, it was still secular, as befit its former Soviet pedigree—although with a high concentration of Shiite Muslims, and Iran only about a hundred miles away, how long that would continue was probably just a matter of time. One by one, the "secular" Muslim countries had fallen, been reconquered, along the southern rim of the Mediterranean in what had been for hundreds of years the old Roman empire, up to and including Turkey, the home of Atatürk and his bold Kemalist revolution—now, less than a century on, despised and forgotten.

Never underestimate the power of religion—or, as he preferred to think of it, deplorable superstition. A powerful, irrational, absurd force—and one that he intended to use to its fullest extent.

What a fool he had been all these years, fighting religion when he could have been using it. He cursed his childhood, the death—make that the murder—of his parents, his upbringing by one of the heroes of the Reich. The atheist, anti-Semitic and unchristian Reich that had sought to purge the world of such primitive belief and instead return it to an older, purer form of savagery, unleavened by the bread of the Hebrews or the love of Jesus. How right they were, and how wrong.

For now he could see, as plainly as if Jesus himself were to sail down from the clouds, separating the wheat from the chaff, the blessed from the damned; whether he came alone or at the side of Allah mattered not. To Emanuel Skorzeny, it was all the same totem, a talisman he would never touch.

But which he could use. "Do you know about the astronauts of Apollo 11?" he asked.

There were two women in the room with him.

The first was Amanda Harrington, the City financial whiz who had run his philanthropic Skorzeny Foundation until she had tried to betray him with one of his own men. He had given her a lesson that she would never forget—nearly killed her, in fact, with a dose of tetrodotoxin—but he had succeeded in breaking her in both body and spirit and now here she was, back on the job, back in his arms and in his bed when he desired her, docile as a lamb.

The second was Emanuelle Derrida, his assistant. That Ms. Derrida was not interested in the male of the species did not bother him in the slightest. She was a beautiful woman, her surname amused him no end, and, of course, he thought her Christian name a thing of beauty, even though she was probably even less of a Christian than he was. Unlike the late M. Paul Pilier, his former aide-de-camp, she was absolutely conscienceless, never blanched at any of his requests, kept the living quarters of his Boeing 707 in pristine condition, as befit a man of his sensibilities. He trusted her—well, he almost trusted her—implicitly and he knew that an order thought was an order carried out.

He wished she did not so obviously desire Miss Harrington, but he was secure in the knowledge that she dare not cross him again.

This must be what true love is, he thought. Then again, there was no point in desiring Mlle. Derrida, which was one of the reasons he had hired her in the first place. After all, carnal and emotional pleasure had to take a backseat to the culmination of his life's work.

There was no answer about the astronauts, and upon this occasion he was not feeling professorial or instructive. "Very well, then," he said. "Report."

The command was directed at Miss Harrington.

"Yes, sir," she began. It was just like old times again, him and her, the recent unpleasantness long since forgotten if not forgiven.

"Through the timely application of Foundation funds, we have increased the number of safe-harbor sites to which we might repair should the occasion warrant," she said. "The number of countries willing to give us admittance or to at least turn a blind eye to our presence has increased threefold since last year. And I am very pleased to tell you, sir, that France may soon join their ranks."

Skorzeny permitted himself a small smile and a brief memory. "I do miss my home there in the rue Boutarel," he said, "as I'm sure you do as well, Miss Harrington, Mlle. Derrida. When this is all over, we shall return in triumph and disport ourselves at several of the city's finest gastronomic shrines. What else?"

Amanda Harrington swallowed her distaste for the monster sitting opposite her, said a silent prayer of thanks that he was well across the room, and continued.

"Despite the reversal of fortune that was suffered after the school-hostage crisis in Illinois, the failure of our EMP attack upon the East Coast of America and the considerable blowback after the successful assault on Times Square, the Foundation nevertheless saw its net assets increase, even in the teeth of the ongoing worldwide recession."

Skorzeny laughed. "Recessions mean nothing to me, Miss Harrington," he said. "I can create them, prolong them, or end them as I choose. In ancient times, Croesus actually needed to have gold, silver, and jewelry on hand to display his wealth; later plutocrats demanded specie. All I need is a functioning iPad. Which is why, right now, for financial reasons, it amuses me to prolong this one."

He rose. Amanda shuddered. Luckily, he went to the window to gaze out upon the Caspian Sea instead of upon her.

"How easy it is to make this thing called 'money,' once you realize that it isn't money anymore. Not a storehouse of value. Not even a worthless piece of paper emblazoned with some country's boastful trappings of sovereignty. Just blips on a computer screen, imaginary numbers rendered temporarily real by equally imaginary flashes of light. And why?"

He turned. This was one of those Skorzeny rhetorical questions that demanded an answer. "And why?"

Emanuelle Derrida said nothing, as she usually did. "I'm sure I don't know, Mr. Skorzeny," replied Amanda. She hoped her nonresponse would keep him on the other side of the room, lecturing instead of leching.

"Because people *believe* in them, Miss Harrington, as well you should know. They believe in the purchasing power of imaginary numbers, the way European peasants once believed in putting pigs on trial for witchcraft. They believe in them because they have no alternative, but the fiction has more power than the reality. Because no one can cart around a storehouse of wealth in precious metals and expect to exchange a tiny sliver of it for a loaf of bread. Because modern life is too complicated, too complex. And so we turn to totems and talismans. To substitution ciphers, representations of reality that obscure more than illuminate. To signs and symbols and portents."

He turned away from the sea and looked directly at her. "Do you understand, Miss Harrington?" he inquired.

"Yes, sir," she answered. "I think I do, sir."

"Very well, then," he said. "Report. You know whom I'm talking about."

Amanda knew whom he meant. Even with the boss on the run, Skorzeny's private intelligence service was very good, and his immense wealth gave him access to figures well-placed in both the American government and its security services.

"As far as we can tell, sir—" she began.

"And as I calculate these things, that ought to be pretty damn far," observed Skorzeny from his window perch.

"He's gone to ground, sir," she responded, quietly.

That got his attention. The old anger flashed. At what age did the fires finally tamp down and die? Did the seven deadly sins, particularly lust and greed, finally fade to memory? Perhaps only when they faded to black.

"What do you mean, Miss Harrington, 'gone to ground'?" he barked. "There is not my equal on this planet, as you well know, and this bastard surely cannot elude my holy wrath, no matter how fiendish his cleverness."

Skorzeny turned his attention back out the window, looking south, watching the ships on their stately progress toward Bandar Anzali in Iran, or one of the Islamic Republic's other port cities. That was where *she* would be headed soon, drugged, bound, gagged, a piece of baggage being delivered in the custody of Miss Harrington to her new, er, interlocutors, her last words already written and posted to Washington. From Bandar Anzali, he knew, it was but a short ride into Tehran, through Rasht and Qazvin and then along Highway One to the capital, and Doom.

Before she could open her mouth, she became aware that

he had switched something on—a dirge she recognized at once. Thank God, it wasn't the *Metamorphosen* by Strauss, which he had forced her to listen to as he'd poisoned her with the fugu fish toxin back in France. No, not Strauss. Instead, it was the funeral march from Beethoven's "Eroica" Symphony.

Skorzeny could feel the vipress's eyes on him, her thoughts boring into him. But hatred and love were two sides of the same coin, one the obverse of the other; as long as strong emotion was involved, all was right with the world. If Amanda hated him now, it was of no consequence. That hate could easily turn back to the love she had once bestowed upon him. All it would take was continued proximity.

Besides, it was a challenge, and there was nothing Emanuel Skorzeny loved more in this life than a challenge. Especially one involving a woman.

"Gone to ground? Impossible."

How he had wanted to kill Maryam himself, and how it had pained him to have to let her go—not only for monetary reasons, for the price on her head was quite high, but for geopolitical reasons as well. The Iranians were still not quite sure whether to trust him, not after what had happened to their operative Kohanloo on the East River in New York. On the other hand, they were all in this together now, and they needed him far more than he needed them. So off-loading the devil's mistress had been a business decision.

"Gone to ground, Mr. Skorzeny," repeated Amanda. "Vanished. We have put out every feeler we can, even upped our payments to certain political columnists well-fed on the Georgetown party circuit, men and women who can hold their liquor when all around them are losing theirs. Nothing." She waited a beat. "Perhaps he's dead, sir."

Her observation had the desired effect. Skorzeny suddenly exploded in rage and anger.

"Dead!" he shouted. "Impossible. Impossible! I cannot, I

will not let some Fort Meade bureaucrat cheat me out of what is rightfully mine!" He was nearly apoplectic.

"M. Skorzeny—*si'l vous plaît*," said Mlle. Derrida, barely looking up from some French fashion magazine she was reading. Mlle. Derrida was very fond of French fashion magazines, mostly because she was very fond of French fashion models. In fact, with her slender body, long legs and cascading hair, she rather looked like one. "Your health."

Skorzeny took a breath and started to calm. "What I mean to say is, it is not possible that he has been terminated. I would know it—perhaps not in my head but in my heart."

Miss Harrington let out an involuntary laugh, which she quickly covered with a cough. If this creature had a heart it would have to be donated to science upon his death as a perfectly preserved example of a nonfunctioning organ that had somehow managed to keep its host alive for decades. "Excuse me, sir," she said.

Fortunately, he hadn't noticed. "No," muttered Skorzeny, "he is still out there. Plotting against me. Let this be a lesson to you ladies—never fail to have done yesterday what you cannot do today and may no longer be able to do tomorrow. Do I make myself clear?"

"Yes, sir," replied Amanda. Mlle. Derrida didn't bother to respond.

"No secure traffic about this woman, Maryam?"

Miss Harrington pretended to consult some notes on her iPad. "None, sir. Upon receipt of her letter, the entire network went dark. It's as if neither of them had ever existed."

"Which is, of course, the perfect proof that they're still alive," retorted Skorzeny. He left his seat by the window and moved back into the room. "If there were a God, wouldn't he be more likely to speak to us by his absence then by his presence? What faith does it require to believe in a being standing right in front of you?"

He sniffed the air, as if seeking either the divine or the diabolical via his olfactory sense. "And President Tyler?"

Amanda let out an inaudible sigh of relief. At last, he was back on ground she could stand on. "President Tyler's political fortunes are waning and I can say with a degree of high confidence that it is very unlikely he will be returned to office in the American general election next month."

"Miss Hassett will defeat him? Of this we are sure?"

Amanda consulted her screen. "He is trailing across the board, even in reliably partisan polls that normally favor the other side. She is leading among all age-groups, and among all demographics. If these trends continue, we are looking at an historic repudiation of a sitting president, especially one swept into office so recently on a wave of such electoral enthusiasm."

"We may have played some small role in that," said Skorzeny.

"Indeed, sir. For a price. Your subsidies to Mr. Sinclair have been rising steeply, I note."

That would be Jake Sinclair, the head of the largest media conglomerate in America. Sinclair's empire was fully behind Angela Hassett, the governor of the smallest state in the union, a woman who guarded both her past and her private life jealously. But, as few contemporary politicians did, she realized that she was not selling the past, but the future. It didn't really matter who she was, or even what she had accomplished. She was the embodiment of the Future, and the compliant and complicit Sinclair media were with her every step of the way, blocking unwanted inquiries, refocusing the debate when the debate needed refocusing. They carried the water and did the dirty work and no doubt they expected to be rewarded handsomely with policy preferences and Oval Office access once the formality of the presidential election was past.

"An investment, Miss Harrington, an investment." Tyler didn't have a Chinaman's chance, as they used to say in pre-PC America.

"In short, Mr. Skorzeny, President Tyler looks to be a one-term president, his appeal to the ladies notwithstanding, and we should plan accordingly."

"Duly noted, Miss Harrington, so proceed accordingly."

"Yes, sir."

"Then perhaps all the rest doesn't matter. A new president will appoint a new head of the National Security Agency and therefore of the CSS and so will rid us of this meddlesome general, Seelye, and his unholy crew."

"I would expect so, sir, yes."

"Very good," said Skorzeny.

He went to the desk, opened a drawer, and extracted a new laptop computer, which he placed on the clean desktop. It was not his computer, as everyone in the room knew. It was Maryam's. The computer she had with her in the hotel room in Hungary. The computer issued by the National Security Agency/Central Security Service of Fort Meade, Maryland. God alone knew what secrets it contained.

An astonishing breach of op-sec, thought Skorzeny, as he contemplated the machine. To let such a valuable object fall into a stranger's hands . . . into his hands . . .

Which is why he was not going to touch it. The damn thing would be booby-trapped six ways from the Sabbath, whichever Sabbath the impudent devil observed. To even lift its lid was asking for trouble. Any number of things could happen, all of them bad. It could explode. It could melt down, taking his hands with it. It could . . . well, it could do whatever the bastard's mind could conceive of.

For surely he would not have let it be captured so easily. No man, not even one besotted with a woman as lovely as Maryam, would be so blithe. There must be a catch to it—yes, that was it. The devil had *wanted* it to fall into his hands, had *offered* Maryam to him, had *intended* for her to become his prisoner.

Skorzeny took a deep breath.

It was a play worthy of himself. The perfect poisoned pawn. And he had almost fallen for it!

He glanced up at Miss Harrington. Time really was a harsh mistress. The luscious young thing stripping off to her knickers soon enough stood revealed as a withered hag, smothering you in her foul embrace. What if she were to betray him again? He was implicitly sure of his power over her—she was nothing without him—but, still . . . Out of some misguided feminine revenge, although for what he could not think. What if she were to somehow free the woman, double-cross him, sell him out?

Why then, much as it would pain him to do so, especially after all they'd been through, he would have to kill her.

But he didn't want to kill her. He had tried that, almost, once before, and look what had happened. The whelp had followed the trail right to his lair, and nearly killed him as he'd slithered down his escape hatch. Truly, a viper unto his breast.

Which begged the question: To open or not to open? Treasures untold within, but corrupted. Gratification, followed by death. A window into the soul of the enemy—whose bile would spatter you and take you down the road to perdition.

His hands hovered over the laptop. Damn the woman for closing it as they'd entered the room. Damn her to the hell she was even now experiencing in her place of confinement.

Or was she?

Could he trust Miss Harrington?

The laptop. The woman. The women.

Him.

He looked around the room, at Miss Harrington and Mlle. Derrida. "Now," he said, "about Apollo 11 . . ."

CHAPTER ELEVEN

New York City

The news was breaking as Jake Sinclair entered the offices on Sixth Avenue. Normally he didn't come to New York much, certainly not since they'd moved the corporate base of operations to Los Angeles in some choice Century City property he just happened to own.

He'd flown in on his private jet, and if there was one rule he had on his private jet it was that he was not to be disturbed for any reason whatsoever, short of Selenites landing at Bowling Green or, worse, Carbon Beach. Or Elvis, reappearing in Branson on a comeback tour.

"What is it, Benny?" he said to Ben Bernstein as he entered the editor in chief's office. Once the job had been called executive editor, and to be the executive editor of the *New York Times* had been the pinnacle of American journalism. So of course that had to go—*he*, Jake Sinclair, was the pinnacle of American journalism, and there would never be another one of him. Editor in chief was as far as he would go with people whose salaries he paid.

"Cows, Mr. Sinclair," came the reply. "Lots and lots of cows."

"So what? We got cows right here in New York state, somewhere. Cows all over the Midwest. Cows in India, sacred cows I think they call them. What's so special about these cows?"

Bernstein kept a poker face. He had no opinion about his new boss and he did his damnedest to make sure his expression reflected that scrupulous neutrality. "These cows are all dead," he said.

"Where?"

"On a big cattle ranch up near Coalinga."

Sinclair's visage expressed his distaste for Twenty Questions. "Where's that?"

"Central California, sir," replied Bernstein, backtracking. "I assumed that, since you're from there, California I mean, that—"

"You think I drive to San Francisco?" Sinclair was rapidly losing interest in the story. "What does it mean? Is steak going to be more expensive? Is it news I can use?"

In Bernstein's experience, the only story the chief was really interested in was the ongoing political story, so he quickly reframed. "It means Tyler's got another disaster on his hands, sir. Somebody's poisoned the California water supply or something."

That stopped Sinclair in his tracks. "What?" Then he was moving again, double-time.

Bernstein watched the boss disappear into his private office at the end of the hall. He'd only been inside it once or twice, but from what he'd seen it was more like a fortress than an office, completely secure, with dedicated phone lines and all the latest electronic gadgetry. Not that Sinclair knew how to use most of it, but to men like Jake Sinclair the display of such equipment was at least as important as its actual use.

Sinclair shut the door behind him and turned to the ranks of TV monitors. The sun may have set on the British Empire, but it was always coming up somewhere on his. Sure enough, Bernstein was right—dead cows everywhere. He didn't much care how the paper played the story the next day—newspapers were so retro they were almost chic—but he very much cared how his news networks were handling it—and so far he was not seeing what he wanted to see.

He reached for one of the secure lines and dialed her secure number. She answered on the second ring. She spoke first.

"Remember what I told you about puzzles? Ciphers? Cryptograms?" He did remember. That was the day they were in the bathroom at his office in Century City, with the shower on, the day she'd pulled him toward her in the steam, kissed him and told him that if he was ever late for another meeting with her she would kill him. "Well, this is the piece of the puzzle we've been waiting for. Now use it."

"I'm not sure I under—"

"How did you ever manage to get anywhere in this life?" came the voice at the other end of the line. He had no idea where she was at this moment, somewhere out on the hustings, as they used to call them, whatever hustings were. Somewhere putting their plan into action. "Honestly, I think you are the stupidest man I have ever met in my life."

There was nothing to say. His job was to say nothing. So far, so good.

"Have you got the package ready? The October Surprise?"

That would be the complete dossier on Jeb Tyler—every bit of dirt and mud and slur and slander and innuendo that the combined newsgathering forces of the Sinclair Empire could dig up. And was there ever plenty of it. It was so explosive that it would finish Tyler before the voters went to the polls, except that they would not be merciful. The material would not be released all at once. No, it would dribble out day by day, each story more damaging than the last, some on TV, some on the radio, some in the papers and magazines.

Beginning the third week of October, every day would be sheer misery for the incumbent president, but there would be nothing he could do about it. He could not withdraw from the campaign, because it would be too late to replace him on the ballot. He couldn't concede in advance, because the propriety of elections would have to be observed. Day after day he was going to have to sit there in the Oval Office and take his beating like a man. And then be destroyed the first Tuesday in November.

Now that was something Jake Sinclair was really looking forward to. And he knew two other people who would enjoy the spectacle even more than he did. The first was the woman on the other end of the phone, Angela Hassett, the governor of Rhode Island, whose meteoric rise to power was about to be crowned with the highest office in the land.

The other was a man he had never met, never seen, and never spoken to—only communicated with by cutouts and go-betweens, each similarly invisible. But a very rich man and the man who had made him, Jake Sinclair, a modestly rich man by his lofty standards. This man who wanted Jeb Tyler gone and would spend any amount of money to achieve that objective.

Anonymously, of course. Untraceably, of course. Electoral proprieties must be observed.

"Tell me that you have it. Tell me that you have everything," she commanded. Involuntarily, he glanced over his shoulder. Even here in his inner sanctum, he could feel her presence, and it wouldn't have surprised him at all to learn that, somehow, she'd had him bugged.

"I've got it—well, almost all of it. There's still a couple of things we're trying to chase down, but I have top people on it. Top people."

Was that a chuckle or a chortle coming through the ether? "I'll bet you do," said Angela Hassett, "and I'll bet I know just who she is, too."

The line went dead. He was alone.

Sinclair sat in his chair, looking out the window at Midtown Manhattan. That woman did something to him. He could feel it. There was something deliciously erotic in fantasizing about an affair with the next president of the United States. With the first female president of the United States. With her. So what if they were both married? He still hadn't quite decided Jenny II's fate yet, and as for Angela's husband . . . well, he could be dealt with down the line.

Somewhere, a soft chime sounded, like something you'd hear in a Buddhist rock garden. Jake Sinclair hated buzzers and refused to be interrupted by the ring of a telephone, the dull thunk of an incoming e-mail message, or God forbid, one of those Twitter things.

"What is it?" The chime automatically activated a microphone that allowed him to communicate with his secretary, whose name he could never quite remember.

"Ms. Stanley, sir."

Just the girl he wanted to see. "Send her in."

The lock on the door buzzed and in walked his favorite television correspondent. Her work during the siege of Times Square had been outstanding, and the fact that she'd gotten herself temporarily kidnapped by, well, they never did figure out exactly who, had been a career enhancer.

"Mr. Sinclair?" she said.

She was beautiful, even more beautiful than she was on television, full-figured but wholesome, sexy but innocent—just the way the viewers liked them. About the only thing that had changed was her hair, but it was growing back nicely. On the air, she wore a wig, so nobody could tell she had been practically scalped.

He didn't rise. To get up would signal weakness to the help. She didn't sit down. To sit down would signal servility toward the boss.

"Have you been looking into what I asked you, Principessa?" he inquired. He loved that name, and wondered if it was really hers.

"Yes, Mr. Sinclair," she said. She moved forward to the desk and now was standing just opposite him, towering over him. "Just a couple more pieces of the puzzle left to gather."

He smiled. "Very good. How long do I have to wait?"

She smiled back. What a smile she had. "Won't be long now. In the meantime, there's this."

She put an old BlackBerry down on his desk. "What I am supposed to do with this?" he asked.

"Nothing," she said. "Just listen."

Who knew that BlackBerrys doubled as tape recorders? That they had little voice-memo doohickies (what did the kids call them today. Applications—yes, "apps") and that they could record—

The babble coming out the smartphone was like no language he had ever heard before. Arabic or Iranian, rapid-fire, and then, at the end, this:

"Because I am sending you to hell."

"What's that supposed to mean?" he asked, reaching for the phone, but Principessa swept it back up and slipped it into her pocket.

"You wanted a puzzle, I got you a puzzle," she said. "Now all you have to do is figure it out."

She was already at the door:

"That's what I pay you for," he said.

"Pay me more," she replied, and then she was gone.

CHAPTER TWELVE

Central California

It was just like old times. The phone buzzed softly, in a pre-arranged signal of long and shorts. He knew who it was without even looking at it. He didn't care. He had better things to do than jump when barked at. He was under suspicion, in the soup, off the job, sent on uncompassionate leave—whatever. The soup was happening here, now.

He had made good time getting up from California City. There had been no reports of poisoned drinking water in the cities—not on the radio, and not from his secure sources back at Fort Meade.

He didn't have to think twice about who might have done this. It had *his* fingerprints all over it. All the plots they'd broken up involving water had to do with city reservoirs, with the drinking supplies. Oh, they'd tried, but through a combination of luck and terrorist ineptitude, every last plot had been stopped—some just in time, to be sure, but stopped.

But this . . . this was classic Skorzeny. For one thing— and he knew he could take this to Skorzeny's Swiss bank—it was a misdirection, an attention-getter while the real action unfolded elsewhere. That had been the man's MO back in Edwardsville as he played on the sentiment of a nation while he tried to get his ships into port to launch the EMP devices, one on each coast. He was still new to the game, though, and had let his man Milverton get too cocky, and Devlin had managed to stop both of them—one of them terminally.

His hand stole to his shoulder, where Milverton had wounded him so grievously, where Skorzeny had kicked him as he dove down his escape hatch in Clairvaux. He'd had the bastard in his hands, and his weaknesses had defeated him. If it weren't for Maryam . . . his guardian angel . . .

The secure Android buzzed again. He ignored it.

The attack on Midtown Manhattan had been several orders of magnitude greater, but again Skorzeny had underestimated him, sent a child to do a man's job. Devlin regretted having to kill Raymond Crankheit as brutally as he did, but it was a mercy killing. The boy had reminded him of himself, and he'd had to cut him off in his amateur prime, before anyone else got ahold of him and turned him into a really lethal weapon. He'd been up against the best the SAS had to offer in Milverton, and some punk, and between the two of them the punk had scared him more.

The goddamn phone was not to be ignored. He activated all necessary security measures, and knew that the party on the other end of the line had done so as well.

"Speak," he commanded.

"This is President Jeb Tyler," came the voice.

"Save your breath, sir. I know who you are. You fired me, remember?"

"That was then and this was now."

"Do I sense my dad and the SecDef there with you?"

"You do, as per their authorization."

"We have to stop meeting like this."

The president replied: "I need you back."

"If it's about the cows, I'm already on my way."

To Devlin's surprise, there was a moment of silence. Tyler was usually quick with a snappy comeback; Devlin half thought that the president was amused by his rudeness, since Devlin was the only man on earth who could get away with being insubordinate to the commander in chief.

"I've got bigger problems than a bunch of dead cows."

"I'll say. You've got an election to lose, and I must say you're doing a damn good job of losing it, sir."

"Believe it or not, the election is only second on my list of worries. General Seelye?"

"Hi, Pop," said Devlin before the director of the National Security Agency could say anything. That was just to get under Seelye's skin. If there was anybody in this world he hated almost as much as hated Skorzeny, it was Seelye—the surrogate father who had raised him after the deaths of his parents in Rome on that horrible day back in 1985. The day he saw his father die and his mother die in his arms when he was eight years old.

"What do you know about the Mahdi?"

"Laurence Olivier played him in *Khartoum*. Is this a serious question?"

"There's something afoot in Iran," said Tyler.

"There's always something afoot in Iran. There's been something afoot in Iran since 1979. Carter should have done something about it. Reagan should have done something about it. These bastards have been killing our people, either directly or through surrogates, since just after their glorious revolution. They are the leading sponsor of state terrorism in the world. And yet your predecessor did nothing about them, despite all his brave talk, and you've done nothing about them. Don't tell me you're finally growing a pair."

"Why don't you shut up before I fire you again?"

"Why don't you put Maryam on the case? She's already in country, I believe." That hurt, hurt him more than it hurt them, but he might as well get it out there, clear the air, get at least one ghost out of the way before anybody else got killed.

"This is no time for jokes," came a female voice, which he knew belonged to Shalika Johnson. Johnson had fought her way up the ladder, from Philadelphia to prison to rehab to the Army to the officer corps to the general staff. She was mean and tough, an affirmative-action wet dream who had earned every last one of her plaudits, which meant she had exactly zero sympathy with bullshit gold-bricking diplomacy, political correctness, or half-measures. Although she had yet to fight her first war, everybody knew that when she did, and if Tyler took the gloves off, she'd finish the job in record time.

Of course, she could also finish him.

Then again, if Tyler lost, as now seemed probable, she'd also be out of a job. As would Seelye, in all likelihood. So maybe the smart play was to work against all of them, fuck up royally, and then disappear somewhere, forever.

Nah . . . they'd hunt him down—either they or their successors. He was walking a tightrope with no net, and the only way to go from here was straight to hell.

"You're right, Shalika," he said, "so cut the crap and tell me why you're all bothering me."

"That is *Secretary Johnson* to you, mister—"

"Listen, you two," said Tyler, "you can work out your insubordination issues later. Right now—"

"There is no *right now*, Mr. President," said Devlin. "You know the drill and you know the deal, and if little Miss Your Name Here until November at the DoD doesn't like it, she can go piss up a rope. I don't care. But this talk about Iran interests me, so get to it before I change my mind. Send me the dossier, and I'll let you know what I decide, and what my conditions are."

He could hear Tyler exploding in the background; then

the voice transmission went to mute. He gave them thirty seconds to get back to him and then he'd ring off.

He was down to seven in his countdown when Tyler came back on. "Deal."

"It's always a deal," replied Devlin. "It's either our deal or it's nothing. Ready to send?"

"Coming through in three minutes. You'll get some security misdirects first."

"Okay. But whatever it is, first I have to get up to Lemoore and pick up some reinforcements. Plus there's the matter of all the dead livestock."

"We're already on that," said Tyler. "Botulism in the feed, caused by Congress's cuts to agricultural subsidies—that's the official explanation for now. The outbreak seems to be limited to a fifty-mile radius centered around Visalia, running up as far as Fresno. We don't like it, but we can handle it while we figure out what it really is. Take a look at this report from Tehran."

Devlin closed his eyes and let his mind race. This was the moment he had been waiting for—not for months but for years. This was the moment when he could tell the lot of them to go hang. This was the moment he could simply walk away, the moment when his life sentence was lifted, when a sudden, miraculous deus ex machina pardon had suddenly descended from the sky. All he had to do was say no—which under the terms of his indentured-servitude contract, he was now free to do—and that would be the end of it.

Only one thing stood in his way.

Her.

Had she betrayed him, like everybody thought?

Had she double-crossed him, been an Iranian plant all along? Set him up, established her legend with him as far back as that day in Paris, seven years before his final confrontation with Milverton? The Iranians, the inheritors of a thousand-year empire, knew how to play the long game, that was for sure. But did she? Would she? Could she?

He had bet his life on the proposition that she could not. Based on absolutely nothing but a hunch, he had staked his fortune on twenty-two black, just like in *Casablanca*—one spin of the wheel for all the chips, and devil take the come what may.

"Send it through."

Now it was Tyler's turn to pause. They were locked in a loveless embrace, he and the U.S. government, neither side able to live without the other, but wishing passionately that it could be otherwise. "On its way."

The Android started to buzz. That would be the security check.

"One more thing." This time the voice was Seelye's. "One more thing I thought you'd like to know. That compromised computer?"

That would be the computer he had entrusted to her before he dove under the Hudson River, on his way into Times Square to take up the fight against the terrorists. She had taken it with her to Hungary, at his command, and whatever had happened there, it had disappeared along with her.

"What about it?"

"Nothing. It has not self-destructed, nor has been accessed in any way that we can tell. So either it's lost, they haven't touched it, or . . ."

"Or she didn't defect, and it's still with her."

"I figured I'd throw that in as a deal-sweetener. What do you think?

Devlin waited a beat before responding. He couldn't let his hopes get up, it was unprofessional. But there was no reason he could not dream.

"I think it's sweet," he said, and rang off. Anyone attempting to listen in would have heard nothing. They would not even have heard scrambled noise. Instead, they would have picked up some perfectly banal conversation between a mother in Bemidji, Minnesota, and her middle-aged son in Merced, recorded by NSA ops and used just once, on this occasion.

He could imagine the SecDef's rage. She wasn't used to being spoken to like that, and was probably still laboring under some quaint delusion about the sanctity of the chain of command. She was new to the operation of Branch 4, new to his unit and its strict protocols. If he could have his way, he would cut the secretary completely out of the loop, but since Branch 4 had operational authority in any theater of war, he was just going to have to live with it.

Oh well, the election was coming right up and it would all soon be over, one way or another. He was already past Bakersfield, so there was only another sixty miles or so to go, and he could make that in no time. There were no Chippers out here in the desert, and if one stopped him, well, that wouldn't work out so well for the Highway Patrol. He had neither the time nor the inclination to fuck around with some dickhead with a badge.

He let his mind drift back to California City. The rose was still on the seat beside him.

Had he dreamed the whole thing? Jacinta, the mute driver, Father Gonsalves? He still had the priest's money in his pocket, so that part at least was real. That part and the rose.

Whether he'd really seen something, there was no way to tell. He fished around in the seat for the Polaroid photos, but couldn't find them right away.

The Android gave off a series of beeps. That would be the incoming. As prescribed, he didn't touch the PDA for at least two minutes after the receipt of the information; anyone trying to intercept it would be eager to open it, and that would destroy all the data, plus send a locator to the Building. Accidents happened quickly once NSA headquarters got a tracer on you, including sudden car crashes that couldn't quite be explained, house fires, and gas explosions. Operational security was everything, or else it was nothing.

He didn't even have to look at the material to be able to guess what it was. As he had told the President in the aftermath of the failed operation to snatch Skorzeny from his lair in France, the crazy bastard was at war with the West, so his common cause with Kohanloo in the Times Square assault came as no surprise.

"An atheist's apocalypse," he had said. "End-times craziness." It would be just like Skorzeny to sign on to the Shiite eschatology, and use their religious belief as the tip of Klingsor's spear—and to plunge it not into Parsifal, but into Christ's side one last time.

Maybe all of this was related. Maybe the vision in the desert had something to do with whatever was happening in Iran. There didn't have to be a supernatural explanation for any of it, but the thematic relationship was irresistible. That would be how Skorzeny would want it, Klingsor the magician, always signing his dirty work with the hand of the master, the last civilized man eager to put out the lights of the West before death finally took him and carried him, screaming, only God knew where.

Only one caveat—sending the bastard to hell was his job, not God's. And that was one job he planned to finish this time, no matter what.

That and find her. If Maryam really was in Iran, then Skorzeny couldn't be far behind.

Now that was a twofer.

CHAPTER THIRTEEN

San Sebastian de Garabandal, Spain

They were passing by the church, as they did every day after school, four of them, four schoolgirls, two named Mari, after the Virgin, and Jacinta, and Conchita. Just like the girls back in the early sixties, same first names and all, the ones who had seen the vision, and heard the warning about the Great Chastisement that was sure to come if her words were not heeded.

Like schoolgirls everywhere, they babbled and giggled as they passed the parish church. The time was long past that they thought maybe they just might catch a glimpse of what those girls had seen so long ago: a vision of radiant loveliness, her face creased with sorrow, her message stern: *Repent.*

It had been easier to believe when they were children. It was easy to repent of sins you had not yet committed, not even in your heart, and yet almost impossible to imagine what those sins could really be. They were things only whispered about, to be savored and to be feared.

The first message had been delivered on October 18, 1961: *We must make sacrifices, perform much penance, and visit the Blessed Sacrament frequently. But first, we must lead good lives. If we do not, a chastisement will befall us. The cup is already filling up and if we do not change, a very great chastisement will come upon us.*

Chastisement was a word they all understood. Franco's Spain died long before they were born, but its memory lingered on, especially here in northern Spain, not far from Santander. Chastisement meant punishment and pain. Especially in light of the second message, the one Conchita alone received:

Previously, the Cup was filling; now it is brimming over. Many priests are following the road to perdition, and with them they are taking many more souls. . . . We should turn the wrath of God away from us by our own efforts. If you ask His forgiveness with a sincere heart, He will pardon you. . . . You are now being given the last warnings. . . . Reflect on the Passion of Jesus.

They could all recite the words by heart, for they had been hearing them all their lives. Tourists came and went through the small village and occasionally a man from the Vatican, which was still investigating the apparition, trying to decide whether it was real or fake. Of the hundreds and thousands of Marian apparitions around the world, fewer than a dozen were officially recognized by the Catholic Church.

So there was no reason to suspect that this glorious October day would be any different from all the others—or that it would be the same as that day back in 1961.

It was early morning, and at first they thought it was the glistening of the sun, past its summer prime. Later, in talking to the villagers and to the newspeople who showed up at their doorsteps, they described it as a blinding flash of light that caught them all in the eyes, as if someone were shining a very powerful searchlight directly at them. And yet, it was focused on each them, individually.

It took a few moments for them to begin to be able to see clearly once more as their retinas began to synthesize the light and the image.

She was framed against what appeared to be a celestial doorway, but on later reflection they realized it was the portals of the simple parish church that served the spiritual needs of the three hundred souls living near the Bay of Biscay. She wore a crown and a cloak. They could see her clearly, silhouetted against an impossible backdrop of the clear blue sky and the shining sun.

But all these details came later. Because, for many weeks, after the apparition, they could not really remember what the Lady had looked like, or how she was dressed, or whether she was holding anything in her arms. They could only remember that her lips were moving but that, strain as they might, they could not hear what she was saying.

But they could see her clearly enough, and that was all that young Jacinta needed. For Jacinta was deaf and she had learned to read lips—not only in Spanish but in Basque and border French—from the time she was young. St. Bernadette, who had seen her own famous vision not terribly far from here, in Lourdes, had heard the Lady speak in Pyrenean patois: *"Que soy era immaculada concepciou."* And so had Jacinta—not heard, but seen.

And this was the proof, the evidence, that what they had seen was not an illusion, not a fake like so many of the so-called apparitions. This was real, in the way that Guadalupe had been real, and Lourdes had been real, and Fatima had been real. The Virgin had not spoken to them in Castilian Spanish, but in their Cantabrian dialect. Halfway between the Basque country and the French Pyrenees. This was the reason that at first hundreds, then thousands, and then tens of thousands of pilgrims had flocked to Garabandal back in the day. This was the reason they were now on the news.

Because they knew the secret. They knew the Word.

And what a sacred word it was. It was the word the Lady had been saying for a hundred years—an eternity to them, but the blink of an eye to the Lady, who was still mourning the death of her Son and yet celebrating His coming apotheosis. There could be no final triumph without trouble, no everlasting transfiguration without confrontation. The final battle between good and evil must be enjoined, and Jacinta knew that it was her sacred and spiritual duty to make that happen as fast as possible.

Therefore, no matter how rigorous the questioning from the priests—some of them Spanish, some of them French, some of them black Africans and races she had never even imagined before, not here in her little village of Garabandal— she had stuck to her story, *their* story. Jacinta had emerged as their leader, and the leader she would stay. Even if she was only twelve years old.

For the Lady had spoken but a single word, but that one word was chilling in its simplicity, and its warning:

"Repent!"

CHAPTER FOURTEEN

New York City

"There something I don't like, boss," said Lannie Saleh to Captain Francis X. Byrne. Byrne was the commander of the Counter-Terrorism Unit of the New York City Police Department and Aslan Saleh was his subordinate, but he didn't act much like it. Which was one of the things Frankie Byrne liked about him.

"Haven't you Arabs caused enough trouble around here already?" replied Byrne. They were in CTU command headquarters in Chelsea, still picking up the pieces of the assault on Times Square.

"Iranians aren't Arabs, remember? Shiites aren't Sunnis."

"But you all look alike," said Byrne. "What's the difference?"

"What's the difference between Orangemen and Catholics in Londonderry, Northern Ireland?"

"You mean Derry, Ulster."

"I rest my case."

"Then take your case and shove it up your ass. Don't you

realize that the Irish are the only people on the planet with legitimate grievances?"

"What about the Jews, boss?" sang out Sid Sheinberg. "We've got plenty of legitimate grievances."

"That's all you got, Sheinberg," cracked Lannie. "Grievances. Comin' out your ears."

Byrne let them go. That was the way it used to be in the old days, when he and Sy Sheinberg, and Matt White had all been young, before the lawyers and the politicians had infected everything with their sophistry, corrupted everything with their relativism, blocked everything with their protocols, outlawed both thought and deed, word and action, and criminalized emotions in the name of . . . well, superior emotion.

Police work was so much easier in the old days. Law in one hand, nightstick in the other. That was how New York had been tamed of the likes of Happy Jack and Owney Madden, back in the days when the Irish ruled the roost, on Fourteenth Street, at Tammany Hall, and on the wild West Side, on Battle Row and in the sanctuary at St. Mike's, and in the Gopher hidey-holes under the docks and under the streets and up your arse if you weren't careful. Law of the jungle, when you stopped to think about it, worked every time it was tried.

Only cowards and lawyers feared the law of the jungle. And now they, along with the women and the eunuchs, were running the show. Today, it was like *1984*, with Big Brother on every corner, CCTV everywhere, revenue and citizen control directed straight from Gracie Mansion, for your safety and protection. Fascism could be fun, if only you would shut up and let it have its way.

What had happened to his country?

No time to worry about that now. Saving the world was not part of his job description. Keeping Matt White happy was.

Frankie looked at his men. And yes, they were all men. It was a good thing the names of all the members of the CTU were secret, just as their location was secret, or else the bow-tied bed-wetters at *The New York Times* would have a conniption, railing from the anonymous safety of their homes in Riverdale and Bronxville and Scarsdale about the unfairness of it all and exposing his men's identities for all to read. Everyone single one of Byrne's men lived within the five boroughs of the City of New York, joined since 1898, fifteen years after the Brooklyn Bridge and the father-and-son team of John and Washington Roebling had transformed a small island into the capital city of the country, in deed if not in word.

New York needed fewer lawyers, and more men like the Roeblings, if it ever wanted to get anything done again. One look at the hole downtown, where the World Trade Center had once stood, told you everything you needed to know about the state of America these days. Sue everybody, accomplish nothing, and have the *Times* cheer your uselessness on. And on and on and on . . .

Until the next attack.

Until the next deaths.

Until the next opportunity for grief counselors and shrinks and candlelight vigils and makeshift memorials and weeping, as if the dead were just so many John Lennons writ small, never-were celebrities made briefly less anonymous by the arbitrary hand of the Reaper and the tabloids and the network news shows' crocodile tears in the pursuit of transient ratings.

What was their motto? "We don't have to be right. We just have to be right today."

Byrne's shoulder had pretty much healed, but Sid Sheinberg's broken leg was never going to be the same: he was looking at a lifetime of desk duty. But the gunshot wound that Byrne had sustained in his duel with Ben Addison, Jr., otherwise known as the late Ismail bin-Abdul al-Amriki, was the least of his problems. Arash Kohanloo's coordinated attack had been a very near thing: their electronic eyes blinded; their computers crashed; billions of dollars worth of damage to Forty-second Street, Times Square itself, the subway lines, the surrounding buildings . . .

He was lucky he hadn't lost his job. His personal heroism that day had won him yet another medal from the mayor, but he was acutely aware of how signally they had failed their city. After 9/11, the NYPD had adopted the Israelis' motto of "never again," but again it was, 9/11 all over again, this time perhaps even worse. Because all their equipment and their independence and their courage had been defeated by a denial-of-service attack from somewhere thousands of miles away. Just a few minutes was all it took to render them eyeless in Gaza, for the bad guys to smuggle in the weapons through the same old riverside tunnels and hidey-holes the Gopher Gang was probably using back when Madden was a pup.

The worst of it was that they had recruited so many Americans—not just Ben Addison, Jr., a converted con, but hillbillies like the kid they found with his head blown off in the pump house under the Central Park Reservoir. They'd probably never get a firm ID on him, since whoever killed him had made damn sure there no prints, teeth, or any other identifying characteristics. Sure, they could grab some DNA, but unless the punk was in the database—which he wasn't—he would molder forever in an unmarked grave, unclaimed and unmourned—just another stiff in the ongoing history of the island of the Manhattoes.

Byrne had promised himself that he would find the man's killer. Not necessarily to bring him to justice, or to shake his hand and thank him for a job well done, but to come face-to-face with a man he very much wanted to meet. The man who had saved him from Ben Addison, Jr., the man who had cleaned his gunshot wound and left him safe in the mael-

strom of Forty-second Street. The man who had guided him
to the chopper, to the shooter, and to the final confrontation
with Kohanloo on the East River.

"We shoulda struck back, right away, hard," said Sid, still
walking with a cane. Sid was the nephew of Frankie's old
friend, rabbi, and mentor, Sy Sheinberg. That was back in
the day when medical examiners were hard-drinking stand-
up comics, not civil servants as bloodless as the corpses they
dissected for fun and profit at the taxpayers' expense.

"At who?" snapped Lannie. He was that rarity, a real
street Arab turned American, a Palestinian kid whose grand-
parents had come over during the first oil shock to run first
one gas station, then two, then ten, then fifty in Brooklyn. He
had money but he didn't act like it, which Byrne admired,
and he had street cred, which Byrne prized. The country
needed more people like Lannie Saleh. Especially when they
spoke both Arabic and Farsi.

"I dunno," said Sid, sitting down. There were computer
terminals at every workstation, and Sid's hands uncon-
sciously flew over the keys, bringing the instrument to life.
Both he and Lannie were virtuosi, and their rivalry was intense. So was their friendship. "Anywhere in the Middle
East, ex—"

"Except Israel. Right," said Lannie. "Anyway, Boss, as I
was saying, there's something I don't like, and I don't just
mean Sheinberg here. What I don't like is—"

At that moment the door opened and everybody shot to
their feet. For the figure in the door was none other than
J. Arness White, commissioner of police, otherwise known
as Matt to the troops. He was the *capo di tutti capi* of the
NYPD, he was big, he was black, and he was Frankie
Byrne's best friend in the whole world. He was also the only
thing that stood between Byrne and forced retirement.

"What *I* don't like," said White in his booming Texas
voice, "what I cannot stand, is failure. You want failure, you

work for some other city department. They'll show you failure. You want failure, you try your hand at teaching in the public schools, or collecting the garbage in a snowstorm, or passing laws against smoking cigarettes on the sidewalk or at Coney Island or in some Mafia social club on Mulberry Street where the goombahs got more firepower than we do. That, my friends, is failure—baked in the cake.

"You want failure, I will happily shove it up your rear end, like Tiny on his wedding night with a Rikers Island virgin, but not that much fun. You want failure, I will give it to you like a gambler about to have his kneecaps broken by a baseball bat on account of nonpayment. You want failure, I will show it to you, the way Patton showed the krauts failure at the Battle of the Bulge. We are talking epic fail here, people, and it cannot and will not be repeated. Are we clear?"

"Sir, yes, sir!"

Without another word, White chose a seat—Frankie's seat. Everybody got the message. The Big Dog was in the house.

"What *I* don't like," continued White, "is a bunch of screwups, accountable to nobody, who let my beloved city suffer an even worse indignity than 9/11. Even worse, a bunch of unaccountable screwups responsible only to my sorry black behind. Is my meaning clear?"

Matt was glowering. Not a pretty sight. Nobody liked it when Matt was glowering. Least of all Byrne. They might be old friends, they might even have something or two on each other, but that didn't mean White couldn't fire him any time he chose. And that Frankie wouldn't accept his fate quietly. That was their unspoken deal, and Byrne would be damned if he'd be the one to break it.

"What the commissioner is saying," Byrne began, "is that failure of any kind is no longer an option. And this failure, when you get right down to it, was mine."

Byrne moved toward the front of the room. "Lads," he

began, "Commissioner White and I have been friends and partners for nearly twenty years. We've been through a lot together—and I don't think I have to explain to you what 'a lot' means in this day and age. There is no space between us, zip, zero, nada—you want to speak to Matt, you speak to me. I love this man like a brother—no, belay that. I love this man like I love myself, and you bastards all know in what a high regard I keep myself and my family."

Well, that was a lie and everybody who worked for him knew it.

"What about your real brother, Captain?" came a voice from the back of the room. Byrne knew who it was, but didn't feel like making a fuss. Besides, the guy was right. What about his real brother?

His goddamned brother. The deputy director of the FBI. And the sonofabitch who now had President Tyler's ear. That was the one question he didn't want to answer. The one question he'd never wanted to answer.

Frankie didn't want to have to think about the variegated ways his brother had him over the proverbial barrel. Misprision of felony, for starters. And so much else. You couldn't do time for things that happened when you were kids, but if you could do time, Frankie knew, either he or his brother would be in the slammer simply for imagining what was coming down the line.

In the future, everybody would be a criminal for at least fifteen minutes, whether they wanted to be or not. Which meant that everybody would be a victim, too.

"With the exception of my brother, Tom," he said with a smile. "But he has a job to do, just like I have a job to do, just like we all have a job to do, and sometimes those jobs are going to come into conflict with each other. But we can't worry about that. So let's do our jobs. Sid, what have we got? Make it snappy, because Matt doesn't have all day."

Sid Sheinberg turned away from his ranks of computers

to address the group. "We took a hit, no question. A good part of Forty-second Street was destroyed, along with much of the Times Square subway station, which took out a good deal of the MTA's capacity until a work-around was found. That necessitated opening up some of the disused stations, and it's been wonderful what we've found, but that's just about the only silver lining in the transportation cloud for the nonce.

"We're still finding bits of bodies around the Times Square area, including pieces of bone and teeth embedded in buildings six stories up from the force of the blasts. This was a very sophisticated operation, far worse than Bombay, and if the ringleader had not been so quickly identified and taken out . . ."

Everybody looked at Frankie. They all knew that it was he who'd fired the shots that killed Arash Kohanloo, the Iranian operative whose name, miraculously, had not yet found its way into the papers or the blogosphere, and with luck, never would.

"Right," said Frankie. "Thanks, Sid. Lannie?"

Lannie gave Sid's curly hair a tousle as he rose and walked to the front of the room. In the heat of the battle, he had saved Sid's life, and forged a bond that could never be broken. He signaled to Sid for the start of the AV presentation.

"Arash Kohanloo was a real piece of work," he began, as a picture of Kohanloo flashed on one of the main monitors. "A favorite of the regime, he was able to move freely between the *dar al-Harb* and the *dar al-Islam,* between the world of War, which is where we live, and the world of the perfect peace of Islam—which is where everyone will live when the final triumph of Islam is wrought by the sword and by submission.

"The mullahs liked Kohanloo because of his business interests. He brought a lot of hard currency into a country that's basically broke. An oil-exporter that has to import gasoline. A no-fun society brimming with hormonal young people. A country with some of the most beautiful women in the world, walking around in body bags. A great urban culture that was conquered by a desert civilization and forced to adopt its religion and its mores. Was forced to renounce and destroy its representative art, its music, its former religion—everything."

"Which means what, Lannie?" asked Frankie.

"Which means that Iran is doomed and it knows it's doomed. Unless . . . and this is where I admit it gets pretty crazy—unless it can bring on the end times and effect the final triumph of Islam. After that, it doesn't care what happens, since its job is to prove the superiority of Shiite Islam over the Arabs and their Sunni form of the faith, and to bring about the coming of the Mahdi, the Expected One."

"And how do they do that?" asked someone.

"By creating as much chaos as possible. The Mahdi can only emerge from the holy well in Qom—"

"You've got to be fucking kidding me," came another voice.

"Belay that," barked Matt.

". . . the holy well in Qom when the world is torn by strife. Then, according to Shiite belief, he will arrive with Jesus by his side, to proclaim the final triumph of Islam."

"And then what happens?" asked Byrne.

"A whole lot of people die, boss," said Lannie.

"The end times," said Matt White. "My pappy used to whup us real good when we was growin' up back home in Houston, Texas," he mused; Matt often slipped into homespun speech whenever he thought of home. "Said it was getting us ready for the end times."

"Christians have the same thing," added Byrne. "Death and destruction and a big fat sorting-out at the end. Isn't that what those prophecies at Fatima were all about? You know, the ones that everybody was afraid were going to signal the end of the world?"

Lannie chuckled.

"What's so funny?"

"You guys really crack me up," he said. "I've heard about this Fatima stuff for years. Do you know who 'Fatimah' was?"

Byrne smiled. "A town in Portugal, where little shepherd kids—wait a minute, I think I can even remember their names . . . yeah, Lucia, Francisco and Jacinta . . . saw the BVM. That's the Blessed Virgin Mary to you, infidel."

Lannie was still smiling. "I didn't ask where it was, boss. I asked who." When nobody replied, Lannie continued. "Fatimah was Mohammed's daughter, the most perfect of women. Mohammed said of her: 'She has the highest place in heaven after the Virgin Mary.' That place in Portugal is named after her. Because the Muslims conquered the Iberian peninsula . . . or did you forget?"

They had wandered far afield from the purpose of this meeting, and Byrne was about to bring it back to order when a phone call came through the secure switchboard. "What is it?" barked Byrne.

"Call from Mount Sinai Hospital," said the disembodied voice of the operator. "For Detective Saleh."

"Put it through," said Byrne. He spoke to Sheinberg. "Put it up so we can all hear it."

A nervous woman came on the line. "Detective Saleh?" she inquired.

"This is Lannie Saleh, yes," said Lannie.

"Are we speaking privately, Detective?"

"Of course we are. What can I do for you?"

Celina Selena swallowed hard. "This is Celina S. Gomez at Mount Sinai Hospital. We got a phone call that I thought you should know about," she began. "At first, I thought he was asking for a Dr. Saleh, and I told him there were no doctors in radiology by that name."

Radiology? Everybody went on full alert. Byrne nodded to Lannie—

"You work in the department of radiology?" he asked.

"Yes, sir, in nuclear medicine." This was getting worse by the second. "Then the man corrected himself and said he had misdialed, that he really had been trying to call the New York City Police Department's Counter-Terrorism Unit. So, naturally, I . . ."

"What did he say, Ms. Gomez?"

"He said he had an urgent message for you. I have it right here. Right here somewhere . . . oh yes, here it is: 'We are discovered. Save yourself.' "

Nobody breathed. Lannie had the ball and Frankie was letting him run with it. "Your sure that's all he said?"

"Oh yes, Officer—excuse me, Detective. I wrote it down. In fact, I even asked him to repeat it."

"And did he? Repeat it?"

"Yes, well that's the funny part. I could kick myself, but I should have turned on the voice recorder much sooner than I did. Forgot all about it. So . . ."

Lannie tried to control the excitement in his voice. "So you have him on tape?"

"Well, it's not really tape, but we call it tape, even though these machines don't use tape anymore. I don't know how they—"

"Can you play it for me, please, Ms. Gomez?"

"Yes, sir. Of course. Just give me a minute . . ."

The wait was agonizing.

Then came the voice.

"Can you play that back to me again, please?" asked Lannie, and again came the voice: low, guttural to American

ears. "Thank you, Ms. Gomez. Please preserve that recording and play it for no one else. Do you understand? That
recording is now property of the NYPD, and someone will
be along to collect it from you and take an official statement
shortly. Are we clear on this?"

"Oh yes, Detective. I thought he sounded a little funny."

"Thank you, Ms. Gomez."

"Just trying to do my duty as a New Yorker, Detective,"
she said, and rang off.

For a moment, nobody spoke. Then—

"What the hell was that, Lannie?" said Byrne.

"Farsi. The language of Iran."

"Fuck," said Byrne. "But Kohanloo is dead. I killed him
myself, on the East River. . . . So who . . . what did he say?"

Lannie took a deep breath. This was not going to be easy,
or fun. "Well, you heard the first message in English. I don't
know what that's supposed to mean, but—"

"It's a line from *Have His Carcase*," said Sid, who had already Googled it. "It's the clear text of some sort of code.
'We are discovered. Save yourself.' "

"So our man's a lover of thirties English mysteries," said
Matt, who was, too. "And an aficionado of the Playfair cipher." Byrne looked admiringly at his old friend, who never
ceased to amaze him. "But what did he say in Farsi? The
same thing?"

"Actually," began Lannie, "he only said one thing. But he
said it three times. '*Taubeh kon! Taubeh kon! Taubeh kon!*' It
means: *Repent*. And it's not a suggestion—it's a command."

Byrne thought for a moment, putting the pieces together.
Radiology. Nuclear Medicine. An order to repent. He thought
they had cleaned up all the loose ends after the battle of
Times Square, but did they miss something? "I never real-
ized Our Lady spoke Farsi," he said. "I thought she spoke
Aramaic. Or Irish."

The bulk of the attack had come along Forty-second Street and the rest in the square. But there was that one outlier, that dead kid under the Central Park Reservoir, who was the gunman behind the attack on the Ninety-second Street Y. Which was not far from . . .

Mount Sinai Hospital.

They missed something. Something whoever was behind the attack—not Kohanloo, he was as dead as Darius—wanted them to know about. Something he had to taunt them about. Something the NYPD couldn't do anything about.

Unless they were smarter than him.

That was a bet Byrne was willing to take.

"Lannie, call the bomb squad and meet me uptown. Sid, I want that stiff we found under the Reservoir dug up and positively ID'd and I don't care how the M.E. does it—your uncle would have that boy whistling 'Dixie' on the autopsy table, because I've seen him do it, so let's hope his successor is up to the job. The rest of you, I want all systems on stun, I want a flyover of Mount Sinai—use a chopper—with our best radiation-detection equipment, and I want it all done before Lannie and I get there. Capisce?"

Everybody capisced. Matt blocked his way as he headed out the door. "I don't have to tell you to be careful, Irish. 'Cause I know you won't be. But we can't afford to lose this one, pardner. If there's something there—you take it out. By any means necessary. You got me on that? By any means necessary."

"I got you, Matt," said Frankie, "just as long as you've got my back."

"When haven't I had your back?" said Matt, but Byrne was already out the door.

CHAPTER FIFTEEN

Zeitoun, Egypt

Ahmed Ali hated Christians. He also hated Jews, as the Holy Qu'ran instructed him to do, but there were precious few Jews in Egypt anymore. Most of them had fled to Israel or America long ago, their way made safe by the traitors Sadat and Mubarak, curse them both. The Coming could not be effected until the war against the Little Satan and the Great Satan was fully effected and, as the mullahs preached every Friday in the mosque, that day was coming. It was the religious duty of every one of the Believers to hasten it. Sunni or Shia, that was one article of faith on which both sides of the schism could agree.

It was nearing sundown. Ahmed Ali suppressed a small chuckle as he passed the Coptic Christian cathedral of Zeitoun. He had seen real cathedrals, visiting his relatives in Paris—great structures of stone, with rose windows and flying buttresses and other architectural marvels of which the Arab world could only dream. In fact, the last time he had seen that branch of the family was outside the whore's temple the Christians called Notre Dame, a blasphemous structure adorned and ornamented with idolatrous statues, a synagogue of sin, as befit this bastard of the Jew religion. When the Cleansing finally came, this filth would all be swept away in Allah's purifying rain of fire.

True, some of the great mosques were on a par with what the savage Europeans had wrought a millennium ago. But, as Ahmed Ali had to admit, many of the holiest places in the *ummah* were merely converted cathedrals, such as the mosque at St. Sophia in Istanbul, or what had once been the Great Mosque of Cordoba in al-Andalus—a former Christian cathedral that had reverted back to its infidel origins after the unfortunate *Reconquista*. Someday, Notre Dame—the Cathedral of Our Lady—would be converted as well, since it was named after Her. Maryam.

They would get it back. Islam would get it all back—not only Spain, but France as well (that conquest was well advanced, with no Charles Martel in sight), and the Low Countries and even Britain. They would turn the West's weaknesses against it—the fetish for "tolerance," the falling birthrate, the lack of will. In the *dar al-Harb*, Islam had both the will, which derived from the sacred scriptures, and the way: All a Believer had to do was get to Italy from North Africa, and the rest of the European Union lay spread open like a virgin on her wedding night.

But, for the moment, Ahmed Ali was stuck here, in el-Zeitoun, the olive. There was nothing about this district of Cairo to recommend it. Those who knew of it tended to be infidels, drawn here by the apparition of Holy Maryam in the sixties. Millions had seen her figure, the woman mentioned many more times in the holy Qu'ran than in the Christian Bible, and of course mentioned not at all in the Jewish Torah. Millions of holy Muslims and Christians and tourists and other infidels had flocked to the domed church, to witness the miracle, including Abdul Nasser, the last leader of Egypt not in league with the Jews or the Americans.

Few of the infidel Christians knew of the Muslim devotion to Maryam. There were no fewer than thirty-four references to her in the word of Allah, and an entire *sura* was named after her. As the Prophet said in one *hadith*: "Every child is touched by the devil as soon as he is born and this contact makes him cry. Excepted are Mary and her Son." She was the one pure woman, who gave birth to the second greatest of all Muslims: *Issa ibn Maryam.* Jesus, son of Maryam.

Although tensions had been high between the small Christian community, resident in Egypt practically since the time of Christ, and the dominant Muslims, Ahmed Ali had often thought of the Zeitoun miracle. The story was told by every family in the district, Muslim and Christian alike, and Ali suspected that those who claimed to have witnessed the holy sight greatly outnumbered the entire population of the capital city at the time. How Maryam herself had appeared, high on the church's dome, day after day, for more than a year. How the blind, the lame, the halt, and the cancer-ridden were cured. Millions saw her, photographed her. The Orthodox Church under Pope Kyrillos VI had confirmed the validity of the miracle. There could be no doubt.

Which was why, as he trudged home on this cool evening, it was almost not a surprise when he looked up at one of the church's five domes—one at each corner, each standing nine meters high, and a great central dome, twelve meters above the ground, one meter for each of the holy apostles—and saw her. After all, the church was named for her, and if only a minority of Coptic Christians worshipped there, the building was still deserving of some respect for its name alone.

Ahmet Ali stopped. Cairo was a teeming city, but at this moment it was as if he were alone in the great metropolis. In every direction, the minarets stretched into the distance, proof of the rightness of the Prophet's holy vision. Everything that had come before—the pharaohs, the Greeks, the

Turks, the British—was as nothing among the sands of time. Many were the miracles witnessed here, near the sacred Nile; the history of humanity itself was writ here, not large, for the sands ultimately swept everything away, the desert consuming all. Everything, that was, except Islam.

It was the motion that first caught his eye. At first, in the fading of the light, the glow had eluded him, and all he saw out of the corner of one eye was something moving back and forth, atop the highest dome. Then, as his sight adjusted, he saw the silhouette—the outline of a chaste female body, gleaming white and crowned by a halo. It was just as he had seen it in the photographs from half a century ago. Only this time, the image was moving.

Corporeal, and yet not corporeal. He could not see through the figure—all was a dazzling whiteness—and yet it moved through space effortlessly, like a projection. Later, Ahmed Ali would remember small birdlike figures around the central apparition, pulsating images that swooped and hovered protectively around the sainted head. But not now.

Now, all he could do was watch. He was not sure what to expect. Was he dreaming? Was he perhaps dead? Had Allah summarily delivered him to the oasis at which the virgins awaited him, Ahmed Ali, named after the Prophet's own kin, a good and decent man who had tried all his life to be true to the precepts of the holy faith? At great expense to himself and his poor family, he had even made the pilgrimage to Mecca, and had worshipped at the Grand Mosque, the *Masjid al-Haram* that sheltered the sacred Kaaba, toward which all Muslims bowed and prayed five times a day. It was yet his dream to worship at the Dome of the Rock in al-Quds, and maybe even journey all the way to infidel Iran, to the holy well at Jamkaran, just in case. Ahmed Ali was among the most pious of men.

But now, all this had flown from his mind. For there She

was, the Holy Mother, the most blessed of women, as even the Prophet had said. The Immaculate Conception, untouched by sin.

Now he became aware that a crowd had gathered around him. He was no longer alone in the great city, but just one man among many. And yet it was deadly silent, as if no one were there—or, rather, as if each individual were, alone, there, alone with the holy visitor.

Soon enough the reporters and camera crews arrived, jostling their way forward through the crowd, setting up to get their shots. Ahmet Ali had no idea whether the apparition would permit herself to be revealed on film, but it was at this moment that he remembered his cell phone. He took it from his pocket and began taking pictures as well.

He could see the image clearly as he framed it in the viewfinder. These phones were most likely the work of the devil, but with them he could talk to his family all over the world—in London and in Michigan and even his brother in the Philippines. They might not believe him if he just told them what he was seeing—"Ahmed Ali," they would say, "surely these are hallucinations. Purify yourself and go to the imam for guidance"—but with this evidence, what could they say?

She was moving now, moving along the top of the large dome. If he looked hard, looked through the radiant light streaming from her body, he thought he could make out another image, perhaps that of a small child. But he could not really tell.

The street in front of the church was nearly silent. Traffic had long since stopped and even the incessant honking of Cairo traffic had receded as a kind of calm radiated out from the center. Ahmed Ali took his eyes off the Lady for a moment to steal a glance at his fellow witnesses. Their faces were rapt, aglow. He wondered if he looked like them.

How long he stood there he could not tell. It was quite
dark now and the brilliance of the light was even more striking. It was beginning to hurt his eyes. He had to look away.
He looked away. . . .

And then, with a flash, she was gone. The light winked
out, and all was darkness.

For many moments, nobody said a word. A few murmurs,
some half-mouthed prayers in several languages. Some of
the infidel women made the sign of the cross.

And then a low sound rippled through the crowd, like a
great moan, but one born not out of pain but from joy. It
swelled, other voices joining until it became a mighty cho-
rus. Many of those in the crowd fell to their knees as it burst
forth, divinely summoned, from a thousand throats:

"Allahu akbar! Allahu akbar! Allahu akbar!"

And that's when the trouble began.

No one knew who threw the first rock, whether it was a
Muslim or a Christian. But one rock led to more rocks, and
pieces of paving stone, and then pipes and other metal ob-
jects. A full-scale riot broke out as Muslims attacked the
Christians, and Christians attacked the Muslims. And
Ahmed Ali was in the middle of it all.

When the fighting started, he snapped out of his reverie
and began throwing punches in all directions. There was
something liberating about physical combat and, after the
spirituality of the apparition, it seemed only right to indulge
in the profane joy of violence.

Then the fires started. The Cairo police stayed well away
from the melee for as long as they could and then they, too,
waded in, truncheons flying. One unit deployed a water can-
non; another opened fire on the mob. Tourists screamed and
ran and died. Flames consumed some of the buildings.

Despite the police, the riot quickly spread to other areas
of the city, and then to other cities in Egypt. Long-simmering

animosities that had been kept under control by the previous regime caught fire and exploded.

The Copts suffered the most. They made up about 10 percent of the Egyptian population, and had been resident in the land since A.D. 42, but over the course of the next three days many of their churches were burned, their houses destroyed, their lives ruined.

Only the Church of St. Mary was, miraculously, relatively unscathed.

When the riot was finally put down, two hundred fifty-six people had been killed and millions of dollars in property damage had been done. Egypt was a tinderbox, just waiting for the next match to explode once more.

CHAPTER SIXTEEN

Bandar Anzali, Iran

After she'd returned home to Kensington Park Gardens in London, home to that awful empty house, home to that place where she was monitored by *him* at all times, with nowhere in that vast house, one of the finest in London, to run, to escape, to forget. With nothing to do but heal and think and ponder and plot her revenge. In those moments she had become the Black Widow: just like the Cray supercomputer that saw everything and heard everything and knew everything, the creature that gave the Americans and their National Security Agency an advantage—that gave Skorzeny's mortal enemy an advantage.

An advantage Amanda Harrington now turned to her advantage.

"Maryam, can you hear me?" she whispered in the hold of the ship, the *Izbavitel*.

The beautiful dark-haired Iranian woman lying tied up before her didn't move. Didn't open her eyes. She might have been dead, but Amanda knew she wasn't. Not if she was going through what she herself had gone through. Paralyzed, her breath almost nonexistent, her body wracked by pain but her face unable to show it. The poison was dreadful, and he had long since mastered the art of administering it in a dose just this side of lethal. To all outward appearance, Maryam was dead.

Which did not mean Amanda could not communicate with her.

Amanda knew she was playing a dangerous game, but it was worth it. No matter what happened, it was worth it. After what he had done to her, raped her, nearly killed her, caused her lover's death and the loss of her most precious possession, anything she did to him in return was nothing. A normal human being would have suspected her loyalties, but not him. His monstrous ego, bolstered by his immense wealth and his utter self-assurance, prevented it. It was his weakness, his Achilles' heel, and she was determined to use it against him.

"Can you hear me, Maryam?" she repeated. When the situation had been reversed, when she had been sitting there in that double prison—the prison of Clairvaux and the prison of her own body—the best Maryam could do was give her a searching, sympathetic look. Amanda could not know then that her rescue was already under way.

And now she held the cards. "Can you hear me, Maryam?" she whispered again.

The boat heaved from side to side. The Caspian was far from the roughest of seas, not at all like the Channel, but Amanda had never liked the water, never wished to be a sailor. She struggled to control herself as the ship tossed, then righted itself. The monster Skorzeny had booked her back by private car from Bandar Anzali, one of the very few things for which she was grateful to him.

Not that she intended to use it.

Almost imperceptibly, Maryam's eyelids fluttered. Anyone else would have missed it, but Amanda was looking for it. Good enough: she could hear.

"I'm getting you out of here. But you must do exactly as I tell you. No deviation. No thinking for yourself. You must trust me."

Amanda looked again for some telltale motion, but this time there was nothing. No matter—she knew. She knew she knew.

There was no real antidote for severe tetrodotoxin poisoning, that she knew from personal experience. Each year in Japan, half a dozen or so sushi fanciers died from ingesting an imperfectly sliced fugu fish, and in the old days, the sushi chef was obligated to kill himself from the shame. But a nonlethal dose was different. It mimicked death as perfectly as any poison could, but in this case, Amanda knew, the dose would not have been as high as it was in her case. After all, Skorzeny did not want to kill Maryam, he wanted to sell her—to use her as a bargaining chip, the way he had been using human beings ever since he was a boy in the collapsing Third Reich.

She placed the oxygen mask over Maryam's face and opened the tank. Fugu poisoning shut down the body's organs, especially the respiratory system, so it was crucial to keep her supplied with oxygen on the voyage. In fact, Skorzeny himself had insisted on it. He always liked to get his money's worth. All Amanda was doing was protecting his investment by spending a little more of his money.

The eyelids flickered again. Good.

"Maryam, listen to me. You're with a friend. We both know who and what he is."

The motion subsided. She was losing her.

Another shot of oxygen. Another shot of life.

"Stay with me. I've been there. You saw me. You saved me. Now let me help you."

Amanda put her head on Maryam's breast. Faintly, faintly, she could hear her breathing. She was still with her.

"Listen . . ."

The *Izbavitel* docked without incident. Amanda Harrington's papers were in order, as were the shipping documents for what she was bringing with her. The panel truck was right where it was supposed to be.

There would be almost no time. Everything had to go perfectly. Everything *would* go perfectly.

She had not worked with Emanuel Skorzeny for so long without learning something about secrecy, speed, and efficiency. As head of the Skorzeny Foundation, she had watched funds rocket around the world, moving them like chess pieces, always to the precise spot where they were most needed and could do him the most good. The sheer size of his fortune brought with it an aura of intimidation, and he used it as a blunt instrument on rivals and whole nations. He was the master of the tactical surprise, as well as the strategic plan.

Their banking relationships in the Islamic Republic were first-rate, both with Bank Melli and the Saderat Bank. The whole notion of banking was, at root, un-Islamic, but the Iranians needed an interface with the West, as well as a way to transfer funds quickly to some of their most favored proxies. Naturally, Skorzeny was not averse to doing business with them.

The two men who met her and her cargo at the port were not at all what she first expected. She had expected big gruff true believers; what she got were a couple of kids who looked like they would be equally at home in London or Los Angeles. Then she remembered that Iran was almost entirely a country of young people, brimming with ill-concealed resentment against the fundamentalism of the mullahs: you could practically smell the coming revolution.

Of course, they both spoke English.

"I am Habib," said the first one, a curly-haired boy of

about twenty. "And this is my brother, Mehrdad." They were practically indistinguishable.

They loaded Amanda's cargo, which had cleared customs easily, into the back of the truck. They treated it carefully and with great respect.

They should. It was a coffin. Nobody said anything as they loaded it into the rear of the panel truck and closed the doors.

"Where you want to sit, miss?" asked Habib.

It was not an idle question. Here, at the port, there was an international mixture of Persians, Russians, Armenians, Azerbaijanis, and Turks, but in Tehran itself an unveiled Western woman, riding with two unrelated men, might be an object for scrutiny. "I'll sit in the back," she said.

"At your service, miss," smiled Mehrdad, and off they went.

Amanda looked at the time on her secure BlackBerry, the one he had given her especially for this trip. With it, she was supposed to check in at pre-arranged intervals, reporting on their progress by means of short transmission bursts. He knew she would be monitored wherever she went, and so had arranged for a direct satellite uplink relay; even if the mullahs shut down the entire Internet and the wireless services, she'd still be able to get signals in and out.

The two boys in the front seat were laughing and joking a mile a minute in Farsi. She liked the Shiites, Amanda reflected. To her mind, they were far preferable to the Sunnis, consumed by tribalism and with nothing to show for thousands of years of existence except their faith and the oil the West had found for them. The Sunnis, mostly Pakistanis, dominated London's Muslim society, and were busily transforming old Industrial Revolution backwaters like Leeds and Birmingham into Pakistani colonies—the colonial chickens coming home to roost. The visiting Arabs from the Kingdom and Emirates knew how to throw money around on opulence and women, but she had always found them charmless, overbearing, and desperately embarrassingly horny.

The Shiites were different, especially the Persians. This part of Iran wasn't much to look at, but as the car sped southeast toward the capital, the landscape began to change and you really could imagine yourself going back in time— not to the time of the Islamic conquest but before, to the Sassanid Empire. *Someday,* she thought. *Someday . . .*

"If you don't mind my asking, who has died, miss?" inquired Mehrdad, turning around to look at her. "Not a relative, I hope."

"No," she replied. "A native, going home."

"I am very sorry to hear of this," said Habib, "but it is good that she has come back."

She? Did they know something? What message had Skorzeny passed to them, if any? Were they someone's sons, someone who owed him a favor? Or were they sent to dispose both of Maryam and of her?

No, that could not be. It made precisely no sense for Skorzeny to trust her after what had happened, and yet it made perfect sense. She was the old fool's one human weakness, the one person on the planet he trusted for the simple reason that he ought not to trust her, so convinced was he of his power over her, and of his own magnetism. Her freedom, however temporary, was both the ultimate compliment and the ultimate insult.

"How do you like Iran, miss?"

"I like Iran very much, thank you, Mehrdad." She had almost no Farsi, but she knew that Mehrdad meant "gift of the sun," and was a highly prized first name among Persian boys.

"I would be most delighted to show you the sights if you are willing," he said, switching to English.

"Thank you. I shall certainly consider your generous offer after my business in Tehran is settled," she said, "but only if your most handsome and charming brother accompanies us."

She smiled and dropped her eyes demurely, a signal for Mehrdad to turn back around and leave her alone. It was time to think about money. Lots of money.

Which is exactly what she had access to. For years, she had been skimming from Skorzeny, ever so slightly, but even a little skim off the top of the immense sums of money laundered through the Foundation added up to a lot, and she had stashed it at private banks all over the world, hidden in plain sight among the Foundation's legitimate assets, until such time as she really needed it.

This was such a time.

Near Ghazvin they stopped for petrol. This was the moment she had been waiting for. "Habib?" she said. "Would you and your brother mind giving me a spot of privacy? I'd like to change into something more modest."

"Of course, miss," said Habib with only the slightest trace of a leer. Amanda was well aware that even the best-intentioned young Muslim men could not help but view a Western woman as both a Madonna and a whore, a prize to be wooed and won, and then kicked to the curb. "We come back quick."

"No," she said. "Take your time. I'm a slow undresser." This time they both smiled.

Now.

She got the coffin open. The breathing mask was right where it should be, the oxygen tank nestled under Maryam's right arm. The woman looked as if she were sleeping, although Amanda knew from bitter personal experience that she had probably been awake the whole time she was in her own grave.

"Maryam, can you hear me?" Once again, the eyelids fluttered. "Good. Now listen very, very carefully. I am going to give you a much stronger dose of oxygen and an adrenaline injection. You're going to wake up. You're going to feel terrible, but you'll be functional. The dose he gave you was nowhere near as strong as the one he gave me."

She didn't tell Maryam just why that was, although she supposed she could guess. Skorzeny had a special use in mind for Maryam, and damaged goods would not have served his purpose. That would work to their advantage.

Amanda turned up the oxygen and sank the needle into a vein in Maryam's chest. Almost instantly, her eyes shot open and she struggled to get up.

"No, stay still. I'm going to have to keep you right here, but don't worry. I'll be with you the whole time. You will not be out of my sight."

For the first time, Maryam tried to speak. Amanda brought water to her parched lips. She knew Maryam would be desperately thirsty, but she had to control her water intake, so she wouldn't drown herself.

Inside the coffin were several bottles of water with a feeding straw attached to each. The straw would control the flow, so that Maryam could hydrate herself while shut away in the darkness. She was probably going to have to wet herself, but that couldn't be helped. In any case, that was the least of their worries.

"Why?" she croaked.

"Because you saved my life once," replied Amanda, stripping off fast and climbing into a modest dress. Before the revolution, Iranian women had been among the most stylish in the world and such a look was still not entirely out of place, especially for a foreigner.

"And now we're even." Maryam was strong, coming round quickly.

"No, not even. Not until I see you safe." She pulled the dress on, rolled up her traveling clothes, and tossed them into a bag.

Maryam smiled. "Safe is a word I don't understand." She

shook her head lightly, trying to clear out the cobwebs. Amanda watched the change of light in her eyes, and could see that slowly the realization of what had happened to her was taking hold of her conscious mind. "Go ahead," Amanda said. "Ask me anything—but quickly. They'll be back any minute."

Amanda glanced outside, but there was no sign of the boys. She turned back to Maryam.

"You know" was all she said.

Voices, nearing.

"I'm sorry, Maryam," she said, closing the coffin lid.

Amanda was applying the final touches to her makeup as the boys climbed back into the car.

"You look good, miss," said Habib, starting the engine and pulling out.

"Very good, miss," said Mehrdad. "Very good indeed."

CHAPTER SEVENTEEN

Lemoore Naval Air Station, California

There were a lot of things you could say about Lemoore, but most of the nice ones wouldn't be true. It was located, or so the brochures said, in a rich agricultural area, which meant it was hot, flat, dry, and dusty. It was, if you believed the base PR guy, close to the playgrounds of San Francisco and Los Angeles, which meant it was roughly halfway between them in the part of the Golden State where nobody wanted to live anymore. It provided a small-town, hometown atmosphere for the poor bastards unlucky enough to catch duty here, which meant that no one would in his right mind ever want to dwell in nearby Hanford, Tulare, or Visalia.

It had exactly one thing going for it—it was the location of STRKFIGHTWINGPAC, the Pacific Strike Fighter Wing, which meant it was home to some of the most bad-assed Navy fliers in the service, hot-shit F/A-18 Hornet jockeys who flew their steeds five hundred miles inside enemy air defenses, bombed the crap out of whatever was pissing them off, and then fought their way out and were home before

breakfast. Once upon a time, you didn't want to fuck with
STRKFIGHTWINGPAC.

And yet, today, most of the F-18 units had been moved
east, to the naval air station at Oceana, in Virginia Beach, to
be closer to the Navy bases at Norfolk and Hampton Roads.
All part of the downsizing of the services that had started
with Clinton after the end of the Cold War, and continued
steadily through the Bush administration. Much of the training had moved over to Fallon in Nevada, but there was still a
presence here. It was the perfect symbol for an America in
decline, just as California was: The Golden State had been
created from nothing, and to nothing it was returning. All
except the coastal cities, which would be the last to fall.

Someday, reflected Danny, West Los Angeles and Pacific
Heights would get to experience the sensations felt by the in-
habitants of fifth-century Rome as the Vandals poured
through the gates. No doubt they would be congratulating
themselves on their tolerance as their necks were stretched
for the knife.

Danny had expected a bit of trouble from the MP at the
gate, but he, Hope, and the kids were waved right through.
"There's a canteen just up ahead, sir," said the guard, who
couldn't have been more than twenty, "if y'all want to wash
up. Admiral Atchison's been notified and he'll send someone
round to collect you shortly."

"I'm sorry to bother the admiral so early in the morning,"
said Danny. The sun was just coming up. Hope dozed beside
him and the kids were all sound asleep.

"No bother at all, sir. Around here, we never sleep."

"Just in case some bad guys need their ass kicked?"

"You said it, sir." He paused; it was lonely on sentry duty.
"Heard about them dead cows?"

"We saw them. Awful."

"Radio says something about botulism in the feed. Gonna
be hell to pay for that, for sure."

"Going to be hell paying for a hamburger, you bet."

"Myself, don't eat much meat. Tryin' to stay lean and fit."

"You're doing a good job, sailor."

"Thank you, sir. Y'all have a nice day now."

"You too. And thanks."

Danny drove slowly toward the PX, the commissary, and a cluster of other small buildings. He hadn't been on a post in a long time, not officially anyway, not since his days with the Night Stalkers. That would be the 160th Special Operations Aviation Regiment (Airborne), 2nd Battalion, based at Fort Campbell, Kentucky, where he had learned his craft and become, if he did say so himself, the finest chopper stud in the country.

"What?" said Hope drowsily.

"Sleep," he whispered.

There was something about being on a base, something both forbidding and comforting. It was a closed community, off-limits to outsiders, a community of like-minded men and women, all self-selected and assembled by merit to get the job done. It was the thing he missed most about military life, and even though he had lived among the civilians for many years now, even though he wouldn't trade his comfortable home in Los Feliz and the money he made from Xe (the old Blackwater) and his other freelance assignments, there were times. There were times. . . .

The PX was closed, but the commissary was just opening. The canteen was attached to it, so they could get something to eat there while they were waiting for the base commander. They were all frazzled from their experiences of the night before.

What the hell had happened back there? The only miracles Danny believed in were the ones he performed himself at the controls of a helicopter. Taking out that punk on the East River had been fun, just like old times, darting over and under the East River bridges until they'd finally trapped the bastard on his boat and that cop in the air with him putting a couple of .50-caliber rounds into the sonofabitch.

His phone vibrated. He looked at the display: HARRIS.

He switched on encryption. They wouldn't be using voice contact at this point, certainly not here. All their traffic would be monitored as a matter of course; on a base like this, every computer terminal on post would be equipped with keystroke-loggers, and all voice traffic would be intercepted and analyzed, then sent back to Washington to the Defense Intelligence Agency and to the Central Security Service in Fort Meade. Op-sec was everything, even here in small-town, hometown America.

SEEING THE SIGHTS?
THE VALLEY IS LOVELY THIS TIME OF YEAR

Well, that made it official. The trip to San Francisco was going to have to wait. The proposal was going to have to wait. The new life that they both wanted to start together was going to have to wait.

He glanced over at Hope, but she was fast asleep once more.

SO I GATHER

That meant he was in, although that was a foregone conclusion. When "Bert Harris," or whatever name he was using at the moment, called, Danny was in. They had been together too long for him to question either the operation or its necessity. It would be high-risk, high-reward, that much he already knew, and it would be a matter of national security.

What did a bunch of dead cows have to do with all that? He'd find out soon enough. He reached for Hope's hand—

The rap on the window startled him; he must be getting

old, to let someone sneak up like that on him. Or soft. Or maybe just in love.

"Sir?" he heard as he rolled down the window. "Admiral Atchison requests that you follow me, please."

The lieutenant commander glanced into the backseat. "Nice-looking bunch of kids you folks got there," he said.

Hope awoke. "Why, thank you, Officer," she said.

"This way, sir," said the lieutenant commander, getting into an official vehicle. Danny swung in behind him as they headed toward the officers' housing area.

"You call cops 'officers,'" he said to Hope with a smile. "In the service, you call them by their rank."

"How do you know what rank they are?"

"You look on their shoulders—dead giveaway."

"But—"

Danny leaned over and gave Hope a quick kiss. "Good morning to you, too."

She smiled, softened—and then remembered where they had been and what had happened. "Is everything okay? What does the radio say? What happened? Why were those men shooting at us?"

The enlisted men's barracks gave way to the BOQ and then to the senior officers' housing area. These homes were quite nice, and the higher up the ladder you stood, the nicer house you got. The base commander, Admiral Atchison, would have the nicest home of all.

As indeed he did. They pulled in front of a large, two-story house with a well-tended lawn and a basketball hoop in the driveway, which Rory eyed enviously. An attractive woman of about forty greeted them at the door.

"Hello," she said, "I'm Melinda Atchison. Please come in. You must be exhausted."

Danny introduced Hope, Emma, Rory, and Jade. "You three come with me," ordered Mrs. Atchison. "Breakfast is served." She turned to Hope and Danny. "Would you like some coffee?"

Hope understood that her place at the moment was with the children. "Let me help you," she said. Then, to Danny, softly: "Good luck."

"You can wait in the living room," said Mrs. Atchison, and then she and Hope disappeared into the kitchen with the three children.

The living room was well furnished and well appointed. Souvenirs from various duty stations were on the mantel and art that the Atchisons had collected at various stops around the world hung on the walls. They had taste and class—typical of today's well-educated officer corps.

"That's for you, Mr. Barker," came a voice behind him.

Danny turned to see the admiral entering the room. As they shook hands, the admiral said, "I found it here this morning."

It was a PDA, but unlike any that Danny had ever seen before.

"You obviously have friends in very high places. About four this morning, I received classified instructions to extend you every courtesy of the base, and that's precisely what I intend to do," said Atchison. "Whatever you need in the way of men and materiel, all you have to do is ask."

Danny wondered just what sort of materiel this operation was going to entail, but he would be very surprised if it didn't have something to do with the Hornets. "What do we know about the cattle deaths?" he asked.

"Officially or unofficially?"

"Your call."

"Officially, it's botulism, as you may have heard. Unofficially . . . we don't have the slightest idea. Something—not a poison—killed the livestock, and I mean killed them dead."

"I know. We saw it."

The admiral gestured to the sofa and invited Danny to sit.

"Best guess, some kind of space-originated laser, possibly from a satellite."

"Surely your men would have picked it up?"

At that moment, the PDA squawked to life. He had been listening the whole time:

"Not necessarily." The voice was altered, but Danny knew its cadences.

"Hello, Bert," he said.

"Lasers have come a long way since science-fiction movies," said the man calling himself Bert Harris. "They're far more focused, harder to pick up; they leave almost no footprint. Think of it as firing a rifle to hit a something the size of a dime from two miles away. Who the hell is going to notice that?"

"You're talking about the SBL program."

"Right," came the voice. "Space Based Lasers. Developed for use as anti-missile devices, but we all know they have a lot more potential uses than just that. But there's even more to it. There's the LLRE."

"What's that?" asked Danny.

"Admiral?"

Atchison didn't seem to mind that he was taking orders from a glorified squawk box. "It began as a way to measure the distance from the earth to the moon," he began. "The Apollo 11 astronauts left retroreflectors on the lunar surface, and Apollo 14 and 15 continued the mission. From various points on earth—the Côte d'Azur Observatory is one, there are others in Germany, New Mexico, Australia—you can fire a laser beam at the moon and have it come rocketing right back at you."

"And you think maybe this is what killed all those cows?" asked Danny.

"It's possible. From what we can tell, something altered the brains of the cattle and turned them to mush."

Danny wasn't sure if this was the right time to mention it,

but plunged ahead. "And how does that explain what I saw on the wall of an overpass?"

Silence for a moment. "What did you see?" That was Harris, not the admiral.

Might as well come right out with it. "I saw the Virgin of Guadalupe, and so did about a hundred other people, mostly Mexican farmworkers."

A longer pause this time, then: "You're sure?"

"Her image is on every votive candle, coffee mug, and tea towel in southern California," said Danny. "Of course I'm sure."

"Well, then . . . I guess we're going to have to talk about this some more. . . . Admiral, Mr. Barker and I may need three of your Hornets and your best flight crews."

"You've got 'em. Just say the word."

"Thank you. You're going to have to conceal their absence, of course, because officially they will not leave your base. Understood?"

"Yes, sir," replied the admiral.

"I may have to take them very far away, perhaps to the Af-Pak theater."

"We'll get them there for you."

"Thank you. Stand by for further instructions."

The line went dead. That didn't mean anything. "Bert Harris" would not be far away.

Danny picked up the device and slipped it into his pocket. "I'm not sure just what this is all about, or how it's going to play out," he said.

"Welcome to the Navy," said Admiral Atchison.

CHAPTER EIGHTEEN

Tehran

The boys delivered the coffin precisely where Skorzeny had demanded, to the basement of the Azadi Grand Hotel. The hotel wasn't all that grand, but it would have to do.

They put the coffin in a storage room, locked it, and gave Amanda a key.

"Thank you, Habib. Thank you, Mehrdad," said Amanda tipping them in rials, which disappointed them both. They would have wanted British pounds, or euros or, failing that, American dollars, but there was no sense in getting into trouble over currency irregularities for nothing. An illegal currency transaction, however innocuous, was just the kind of thing that landed you in hot water if you were not careful, especially when you didn't trust the people you were dealing with. And she didn't trust either of the brothers.

"You need help to your room, miss?" Mehrdad said. He was a little pushier than she would have liked, so it was time to put him in his place.

She gave him a come-hither smile and he drew close, as she knew he would. An Iranian male could never resist a

Western woman, unless she was spectacularly ugly, and even then he would have to think about it. Restricted from sex in their own culture, a Western woman was just about the easiest lay they were ever going to get. If they could get it.

"That is very thoughtful of you, Mehrdad," she said, slipping her hand behind his head and bringing his ear close to her lips. "But I wouldn't want to hurt your feelings if you came upstairs and I got a look at your shriveled little dick that would never be able to stand up properly because I am too much woman for you. So why don't you go home and practice with one of your sisters, or perhaps a goat, and spare yourself needless humiliation?"

She said all this with a radiant smile, batting her eyes at Habib as she spoke to his brother. Habib's teeth flashed in delight, and no doubt he would soon be pressing Mehrdad for the joy that was sure to await them later that evening. How puzzled he would be when Mehrdad refused to talk about it, or suggested some other avenue of delight. For Mehrdad would never repeat what she'd said—it would be too shameful—and so her little stunt might also drive a wedge between the brothers, as Habib would be convinced that Mehrdad was concealing something from him. And that would keep the both of them away from her this evening.

One evening was all she would need she put her plan into motion.

She bid both boys good-bye, kissed them on the cheek, and went upstairs.

The room was plain, as she expected. There was a television, but it only got six local Persian channels plus the BBC and CNN international. There was limited wireless Internet service, so heavily filtered by the government that it might as well be dial-up. Room service, but no wine. No matter, she didn't need it.

She kicked off her shoes and stretched. Were there hidden cameras in the room? It would be just like them to have a snooping device in the rooms, just so they could see a Western woman naked.

She pulled her dress over her head and stood there in her bra and panties. If they wanted to have a limited look, now was the time.

Skorzeny had given her one of his little toys, a bug scanner that would instantly locate—and neutralize, if the bearer wished—and listening or video devices in the room.

She went into the bedroom, pulled the curtains, took off her clothes, and turned off the lights and let out a curse. "Damn, I dropped an earring," she said for the benefit of her minders.

She got down on her knees and reached under the bed. The infrareds couldn't penetrate under the bed, so that's where she activated the device. Any watchers would be too fixated on her bare ass to wonder why she was looking under the bed.

Three devices: one in the bedroom, one in the sitting room, and one in the bathroom.

Fucking pervs.

She decided to leave the one in the bathroom and take out the other two, lest a clean sweep arouse their suspicions. She didn't care if they saw her naked, if they went home after jerking off; at least it would give their wives some peace. Not to mention the goats.

When the techies finally got around to investigating, each device's failure would be chalked up to a different cause: the wiring here, a transistor there. And by that time she'd be long gone.

She threw herself down on the bed and tried not to think of Maryam—which meant, of course, she thought about Maryam. Who the hell was she? Why was she working for the Americans? What was her surname? How had she come to know the man Skorzeny called "Devlin"? Which side was she really working for?

None of that mattered. What mattered was that Maryam—whatever her real name was—had tried to save her in Clairvaux—in fact, had saved her in Clairvaux, at that awful prison Skorzeny called "the country house," the maximum-security French prison that had once been a famous monastery, and where the devil kept a suite of rooms on the not-unreasonable theory that he would be safe there.

As indeed, he had been, until Maryam showed up.

Amanda let the long-repressed image play again in her mind, hearing the music as well. Skorzeny had ordered a private orchestra to play one of his favorite pieces, Richard Strauss's *Metamorphosen* for twenty-three solo strings. He liked it because of what it represented: the end of Western civilization and the beginning of the descent into eternal cultural darkness. For Skorzeny, the West was finished, a suicidal basket case that needed only one good push to finish it off. For him, the destruction of what used to be called Christian civilization was a mercy killing, which is why he had so eagerly made common cause with the Islamists: The enemy of my enemy is my friend.

Except that civilization was not really Skorzeny's enemy. He had made too much money from it, and no matter what had happened to him as a youth in Nazi Germany—no matter what terrible things he'd been forced to do after his parents were hanged by Hitler and he was entrusted to the care of none other than Otto Skorzeny, the most dashing figure in the Reich—he still loved the culture of the West with a mad passion. The music, the paintings, the great cathedrals—these were as mother's milk to a boy who had never really known mother's milk.

In his mind, he was not destroying it, but preserving it, preserving it as it was, frozen in time, frozen at its apogee, before times had changed, before people stopped caring, before the capitalist West descended into that long night of its long-forgotten and long-disparaged soul.

And now she was so very far away. She was here, in the heart of the Islamic Republic, in the heart of Shiia Islam itself, an Islam poised on the verge of earth-shattering things. An Islam that *believed*, as the West no longer did. An Islam that was not simply about oil and control and retribution, but the other Islam, the Islam that sat atop one of the world's great civilizations, a culture that had battled Alexander and Sparta and Rome alike, a culture that proved its mettle, even in defeat.

She rose and padded over to the window and pulled the curtains: there were the great mountains in the distance, snowcapped already.

How far she had come.

She left the curtains open and sank back on the bed. Sometimes she thought about him, about the man who'd called himself Milverton, the man who had nearly freed her from Skorzeny. Together they had nearly killed Skorzeny with the missile that destroyed the London Eye, but they had both paid for that act of lèse-majesté—he with his life and she very nearly with hers. She had been ready to die on that day, by the Thames, and she was no less ready today—as long as she could take him with her.

And who had killed Milverton? Why, none other than the lover of the woman in the coffin down below.

Two broken circles, very nearly contiguous. And she had the power to fix one of them, to make it whole again.

Which would it be?

She rose and stepped into the shower. At least the place had hot water. She didn't care who was watching.

A knock at the door, which she discerned only dimly as she toweled off. One of those intrusive hotel "welcome" packages that they reserved for VIPs, or people with money, or both. Iran still admired money, in a way the West did not. Maybe that was because the West didn't have money anymore.

She wrapped the hotel bathrobe tightly around her and went to the door—

And caught herself. What the hell was she doing? You didn't answer the door in a strange place, in a strange hotel room, in a place where you knew nobody. She had already learned that lesson from Maryam.

She looked for the peephole, but there was none.

Another knock.

"Who is it?" she said, in what she hoped was a weak, helpless feminine voice. If there was going to be trouble, that would trigger it.

Instead, nothing.

She got out her device, pressed a button, and pointed it at the door.

It worked like ground-penetrating radar, only now she could see whomever was standing on the other side of the door on the screen. Not clearly, but at least the outline of the body, from which she could deduce whether it was animal, vegetable or mineral, male or female, young or old, friend or foe. Well, not quite that, but from the preceding, she could make an educated guess.

Two men. Habib and Mehrdad, no doubt, unable to take no for an answer.

They shouldn't be here—they shouldn't even be allowed upstairs and, according to the Islamic law, they should not be visiting a single, unrelated woman, even if she was an English Christian whore.

Another knock.

She looked at her device. Hell, it was still a phone—with a direct satellite uplink.

She called Skorzeny.

He answered.

She explained the situation.

He hung up.

Unless they had a key, she would be safe. She turned on

the BBC and turned the volume all the way up. It was good to hear the accents of home.

She did not hear the footsteps in the hallway. She did not hear the sounds of heads cracking, of bodies falling to the carpet and being dragged away.

She was watching an ancient rerun of *The Dukes of Hazzard.* She had been hoping for *Dynasty*, but this would have to do.

After five minutes or so, the infernal machine buzzed. She picked up on the second buzz. "Yes?"

"It's done. And so to bed."

"And so to work, you mean."

"We, each of us, have our priorities." In the background she could hear the usual lugubrious music. She wondered if Mlle. Derrida were there. She wondered if she, too, were nude. Mlle. Derrida, as everybody knew, had no interest in Emanuel Skorzeny's masculinity, but she very much did have an interest in his fortune, and it would be just like him to consider her conquered when she merely considered herself rented. Maybe that was the real definition of a whore.

"Emanuel," she said, thinking of the two Iranian boys she had just condemned to death. Or did they condemn themselves? After all, she had warned them, and yet they came.

"Yes, Amanda?" he said. He almost never called her by her Christian name.

"I'm sorry."

"I know you are, my dear. Which is why I trust you."

"I'm glad you do."

"Why else would I let you out of my sight? Had I not trusted you, you would be long since dead. As I'm sure you understand."

"I do, Emanuel."

"I do, too, Amanda. Now finish your business and come home. Even the sight of Mlle. Derrida's delicious body, which I am forbidden by contract to touch, does not compensate me for the loss of your company."

So there it was. The one weakness he could never overcome. His Achilles' heel, located right between the old goat's legs.

She let the line dangle for a moment; she still had the power of a woman over him, could still dictate the tenor and the rhythm of the conversation:

"Emanuel, are you still there?"

Now it was his turn to pause. "Of course, my dear, of course I am still here. Is the package ready for pickup?"

"Yes, in the basement, in a secure room."

"Excellent. Your flight from Imam Khomeini Airport to Baku is booked. You may check in at the airport, or at your hotel desk. Don't worry, there's no bother about customs. It's all taken care of."

"Thank you, Emanuel."

"Hurry home, my darling."

"Yes, my love." If she could have torn her tongue out by the roots rather than utter those loathsome words, she would have. But she had no choice.

There was no response from the other end of the line. Which, actually, was all to the good. Had he suspected her, had he had the slightest inkling that something in her heart was awry, he would have kept her on the line, kept her whispering sweet nothings until he could track her down and kill her.

She exhaled.

Cautiously, she opened the door. There might have been a bloodstain on the carpet, there might not have been. God or Allah only knew what these hotel corridors had seen.

She closed the door. Went to her suitcase. Pulled on an all-black outfit of form-hugging clothes. She was like Catwoman in the old *Batman* TV series, only slinkier. Grabbed a bag she had prepared. Left the room.

No one would see her. No one would hear her. Only Maryam, alone in her grave, in the bowels of the building, awaiting she knew not what, had any inkling what she was about to do.

But she, Amanda Harrington, knew. Once the darling of the City, the darling of the Street, the head of one of the most powerful charities in the world, a woman known by sight to every one of the London paparazzi, a woman whose love life had been the topic of speculation in every London tabloid, page three after every night at the old Annabel's, every night at the Groucho Club, every night at one of the anonymous casinos at which the Sunni Arabs from Yemen and Abu Dhabi had tried their luck with the roulette wheels, the cards, the loaded dice, and the compromised women, dragged from one den of iniquity to another knocking shop, the Empire turned on its head, the maid made mistress, *La serva padrona*, the end of the world.

She turned on the television again. Whatever had happened to Habib and Mehrdad was no concern of hers. No doubt the hotel would report it, but Skorzeny's money would see to a satisfactory resolution of the attempted rape of a British woman by a couple of priapic Tehranians. Such things were to be expected at the interstices of the conflict between the West and Islam. Shit happened.

Something was going on in the holy city of Qom.

The government cameras were inside the mosque at Jamkaran, homing in on the sacred well. From the outside, it was not much to look at, enclosed above ground level by some sort of structure that allowed the faithful to fold up a slip of paper and then insert it into the narrowing openings of concentric squares. It was like the Wailing Wall, only rotated ninety degrees, and just as indifferent to the prayers of the petitioners.

Nevertheless, legions of the faithful, each bearing tiny folded-up oracular origami, were shuffling toward the sacred well, bowing, mouthing prayers, and inserting the pieces of paper into the slots provided by the nonrepresentational design. On any other planet not corrupted by the absurd ghost of political correctness—which, in some perversion of Christianity, posited that the wrong were always right, and the weak were really strong—such petitioners would have been dismissed as the fools they were. But not here. Not now.

Skorzeny was right. Superstition had taken over the earth, belief had trumped science, man had defeated a pitiful, helpless God

The Great Chastisement was nigh—but whether it came from above or below was not exactly clear.

It was time to move.

She stepped out in the hall and closed the door. She had her camera killer ready, and she was ready to use it.

CHAPTER NINETEEN

Lemoore Naval Air Station

Danny had always known it would come like this, fired on from behind, the one sound in his entire life he would not hear and never would hear. Every op in his business, no matter how high or how low, knew this for a dead-solid fact. It might come from a friend or it might come from an enemy, but come it would. The only way out of the business was feet-first.

"Keep walking."

Well, that was a start. At least he was hearing it. At least he was able to keep walking.

They were on the outskirts of the base. He had driven to where "Bert Harris" had told him to drive, and then walked across the Little League baseball field, across the field in front of the social center, past the boathouse for the artificial lake that the genius of the American mind had created out here in the Central Valley, a valley only in geography, unwatered and unirrigated until the Okies and Harvard boys and the Nevada silver miners and the Appalachian coal miners and the failed farmers from the Upper Midwest had all arrived and seen the possibilities and realized them. That was California in the old days, a melting pot of minds, not races, a cooperative of farmers, not ethnicities, a state that worked instead of a state that had failed.

"Don't worry. And I won't look back."

"They might be gaining on you."

"Am I talking to Bert Harris or Satchel Paige?"

"Does it make a difference?"

"At this moment, no."

"Right answer."

They were past the irrigated fields now, past the ball fields, past the garden plots. This may have been California, where everything grew year-round, but Danny knew that was an illusion—nothing grew here in the saline desert, so hard by the ocean, unless man made it grow. California was Schopenhauer's world as will and idea, and after more than a century, both the will and the idea were failing.

"No roses. Have you noticed?" The voice came from behind, unfamiliar but familiar. New in intonation and yet old in rhythm.

"No roses."

"None. The ones the housewives try to grow are shitty. Crap. Roses need rain. Why do you suppose that is?"

Danny thought. "Because roses really do need rain?"

He could feel something in the small of his back. "Precisely. Because roses really do need rain. Because man needs woman. Because the internal-combustion engine needs gasoline. Because universities need people who could never get jobs elsewhere, to teach idiots who will never get jobs elsewhere that they have no chance of ever getting a job elsewhere, which is why they need to stay in universities. You get my drift?"

"Loud and clear, sir."

"Good. I like that word, *sir*. Nobody ever calls me sir."

"And yet you can kill just about anybody you want, whenever you want.'

"That doesn't mean they have to call me sir or else I kill them."

"That's white of you."

"Nobody says that anymore. It's un-PC."

"I know."

Danny stopped and was about to turn around.

"Don't. Keep walking. Do not look upon me."

"You know, I'm sick of this shit. How long have we been working together?"

"Not long enough for us to meet. Keep moving."

Danny stopped again. If Bert Harris wanted to put a bullet through his spine, now was as good a time as any. "No. You're either going to have to shoot me or talk to me. I'm not the guy you used to know."

"So I see."

"Do you? My wife died at the Grove, and Jade nearly did too. Hope's husband died at Edwardsville. Emma damn near died when that bastard kidnapped her. Everywhere you go there's trouble. Everything you touch turns to shit for somebody else. And yet you always walk away, Casper the unfriendly ghost. Who the hell are you, anyway?"

The reply was soft. "I am the Angel of Death."

"So you always say. In fact, I've heard you say it."

"It's the only way I can live with myself. But sometimes even the Angel of Death needs a guardian angel."

They were on the far outskirts of the base now. "So here's the deal," said Bert Harris. "Do you want to die now or die later?"

Danny had no fear. He knew that the man behind him, who could end his life and who had ended the lives of many, would not now harm him. They had been together too long—not that that counted for anything but that they knew each other—and trusted each other, and with a big job ahead of them, this was the only time they were going to have to get the ground rules straight. "That's pretty much the same choice everybody has every day, so what's so special about it today?"

"Because we're going to Iran and we may not come back."

"Iran? Where?"

"How does Desert One sound? Payback time."

"Tabas," said Danny. "Eagle Claw."

"Eagle Clusterfuck was more like it. Your unit was born in its wake. Interested in a little payback?"

They were nearly at the wire now, the demarcation line that separated the base from the civilians. It looked like an innocent chain-link fence with barbed wire on the top, but Danny could tell at a glance that it was far more than that. Everything that came near the fence was photographed, recorded, monitored. If by chance some miscreant attempted to scale the wire with a cell phone on him, the SKIPJACK chip that Apple had agreed with the government to insert in every phone in order to trace its owner's movements would give him away.

"So where are we going with this?" asked Danny. "I was going to tell you that I wanted out. I'm getting married again. To Hope. You remember Hope."

The voice was soft. "I ought to. I saved her son."

"And you got her husband killed. I guess I ought to thank you for that. Funny how life works out. And we both saved her daughter. *My* daughter now. So why should I listen to you?"

"Because you don't have any choice. Listen up and listen good . . ."

For the next five minutes, Danny heard just about everything he had never wanted to hear in his life, his worst fears. Only a few men could prevent them from full realization, and two of them were standing out in field in the Central Valley of California, in a godforsaken part of the world, trying to decide what to do.

"That doesn't explain what I saw in Coalinga," said Danny.

"Or what I saw in California City," said Devlin.

"Which was?"

"Roses. Roses and hyacinths . . . but let's stopping worrying about what we may or may not have seen—what we *think* we saw—and start worrying about how we're going to fix our problem. Because if we don't, the whole world is going to have a problem."

Danny started to say something and then, without warning, wheeled around. If Bert Harris or Tom Powers of any of the other names he had used in their work together over the years was going to kill him . . . well, let it happen, here, now, in front of the security cameras. Danny had so much to live for now that he almost didn't care—if he died on the spot, he would die happy, his life once again given meaning and shape.

He was not surprised that the man he was suddenly confronting was so ordinary. It was entirely possible that he had walked past him every day for years, that he had seen on the street in L.A., or in a diner in Kansas City, or in a thousand other places both at home and abroad. His was the kind of face you saw all the time and never noticed: not handsome, not ugly, not remarkable but not plain either.

It was only when you looked into those deep blue eyes that you saw what was special about him: cold, unemotional, lethal. The perfect killing machine on behalf of president and country disguised as Everyman. No wonder he was so effective. No wonder he was so miserable.

Because Danny also was not surprised to find that, no matter how fast he had been, the man was holding a knife to his throat.

"Are you in or are you out?" was all he said.

Danny didn't even have to think. "Payback's going to be a
real bitch. When do we leave?"

"An hour soon enough? First stop, Washington. There's
some folks you need to meet."

"What about . . . you know?"

"They'll be safe here. Admiral Atchison extends his hospitality. Rory will have the run of the base. Girls will be
girls."

"Deal," said Danny.

But Devlin was already gone.

CHAPTER TWENTY

Tehran

The lights in the stairwells were either dim or nonexistent. For a rich country, Iran was remarkably poor. Everything was just this side of shabby, even in a nice hotel, the modern carpets already threadbare. The workmanship was poor. Revolutions would do that to a country.

She moved softly, purposefully. This was the only part of her plan that she could not foresee. If she encountered anyone . . .

But she did not. She made it to the basement without incident. She might have been picked up on a camera, but she was sure the chances that the indolent public servants would have noticed on their monitors were nil. And if anyone looked at the tapes later, all they would see was darkness.

There was the room. She produced her key, unlocked it, and slipped inside.

There were no lights in the little storage room, because neither luggage nor the dead needed lights. She would have to work by the light of her phone.

She unfastened the top of the coffin. Even before she got it off she could hear the sound of Maryam's breathing, strong and regular. "Are you all right?" she asked.

Maryam sat up. There was a puddle at the bottom of the box, but that was a good sign. It meant she had been drinking the water, and flushing the poison from her internal organs.

"Yes. Now let's get out of here."

This was the worst part of the plan. Now that she was faced with the moment, Amanda Harrington wasn't sure she could go through with it. But she had to go through with it. The Black Widow would have her revenge, at whatever personal cost to herself.

She gave Maryam the bag. "Clothes and some other things. I think they'll fit you."

"Where are we?"

"The Azadi Grand. You know it?"

"Yes."

"Good. Because this is where we must part."

"What?" Maryam's head was clearing, her limbs moving again. She could feel her strength coming back. She still had little memory of what had happened that night in Hungary, but she remembered Amanda, and she trusted her. She had to. "Where are you going?"

"I'm not going anywhere." Amanda threw a blanket down on the bottom of the coffin. She was a little taller than Maryam, but she would fit. "You're leaving, to do whatever you have to do. I'm staying."

"You're kidding, right?"

"Listen to me," said Amanda urgently. "We don't have much time. Skorzeny has sent someone to pick up the coffin. He expects someone to be in it. I don't know who's supposed to pick you up, but I can only imagine what your fate was going to be. That's why I'm taking your place."

"I can't let you."

"You have to let me. You have to get away and stop this monster. He's got something going with the mullahs. He didn't tell me because he doesn't trust me the way he used to, but it has something to do with lasers. He's going to attack the West again, but this time he'll have the force of a nuclear state behind him. And the West will be too weak to try and stop him. So we're going to have to."

Amanda clambered inside the coffin. There was still plenty of water, and the tank still held oxygen. If she closed her eyes, she could pretend she was sleeping peacefully in her lover's arms, instead of the arms of Morpheus.

"They're in Baku," she continued. "He still has your computer, but he hasn't touched it yet. He knows it's rigged or that it will give away its position the minute he turns it on. He wants to use it as a bargaining chip or, rather, a homing device, to bring . . . to bring . . ."

"Frank Ross. That's the name I call him. Frank Ross."

"To bring 'Frank Ross' into his orbit. So he can finally kill him."

Maryam hardly dared ask, but she did. "What news of him? Of Frank?"

"Gone to ground. We think he was cashiered after they got word of your defection. You probably don't remember signing the postcard. Just before Skorzeny drugged you into insensibility, he had you send a message from the laptop, which he redirected through an IP address in Tehran. So 'Frank Ross' thinks you're here, in Iran. And now you are." Amanda smiled, her teeth white in the faint light of the PDA. "So maybe it will all work out somehow."

"Maybe." Mixed news indeed. Frank might be on his way here—but to rescue her or to kill her? She had to get a message to him somehow.

"There's a plane ticket waiting for you at the airport under my name," continued Amanda. "My identity documents are in that bag. We look enough alike that you can pass for me in a pinch. I figure we have maybe to the end of the day before he begins to suspect something is amiss. . . ."

"And by that time, he may have a nasty surprise coming to him," finished Maryam.

"Who do you suppose they're sending for you?"

"I don't know. Some goons. But I think I know where they're taking me—taking you. Evin University. That's what we call it, anyway. It's really Evin prison. It's where they hold the political prisoners. Where they execute them."

Evin prison was the most notorious in Iran. Built on the site of the home of a former prime minister, it sat at the foot of Alborz Mountains in northwestern Tehran, the natural beauty of the setting contrasting vilely with the horrors within.

Amanda was still sitting up. She stuck out her hand. "Sorry, forgot my manners. I'm Amanda Harrington," she said.

"Maryam."

"That's all? Just Maryam?"

"That's all."

"Good luck, Maryam-that's-all."

"I'll come back for you. As soon as they see you're not me, they won't hurt you." She wasn't exactly certain that was true, but that was about the only reassurance she had on offer at the moment.

"I know you will," said Amanda. "One more thing. Something's happening in Qom, in the mosque."

"The well at Jamkaran, where Ali, the Mahdi, lies occluded and dreaming."

"Yes. Whatever Skorzeny is up to, I think it has something to do with that." She paused and collected herself. "Now, fasten the top down and get out of here."

Amanda lay back. There was nothing more to say.

Maryam fastened the top down. Then she picked up the bag and left the room, locking the door behind her.

She exited the hotel by a side door and glanced in the bag. Amanda had thought of everything: clothes, documents, money in various currencies. Best of all—her secure PDA. How Amanda had sneaked that out, past Skorzeny, Maryam would never know. But Amanda didn't have to worry about his finding out, because she wasn't planning to return anyway.

She could handle this.

The sun was coming up as she stepped into the street and breathed in the familiar smells.

She was back home in Tehran. With a few innocuous phone calls, she'd be back in touch with the NCRI network. They'd taken a beating during the recent protests against the government, and some of them had wound up either shot to death on the street or taking classes for extra credit at Evin University, but the mullahs couldn't get them all.

She'd be in Qom in couple of hours. But there was something she had to do first.

CHAPTER TWENTY-ONE

Baku

Dawn over the Caspian was a beautiful sight, but Emanuel Skorzeny was not contemplating that kind of beauty. Instead, he lay dreaming—not of resurrection but of death.

Later, when he awoke from his uneasy slumbers, he would realize that these dreams were coming more often now. Skorzeny didn't believe in signs from the heavens; he knew they were messages his own brain was sending to him, not communications from some imaginary higher power. Nevertheless, they disturbed him, and he was not a man who enjoyed being disturbed.

He was back in Dresden, in 1945. Winter. Mid-February. Very cold. Working with *Vater Otto* in rooting out the hidden enemies of the Reich. And who better than him, since his parents had once been among those hidden enemies?

They were in a restaurant. Everyone was singing—Schubert's "Erlkönig." That's when they heard the sirens.

You rarely heard sirens in Dresden. The beautiful city on the Elbe was far inland, far removed from the western front. True, the Americans and the British were flying relentless sorties over the other major German cities, pounding the Reich into rubble while Goering's useless Luftwaffe sat on the ground, unable to attack and unable to defend. Teenaged boys, he had heard, boys his age, were manning the anti-aircraft guns in Berlin.

But in Dresden they didn't worry much about bombing raids. True, there had been a couple of attacks on the rail yards, but the Florence of the Elbe had no military targets to speak of, and its status as one of the architectural wonders of Europe, the visible manifestation of all that was great about German *Kultur,* would certainly spare it from destruction. The real worry was the Russians to the east. They were coming and, since the epic defeat at Stalingrad, there was no one to stop them. That had been two years ago, almost to this day, and the rest was commentary. Indeed, Father Otto was already making arrangements for their escape.

He knew, because at night, asleep upstairs in their small house, he could hear voices, talking treason. The war was lost, they all said, and now the only question was what to do about it, and where to flee. After all, Father Otto was among the most-wanted men in the Reich, but he had got out of tougher spots than this in the past. He would think of something. And he would not leave his *Sippenhaft* son behind.

They were celebrating Shrove Tuesday, the day before the beginning of Lent, not that either he or Father Otto cared about such things. Religion was something that had abandoned him with the death of his parents, a death they forced him to watch as part of his reeducation as a loyal and dedicated citizen of the Reich.

It was just before ten o'clock in the evening; at midnight, it would be *Ascher Mittwoch*, the beginning of the penitential season that would culminate with Christ's resurrection on Easter Sunday forty days later.

At the sirens, Father Otto knew right away what was coming, that much was clear. He rose immediately and, without a hint of concern, took Emanuel by the arm and led him into the cellar. And then he did a remarkable thing. He picked up one of the chairs and smashed right through the foundation of the building, opening a hole into the next building.

That was impossible. German cellars were famous for their thick stone walls. But in many of the Dresden buildings, the cellar walls had been replaced by mere partitions, so that people would not get trapped in them if the house above collapsed after a bombing. Father Otto knew that. Father Otto knew everything.

But in the dream, Skorzeny did not know that. In the dream he watched in wonder as the wall vanished and they dashed through where the stones once had been.

The bombs were already falling as they emerged into the street. Not ordinary bombs. Firebombs. Much of the city center was already in flames.

"Run, Kurt, run!" commanded Father Otto. Kurt was his new name, the one they gave him when they placed him with Father Otto. He could barely remember his old name.

They ran.

Over dead bodies, past people aflame. The heat was already incredibly high, so high that those closest to the center of the raid had simply burst into flames. Others toppled over from lack of oxygen, which was being sucked into the vortex.

The bastards above knew this was going to happen. They knew, and yet they did it anyway. They had done it to Hamburg, Bomber Harris and the others, and now they were doing it to Dresden.

They were doing it to him, personally. And he would hate them forever for it.

The car was nearby. Emanuel jumped into the front seat as Father Otto landed behind the wheel. People were rushing toward them, imploring them to help them escape, but they had no time for people. They barely had time for themselves.

The attack had come from the east, so it was to the east
they fled as the flames roared up behind them.

Father Otto sang as they drove:

> *Wer reitet so spät durch Nacht und Wind*
> *Es ist der Vater mit seinem Kind*
> *Er hat den Knaben wohl in den Arm*
> *Er faßt ihn sicher, er hält ihn warm*
> *Mein Sohn, was birgst du so bang dein Gesicht?*
> *Siehst Vater Du den Erlkönig nicht?*
> *Der Erlkönig mit Kron' und Schweif?*
> *Mein Sohn, es ist ein Nebelstreif*

Something hit the roof, hard. It sounded like one of the
balls from the *Kegelbahn*. "Why are they throwing things at
us, Father?" he cried.

Another bowling ball hit the roof, only this time it wob-
bled and then rolled down the windscreen and onto the hood.
It wasn't a bowling ball, it was a human head.

Then another, and then another.

Not only heads but limbs were flying through the air,
some of them on fire. Arms and legs and hands and feet. A
legless, headless, and armless torso hit the street right in
front of them, but Father Otto just drove right over it.

Emanuel turned back to look at the city, which was now a
gigantic fireball. The planes were coming in ranks, their
progress barely disturbed by the antiaircraft fire.

"I hope that fat pig Goering burns in hell," said Father
Otto.

They were leaving the city. There was no urban sprawl in
the Germany of that time; the city simply ended and the
countryside began. Soon they were in a deep forest, the big
Benz bouncing over potholed and damaged roads but making good time, speeding, speeding always toward the east.
He saw a sign for Görlitz.

Then, even in his dream, he fell asleep.

When he awoke they had stopped somewhere in a clearing. There were no signs of life anywhere near them. Father Otto was rooting around in the trunk of the car, searching for something.

"What is it, Father? What are you looking for."

Instead of answering, Father Otto turned his gaze past his foster son, to the west, toward where the proud baroque jewel had once stood on the banks of the Elbe, and wept.

This was an extraordinary thing. The great Skorzeny, the rescuer of *il Duce*, the bravest man in the Reich, a dashing figure in his SS uniform, his face creased by a dueling scar, was weeping. Emanuel could scarcely credit his eyes.

"It's over," he said. "And now it's time for *Operation Greif.*"

He handed Emanuel a rucksack. "Everything you'll need is in there. Clothes, new identity papers, some dried beef. You know how to find food in the forest, I know you do. Keep away from the bears and the boars and you'll be safe enough."

"You're not leaving me here, Father!" he cried.

"I have to. Where I go now you cannot follow. The war is lost and soon all Germany will be under the boots of the Russians and the Americans. We are too far from the western front for me to get you to the Americans, who would take care of you. So I must leave you here for the Russians to find."

Now it was his turn to weep. "No, Father, no! Don't leave me here alone in the forest."

"I must. But don't worry. Your new identity papers are your old identity papers—do not show them to any German, lest they shoot you on sight. Instead, when the Russians come, and they will, ask for the officer and show him your papers. You are the son of one of the July plotters against the life of the Führer. They will respect and honor you for that."

Father Otto turned to him. For a moment, Emanuel thought he was going to embrace him, as a real father would, but of course he did not. He had already shown enough weakness for one day.

"You have greatness in you, boy," he said as he got back into the car and fired up the engine.

"But much anger, Father."

"Hold on to that anger. Nurture it. Let it nourish you through the long nights ahead. Love nothing except your own hatred, lest you become soft and weak. Do you understand?"

"Yes, Father."

"Wer reitet so spät durch Nacht und Wind?" Who rides so late through night and wind?

Emanuel answered: *"Es ist der Vater mit seinem Kind."* It is the father with his child.

Otto Skorzeny smiled. "May God be with you, Emanuel," he said, and drove off.

Emanuel watched for a long time until the car was no longer visible. Then he turned back into the forest.

The Erlking, the evil creature who lived in the woods and preyed on children, was waiting for him there. He would find a welcome ally.

Skorzeny was still sleeping when he became aware of the ringing of the secure telephone. Mlle. Derrida lay beside him, indifferent as ever.

He found the phone and looked to see who was calling. It was her. He knew it would be. She had not let him down. He might have just hung up, the information duly conveyed and noted, but he enjoyed the sound of her voice. "Yes?" he said.

"The package has been delivered," came her voice. The connection must be bad, for it was muffled. But it was unmistakably her.

"And you?"

"I'll be back soon."

"Excellent. I shall have Mlle. Derrida prepare us a splendid lunch."

"What a wonderful idea. See you then."

She rang off.

Skorzeny rose, pulled on his robe, slipped the phone in its pocket, and stepped out onto the balcony. How different this sunshine was from that horrid winter in Dresden, the winter that haunted his dreams—which were, of course, not dreams at all but memories, the ghosts of the dead summoned up from the eternal wellspring of hatred that yet burned in his soul. . . .

The Russians had found him a few weeks later, cold and hungry. They had treated him about as well as he could have expected, which was to say not well at all—which was why he treated them not at all well in his business dealings with them. Scores were always meant to be settled, right up to the day of final reckoning.

And now that his package was in Tehran, that day was hastened.

His hand brushed his pocket and bumped into the phone. He remembered that he had not turned it off, so he extracted it and pushed the off button.

Half a world away, at the headquarters of the National Security Agency in Fort Meade, Maryland, the Black Widow made a note of the duration of the phone call, its origin, and its reception; transmitted the audio to one secure destination and initiated a complete transcription, which it encoded; and then signaled to a human operator that its task was complete.

The tech specialist on duty noted the alert and sent it straight to the top, to General Armond Seelye, the DIRNSA, who in turn relayed it to the one man who needed to know about it.

WE'VE FOUND THE BASTARD

In California Devlin looked at the readout and punched back: WHERE?

BAKU, AZERBAIJAN. BUT WAIT—THERE'S MORE
GET TO IT, OLD MAN
HE WAS TALKING TO HARRINGTON. SHE'S IN TEHRAN
MARYAM?
NO CLUE
WILL BE BACK IN WASHINGTON LATER TONIGHT.
GOOD. YOUR HOUSE, AFTER 11. EYES ONLY
WHY?
BECAUSE THE PRESIDENT WOULD LIKE TO SPEAK WITH
YOU PERSONALLY AND EVEN YOU AREN'T THAT RUDE
DON'T BE LATE. I NEED MY SLEEP

CHAPTER TWENTY-TWO

Kaduna, Nigeria

Mobi Babangida was one of the richest men in Kaduna, from one of the richest families. Of course, here in Kaduna, about one hundred miles north of the capital city of Abuja, rich was relative.

"Babangida," in the Hausa language, meant "master of the house," and Mr. Babangida very much considered himself to be just that. Since the founding of the colonial city by the British in 1913, the old provincial capital had been a center of agriculture and trade in central Nigeria, and for a long time, so long as peace was maintained between the Muslims and the Christians, there were fortunes to be made.

But then came the troubles, the riots, the installation of *sharia* as the provincial law, and things had changed. Neighbor distrusted neighbor. When a newspaper columnist idly wrote of an upcoming Miss World pageant in Abuja years ago that even the Holy Prophet, Mohammed, peace and blessings be upon him, would be tempted by the contestants' great beauty to take another wife, twenty churches were burned by the Muslims and eight mosques destroyed by the Christians. These were tense, unhappy times.

Still, Mr. Babangida felt no qualms or unease about moving freely between the Muslim north of the city and the Christian south, for in this it was a mirror of Nigeria itself. One could not be a prosperous businessman if one were not willing to visit both sides of town. Whether in mosque or church, Mobi Bagangida, the master of the house, was among his people.

Besides, that's what well-armed bodyguards were for.

His first thought, when he saw the crowd gathered across from the petrol station at Mohammed Buhari Way and Independence Way, was that there was some sort of official ceremony going on, perhaps a procession coming down from Lugard Hall, where the Assembly met. But as he drew nearer, he could see that the people were looking up at the sky.

Now the sky was not where Mr. Bagangida normally looked. There was nothing to see in the sky except the occasional cloud or the planes coming in and out of the airport or the government helicopters monitoring the populace whenever another riot broke out and, occasionally, strafing them. But he looked anyway—

—and saw the holy Prophet, or someone who looked very much like him.

Mr. Bagangida had never seen the Prophet, except in a few ancient pictures from the infidel Iran. While it was not forbidden to show the sacred likeness, representations of the holy visage were frowned upon, as was representational art in general. The human form was the highest work of divine Art, and mere man could not hope to improve upon Allah. In fact, thought Mr. Bagangida, looking around Kaduna, there was not very much that man could get right; already parts of the city were returning to the nature that the British had found a century ago and, soon enough, he expected, much of the country would follow it into the countryside. The devil was afoot in Nigeria, but it did not much matter, for within a few years, Mr. Bagangida planned to be living in New York City.

Now, face-to-face with the Prophet, he was not so sure. Mohammed's lips were moving, but no sound emerged; he seemed to be floating in the sky, shimmering yet corporeal, imparting instructions to the Faithful, instructions that Mr. Bagangida was not holy or purified enough to hear.

An imam from a nearby mosque must have come on the scene, because suddenly the crowd of men fell to the ground, many of them carrying their prayer rugs, and turned toward Mecca and began to pray while, above them, Mohammed kept talking.

And then—this was something Mr. Bagangida never would have believed had he not seen it with his own eyes— another apparition appeared, this one hovering over the Christian side of the city. She was a beautiful lady, standing atop a bed of fresh rose petals. She said nothing, but merely smiled a smile of a million sadnesses. Soon enough, people noticed her as well, and Christians poured out of their houses by the hundreds to see the holy sight.

And here was Mr. Bagangida, caught in the middle.

He was not sure what to do, or where to turn. The streets were filling up with humanity very rapidly, and he had witnessed firsthand many times what happened when one half of an explosive and restive population came into contact with the other half. He was the master of the house, and so it was high time for him to put aside his business affairs for the day and retire to his domicile.

Now a roar came up from the Muslim crowd. He could hear shouts of "blasphemy" in several tribal languages; as luck would have it, at that moment his eyes turned back to the Lady. Something was happening to the rose petals at her feet. Something unseen was slithering through them, knocking them aside—

A snake. No, a dragon. But the Lady kept her feet on the dragon's neck and, squirm though it might, she would not relent. Still with her smile, she was slowly crushing the life from the dragon, and its death throes were terrible to watch. The beast writhed in agony, but the woman was immovable, and a great cheer went up from the Christian crowd.

He turned back to look at the Messenger of God. A great rage had come across his noble and holy features, like the rage he felt when confronted with the stubbornness of the Jews of Medina. In response to his blessed wrath, a chant went up from the Muslims: *"Kill the blasphemers. Kill the infidel. Allah commands it. Allahu akbar!"*

The Muslim crowd rose to its feet. He could see many machetes flashing. Some had rifles. There was going to be bad trouble.

Surrounded by his bodyguards, Mr. Bagangida backed away, trying to get back to his car. He was very proud of that car. It was a splendid, if used, Mercedes-Benz that he had bought from a German for a trifling sum. It was in tip-top running condition, and he employed several of the neighborhood boys to keep it clean at all times. It would never do for the master of the house to be seen in a dirty vehicle.

He never made it to the car.

The enraged crowd swept everything before it as it rushed to attack the Christians. Bloodcurdling screams were the order of the day, and Mr. Bagangida fell with them echoing in his ears. His guards fired a few shots, but what were their pistols against numbers? A blow from one of the machetes sent him to the ground, minus one of his ears. He tried to pick up the ear—the doctors at the international hospital in Abuja could work miracles—but then he was hit again and lost one of his hands.

Mr. Bagangida had seen what was about to happen next

too many times to have any illusions of escape. It did not matter that he was a prominent businessman, that he gave regularly to charity, that he employed many people, that he took no sides. When the crowd had the wind up, there was no stopping it, no begging or pleading that could affect the great beast. In this moment, being master of the house meant nothing.

He was trying to decide which prayer to utter when his head flew off his shoulders.

What happened next is a matter of historical record. More than seven thousand people were killed in the violence, many houses destroyed, businesses sacked, and even some government offices. The central government was slow to react, and so the conflict spread like a wild blaze, burning north to Niger, west to Benin, Togo, Ghana, and the Ivory Coast, east to Cameroon and Chad and into the Central African Republic. In less than two weeks, any place in black Africa where Christians and Muslim had lived together in uneasy coexistence was the site of a raging civil war.

What happened to the apparitions, no one could say. They simply disappeared.

CHAPTER TWENTY-THREE

New York City

Celina Gomez was right where she said she would be, sitting at the reception desk in Nuclear Medicine. She had to admit it gave her a little thrill when the two plainclothes cops walked in. All she ever saw were doctors and sick people.

"Ms. Gomez? I'm Captain Francis Byrne and this is my associate, Detective Aslan Saleh. We know you're busy, so let's get right to it, shall we?"

Celina had the tape all queued up. "There's something I forgot to tell you on the phone. The man clearly said that Detective Saleh had an appointment right here, in our department. You didn't make an appointment for a stress test, did you, Detective?"

"No, ma'am, I did not," replied Lannie.

"He said it was a matter of life and death."

Byrne was not liking this at all. It was obviously a taunt, a dare—daring them to do something. "Let's hear the tape," he said.

Celina tapped the computer. The voice emerged from the speakers:

"Taubeh kon! Taubeh kon! Taubeh kon!"

". . . the fuck," said Byrne under his breath.

Lannie looked at him. The look in his eyes said it all: *Got it the first time.*

"Do you mind if we look around, Ms. Gomez?" asked Byrne.

"Not at all," she replied. "But of course I will have to clear it with the administrators. And get you a tour guide . . ."

"We're not here for a tour, Ms. Gomez," said Lannie, champing at the bit. The place was dirty, he could feel it. He just didn't want to think about how dirty it was. But it all made sense. If the terrorists had somehow managed to smuggle some kind of dirty bomb or worse onto the island, a hospital was just the place to store it—radiation hiding among radiation. And the Department of Nuclear Medicine would be the best place of all.

"You're all set," said Celina, hanging up the phone. "And Alonzo here will take you where you need to go." Byrne and Lannie turned to see a tall young black man in hospital whites coming round the corner, his hand already outstretched in greeting. "Alonzo Schmidt, at your service," he said. "Your 24/7 guide to the underworld here at Mount Sinai."

They shook hands. "Let's go," said Byrne. "Walk and talk."

"Follow me."

They headed for the nearest elevator. It was one of those huge hospital elevators, with doors that opened on both sides, so big that it could accommodate several gurneys simultaneously, but at this moment it was empty except for the three of them.

"Have you noticed anything different, Mr. Schmidt?" asked Byrne.

"In what way? Every day at a hospital like Mount Sinai is

different. Every night is different, and it doesn't even have to be Passover."

"You know," said Lannie, "something that's not where it belongs, something new that wasn't properly checked in."

The elevator was still descending. Hospital elevators, perhaps because they could carry so much weight, tended to move at a glacial pace. Byrne hated slow elevators; in fact, he pretty much hated all elevators. And he lived in New York City and wouldn't live anywhere else, go figure.

"Since you gentlemen are here in the Department of Nuclear Medicine, I can only surmise that you're talking about something . . . fissionable."

"Any radiation spikes over the course of the past couple of months?" asked Byrne.

"There are always radiation spikes in a hospital, Captain," replied Alonzo. "In our department we mostly deal in gamma rays—you know, like the kind that turned the Incredible Hulk green—and it varies from day to day. Among the isotopes we use are fluorine, krypton, gallium, indium, xenon, and iodine-123—they're used in imaging—yttrium and iodine-131 in various types of therapy."

Byrne had very nearly failed chemistry in high school; this sort of talk made his head ache.

At last, the elevator found its floor. They stepped out into a dark and eerie place, lit only by emergency lighting. It was a large room that contained a series of sealed cubicles, each with thick walls. "Down here we conform to all industry standards and then some," said Alonzo. "Impermeable materials, chemical-resistant worktop surfaces, photo-cell-activated wash-up sinks. Nobody touches anything down here."

"You sure it's safe for us to be here without hazmat suits?" asked Lannie nervously.

"Perfectly safe," said Alonzo. "Everything is sealed at the moment, so let's have a look."

Schmidt went to one of the workstations and punched up some images. "As you can see, the spectrometers are all in the normal zone. 'Normal' is recalculated every day, so that at any given moment it reflects the kind and volume of the work we're doing. As I said, it's never a constant. But it's always ALARA."

"Alara?" asked Lannie.

"As low as reasonably achievable."

"But what about other forms of radiation?" said Byrne. "Do they pick that up, too?"

"Depends on what kind it is. For example—"

"You can spare us the chemistry lesson. Not going to mean anything to me or Detective Saleh here. So let's cut to the chase."

Alonzo stopped. "You're talking about a suitcase nuke, aren't you? Polonium or U-233, with a pair of neutron generators and some sort of power source, either direct electrical or a battery. First, if there are such things—and I gather that the literature is mixed—it would have to be plugged in somewhere or have a very long-lasting and reliable battery. Now, I haven't seen anything sticking into someplace where it ought not to be, if you don't count my brother-in-law, and second, we might—*might*—be able to detect a spike in neutron activity if we recalibrate for it. May take a while."

Byrne and Lannie exchanged glances. Schmidt caught the look. "How long have we got?" he asked.

What had the caller said?

"Three days, max," said Byrne. "Probably less now."

"This is for real, isn't it?" said Alonzo. "Serious, I mean."

"You know the old saying," replied Byrne. "Serious as a heart attack. And I bet you get a lot of those around here."

A few minutes later they were back at ground level, shaking hands with Schmidt in the main entrance. "Thanks very much for all your help, Mr. Schmidt," said Lannie. "I don't have to tell you that—"

"—that it's all completely confidential. I know the drill. And you can count on me."

Byrne and Saleh each handed him a card. "This is where you reach us." Byrne took out a pen and wrote something on the back of his card. "That's my private cell number. You learn anything, you call it any time day or night. Got it?"

"Got it."

They stepped into the street. Byrne's car was parked in front of the hospital. In retrospect that was probably an error, since anyone with functioning eyeballs and half a brain could figure out it was a cop car. And, as luck would have it, such a person was right there.

"Captain Byrne?" The sound of a throaty female voice behind them got both Byrne's and Lannie's attention. As soon as he turned around, though, Byrne immediately regretted it.

She was still wearing a wig, although it was pretty damn lifelike, and she certainly was quite a dish, but Principessa Stanley was the last person in Manhattan Byrne wanted to see at this moment.

"Captain Byrne? I'm Principessa Stanley."

Byrne started walking toward the car. He wished Lannie would learn how to close his jaw.

Principessa kept up with them as they walked. "Captain, I wonder if I might have a word with you."

"I hate ambushes, Miss Stanley," he said.

"I have something I think you ought to listen to." Byrne kept moving. The car wasn't far now. "It's some new evidence about the terrorist incident that's just come to light."

Interesting, but not interesting enough to stop right at this moment.

Stanley sprinted around ahead of them and stopped. She was holding a cell phone in her hand. "Listen, Captain, I know you played a major role in stopping what those animals did to our city, and I know you got wounded doing it. Well, so did I."

There was no way around her. Both men stopped. Byrne clicked the unlock button to signal they had urgent business elsewhere, but that was as rude as he was willing to be, under the circumstances.

"I was buried alive, Captain. He *scalped* me. He was probably going to rape me and he might have killed me. And while I know that he's dead, whoever he was, I think you need to hear this. Because somebody saved my life, and I need to know who that man was."

"How am I supposed to know that?" asked Byrne.

"I thought you might recognize his voice. Because *I do.* Listen."

Even out here on the street, Byrne could tell at once that the man was speaking a foreign language—a language that, in fact, sounded remarkably like the one they had just heard on Celina Gomez's sound capture. Not the same voice, far from the same voice, but the same—

"It's Farsi," said Lannie. "Again."

Principessa turned her famous eyes on Lannie; standing next to him, Byrne could feel him melting, the soles of his shoes fusing with the pavement.

"Great. Let me play it again and perhaps you'll be kind enough, Detective . . . Detective . . . ?"

"Aslan Saleh. My friends call me Lannie."

"Lannie." She pressed PLAY.

" 'Listen, you cocksucker,' " Lannie translated. " 'I am coming for you. O my brother, this will be the last dawn you shall ever see,' or something like that. I'm an Arab, not a Persian."

Principessa paused the playback for a moment. "And then he ends with this," she said, and hit the play button again. "*For I am sending you to hell.*"

"Do you have what you need now, Ms. Stanley?" said Byrne, pushing past her and opening the driver's door. Reluctantly, Lannie followed, climbing in the passenger's side. Byrne started the engine and rolled down the window.

"I know who he is, Captain," shouted Principessa. "And I think you do, too."

"Who's that?" he asked. He recognized the voice, too—it was the man who'd saved him from Ben Addison, Jr. Looks like they shared a guardian angel, not that he was going to tell a reporter that. Whoever the man was, he deserved his anonymity.

"His name is Archibald Grant, and he's a consultant for the RAND Corporation," she shouted. "I heard him give a speech last year in New Orleans on terrorism. Please, you have to help me find him."

The name meant nothing to Byrne, but he would check it out soon enough. "I'll see what I can do, Ms. Stanley," he said, and pulled into the Fifth Avenue traffic, heading back downtown. He had more pressing and urgent issues on his mind than some guy at the RAND Corp., such as whether there was likely to be a radioactive crater at the corner of Ninety-eighth and Fifth. It was highly unlikely that some pasty-faced academic could have done the things Byrne witnessed during that terrible day.

"You got that, Lannie?" he asked as they moved down Fifth. But Lannie was looking out the window at Central Park. As they passed the Metropolitan Museum, he pointed and said, "That's where she was, isn't it? Over there, behind the museum."

"Did you hear a word I said, Detective?" asked Byrne.

"No, Chief."

"The get your head out of her admittedly splendid ass and write this name down. Archibald Grant, RAND Corporation. Got that?"

"Got it, boss."

"Sure you do." Byrne put the flasher on; he didn't feel like fucking around with traffic at this moment. "There's something else you'd rather be getting and we both know what it is, don't we?"

CHAPTER TWENTY-FOUR

Falls Church, Virginia

They were in the secure room of Devlin's home on North West Street. He hadn't spent much time in this house lately, not since it had been assaulted by a hit team from the FBI and he had had to take them all out, including poor Evalina Anderson. Milverton, the rogue SAS operative, had done this to him, had discovered the location of his house while blackmailing poor Senator Hartley, and for a time Devlin thought he would never be able to come back. But the place was too useful and, with a few security modifications, it had been made airtight once more.

They were in the "panic room"—the ultra-secure location from which Devlin could monitor the vast wide world beyond. Even if the house's formidable defenses were penetrated, this room could be instantly sealed off and protected externally by a lethal jolt of electricity. On his desk was the old-fashioned black telephone that looked like something out of *The Roaring Twenties* and really wasn't a telephone at all, but a direct incoming link from the Oval Office, Fort Meade, and the Pentagon.

"Now that's what I call retro," said Danny Impellatieri, reaching for it.

"I wouldn't do that if I were you," said Devlin.

Danny's hand froze in midair. "Booby-trapped, right?"

"You might say that," said Devlin. "For one thing, it's incoming only. For another, only my voice can activate it via voice-recognition software I designed myself; don't ask. For a third, the grip is also a fingerprint reader. Finally, I have to look directly into the instrument within five seconds of its ringing—both the receiver and the transmitter pieces—for a retinal scan."

"What happens if you don't? What happens if someone else picks up?"

"The phone self-destructs in a shrapnel fireball, and that's the end of whoever's fucking with me. Of course, if it gets that far, it means I'm probably already dead. Still, I sleep easier at night."

Danny looked around the room at the range of computers and weapons. That was all that was in the room: multiple laptops and multiple weapons. The place was a cross between Best Buy and an Afghani weapons bazaar.

"Like I said," said Devlin, reading his mind, "I sleep easier at night."

For open-source data mining, there were three laptops, each with a different operating system and a different Web browser. Double-blind passwords, proprietary encryption algorithms. Each of the machines running DB2 and Intelligent Miner and hotlinked separately to the three parallel mainframe servers at the IBM RS/6000 Teraplex Integration Center in Poughkeepsie—the RS/6000 SP, the S/390, and the AS/400. Predictive and descriptive modes, depending on what he was looking for.

True, some of his systems needed updating. He was running Sharpreader on Windows, NetNewsWire on the Mac, Straw on Linux: his in-box was RSS-refreshed on a minute-

by-minute basis, with real-time news. Level Five NSA fire-
wall security, updated regularly. Complete virus, trojan, and
spyware projection, automatically renewed every forty-eight
seconds.

"While we're waiting," said Devlin, "let me show you
something."

He opened the folders the priest had given him. A few ar-
ticles from the *Los Angeles Times* and other local newspapers about the monthly gathering in the California City
desert. Surveillance photos of unknown provenance. Some
background information on "Juan Diego." But the bulk of
the material had to do with the larger phenomenon of what
the true believers referred to as the Marian Apparitions—the
purported manifestations of the BVM at obscure and remote
places around the world, whether in person, as at Fatima and
Lourdes: a reflection or image, as at Knock, in Ireland; or vi-
sualized as a salt stain on a highway underpass, as in
Chicago a few years back.

"This is what I saw," said Danny, pointing to the Chicago
images.

"Those were eventually vandalized and removed," said
Devlin, "but I have to admit the likeness is striking."

Danny kept one eye on the telephone as he spoke. "Do
you think they're really coming? I've never met a president
before."

"You'll get over it pretty quickly."

"And why are you involved in all this?" asked Danny, re-
ferring to the Marian information. During the plane ride to
Washington, they hadn't spent much time in conversation.
Danny was too busy putting together a team for any eventu-
ality, while Devlin mostly slept—although whether he was
sleeping or thinking, it was impossible to tell.

"Because," came the reply. "Because a woman I never
met before asked me to. Because a priest in a deconsecrated
cathedral who probably doesn't really exist gave me these

dossiers. Because I went out to California City and saw something. Because of *this*."

The rose was withered now, but it was still a rose. Danny caught it in midair.

"When was the last time you saw a wild rose in the Mojave?"

"I've never seen a wild rose in the Mojave."

"It's the end of the world. That's what Tyler said. You and I each have a piece of the puzzle. The White House, NSA, maybe Defense—they have their own pieces. We're here to put them all together."

"It's because of her, isn't it?"

Devlin turned and looked at Danny. They had come a long way together, and he had just breached his own most important protocol by bringing the man here. But trusting him was the least of his sins. The real sin, the only sin that mattered, was trusting her.

He had trusted her for absolutely no reason. Everything she had done from the time she'd picked him up in Paris years ago, to their "chance" meeting on board a commercial flight two years ago . . . everything screamed out for closer scrutiny. And yet he had given her none. Instead, he had forced the president to allow her on the Branch 4 team, reporting exclusively to him, his first partner. And then look what had happened.

Was it about her? "You're damn right it's about her. It's always been about her and until the day I die it's going to be about her."

"Which means it's really about you."

"I thought I wanted out."

"Your country needs you in. *She* needs you in. You believe in her, then go get her. Do we know where she is?"

"That's one of the things we're about to find out."

As if on cue, the phone rang—a startlingly old-fashioned loud clanging that did not subside until Devlin had satisfied the security protocols. "I'm listening," he said. He grunted a couple of times and then hung up. "They're on their way."

Devlin closed the panic room and together they headed downstairs. The living room, like everything on the ground floor, was startlingly conventional. Anyone looking through one of the windows would have seen nothing out of the ordinary—but anyone trying to break in would never have broken out again.

They could hear the sound of a car pulling up in front of the house. "They're just going to walk right up to the door and ring the bell?" asked Danny. "What about security? What about decoys? What about—"

"What about just acting like a normal human being?" retorted Devlin. His own existence might be conducted completely in the shadows, but that was no reason not to act normal. His safety was assured by his anonymity; in his experience, the more a target tried to hide from him, the easier he was to find.

He opened the door and greeted the President of the United States. "Mr. President," he said to the first man through the door. Tyler was wearing a baseball cap and dress-down clothes, and had adopted a slouching walk for the occasion. Behind him came Seelye, also in weekend civvies, and then Shalika Johnson, the secretary of defense. He was somewhat surprised to see a fourth person trailing behind, someone who looked more like a desk jockey than a field op. Maybe he should send out for pizza.

Devlin closed the door. "Please sit down." He knew they were not alone, that members of the President's Secret Service detail were outside, passing as pedestrians, waiting in cars, circling the block. But inside his house was one of the most secure locations in the D.C. area, fully vetted by all the relevant agencies.

Seelye made the introductions as President Tyler instinctively headed for best seat in the room. This was Devlin's first encounter with Secretary Johnson, a large, tough woman, and he liked her on sight. No doubt she would prove to be a huge pain in the ass, but that was her job and he suspected she was very good at it.

"And this," said the DIRNSA, "is Major Kent Atwater, the man who cracked the *Dorabella* cipher and has brought us all here together today." Seelye looked at Atwater. "I ought to fire you, but in a time of war, certain liberties—certain judgments—sometimes need to be made. Thank you for making them."

Devlin spoke up. "Mr. President, Madame Secretary, Major, Dad—this is Don Barker. He has my complete confidence. Anything you need to say to me you can say in front of him."

"That's what you said about her," said Seelye.

Devlin struggled to control his rage. *One of these days . . .* "With all due respect to your crack intelligence acumen, Director Seelye, why don't you wait until all the facts are in? For unless I'm very much mistaken, the wheel just took another spin—didn't it, Mr. President?"

Tyler looked at him with a modicum of respect, which is all anyone got out of him. "We've just received an encoded message from somewhere in Iran, outside Tehran. It came through back channels, as if the sender didn't have access to the NSA network, but it got here and it got bumped all they way up the chain of command, so I guess our boy—our girl—knows how the game is played. The trouble is, we don't know what it means."

"May I see it, please?" asked Devlin.

Tyler nodded at Seelye, who handed him a new Android. "No," said Devlin. "Transmit it to me. Don't worry, nothing gets out of this bubble that I don't want to get out."

Seelye pointed the device at Devlin's own Android and pressed a button. "Thanks," said Devlin.

He pressed several keys on his device and suddenly a

piece of a side wall disappeared into the ceiling to reveal a large video screen. "This would be a little faster upstairs, but we can make it work," he said. He thought a moment—

"The message appears to be encrypted inside some sort of video file," said Devlin.

"Yes," said Seelye. "It's a clip of the recent royal wedding."

"Fascinating," said Devlin. "That tells us something already. And what is it?"

No one answered.

"That the sender is definitely a woman. Who else could possibly endure such tedium?"

On the screen, two newly wedded members of the British royal family were waving at their cheering subjects.

"Don't you wish the public would cheer you like that, Mr. President?" said Devlin.

"Look here," said Shalika Johnson, visibly annoyed at Devlin's blithe tone. "I don't like the way you speak to the President. He's the President of the United States, which means he's your Commander-in-Chief, so why don't you show a little respect?" She glared at Devlin, and looked like she was ready to take a poke at him.

"Guess you haven't read the memo," replied Devlin, calmly. "Dad, why don't you explain the facts of life to the secretary later? Right now, if this is what I think it is, we've got a big problem."

They all turned their attention back to the screen. "It's easy to embed a secondary or tertiary file in video material," said Devlin. "We do it all the time, even for fairly routine stuff. That way we can use open-source platforms, publicly accessible things like Facebook, and get messages out easily and quickly. Hiding in plain sight."

"We found it quickly enough," said Major Atwater.

"And did it have anything to do with those codes of yours? It didn't, did it?

The major looked sheepish. "No. I thought it would, but it was just some personal-services chatter—you know, mail-order brides, sex stuff. So we looked elsewhere, and didn't find anything."

"That's because naked is the best disguise." Devlin opened up the hidden file, which was just the sort of thing you could see on any website as an advertisement: *Russian and Persian Brides for You.*

"I didn't want any of that stuff showing up on a government computer," explained Atwater. "You know how sensitive the filters are . . . not to mention the penalties."

Devlin glanced over at Danny. "No wonder we're losing this war. We'd rather be dead than politically incorrect. Okay, Major, watch."

Devlin drilled down into the ads. On a hunch he skipped over the photographs of the alluring Russian women—

"How do you know it isn't in that section?" asked Secretary Johnson.

"Because this message isn't for you. It isn't for General Seelye. It isn't even for that notorious lady-killer Jeb Tyler. It's for me."

He flashed through the Persian brides. He knew exactly what he was looking for, and headed straight to the city of Shiraz. "This is all I know about her," he said while working. "I know you all think she's a double agent, and that I might have been in on it with her. I know that's why you cashiered me"—he looked straight at Tyler—"and I know that's why I'm still alive. Because you thought by sending me on some crackpot mission about miracles in the desert and then wiping your prints off it, you didn't have to admit to anybody who might be watching your little charade that I'd gone rogue. You could ruin me without signaling Skorzeny that you were on to me by killing me. So thanks for that."

Tyler glanced over at Seelye and Johnson, who both

shrugged and shook their heads. But Devlin was too wrapped up in his demonstration to notice.

"Here we go."

A parade of round-faced, olive-skinned women, each one eager to meet an American man, preferably with money.

"You think her picture is just going to turn up in there?" asked Seelye.

"I know it is," said Devlin, running through the sequence.

"Nobody's that stupid," said Seelye.

Devlin turned to his stepfather. "Except you. Now shut up and watch."

With all the photos loaded in, he began to synthesize them using facial-recognition software that he had developed for just such an occasion.

"She didn't use all the girls, just some of them, chosen by a single facial characteristic. Taken together, they're a composite, like one of those gag photos you see on the Internet, where they combine pictures of President Tyler, the mean granny from 'American Gothic,' and a lemur to come up with . . . here we go."

The synthesis was finished. Everybody looked at the screen.

"She probably had very little time," said Devlin with a touch of pride. "Ordinarily, she might have added an additional step or two, made me work a little more. But here she is: Maryam."

It was her, all right, every bit as beautiful as Devlin had remembered her, and stunning to those who had never seen her. He let the moment linger. . . .

"Okay, so that's how we know it's her. We also know that she's got access to some of the proprietary technology I gave her, probably her PDA. We know she's alive and that she's in Iran. Now let's hear what she's got to say."

"She'll use a Playfair cipher, of course," said Major At-water.

"Smart fellow," said Devlin, assembling the first letters of all the names of the women into a row. "We'll have to allow for some English orthographic variations in the notation of Farsi, but it will be close enough."

On the screen, a square—five letters across and five letters deep—suddenly appeared. Rearranged, they spelled out: WE AR ED IS CO VE RE DS AV EY OU RS EL F.

"We are discovered. Save yourself," said Atwater proudly.

"What?" said Seelye suddenly, and started fumbling through some briefing papers.

"The same line from *Have His Carcase* . . ."

"One more step," said Devlin, now using the phrase as the key and re-coding—

TH MA HD II SR IS IN GF RO MT HI SW EL L.

Everyone could read that.

"It all makes sense now," said President Tyler softly. "Sense, assuming you believe in miracles. But put it all together: the Iranian nuclear program. The apparitions of Mohammed and the Virgin Mary."

"Don't forget Farid Belghazi," reminded Devlin. "Maryam and I snatched him in Budapest last year."

"So what?" asked Secretary Johnson. "What's that got to do with—"

"So he had been working at the Organisation Européenne pour la Recherche Nucléaire, better known as CERN—working on the Large Hadron Collider in its search for the Higgs boson. The 'God particle.' "

"And the codes . . . the threats . . . it's all coming together now."

"In more ways than you think, Mr. President," said Seelye, finding what he was looking for. "We got this from a confidential informant inside the New York City Police Department's Counter-Terrorism operation, relayed to us from Deputy Director Thomas A. Byrne of the FBI."

Seelye handed the president a document. "This just came

in. Someone phoned in an enigmatic message to the nuclear-medicine department at Mount Sinai Medical Center in New York, a statement that referenced a detective on the CTU needing to come in for an appointment. They used that exact same phrase—'We are discovered. Save yourself.' NYPD is investigating it as a possible bomb threat."

"It is a bomb threat," said Devlin. "Damn!"

He rose and addressed the group. "Captain Francis Byrne—the head of the CTU—and Mr. Barker here took out Kohanloo while I was tied up under the reservoir with that kid. Manhattan registered clean after we picked up the pieces. But it's possible—not probable, but possible—that Kohanloo got the kid to deliver a . . . a *nuclear* device to Mount Sinai, which is where it's been hiding in semi-plain sight for months now."

"But why warn us about it? That's the kind of thing villains only do in the movies."

"It's not a warning. It means they're ready to make their move." It was all clear to Devlin now. "There's a sect of Shiites known as the Twelvers. They believe the Twelfth Imam, Ali, has been occluded at the bottom of a well in Qom for centuries, but that he will return, with Jesus by his side, at a time of maximum strife, discord, and bloodshed. And for that to happen, somebody has to cause that strife and bloodshed."

"The apparitions," said Secretary Johnson, getting it.

"Correct," said Devlin. "Spain only started a media frenzy, Zeitoun a riot. But the one in Nigeria has set off an entire continental civil war. Let's hope the Virgin Mary and Mohammed don't start showing up in Jerusalem."

"The end of the world," muttered the president. "Even worse, the end of my administration. Hassett will kill me."

"She's already killing you, Mr. President," said Devlin. "The question is, what are you prepared to do about it? This stuff isn't just happening—somebody's making it happen.

Somebody without a national allegiance, somebody who can manipulate currencies, bribe officials with his limitless wealth—and somebody with a high personal animus against the West. Iran is only partly behind this; the mullahs that run that poor country are insane, and we can bring them down any time we want." He directed that last remark to President Tyler.

"But we all know who's behind this. I told you this after the EMP attempts on Los Angeles and Baltimore. This apocalypse isn't religious—it's atheistic. The revenge of one lone lost soul on a world he inherited and would now unmake."

"Skorzeny."

"Request permission to terminate with extreme prejudice, sir."

"Request granted. Anything you need, you talk to Seelye and Johnson."

"I'm going to need to get in touch with this Captain Byrne. As it turns out, I know him by sight—I saved his life on Forty-second street when the hot-dog vendor was about to kill him."

"I know him, too," said Danny. "He was the sharpshooter on the chopper when we got Kohanloo."

"But we have no time," said Devlin. "Mr. Barker here and I will be in Virginia Beach later, and we fly out from Oceana tomorrow."

"If there's a bomb in New York, the FBI—"

"If there's a bomb in New York, Mr. President, the NYPD is best equipped to handle it. If I were you, I'd keep Deputy Director Byrne as far away from his brother as possible."

Tyler didn't like it, and Devlin knew that when Tyler didn't like something, he had no intention of listening to anybody else. "Maybe, but . . ."

"It's your call, sir." A thought suddenly struck him. "If Tom Byrne has a source inside his brother's unit, we're going to need a secure line of communication to Captain

Byrne. Someone whom both Mr. Barker and I trust implicitly. Someone whose loyalty is unquestioned. And I think I
know just who that person is."

"Put him on the case," ordered the President.

"Her." Devlin looked at Danny. They both knew whom
Devlin was talking about. "We'll need special air transport
from Lemoore to New York immediately, party of four."

"Four?" asked Seelye.

"Just do it, Army," said Tyler.

"And some special communications equipment—you know
what I mean, right, Dad?"

Seelye said nothing.

"Okay, then that's settled."

Secretary Johnson spoke up. "If this bastard is going to
try and hit us . . . let me just say that in my neighborhood in
Philadelphia, we know how to handle this kind of shit."

"And now," said the President, rising to signal the end of
the meeting, "I'm going home to the White House to study
my polling data and drink myself to death."

CHAPTER TWENTY-FIVE

Tehran

Amanda Harrington had already decided that she would prefer to be cremated than buried when she felt Maryam's coffin move. Even for a corpse, being nailed inside a box was no way to enter the afterlife.

Then she heard the voices, muffled, male. She could not understand the words, but she knew curses when she heard them. And when one of the men dropped his end of the coffin and she very nearly toppled over, the imprecations and oaths were unmistakable.

They loaded her into some sort of vehicle—she doubted if it was a hearse—and then she felt the motor start and they were on their way. But where?

She had lost track of time. The coffin was too narrow for her to see the display on her PDA and she wouldn't have wanted to use it anyway. At first she tried to sleep, but how could you sleep in a place like this when you weren't already dead? It was the fear of death that kept you awake. From time to time she supposed she must have dozed and she found herself half-wishing she might have a shot of the fugu fish poison once more, just to make the torture a little more endurable.

He must know that something was wrong by now. She tried to imagine his reaction, just for the small pleasure it gave her. That he eventually would kill her, she had no doubt. Death was something to which she'd condemned herself with her affair with Milverton. But he couldn't just murder her; no, he needed her submission first, her groveling apology, her protestations of eternal fidelity. Emanuel Skorzeny could endure many things, but abandonment was something he simply could not accept.

What would he do? Go ahead with his plan, she supposed. She was never entirely clear on what was going to happen to Maryam once they'd arrived in Tehran—she was being traded to the mullahs for something, but what? So now, like a nude girl popping out of a cake at a bachelor party, she would be the surprise guest at whatever event was scheduled.

She steeled herself. Yes, steeled. She loved that fine old English expression, now sadly fallen into disuse. No one steeled herself anymore; instead they whined and complained and begged and sniveled. St. George wasn't interested in slaying the dragon and rescuing the damsel in distress anymore; he'd rather get drunk with his mates and beat the crap out of some queers.

No more stop-and-go traffic. The car was moving along an open road. They were out of the city. So it wasn't to be Tehran after all? Where?

She could not possibly imagine.

Chapter Twenty-six

Qom, Iran

Attired head to toe in the chador, Maryam moved through the streets of the holy city. Although it was not required, she also wore a veil pulled across the lower half of her face. If the Islamic dress code was going to make it easy for her to walk publicly and in disguise, why not?

Most of her strength had returned to her, which was a good sign and also a bad sign. Good for her, bad for Amanda, since it meant that Skorzeny had been keeping her alive and in reasonably good shape in order to deliver her to something far worse than death by paralysis.

It was possible that he had deciphered her background; after all, she had been trailing his man Milverton as long as Frank Ross had. Skorzeny left absolutely nothing to chance and he certainly would have moved heaven and earth to learn more about her. What protected her was that there was so little to learn.

Her parents were both dead. The Revolution had seen to that. Her father had been a scientist, her mother a professional woman, such as used to exist in the Shah's Iran—a judge, in fact. But the Islamic Republic had no use for women in positions of authority over men, and so, despite the fact that she had been an enthusiastic supporter of the Ayatollah Khomeini when he first arrived back from Paris, the regime quickly soured on her and she was soon fired, demoted to charwoman where once she had held court.

Her father, too, was devoured by the Revolution, as someone who had held a privileged position under the Shah—he had been one of the earliest Iranian scientists working on the quest for peaceful atomic energy, all the rage in the 1950s. He had in fact spent some time at the Lawrence Livermore laboratory as a research fellow at Cal Berkeley, which was why he'd been forced to undergo a political cleansing process. At first, he went along with the charade, but soon enough no demonstration of ideological and religious fealty was enough—no matter how much he cast off his Western ways, forced the women in his family to conform to the new normal, or otherwise showed his enthusiastic support for the Revolution, it was impossible for him to be pure enough. One day the secret police came for him and she never saw him again.

Her mother died shortly thereafter, her dreams shattered, and Maryam was left to be raised by family under the strict supervision of the religious police. The last thing the Revolution wanted was an angry young orphan who blamed it for the death of her parents. But that was exactly what it got.

The mosque at Jamkaran was dead ahead. There was some activity in the square, as workmen were busily finishing a substantial speaker's platform, which was flanked by two large video screens. Such spontaneous religious harangues were not uncommon in the Islamic Republic.

From the outside, the mosque resembled a smaller version of the Taj Mahal, its large central dome flanked by the pillars of the muezzin. Inside, there would be segregation of the sexes and in fact the women's area had its own version of the holy well, to which, using pieces of string, the faithful could attach their written prayers to the Occluded Twelfth Imam, in the hopes that he would grant their wishes on the fateful day of his return.

She knew just what she was going to wish for.

Maryam listened to the conversations around her as she approached the mosque. Normally they were the usual idle chatter of daily life, but there was something different about this group—a tone of hushed, expectant reverence. From snatches of conversation, it was clear that some sort of awful battle between Islam and Christianity was taking place in central Africa. Hundreds of thousands of people were dead, and the battles were still raging.

She entered the mosque and made her way toward the women's well, her written prayer clutched in her hand. When it came her turn, she knotted it into the strings that hung from the slats protecting the sacred waters below and slipped away. In the morning, the strings would be cut, the prayers would tumble into the well for Imam Ali to read, and the cycle of petition and penitence would begin again.

She emerged back into the light. Around the reflecting pool hundreds of people had gathered. It must be a holy man, she thought to herself, come to entertain and enlighten the Islamic tourists on a pilgrimage to one of the holy sites in Shia Islam. That was the reason for the low voices and reverential atmosphere.

The holy man was mounting the platform. An acolyte switched on the loudspeakers. Suddenly, Maryam realized whom she was looking at: none other than the Grand Ayatollah Ali Ahmed Hussein Mustafa Mohammed Fadlallah al-Sadiq, one of the most powerful men in the government.

"O Muslims!" he began. "Raise your voices in prayer, for today a great sign is to be given to you here at this holy place."

The Ayatollah held up his right hand, its image clear and strong on the video screens. Everyone could see a black mark on it—the healed wound, complete with powder burns permanently embedded in the skin, from an assassination attempt many years ago, as the mullahs had struggled to consolidate their power after the death of Khomeini.

"Am I not from the province of Khorasan, as prophesied in the hadith? Do I not have the mark upon the right hand, as is written in the hadith? And do not all holy Muslims, Sunnis and Shia alike, accept that the great imam, Seyed Khorasani, will arise in the east to hand the holy banner of Islam to the Mahdi?"

An ululation went up from the women in the crowd, signifying the immanence of the moment.

"Is it not written that Khorasani must make the way clear and straight for the Twelfth Imam, in order to lead him into a world rent by death and destruction, by terror and oppression of Allah's chosen people?"

A cry went up from the men, as one, full-voiced and throaty.

The Grand Ayatollah was a master speaker, and he knew how to play to a crowd. Maryam looked around and noticed that the mosque was entirely surrounded by the faithful, come to witness the holy miracle in the flesh.

"Today, in Africa, the faithful battle the forces of iniquity as the *ummah* rises up in righteous anger to slaughter the Christian descendants of the apes and pigs the world knows as the Jews. In the hadith of Sahih Bukhari, are we not instructed that the Day of Resurrection will not arrive until the Muslims make war against the Jews and kill them, and until a Jew is hiding behind a rock and tree, and the rock and tree say, 'O Muslim, O servant of Allah, there is a Jew behind me, come and kill him!' "

"Allahu akbar! Allahu akbar! Allahu akbar!"

"O Muslims, surely the day is at hand!"

"Allahu akbar! Allahu akbar! Allahu akbar!"

"O Muslims, the time has come to bring about the coming of the Twelfth Imam!"

"Allahu akbar! Allahu akbar! Allahu akbar!"

"O Muslims, will you not join me? For I am no longer Ali Ahmed Hussein Mustafa Mohammed Fadlallah al-Sadiq . . ."

"Allahu akbar! Allahu akbar! Allahu akbar!"

". . . but Seyed Khorasani, the living embodiment of the holy prophecy. Make way! Make way for the Blessed Mahdi, Abu' Qasim Hujjat ibn Hasan ibn 'Ali."

At that instant, the vision of Mohammed that the Nigerians had seen appeared in the sky above the Ayatollah's head. Maryam felt a chill pass over her as she, like everyone else in the square but the Grand Ayatollah, prostrated herself before the Prophet's majesty.

It all made sense, thought Maryam, lying there eating the holy dust of the holy city. Not the vision—if that was real then there was no point to anything she was about to do. It was the end of the world and the world was just going to have to accept it.

But the resurrection of the Mahdi—that could be explained.

In the fall of 2009, the West had been astonished to learn that the holy city was also the site of a hitherto-unknown uranium-enrichment facility located on one of the Islamic Revolutionary Council bases nearby. The mullahs had, of course, lied about it to international inspectors and naturally the willing fool who ran the International Atomic Energy Agency was only too willing to accept their lies. He was, after all, a faithful Muslim, and *taqqiya*—bald-faced lying—was an acceptable practice when you were prevaricating with infidels. But the atomic energy program her father had begun for the Shainshah was finally about to bear a hideous, poisoned fruit.

That's why Skorzeny had used her as a bargaining chip.

When the first Iranian bomb exploded, what better propaganda coup could the mullahs have than to parade the daughter of the Shah's greatest scientist, the father of the Iranian nuclear program—and blame it all on her family? She would at once be a heroine and a martyr, to be exhibited and then publicly executed in Evin Prison as a traitor to the Revolution and an object lesson for the masses.

Let the West cavil—the true believers in Tehran would have their apocalypse.

And so would Skorzeny. "Frank Ross" had been right all along—this was not the end times, this was the endgame of Emanuel Skorzeny's long war against the West and its religions. If he had to subvert Islam to accomplish his ends, so be it. "Dying, you destroyed our life. Rising, you restored our life. Lord Jesus, come again in glory." That was the Memorial Acclamation of Christian worship, now perverted to his will.

They had to stop it. And she would have to do what she could, no matter what the cost. Not to save the world—the world had no lien on her loyalty. No, it was to save her country, to save herself—and to save *him*.

A less likely pair could hardly be imagined. Both orphans, both killers, both lovers. Adrift in a world they never made, and battling another orphan who would unmake it forever.

She got to her feet as the rest of the crowd rose. She glanced from side to side at the other women, some of them veiled, some not, but all clad in the chador on this holy occasion. What were they thinking? Did they think of their mothers, those laughing, smiling women whose photographs they kept hidden and out of sight in the innermost recesses of their homes and their minds, the young college girls of the fifties and sixties of short skirts and tight sweaters and quick laughs, the mothers and torchbearers of two thousand years of civilization and high culture in the darkness of central

Asia? The women who counted Jews and Assyrian Christians among their friends and neighbors, who drank in the bistros of Tehran and dined openly in the best restaurants and spent the summers at their fathers' country houses on the Caspian, where they ate beluga caviar for breakfast and made love on the beach at night?

Subjugated now, all subjugated by an alien desert misogyny, imposed by force and maintained by terror.

"O Muslims," shouted the Grand Ayatollah, pointing toward the holy mosque, wherein lay the holy well. "Your prayers are about to be answered!"

CHAPTER TWENTY-SEVEN

Oceana Naval Air Station, Virginia

The three Super Hornets were waiting for them, as promised, at Oceana, right there on Tomcat Boulevard in Virginia City, an homage to the old Grumman F-14 Tomcats. Room for one pilot and one passenger in each. Twenty percent larger than the Legacy Hornet, and fifteen thousand pounds heavier at max weight, with a third more fuel capacity, the F/A-18F Super Hornets could kick just about anything's ass. At fifty-five million dollars a pop, they'd better.

"Don't wreck 'em, okay?" said Commander Stephen Joseph. "These babies almost cost real money."

"Range?" asked Devlin. "And don't bullshit me, because I'll know."

"Twelve hundred nautical miles, in and out."

"Airborne refueled?" asked Danny.

"What, do I look stupid?"

"Radar?" Devlin again.

"If they're looking you in the face or up the ass, they ain't gonna see ya. Not quite Stealth level, but good enough for government work. Full ECM. But try to fly straight."

Danny was walking around one of the three Super Hornets. "Weapons? I see a twenty-millimeter Gatling, four Sidewinders, JDAMs. . . ."

"And you can get them in red if you don't like them in white or blue," said Joseph. "Sparrows, Mavericks . . ."

"JDAM bombs. I like that," said Danny. "I hear CBU Clusters, too."

"If you say pretty please."

Danny kicked one of the tires. "We'll take three," he said.

"Where to, sir?" asked Commander Joseph.

"Diego Garcia, and we'll take it from there," said Devlin.

Diego Garcia was a small atoll in the Indian Ocean south of the subcontinent. Administratively, it belonged to the BIOT, the British Indian Ocean Territory, but in practice its forty-four square kilometers were entirely given over to a joint forward operating base of the Americans and the Brits. Basically, it was a stationary aircraft carrier fashioned from a coral reef. Strategically situated among East Africa, Saudi Arabia and the Emirates, India, Indonesia, and, at a stretch, Australia, Diego Garcia controlled one of the most critical areas on the planet.

"What about you, Mr. Harris?" asked Joseph. "And you, Mr. Barker?"

"We're headed elsewhere."

"We'll need some choppers, too," said Danny. "Carrier-based in the Gulf of Oman. The *Eisenhower* will do just fine."

"Heavy lifting? MH-47s? We can have those there as well."

Danny shook his head. "More along the lines of MH-60Ks. The new ones, with Stealth technology. Six will do just fine."

Commander Joseph smiled. " 'Night Stalkers Don't Quit,' huh?"

"They never die, either."

Joseph looked at the two men standing before him. This was probably the last time he would ever see them, no matter whether the mission was a success or a failure, whether they lived or died. But he was proud to be serving with them.

"I suppose this is all classified."

"Got it in one."

"Dangerous? I mean, more so than usual?"

"Any man KIA, his family will be taken care of. No worries there. But I'd prefer bachelors, if you catch my drift."

"Got three hot-sticks flight teams itching to mix it up."

"They're going to get to scratch that itch. And if you know your men, Commander, they'll all be coming home."

"Outstanding," said Commander Joseph.

"Now load those suckers up with JDAMS and get them in the air."

Devlin and Danny started to walk away. They were heading back to Washington to go over the plan with Danny's Xe ops once more and then they'd be in the air, and on their way to the Al Dhafra Air Base in the Emirates, which would be their jumping-off point. Joseph called out after them.

"We're going to get it right this time, aren't we?"

Smart fellow.

Devlin turned and gave a thumbs-up, and then they were gone.

CHAPTER TWENTY-EIGHT

St. Louis

"I hate Missouri," said Angela Hassett. "I hate everything about it. I hate the weather, I hate the humidity, I hate the cold, I hate the damp, I hate the symphony, I hate the people, I hate the blacks, I hate the whites. I hate the French and the Germans who founded it. I hate the Okies in the Ozarks. I even hate Branson."

She was naked, sitting upright in the bed at the old Adam's Mark in downtown St. Louis.

"I thought you loved humanity," said Jake Sinclair, just as naked, beside her.

"I do love humanity," she replied. "It's just people I can't stand."

Sinclair kissed her and then rolled back over on his pillow. They had made love three times already and he was exhausted, although he would never admit it. "In that case," he said, "you'll make a great president."

Now it was her turn to kiss him. The press was probably downstairs, but she didn't care. The press fed from her virgin hand every morning, noon, and night. The press was her best friend, her protector. She told them almost nothing, her campaign told them less than nothing, but the press was so wedded to the notion of the First Woman President—historic!—that they would do anything to see it become reality. "When the legend becomes fact, print the legend," said the wise reporter in *The Man Who Shot Liberty Valance*.

How easy it had all been; nothing to it, really. All you needed was a gimmick, an angle, a "first" for the narrative and the media would block and tackle for you all the way to the end zone, which was 1600 Pennsylvania Avenue. She had quickly learned the First Lesson of Media, which was that nearly all reporters hated being reporters, hated being servile toward those they regarded at the very most as their social equals and, at worst, their inferiors. After all, they had all gone to the same schools together, they socialized together, they lived in the same neighborhoods in Georgetown and on the Upper West Side of Manhattan. But the power imbalance thing really pissed off the ladies and gentlemen of the press, which is why they had, in effect, created their own shadow government, a government-in-permanent-exile but always on the job, and an endless round of television shows on which they interviewed each other, hounded some hapless office-holding nitwit, and then interviewed each other about the interviews they'd just done. A more perfect circle of jerks could hardly be imagined.

The Second Lesson of Media was corollary to the first: Most reporters wanted to be something else. The ones who could write a little wanted to be Real Writers. The ones who couldn't write very well wanted to be Hollywood screenwriters. And the ones who couldn't write at all wanted to be movie producers. Every story came with an angle, and that angle had to be Option Money. Every series of stories had to build a Narrative. And that Narrative could only be one thing:

Oppressed Minority Triumphs Over White Men.

Well, she certainly qualified. And now she was wiping the floor with John Edward Bilodeau Tyler.

She had worked hard at establishing the legend, from the time she first burst on the scene as the governor of Rhode Island. Rhode Island! Thank God for federalism, for where else in the world could you and your gang take over a dinky-ass state like Rhode Island and be taken seriously? To burnish the legend, she had moved quickly to toss the Italian mobsters who had been running the joint for decades into the federal pen—they had supported her, even helped her buy some choice real estate in Newport, but now that their usefulness was at an end, they had to be made an example of. Hello, Supermax, the ultimate no-tell motel.

And the media had been a part of it, which was why she found herself at this moment in bed with the loathsome Jake Sinclair. This was a consenting adult, two-way-street trans-action, a fuck for access and endorsement. In a few weeks it would be all over, and she would never again have to have his hands on her body. She would send him packing back to whatever little chippie named Jenny he was currently married to, and then, when all the reports of campaign irregularities surfaced via leaks from her press office, she'd have him arrested and thrown in jail, preferably for life.

"You're up across the board," said Sinclair, consulting his iPhone. His newspaper had broken the recent reports of the special tracking chip implanted in every iPhone, which made him laugh, since anyone with a source in Washington had known for years that the iPhone incorporated the SKIP-JACK technology from the Clinton Administration: Big Brother was watching you, for your own safety. Naturally, Tyler got the blame. "Eighteen points, in some states."

Don't get cocky—that was a lesson she had learned long ago, when she was a girl. Never trust a fixed fight until the fight is over and the bum you bet on has his hand raised in triumph. Now that bum was her, and the hand being raised was the one that would not be on the Bible as she took the oath of office on January 20.

It was amazing how stupid the media was, how gullible. They were just like Churchill's description of the Germans: either at your feet or at your throat. And the only thing you needed to do to keep them away from your throat was to feed them—in this case, information. Information on the other guy. Once they had made up their mind that their precious "narrative" dictated that you were the good guy and the other guy was the bad guy, you had it made in the shade.

Just as long as you didn't do anything stupid. And the later into the election season it got, the smarter you became. At this rate, she wouldn't even need the collapse of the dollar that a certain quiet campaign backer had told her he could deliver. In fact, she'd have to really fuck up now to lose. Either that, or the other guy would have to get awfully lucky. And Jeb Tyler's luck had run out.

Her private phone rang. Sinclair tried to snoop over her shoulder as she looked at the display, but she turned away from him. "I have to take this," she said, rising and heading for the bathroom.

"Another lover, I suppose?" he said and then flopped back on the pillow. He was very proud of himself, Mr. Sinclair was, getting to advance-fuck a president of the United States.

She closed the bathroom door. "Yes?"

"Are you alone?"

"I am now."

"Don't tell me it's that awful Sinclair. Really, my dear, I thought you had better taste than that."

"Yeah, well, you do what you have to. Everything in place?"

At the other end of the line, Emanuel Skorzeny had an uncharacteristic moment of hesitation. "Yes, of course."

"Don't fuck with me, old man," she said, her voice rising,

"Need some help in there?" came Sinclair's voice from the bedroom.

"We have a deal and I expect that deal to go off without a hitch. I need to put this bastard Tyler in the ground, six feet under, so that by Election Day he'll be lucky to carry his home state of Louisiana. The country's sick of his ineptitude. It's sick of watching the body count rise on his watch. One more push and he's done."

"Do not underestimate him, Angela," said Skorzeny. "I made that mistake once and it cost me a considerable amount of money, staff, and personal happiness."

"That's your problem. You can always find more money, I'm sure you can find staff, and as for your personal happiness, I don't give a shit. Just tell me our little surprise is going to go off without a hitch."

"Haven't you been reading the papers? Watching television? I noticed you haven't said a word about the trouble in Africa."

"Why should I? There's no votes in it, and besides it's more fun to watch Tyler flounder and stew. As far as I'm concerned, that's for your amusement. I want the bang for my buck you promised me."

"Oh, you'll get it, all right," said Skorzeny, "and right on schedule. Just one thing, Angela . . ."

"What's that?"

"Do be prepared for Tyler to have a little October Surprise of his own. The man has the cunning of a snake, and if you're going to beat him, you're going to need to be utterly ruthless."

Angela Hassett smiled. "I think I've done pretty well in that department so far," she said.

A loud knock on the door. "You going to stay in there all day? I gotta go."

"Keep your pants on, big boy," she said sweetly, "and let a girl do what a girl's gotta do."

"Okay, but hurry up. Jeez . . ."

"What an idiot," said Skorzeny.

"Yes, but he's our idiot for now," she replied. "And when he's no longer useful . . . 'ruthless,' you were saying?"

"Listen to me, Angela. It's not just Tyler. He has people—one man in particular. This man might well be the most dangerous man on the planet, next to me. Pray you never meet him."

A voice from outside the door. "Aw, Angela, come on. . . ."

"I think I can handle men," she said to Skorzeny. "Just do your job."

She rang off, splashed some water on her face, and looked at herself. In less than a month she would be looking at the president-elect and, a couple of months later, the POTUS herself. That's when the real fun would begin, when fortunes would be made and unmade, and when social transformation would begin in earnest.

She stepped back and examined her body in the mirror: not bad for an old broad.

"Angela . . ." He was starting to whine now.

She threw open the door to catch him hopping around like a two-year-old; some men just couldn't hold their water. She caught him as he rushed past her and kissed him. That would get his attention, and pretty soon his mind would be right back where she wanted it to be, which was between her breasts and other parts of her anatomy.

Men were such fools.

CHAPTER TWENTY-NINE

Lemoore Naval Air Station

The kids were already in bed. Hope felt bad about waking them up, but she had no choice.

Mrs. Atchison helped her get their things together. "It's all right, honey," she said to Jade as Hope tended to Rory and Emma. "You're all going to New York City. Won't that be fun?"

Jade didn't care much one way or the other about New York City, but she doubted that either Rory or Emma would be looking forward to the trip, not after what happened to them there the last time.

"Thank you, Mrs. Atchison. Will I get to see my dad?"

Mrs. Atchison had obviously been fully briefed, because she drew Jade close and whispered in her ear: "Take care of them now. You all have to be strong for one another."

Jade nodded. Tragedy was something she and the Gardner kids had in common. The loss of a parent. Of course, she hadn't had to endure what Emma had; she wondered if she would have been able to hold up as well, or emerge so relatively normal.

The admiral appeared in the doorway. "It's time."

A driver took them to the airfield, where a transport plane was fueled and ready; both the admiral and his wife came along.

"Cool!" shouted Rory as he saw the interior of the plane.

"Just like being a real soldier or sailor, Rory," said the admiral. "Do you think you'd like to the try that someday?"

"Would I ever!" exclaimed Rory.

"Then, when you're old enough, you be sure to write to me and I'll see what I can do."

"Wow! Thank you, Admiral Atchison."

As Mrs. Atchison helped get the kids strapped in, the admiral took Hope aside. "Listen," he began, "I'm not privy to any of the details, but I do know that this operation involves you. Don't worry, it's not going to be dangerous. But your husband needs someone he can trust to act as a go-between in a very sensitive situation, and he asked for you."

"He's not my husband," said Hope softly.

"My error."

Hope blushed a little. "I think he was going to propose to me in San Francisco. That's why we were heading up there, when . . . The last time we were in New York . . . well, you probably know."

"I heard. You and your kids have been through a lot."

"Is Danny going to meet us there?"

"I'm sorry, ma'am, I can't tell you that. I don't know—but even if I did, I couldn't."

"I understand. Thank you for everything, Admiral."

"Anything we can do . . ."

They left. The crew shut the doors. The plane rumbled down the taxiway and soared into the sky.

CHAPTER THIRTY

Baku

"I am beginning to be concerned, Mlle. Derrida."

She looked up from her reading. There was nothing to do in this godforsaken town. It still had the old Soviet smell about it, the same hopelessness, the same rundown atmosphere, as if tomorrow was inevitably going to be worse than today and there was not a damn thing anybody could about it.

She'd admired Baku Bay, seen the Azerbaijan State Philharmonic Hall, traipsed up and down the Maiden Tower, from which some princess or other was said to have thrown herself in an attempt to escape the place. She could certainly understand that.

"It's Iran," she said. "Not France. Things happen."

Skorzeny shot her a look. How unlike his late adjutant and majordomo, M. Paul Pilier, she was. He had been a man of impeccable taste and breeding, and quite handy in a tight spot. She, on the other hand, was a French lesbian intellectual.

The thought of the late M. Pilier got him to thinking about Maryam again—she had shot his man back at Clair-vaux—and his impatience only grew. "Try her again."

"I don't think that's a wise idea, M. Skorzeny," she said. "You're wanted by the American government. You may assume that the Black Widow is tracking any unsecured communication, and no matter how good you think your technology is, theirs is better. So I advise you to maintain operational security and try to enjoy the wonders of Baku."

"I trusted her," he muttered, growing agitated.

"That's your problem," said Mlle. Derrida, and returned to her reading.

He needed to get out of there. He was a man of property as well as principle. A man at home everywhere. "I am going out for a constitutional," he informed her.

"Do you want me to shadow you in case someone tries to grab you?"

"Don't be absurd," he said, and left.

Out on the street he took a deep breath of the sea air. There was, in fact, a man he wanted to meet. A man with whom he had business, and a man whom he counted on for the utmost discretion. He began to reach for his phone, then thought better of it; perhaps Mlle. Derrida was right. There was no point in coming all this way, and getting this far, only to blow it at the end over something as silly as a woman. He trusted her, and that was that.

The building he sought was near Boyukshor Lake, near the steel company. Not very fashionable. But that is exactly what he would have expected.

Slobodan Petrovich had come out of the old Soviet Union—where, exactly, was not clear—and after the collapse of the U.S.S.R. had made a fortune operating in the interstices of communism and capitalism. There were vast sums of money to be made in such tight spots, and Petrovich made them. And yet he lived here, anonymously. He was a man after Skorzeny's own heart.

The taxi stopped in front of a typical Soviet piece of industrial architecture. Skorzeny entered an office and spoke Russian to the functionary; he had not spent all that time as a guest of the Red Army at the end of the war without learning their language. He thought it might be difficult to see Petrovich, or that perhaps he was living there under a pseudonym, but no: he was told exactly where to find the man, and find him soon enough he did.

The door was made of steel. There were no peepholes or any visible security devices, but before he could rap on it, it slid to one side and there stood the financier, a cigar in one hand and a glass of wine in the other. "I've been expecting you," he said, stepping aside to admit Skorzeny.

Skorzeny entered gingerly. He was not used to being a guest in someone else's house; in fact, lately he was not used to being in a home at all. With Tyler's fatwa against him, he had spent most of his recent life on board his specially outfitted Boeing 707, condemned like some latter-day Flying Dutchman to only the most unpleasant ports of call. Ah, but look how well that was going to work out, despite what happened to the late Arash Kohanloo and his merry band of terrorists in New York City.

Petrovich had helped with that operation. It was difficult—although not impossible—to launder money from the air, but to have an ally on the ground, living in a Muslim country but completely at home with the old Soviet ways of evading taxes and getting a maximum return on one's investment . . . well, that was invaluable. He needed a paymaster, fixer, and investor, and in Slobodan Petrovich, he got all three.

"Has the package been delivered?" said Petrovich. The man's tastes ran to the sybaritic, it was true, but then Skorzeny's own handsomely appointed apartments in Vaduz and

Paris, with their priceless art and furnishings, bespoke his sophistication as well.

"Things are under way in Iran, yes," said Skorzeny, not quite sure what to do with himself. Petrovich noticed his social discomfort, and yet did not move to offer him a seat, a cigar, or a drink.

"What about New York?"

"Countdown has begun. Timing is everything, and I believe I can predict with a degree of high confidence that simultaneity will be very nearly achieved. First the one, then the other."

"And our Iranian friends get the blame?"

"Of course. After all, they are the ones who are guilty. You and I are . . . just bystanders."

"And about to make a great deal of money shorting the market. I congratulate you. Now, tell me the real reason you honor my house with your presence. You've lost your girl, haven't you? Or, judging from your demeanor, both of them. There's a line from Oscar Wilde that might be appropriate right about now."

Skorzeny finally chose an uncomfortable-looking chair and sat. He didn't plan to stay long. Just long enough to make sure their business arrangement was solid; later, if he had to, he could have Petrovich killed. In the aftermath of what was about to happen, no one would notice.

"I must say, Emanuel," said Petrovich, relighting his cigar, "so far your plan is going splendidly. Have you seen the news from Africa today? The entire continent is in flames. Blend excitable people with machetes with competing superstitions and you have a prescription for a bloodbath that is making Rwanda look like a warm-up act at a bad Moscow nightclub. You've been to bad Moscow nightclubs, I assume?"

Skorzeny let the question float. "Tomorrow, the Philippines. Muslims and Christians have been fighting there since the Moros. It won't take much for the beheadings to start. Then, Paris—think of the reaction of the Muslims, and how much damage they will be able to do to Notre Dame and San Sulpice before the flics get out of bed. Paris will be lost to tourists forever."

"The girls," prompted Petrovich. "The girls."

Skorzeny thought, then decided to tell the truth. "Radio silence."

"You old fool. She's left you, and taken God only knows what with her."

"Impossible. I am everything to her. And, in any case, it doesn't matter. Should the mullahs get their hands on both of them, well . . . that is one fewer problem for me in the days and weeks ahead." He decided to change the subject. "Where will you go when it happens? Baku seems uncomfortably close to . . . ground zero."

"I have my bolt-holes," replied Petrovich, "as I'm sure do you." He had remained standing throughout the interview, but now moved toward the door. "This conversation is very pleasant, more pleasant than I would have imagined, but as I never mix business with pleasure, it must come to an end, for we are not friends, merely business partners. . . . What do you suppose the damage will be? An idle question, but please indulge me."

"I estimate that up to a million people will be killed in the blast, or will subsequently die from radiation poisoning, and much of the island will be rendered uninhabitable for a very long time. Manhattan will finished as a center for world finance."

"That's it, then." Petrovich helped Skorzeny to his feet and began to propel him to the door. Skorzeny could feel himself getting hot under the collar—nobody was supposed to touch him, and the fact that this parvenu thought he needed assistance was an outrage. He would most definitely deal with Tovarish Petrovich when the time came.

"My man has positioned the device as per your instructions, but, if I may say so, the thing has been well-hidden and not connected to any electrical source. What about the trigger?"

"Leave that to me." said Skorzeny, exiting.

Outside, on the street, he brushed his lapels and his sleeves, then began looking for a taxi.

Typically Soviet, there were no taxis, and he would be damned if he were to stoop to bribing one of the workers for a ride in something that still looked distressingly like a Lada.

Very well, then, he would walk. And when he got back, it would be time to open the delicious little Maryam's precious laptop and see what mischief he could cause before all hell broke loose.

CHAPTER THIRTY-ONE

In the air

Devlin had always been able to sleep on planes, sleep in elevators, sleep standing up, sleep wherever and whenever; in his line of work you never knew where your next nap or good night's sleep was going to come from. But now, here above the Atlantic and on his way to whatever Fate finally had in store for him, he couldn't.

Danny was racked out. Good, he and his boys would have the toughest part of the gig, getting in below Iranian air defenses and putting boots on the ground, in and out as fast as possible but not one second less than the mission called for. And nobody knew what that was going to be.

Devlin's job was, in a sense, simpler: get Maryam the hell out of there. Now that she was free, and roaming loose somewhere in the bowels of the Islamic Republic, she was no doubt amassing a treasure trove of actionable intelligence, something they were going to need when they explained to the world just why America had done what she'd done. But it would be too late for anybody to do anything about it.

Too late for the whiners, for the you-can't-do-that crowd, for the how-dare-you bunch, for the "higher moral authority" gang, for the lofty editorialists in the employ of Jake Sinclair, men and women who had never done a damn thing except learn to type. Too late for the blame-America-first johnnies, for the internationalists, for the one-worlders and the citizens of the planet. Devlin had spent half his life living overseas, spoke his languages better than most of the natives, and was at home everywhere. But he never felt that he was anything but an American.

Maybe that's how you felt when you saw your mother die in the service of her country and then be called a traitor.

Maybe that's how you felt when you saw your father killed trying to save your mother.

Maybe that's how you felt when you were raised by a man you despised, a man who had played both sides of the political street for so long that he'd forgotten which side was his. A man who helped ruin your family and create the monster you were now seeking. The man who raised you to be the perfect, anonymous killing machine, the perfect agent, the perfect invisible man.

Maybe that's how you felt when you could have anything in the world except happiness.

And that's why he, the American, was going into Iran to rescue the Iranian. Because only she offered him a way out. And all he had to do was trust her, implicitly and faithfully.

The roses, glistening in the rainless desert. The doorway. The call to repentance. There could be no rational explanation for what he saw, or why. The vision in the Mojave had been but a prelude for what he was now about to do. Was there really a God? Up 'til now, he'd never seen any evidence for one. But something had happened out there. . . .

Which brought him to the real apparitions. It would have been easy to dismiss the one in Garabandal, a place that seemed to grow a new crop of impressionable schoolgirls every generation. All these BVM stories were depressingly the same—you'd think that when the Virgin finally decided to show, she'd have something new to say, something beyond her usual "repent" and "honor my Son" bromides. And always the same MO, appearing to kids, in Fatima, Lourdes, Medjugorje.

Until now. Maybe the first Zeitoun event, back in the sixties, had been faked—the photographs certainly looked absurd—but millions of people just saw *something*, and set off the tinderbox. And Kaduna . . . the savagery was appalling, especially when Mohammed got into the act. To think that in the twenty-first century human beings were still slaughtering other human beings like cattle, hacking each other to pieces with machetes. And now, according to some information just coming over his Android, there was trouble on Mindanao, where the fighting was said to be especially fierce. It was almost as if—

Wait a minute. Long ago he had learned that it was never "almost as if." The proper formulation was: "It was as if . . ."

No "ifs" about it. Except for the first apparition, the Virgin's appearances had been in places of maximum religious and cultural tension, powder kegs that barely needed a spark. So why in the name of a merciful God would . . .

Merciful God, his foot. This had nothing to do with a merciful God. Somebody was doing this—somebody looking to destabilize as much of the planet as he—or they—could, before . . .

Before what? What was the end game? The Iranian nuclear program made sense; the crazies who controlled the government wanted a fireball, preferably in either Israel or a major American city, precisely because they desired the retaliation that surely must follow. The occluded Mahdi, dreaming for centuries at the bottom of his well, needed a provocation in order to render the apocalypse. But . . .

But what if . . .

But what if there was a puppet master behind even the Iranians? Someone with enough wealth and power and influence and reach to manipulate their superstition and turn it to his own ends?

An atheist's apocalypse. The End Times without an end game. No triumph of good over evil, no submission of all to the will of Allah . . . just an endless, barren emptiness, in which one lone voice could be heard crying out, "I told you so."

Skorzeny. He'd been right about him all along.

Not motivated by money.

Not motivated by greed.

Not motivated by ideology.

Motivated solely by suffering and revenge. That was the meaning of the series of codes Atwater had solved, with its ultimate terminus in the nihilism of the double-cross-plus-one: *XXX marks the spot.*

The world didn't deserve its patrimony, of which Emanuel Skorzeny was very much a part, one of history's gifts to the unenlightened. The world didn't appreciate his taste, his refinement, his genius. The world had grown weak. And so he was going to deprive the world—the Western world, anyway—of its highest glories by unleashing upon it the one force that defined itself in opposition to the West, in opposition to Judeo-Christianity, and which would never rest, would never accept peaceful coexistence, until it destroyed the West, or was itself destroyed:

Radical Islam, led by the millenarian sect of Iranian Shiias.

He is starting a worldwide religious war. That's what this is all about.

Chaos theory in action.

That was what it had always been about, from the time

Skorzeny financed the terrorist operation in Edwardsville, hoping to panic the American public. When he tried to launch an EMP attack on both coasts. The assault on Times Square. But now he was widening the scope of his ambition, not just using freelance proxies but co-opting as much of a religion as possible.

Devlin and his few allies were no longer up against just a man like Milverton, an opportunist like Kohanloo, or a crazy like that kid. They were up against millions. They had no chance.

Unless their plan worked.

The only way to defeat a belief is to discredit it. Christianity and Judaism had been through this many times before: the false messiahs and moshiachs who had gathered unto them hundreds, even thousands of followers, until the day came when the holy man or rabbi died and didn't get back up again. Until the day that the earth was supposed to stand still never happened. Until the end times came and went, and people went on, crying, lamenting, worrying, fearing, fighting, loving.

But Islam had not.

Devlin was not a religious man; the only ghosts that need apply in his world were the ones he dispatched himself. Like the Marines, he had been raised to believe that his job was to keep heaven, or hell, filled with fresh souls. But he'd be lying to himself if he didn't admit that whatever had happened near California City had shaken him profoundly. It didn't make him believe, exactly, nor did it make him a believer—but, he realized with a start, it had made him believe in something. And even if that something was the life of just one human, it was a start on the long road to salvation.

He glanced back over at Danny, still asleep. That was the sign of the true combat vet: get plenty of shut-eye before the shooting started. Danny had so much to live for now, a woman and three children, and the two ghosts who would always be with them.

His ghosts: Devlin's ghosts. The ghosts who had surrounded him since that day in Rome, ghosts all around.

It was time for him to leave the ghosts behind.

It was time for him to rejoin the living.

CHAPTER THIRTY-TWO

Baku

As he walked, Emanuel Skorzeny had a chance to think back over his life, what its purpose had been, and how he had—by sheer force of will—come to this moment. Just as he was doing now, he had always lived in the present. The past was dead, immutable; the future unknowable. One could plan, one could scheme, but in the end, nobody really knew. You placed your bets and hoped for the best.

But the present, that was something else. You were always in the moment, always the master of your own fate. When he fled Dresden with Father Otto, when he survived in the woods on nothing but jerky and water, when he encountered the Russians and made up his mind to survive—then he had been master of his own fate. In the moment there was nothing to the future; each decision you made was sovereign, each step irrevocable. That was how you triumphed.

Take this moment. At this moment he was walking the streets of Baku. In half an hour or so, provided he kept putting one foot in front of another—something that was completely within his power to control—he would be back at the residence and greeting Mlle. Derrida and Miss Harrington. He could not be sure of the latter, but this he knew: that if she was not there, he would consider it enemy action.

Other men might well have cursed themselves for fools, but not Emanuel Skorzeny. His judgment about human nature was unerring. He knew his men, and his women. In his considerable experience, everyone could be bought, bribed, or threatened. The Christian notion of free will he found risible, as ludicrous as the notion that all men really yearned to be free. What foolishness that had been for an American president to sow, and what terrible things would he, Skorzeny, now reap. The human heart was not yearning for freedom, it was pursuing security, always in headlong flight from largely imaginary terrors. Without security, there was nothing and nobody an individual wouldn't cheerfully sell out for the mess of pottage he laughingly called his soul.

And that's why he trusted Amanda Harrington. Because she had nowhere else to go.

That's why she would be there, her flight delayed, the business in Tehran having been slightly more complicated than they expected.

That's why she would be both delighted and relieved to see him, to take her place at his side once more, secure in the notion that no woman could ever possibly be a rival for his affections, not so long as she breathed.

That's why he never even considered betrayal—having ventured away from his orbit once, she had learned a brutal but necessary lesson, and certainly would not repeat that mistake again.

This religion business—what was it, really? Just another search for security, this time in the arms of a fictional deity, the legend of which had been concocted and then handed down by a succession of savage tribes until it had taken on a permanence of its own. True, one branch of the universal superstition had given birth to much of the art and architecture he especially admired, but that religion no longer believed in its own fantasies, and hence was no longer worthy of survival. The church militant that had sent its combative and hormonal young knights off to the Holy Land to do battle with the Saracens now molested altar boys and ran food banks. The sooner it disappeared, the better.

He was just the man to put an end to it, to put the whole Western world out of the prolonged misery caused by its own lack of faith in itself. Had he not already given them good and sufficient warning of his intentions? The school near St. Louis, Times Square, everything else he had tried? And yet the benighted fools would not listen. They were too busy watching sports and their idiotic television programs and arguing about politics to notice what was happening. Soon, perhaps, they would heed him.

Because he was just the man for the job. His whole life had been preparation for this one heroic task. How did Lee Harvey Oswald translate Yeletsky's aria from *Pique Dame*? "I am ready right now to perform a heroic deed of unprecedented prowess for your sake. Oh, darling, confide in me!" His sentiments precisely. After all, Oswald had changed the world with his puny Mannlicher-Carcano; how much greater would his accomplishment be, and how much more would she love him for it.

He was closer now, the smell of brine in the air. He breathed it in. Soon enough he would be in the air, observing the holocaust below with a combination of dispassion over the loss of life and pleasure in the role he had played in it all. Might as well enjoy the scent of earth and sea while he had the chance.

Except in those unbidden reveries, he hardly ever thought about his own past. That had all been prologue to this moment, this glorious present. What emotions of loss and longing still dwelled deep in his breast he rigorously controlled. In his imagination, his father still dangled at the end of a piece of piano wire while Party members cursed and mocked him and a film crew recorded his *Totentanz* for the private amusement of the *Führer*. His mother as well, and the fact that he hardened his heart and consigned that memory to the shades spoke well of his training as a young German. That was what the *Führer* had always preached and what he commanded the SS *Einsatzgruppen* to do as they lined up the Jews, the Slavs, the gypsies and all the other *Untermenschen*: to harden their hearts against all weak and useless feelings of human emotion and to do their duty. And the nation had followed him, right up to the moment when he put the gun in his mouth and pulled the trigger.

The trigger. Yes, the trigger.

That old woman, Petrovich, was worried about the trigger. Did he have no imagination? No trust in Skorzeny's infallibility? That fool, Farid Belghazi, had not brought him news of the Higgs boson when he was Skorzeny's man inside CERN, but the boy was a whiz with both lasers and computers and had given him exactly what he had needed in order to realize the plan that was now unfolding around the world. For CERN was practically the epicenter of GRID computer research, able to reach out anywhere on the Internet that it had been so instrumental in developing. It really was easy when you had the right people in place.

Unfortunately, the bastard who called himself Devlin had grabbed Belghazi and cut off the flow of information, but not before Skorzeny had what he needed.

There was the building, just up ahead.

He felt so much better as he entered. But his mood was ruined almost at once.

Miss Harrington was nowhere to be found.

"Where is she?" he demanded of Mlle. Derrida, who was out on the balcony, sunning herself. He had to admit she looked quite fetching topless.

Mlle. Derrida gave a Gallic shrug and rolled over.

At that moment, his secure PDA buzzed in his pocket. Surely, this was she, messaging him that she was on her way in from the airport.

But the message was not from her. It was from Col. Zarin in Tehran and it read:

WHO IS THIS WOMAN?

The present had just changed. And so he must change with it. "Mlle. Derrida," he barked. "We leave for Tehran at once. See that we are in the air in one hour's time."

He looked at the computer—her computer; no, *his* computer. It was still hard for him to credit that the whelp had used his own lover as a poisoned pawn, but then again, why would he not? Human kindness meant nothing to him. From youth he had been trained by Seelye to hate humanity and kill without remorse. But that was his ethos, Skorzeny's credo, and Devlin was much more a son to him than he ever could be to Armond Seelye. It was a shame to have to kill him, but the thing must and would be done.

He picked up the computer. It, too, would be making the trip to Tehran.

CHAPTER THIRTY-THREE

Qom

She must have dozed, but it was the stopping of the car that woke her up. Not just stopping, slamming on the brakes. She felt the coffin shift. She wasn't sure how much of this she could take.

She had stifled the panic attacks thus far, but she was beginning to lose it. She was not particularly claustrophobic, but the realization that she was trapped inside a box that might never be opened again was gradually sinking in. What if they opened the coffin and just shot her? What if they just buried her? Torture, anything but being shut in here, was starting to seem like a good idea.

She heard the voices again, the sound of the doors opening, and then felt the coffin move. She could feel herself slide across the floor of the vehicle, then fall a little as it cleared the transport and landed with a thud on something. Then that something started to move. She must be on some sort of handcart.

She could hear some doors creaking, then silence for a moment as she was wheeled somewhere. She stopped, and then felt the jerk of what must be an elevator as the lift started to ascend—or maybe descend, it was hard to tell. Her panic was rising now, faster, as it seemed the end of her ordeal might be near. An end that could not come fast enough, no matter how it ended.

She was in a large room now—she could tell by the different acoustical environment. More voices now, but not a crowd. She could even make out some words, but as they were in Farsi, she didn't understand them.

Then a banging on the top of the coffin as someone jimmied a screwdriver or a wedge into the top. She heard someone grunting. Then—*crack*—the top came off the box and she instantly closed her eyes at the unaccustomed light.

Shouts as a man rudely yanked her to her feet. She was soaked in sweat and reeking of urine. A man she couldn't see slapped her. Someone else punched her. She fell back into the coffin, her head spinning. She grabbed the oxygen tank.

Her eyesight was gradually returning. A man was coming forward, toward her. She raised the empty tank above her head and brought it down on his skull. She could hear the crack of the bone as he fell.

Someone grabbed her from behind. She brought an elbow back and caught him in the Adam's apple.

Now half a dozen men were on her, punching her and ripping at her clothes. She clawed and gouged and bit. She could feel flesh rend and hear men scream and curse. She would not go down without a fight, not this close to freedom. Not this close to death.

They were too much for her. When they had finished beating her into submission they stripped her naked and tied both her hands behind her back and hung her on a hook. The pain was excruciating, but she knew she could endure it for a while. She had sworn to herself that she would get Maryam to safety and she would fulfill that promise.

There were about twenty men in the room now, laughing

at her. Spitting at her, fondling her, touching her, slapping her. It was as if at least half of them had never seen a naked woman before, had never come this close to a Western woman before. She was at once an object of scorn and lust, of repulsion and desire. She was the West, helpless before the East and yet somehow still potent, still threatening.

One man ventured a little too close and she struck out with her right foot, smashing his nose. He spouted blood and fell to the floor. It was like throwing chum into a shark tank. His mates turned their attention away from her and circled round him, laughing, pointing. One of them lashed out with a foot, in imitation of her, only this foot was shod and the point of the shoe caught the man right under the chin.

His head snapped back, and that was the signal for the others to fall upon him, beating and cursing him, cursing him for the shame of being bested by a woman, by a naked woman, by a Western woman. Even after he stopped moving and crying out, they continued to beat him like a dead ass in the street whose owner has not realized he has just lost a prized possession, and they kept on beating him, pulping him until—

A gunshot. A single gunshot. It was the most welcome sound she had ever heard.

Two men cut her down, wrapped her in a blanket, and carried her into another room. She was inside some sort of government building, spartan and functional, moving from what looked like a squad room and into more private quarters. Yes: now that her vision had cleared, she could see that the men were wearing uniforms—the uniforms of the Army of the Guardians of the Islamic Revolution, better known as the Revolutionary Guards.

A bearded officer approached her and spoke to her harshly in Farsi. She shook her head: *I don't understand.* He stepped closer, caught sight of her English blue eyes, and recoiled. She was not the woman he had been expecting.

He turned and barked something to the two other men in the room, who quickly departed. Once the door had closed, he lit a cigarette and took a deep drag.

"My name is Col. Navid Zarin. Welcome to Iran," he said.

"I suppose that was your special welcoming committee? Is that how modern Persians greet their guests?"

Col. Zarin smiled. Spunky. Breaking this one was going to be fun. "A guest, yes—but under irregular circumstances. May I get you something to drink? I would offer you coffee, but as you know we observant Muslims do not drink coffee, even though we invented it and the Turks brought it to the gates of Vienna with them. Pity. I did enjoy it when I was a student at UC Irvine, back in the day."

She shook her head, said nothing.

"There is a bathroom through that door," he said. "Please clean yourself up. When you come out, I will have some clothes here. You will put them on, so as not to tempt my men with your beauty. And then we will have a little talk."

He came closer to her, cigarette in hand. "We are not supposed to smoke, either, but old habits die hard. After all, we are not Mormons." He laughed heartily at his own joke.

The cigarette was dangerously close to her face now. She could feel the heat from its glowing tip. She knew that the temperature of the tip of cigarette could reach up to seven hundred degrees Celsius, and leave a mark forever. Closer . . . closer . . .

"You're sure you wouldn't like a drag?" he said, with a smile. She closed her eyes, flinching from the burn she knew was coming.

But it never came. Instead, the officer stubbed the cigarette out and pointed toward the bathroom. "In there. Don't worry, you'll be safe. None of my men will molest you. You have my word as an officer and an Iranian gentleman. Now,

if you will excuse me, I have to make an important telephone call."

Amanda wrapped the blanket tightly around her and
slowly backed away. All her instincts were on alert, but she
couldn't read this man. Would he show traditional Muslim
respect toward a helpless woman, or did he consider her a
Western whore who could be raped or killed without consequence? She supposed she would find out soon enough.

The hot water was a welcome relief. She could stay in the
shower, mean as it was, forever. She found some soap and
scrubbed herself, then washed her hair with it. She wasn't
going to look her best, but then that didn't really matter right
at the moment. She was lucky to be out of Maryam's coffin,
and lucky to be alive.

The moment. She would take a page from Skorzeny's
book, since he had always preached the gospel of the present
to her. The future might hold terrors or wonders or both, but
there was nothing she could do about it for now, except to be
as ready for it as she could.

When she emerged from the shower, still clutching the
blanket to her, the office was empty. There, on one of the
chairs, was a full-length chador, much like the one she had
left for Maryam.

She put it on. She felt like she was going to a costume
party in Mayfair, but this was no joke. She had just finished
dressing when the door opened and the officer walked
back in.

"Beautiful," he said. "Not exactly what we were expecting, but nonetheless beautiful. Now, you will please come
with me, there are several people who would very much like
to meet you."

If Maryam thought the Grand Ayatollah's ringing invoca-
tion was the end of it she was mistaken. As one, the crowd

turned toward the sacred mosque where the vision of the Prophet now floated over the holy place.

"O Muslims, behold!" shouted the Grand Ayatollah. "Until today, was not such a thing forbidden? And yet you are witness. For so I proclaim that I am Seyed Khorasani, in fulfillment of the hadith—I, the man from the East, from our blessed Persian tradition, here to unite two great cultures, and bring together all the *ummah*. O Muslims, this is the beginning of the days you have been awaiting for more than a thousand years. And thus do I proclaim to you that the days of the Occultation are nearing an end, and that the Coming is nearly upon us!"

"Allahu akbar! Allahu akbar! Allahu akbar!"

"O Muslims, behold!"

In the near distance, behind the mosque, three Shahab-3 rockets leaped into the air, heading north, east, and south.

"Let the infidel be warned—this is only a small demonstration of our might. We no longer fear the West. Therefore, I hereby proclaim that we have no alternative but to unleash Allah's holy fire upon the Great Satan's cities and rain down His wrath upon the Zionist entity. The next missiles will go to the West, bearing the most fearsome weapons, and the Faithful will soon be worshipping freely in al-Quds. So it is written, so shall it be done."

Above the mosque, the image of Mohammed slowly faded from view.

"O Muslims, truly the Coming is upon us! Gird yourselves, for the battle will be hard and bloody. But it is only through blood that we are purified and made holy. It is only through jihad that we prove ourselves worthy of Imam Ali and Issa. It is only through them that we will truly find Paradise—when all the world has accepted the Word, or is put to the sword. *Allahu akbar!*"

The crowd burst into a cacophonous roar. Maryam slowly

edged away, heading behind the mosque. She needed to get word out. She needed to warn the world.

Any transmission from this spot, though, she knew would be picked up, if it even got out. The mullahs may have practiced a fundamentalist brand of a seventh-century faith, but they were very much up to date on the latest Western technology, and they were not about to let things get out of control.

Think. What would Frank Ross do?

Two members of the religious police saw her moving away from the crowd and made a beeline for her. Unaccompanied women should not be wandering the streets alone, lest they be thought whores.

She was either going to have to talk her way out of this or fight her way out, and at this point she didn't much care which.

CHAPTER THIRTY-FOUR

Washington, D.C.

It was just the three of them, sitting in the Oval Office. President Tyler had switched off the recording system, a descendant of the one that Johnson had first instituted and that had brought Nixon low. He'd had Seelye's CSS men sweep the place for any bugs and then bubble over the White House so that no transmissions would inadvertently leak out.

Even though the old Soviet Union was dead and buried, the old Soviets were back as the new Russians, still with their ambitions for great power status, still bearing their animus against the U.S., still competitive although greatly diminished in size, population, and capacity. The new Russian president was fighting a rearguard action against the forces of fate, but his dream of reconstituting the Czarist empire was still burning.

And now the country had a more worrisome foe than the Russians. The long, slow, three-hundred-thirty-year sleep-walk from Sobieski's triumph at the gates of Vienna had abruptly ended on 9/11. Or, rather, the age-old conflict between Islam and Judeo-Christianity had begun again anew.

Only this time it was, as the Pentagon liked to say, asymmetrical, with the Muslims using the West's own technology against it and hiding behind the Metternichian fiction of Islamic nation-states while waging war in the name of the *ummah* and Allah. It was settling in to be a long war of attrition.

"The only question, Mr. President," Shalika Johnson was saying, "well . . . there are two 'only' questions. The first is, if we accept the premise of asymmetrical warfare, then what is an acceptable level of casualties on our side? How many people are we and the Europeans prepared to lose each year—to say nothing of the people in Africa and Southeast Asia—so that we can maintain our high moral ground?" She spat the last three words out like the gang member she once was.

"The second 'only' question is this: if you can't answer the first question, then what are you prepared to do about putting an end to this, as asymmetrically and finally as possible?"

"Well, Shalika," said Jeb Tyler, "that's what we're here to discuss, isn't it? Army?"

Seelye pushed a button on his PDA and one of the screens across the room flickered on. "This just occurred in Iran," he said. "This is from their state-run television feed, which was broadcasting a speech by the Grand Ayatollah Ali Ahmed Hussein Mustafa Mohammed Fadlallah al-Sadiq."

"Quite a mouthful of a moniker he's got there," said Tyler.

"Apparently the Ayatollah was giving a speech outside the sacred mosque of Jamkaran—"

"It's not sacred to me," said Tyler quietly, cold steel in his voice.

"Yes, sir. As I was saying, he was giving a speech about the Coming—that's their term for the resurrection of the Mahdi, who is supposed to be down the sacred . . . er, the well, when this happened."

All eyes were on the screen. There was the image of Mohammed, the same image that had set off the horrible rioting
in Africa, which was still raging. As usual, the United Nations had condemned the violence and sent in peacekeepers
to Nigeria and elsewhere, but they were quickly routed by
people with no need to keep the peace. The death toll was
horrendous, and nobody knew what to do about it.

Except Jeb Tyler. "That's the same image that was seen in
Africa, isn't it?" he asked.

"Yes, sir," replied Seelye.

Tyler got up. A drink would have felt good right about
now, but he turned away the temptation. He had to think both
rationally and emotionally. He had to cut this Gordian knot,
end this cycle of constant conflict and misery and death. If
he could do this, then he would be a great president, and it
wouldn't matter if some nobody like Angela Hassett beat
him in the election. For the first time in his life, he saw a way
clear to serving the people—not just the people of the
United States, but the people of the world, even the Muslim
world—instead of serving himself, and by God he was going
to take it.

"I get it," he said softly.

"There's more, Mr. President," said Seelye. Tyler turned
to look at the screen.

"No, I've got it."

A holographic projection of Islam's prophet.

A trio of Shahab-3 rockets, leaping into the sky.

It was so obvious now.

"All our problems are related," said Tyler. "All of them.
The apparitions, the riots, whatever the hell is hidden at
Mount Sinai, the well at Qom, the Iranian nuclear program—all of it is really just One Big It. And that's what
we're going to solve, right here, right now. Am I clear about
this?"

"Yes, Mr. President," said Shalika Johnson.

"Yes, sir," said Army Seelye.

"What were you going to say, Army?"

"That those Shahabs were fully nuclear-operational. All they need is the word from the top and we've got six million more dead Jews."

"And a hundred million dead Muslims," added Shalika. "Israel will not go quietly—and, as you know, sir, we have assured the Israelis that we will retaliate on their behalf as well, which is something the entire Muslim world understands."

"But the Iranians don't care," noted Tyler. "At least, not the bunch running the country. They want the end of the world and they're bound and determined to do it. But this all stops now. All of it."

Neither the NSA director nor the secretary of defense had ever seen Tyler like this. They were used to the boyish Louisiana pol, the say-anything president, the man who preferred to be loved rather than respected. And now he was changing right in front of their eyes.

It was about time.

"STUXNET," said the President.

"It's been deployed at several Iranian nuclear sites. . . ."

"Is Qom one of them?"

"Up to now, no. Qom—actually Fordo—is just an enrichment site, so we and the Israelis concentrated on—"

"Turn the worm loose on Qom. Right now. I want instant results."

Seelye punched in the order and transmitted it back to the Building in Fort Meade. He got a pingback almost immediately. "Sir, the Iranians have mounted very effective defenses against the worm, mainly through patches supplied by Siemens in Germany. There's only one way to introduce the virus at Qom."

"What's that?"

"Somebody has to do it manually. Where's Devlin?"

"Probably in country by now," said Seelye.

"And his team?"

"In place, Mr. President. On the *Eisenhower,* at Al Dhafra, on Diego Garcia."

"Then he'll have to do it manually. Relay the virus and instructions. I want the whole damn system taken down."

"Done," said Seelye.

"That's what the bastards get for using Windows," muttered Tyler. "Next."

Shalika looked at her notes. "We've established that the apparitions are really just laser-carried holographic images being relayed from the surface of the moon. As you know, Mr. President, the Apollo astronauts left retro-reflectors on the moon's surface for use in scientific experiments, so somebody—"

"Skorzeny," said Tyler.

"Skorzeny or somebody has hijacked the experiment."

"Where are the projections originating?"

"The Côte d'Azur."

"Which means somebody at CERN is involved." He looked at Seelye. "What did Devlin say about that Algerian scientist he grabbed . . . what's his name?"

"Farid Belghazi, sir," said Seelye. "He's being held in protective custody at an undisclosed—"

"Disclose it."

"At Mount Olive in West Virginia. Level Five security. He's not a happy puppy."

Tyler's eyes were gleaming now. Sometimes it was good to be president.

"I want him less happy. In fact, I want him fucked up to the maximum level the law allows, and then I want him fucked up just a little bit more, in case his training has prepared him for the maximum level the law allows. And then I want him to sing out Louise. Who do we turn at CERN and how quickly can it be done? I want control of those lasers."

"He has a brother still working there, I believe," said Seelye.

"See that he sees the light, pronto."

Tyler rang for Manuel. The steward appeared in the doorway, ready to take orders. "Three of my favorite libations, please."

"Yes, Mr. President."

"Sir, it's—" began Seelye, but Tyler waved him off. On the screen, the Grand Ayatollah was still ranting and Mohammed was still preaching, in an endless loop. . . .

"Secretary Johnson, belay my request for operational planning involving the bombing of the Iranian nuclear facilities. Skorzeny and the Iranians have just handed us a great gift—and we're going to use it."

Tyler rubbed his hands together. This was it—all the marbles. If he could pull this off, not only would he go down in history as one of America's greatest presidents, he would also land in the same history books as the canniest politicians who ever lived. Which was the higher honor, he wasn't sure.

"We don't have to do it all. We don't have to kill everybody. But we don't have to roll over and play dead, either. They think the End Times are a'comin'—very well then, we're going to give them their End Times. But not the way they think. These will be the End Times to end the End Times—not only in our lifetime, but—if we get it right—for generations to come."

"What are we going to do, sir?" asked Johnson.

Tyler sat back down again, just as Manuel entered with the drinks. "We're going to show them," he said. "We're going to show them that they're half right. We're going to show them that there is no god but Allah—but that there is no Allah. Not in this life, anyway."

He handed the drinks around. "I want our enhanced version of the STUXNET unleashed on the facility of Qom—

and everywhere else. I want those three Super Hornets locked and loaded—make sure they know the rubble needs to bounce, and in the most spectacular fashion they've got. A real fucking *son et lumiére*. I want the Iranians and any other holy warriors to understand: no more Mr. Nice Guy. From now on the Bush Doctrine is in effect: any country that harbors or abets these murderous bastards is going to get it, right in the chops. And I want Emanuel Skorzeny dead. Not brought to justice. Dead. Cheers."

They drank. Tyler looked over at the bust of Lincoln hanging on one of the walls. "Now I know how you felt, you ruthless son of a bitch," he said, and raised his glass to Abraham's ghost.

Chapter Thirty-five

New York City

Alonzo Schmidt would be damned if he was going to let this stump him.

The radiation levels were well within the standard tolerances, but something was amiss. He couldn't quite put his finger on it, but there definitely was something wrong.

Think.

He'd been on duty the day of the attacks, and he'd seen firsthand some of the carnage as they brought the dead and wounded over from the Ninety-second Street Y. It was always the Jews who caught the brunt of things like this, always the Jews who got blamed for everything. Being black in America was hard enough, but being a Jew, he decided, was really tough.

Not that he minded being black in America. He was always being lectured by some baggy-pants, straight-haired Negro or other that the black man had suffered four hundred years of iniquity at the hands of the white man, but then he looked around the hospital and what did he see? A sea of color: white doctors, black doctors, Indian doctors, Arab doctors, Christian doctors, Jewish doctors, even some Muslim doctors. All getting along perfectly fine, all conforming to the discipline of the hospital, all dedicated to precisely one cause, which was saving lives.

He had a good job, a good life, a good wife, great kids. They had their own place in Queens, bought if not yet paid for. He had a nice car, which he left garaged most of the year until spring came and he could take the family out to Sag Harbor to visit relatives. And the hospital made it all possible—the hospital and his skill at his job.

Think. No, better—

Think back.

Chaos that day. Hard to believe that one lone gunman could have done all that damage. Why—

The phone rang. "Schmidt," he said.

"It's Detective Saleh, Mr. Schmidt," came the phone. "Remember me?"

"Sure I do. In fact, I was just thinking about you. You know, there's something at the back of my—"

"Listen, we don't have much time. I'm in the car right now, on my way uptown. Can you clear your schedule?"

"Of course, Detective."

"The M.E. got us an ID on the shooter at the Y. His name was Crankheit, C-R-A-N-K-H-E-I-T, like Walter only different, first name Raymond. Does that ring a bell?'

Alonzo thought for a moment. "Can't say that it does."

"He might have been using another name. Or maybe he never told anybody his name."

"What are you getting at?"

"We think he might have been in the hospital prior to the incident. His head was blown off by whoever took him out, but our guys in the M.E.'s office are whizzes with computers and we think we've got a pretty good idea of what he might have looked like. I'm sending you the picture now. Hold on."

Alonzo Schmidt took the smartphone away from his ear

and watched. Sure enough, in a few seconds the machine let him know he had a photo. He punched it up.

"Nasty-looking little geek, ain't he?" he said to Lannie.

"Mustn't go by looks now," said Lannie. "But he was even nastier than he looked—a real piece of shit."

"I saw what he done to those ladies at the Y," said Alonzo. "He messed them up pretty good. A whole lotta hate in that boy. Whole lotta hate in a lot of people."

"Yeah, love seems in pretty short supply around the world these days. Hang on—we're pulling up now. Meet me out front."

Lannie was coming through the main doors when Alonzo got there. He held out his hand in greeting. Lannie shook it and kept moving. "Someplace private," he said, "where we can talk."

They ducked into a nearby office, empty. "Do you recognize him?"

"Yes," said Alonzo simply.

Lannie turned on the recorder application in his smartphone. "Go."

"I only saw him a couple of times, but I have a pretty good memory for faces, and this one kinda creeped me out. I mean, he seemed nice enough in a weird sort of way, but he wasn't what you'd call friendly, which I thought was odd for a delivery guy."

"Delivery guy?"

"Yeah, from the deli around the corner. People always getting hungry around here, sending out for stuff, and he brought me a corned-beef sandwich a couple of times."

"When was this?"

"Right before the attack. Couple of days."

"What makes you think you'd remember somebody as anonymous as a delivery guy?"

"Celina Selena pointed it out to me. That's what we call her, Celina Selena, on account of her momma loved that singer who got killed. Don't tell her I told you. She likes to keep her middle name private."

"You mean, the technician in nuclear medicine?"

"That's Celina."

Five minutes later they were in one of the unused examining rooms in Nuclear Medicine. "Of course I remember, Detective," Celina was saying. "People tell me I have the best ear for accents of anyone they've ever met."

"Where am I from?"

She didn't hesitate. "Atlantic Avenue, west of the Van Wyck. If I hear you talk some more, I might be able to get within a couple of blocks."

Lannie was impressed but didn't have time for parlor tricks right now. "I'll take you up on that some other time," he said. "Tell me about this guy. What was it about his accent?"

Celina looked at Alonzo. "Well, we were shooting the breeze and he said he was from Wahoo, Nebraska, but I know people from Wahoo, Nebraska—Dr. Lovenberg is from Wahoo, Nebraska."

"Why do you keep saying that. 'Wahoo, Nebraska'?"

"Because that's how they say it. Wahoo, Nebraska, accent on the 'hoo.' And he didn't. He just said Wahoo. So I said, you mean, Wahoo, Nebraska, and he just looked at me. That was when I knew he wasn't from Wahoo."

"Nebraska," finished Lannie.

"Exactly. Plus he accented 'Wa.' "

"Okay, now where did he go? Was he ever carrying anything? Did he walk over here or take a bike?"

"Neither," said Alonzo. "He rode one of those three-wheelers with a compartment up front to put stuff in. You've seen 'em."

Lannie felt his heart racing. "Where's the service entrance?"

They were there eight minutes later. Lannie was punching in text on his phone the whole way.

The room was downstairs, just as he feared.

"Are there any storage rooms around here? Places the service personnel use to store things?"

"It's okay, Ralph," said Schmidt to a big man in a security guard's rig. "Everything cool. Right over here, Detective."

Lannie tried the door. "It's locked."

"Not locked. The door's busted, stuck or something, and we haven't gotten around to getting it fixed. Not a lot of use for it anyway."

"We have to break it down," said Lannie, deadly serious. "Come on, help me."

He and Alonzo threw themselves at it. Nothing. Celina tried as well. They felt it move a little, but that was all. "Come on, Ralph, get your ass over here," said Alonzo.

The fat man added his weight to the mix. The door groaned and buckled but did not give.

"Stand back," said Lannie, drawing his weapon, the Sig P226, the model that was among the standard-issue nine-millimeters in the department. Even his chief, Frankie Byrne, had switched, although more out of necessity than choice. He fired a single round. "Okay, again," he said, and the four of them put their combined weight behind it. . . .

Open. There was the trike. "Fuck a duck," said Lannie.

He raced to the trike and opened the compartment. Empty. It would have been a miracle were it not, and it seemed that for New York City miracles were just about in as short supply as love.

Lannie punched another message, then looked up. "How far could he have gotten with whatever he was carrying before somebody noticed him?"

"Depends on the time of day," said Celina. "Late at night . . ."

Late at night, hospitals were just about the least secure

places in the city. Just the comatose patients and a few over-worked interns heading into the twentieth consecutive hour of work while most of the doctors slept soundly at home in the Oranges or Westchester or Ridgefield in Connecticut, and the help went home to the Bronx and Staten Island. If that kid had gotten entry to the hospital at night, he could have left his package anywhere.

"Thanks, Ralph, you've been very helpful," said Lannie to the fat man, and began to walk away. He dropped his voice as he spoke to Celina and Alonzo. "You're not to speak of this to anybody, you understand. This is police business. Alonzo, get me a radiation check on that trike ASAP. Celina, I need you to start asking around . . . *quietly* . . . among the staff if anybody remembers seeing your boyfriend Raymond one night before the attacks. And I need to see the head administrator, right now."

"I'll take to you Dr. Leopold's office," offered Celina.

"I knew something was wrong," muttered Alonzo. "I felt it. I felt like something was hiding from me"

Celina and Lannie were heading for the elevator that would take them to the administration floor. "Do you think you can feel it one more time?" asked Lannie. "And find it? Our lives are going to depend on it."

"You can count on me, Detective," said Schmidt. "If there's something hot in this place, I'll get it."

"Make it snappy," said Lannie. Then, to Celina, "Let's—"

She was taking an in-house page on her cell phone. The look on her face told Lannie something was terribly wrong. "Can you please repeat that?" she said, signaling frantically to Lannie to come close and listen. "I'm having a hard time hearing you. This is a hospital, you know. It's noisy around here. Wait, let me put you on speakerphone."

She hit the button. Together, they listened to the voice.

"Did you give him my message?"

Lannie signaled for her to play along, string out the conversation, keep him on the line as much as possible as he frantically sent a message back to Sid Sheinberg at CTU headquarters. In hospitals, cell phone service was tied in with Internet service; the relay stations worked off the wireless service. If he could just keep the guy talking long enough, they could get a read on his position.

"Give who the message?"

"Detective Aslan Saleh—" and then the words devolved into some kind of Middle Eastern gibberish again, words that Celina had no chance of ever understanding, no matter how many times she went to Brooklyn.

Lannie was still texting when his ear caught the change of language. A look of disbelief came over his face as he listened, and a sneer of derision appeared on his lips.

"He's right there with you, isn't he?" said the man, speaking in English again. "So this is my message to you, Detective Saleh, you dog son of a thousand whores. There is fatwa against you and your family for the crime of apostasy. There is fatwa against you and your family for the crime of insulting Islam. There is fatwa against you for the crime of collaborating with the infidel. May you make your peace with Allah and beg his most compassionate forgiveness. *Taubeh kon!* For the day of reckoning is at—"

Lannie grabbed the phone. "Listen to me, fella. You can take your goddamn fucking threats and shove them up your ass. This is my town, my country, my home and if you don't like then go blow a camel. You ever show up here, you're dead meat. You wanna see repentance? By the time I'm finished with you, you're gonna confess to murdering Judge Crater. *Capisce?*"

But the bastard had rung off. No matter—he'd kept him on the phone long enough. Sid Sheinberg would track his ass down. The long arm of the NYPD would reach out and take his fucking head right off.

"Everything okay, Detective?" asked Celina.

"Let's get to work," he said.

CHAPTER THIRTY-SIX

Washington, D.C.

Millie Dhouri hated to interrupt the President when he was power napping but the FBI was on the line. "It's Deputy Director Byrne, Mr. President," she said. "On the phone. Says it's a matter of national security."

Jeb Tyler shook his head to clear the cobwebs. What was he, some middle manager? Didn't anybody go through channels anymore? It was easy for the President to say that the door to the Oval Office was always open, but he wasn't supposed to mean it.

Before he took the call he went into the small room just off the Oval Office that one of his predecessors had made famous and splashed some water on his face. He loved playing poker as much as the next good ol' boy, but this was the highest-stakes game he ever hoped to play in. The situation was fluid and changing by the minute. Prophets and Virgins were appearing in the skies, the Iranians had just fired off three Shahabs to make sure everybody was paying attention, he'd just signed off on an op that, if it failed, would ensure that he ranked right up there with Jimmy Carter and the failed hostage rescue attempt in the annals of presidential futility, fecklessness, and infamy.

What was not to like?

"What is it?"

"There's a bomb at Mount Sinai Hospital in Manhattan. The NYPD won't confirm that, but I can."

"What kind of bomb?"

"Suitcase nuke, we think. The media's been telling folks for years there's no such thing, but you and I both know better, don't we, Mr. President?"

Tyler could see why everybody loathed Tom Byrne. The man was rude, crude, and lewd, and probably screwed, blooed, and tattooed as well. Nevertheless he was damn good at his job precisely because of all those unsavory character traits.

"How do you know? Did your brother tell you? And if he didn't, why wasn't I informed?"

"You'll have to ask Frankie that, Mr. President. He and I don't get along so good, as you probably know. But I've got a little bird in the CTU, and he sings like a regular canary."

Tyler felt his blood boiling. Goddamned clannish Irish and their goddamned NYPD blue line and their goddamned mick version of omertá.

"Thank you for informing me, Deputy Director Byrne," said Tyler. "I'll task it to the proper authorities."

It was clear Byrne didn't like getting blown off. "I think you should let the FBI handle it, sir."

"I was thinking more along the lines of Homeland Security."

If he'd been present, Byrne would have laughed in his face. The sneer came through loud and clear over the phone. "You have got to be kidding me, sir."

"I'm the President of the United States," Tyler reminded him.

"Yes, you are, sir. And the statutory authority is clear: This is an FBI matter, Mr. President. So please let us handle it. We have the men, the training, and the equipment. And I have my . . . special relationship . . . with the head of the CTU, as you know."

Tyler ran through the calculations in his head. Results were all that counted now, and there was no time to waste. The thought of dragging that idiot Colangelo into the case and getting him up to speed made him ill. Whatever the bad blood between the Byrne brothers was, it didn't matter at this moment. All that mattered was finding that bomb, defusing it, and getting it the hell out of Manhattan with the public none the wiser.

"If this goes tits up . . ." said Tyler.

"Then we've both got bigger problems than jurisdiction."

"Where are you now?"

"In the Acela, on my way to Penn Station. Will be there in forty-five minutes."

So the die was already cast. After this was over, if somehow he won reelection, he was going to clean house. Except for Seelye and maybe Shalika Johnson, there wouldn't be anybody left standing from the old regime. Well, maybe with one or two exceptions, depending on how well they carried out their current missions. But Thomas A. Byrne, he felt quite sure, was destined for early retirement.

"Deputy Director Byrne?" said the President.

"Yes, Mr. President?"

"Don't fuck up."

"Thank you, sir. And if you ever need a, you know, favor . . ."

Tyler kept him on the line. He didn't have to worry about Byrne hanging up. You didn't hang up on the President, he hung up on you.

"Sir?"

"I'm thinking. . . . Listen, Tom, what's this I hear about you and a certain lady . . . ?"

Thank God for interagency gossip, and his appetite for it.

CHAPTER THIRTY-SEVEN

Al Dhafra, United Arab Emirates

It was more than a little creepy to see the memorial models of the World Trade Center and the Pentagon outside the fire department. At least, thought Devlin, we had some friends in the Arab world. Especially here, in the Emirates and near the other Gulf states. They all had their problems with the United States, but they had an even bigger problem with their Shiite minorities, who were growing more restive by the day, whipped up and egged on by the Iranians and their proxies in the Levant. Thank Allah for the ancient principle that the enemy of my enemy is my friend, or we wouldn't have any friends in the Middle East at all.

They were inside a secure transmission area. The base, a stone's throw from Abu Dhabi and not far from Dubai, was used by the UAE air force, but also by the French and, most important for their purposes, the 380th Air Expeditionary Wing of the U.S. Air Force. Its mission was mostly recon and air refueling, but it could do some damage when it wanted to and its presence there, in the heart of Sunni Arabia, was a powerful reminder that the Great Satan still had some punch left in him.

Both Danny and Devlin knew that every word they said would be recorded and that every keystroke on a computer terminal would be logged. Friendship only went so far, especially among natural enemies. So they were using a double Playfair cipher to disguise the real purpose of their communications with Washington. They had worked out the key phrase and grid on the flight over, and for two experienced pros, it was a fairly simple matter to send back a stream of official-sounding but innocuous reports to the DoD, which would in turn be decoded on the spot and relayed from the SecDef to the Building in Fort Meade.

"You know they're playing us, don't you?" said Devlin when they were back outside. The temperature was over one hundred degrees, and even the waters of the Gulf looked like the beach in hell. "We think we have a mission, but Tyler is as cunning as a snake. He'll piggyback some damn thing or another on top of what we're doing. That way, if things go south and we have to abort, or get captured, he can leave us 'rogues' hanging out to dry and walk away."

"Does it make any difference?"

"Not to me. My official job is track down Emanuel Skorzeny and terminate him. My personal job is to find Maryam and get her out, and muss the Iranians' hair. Your job is to fly me in and fly us out from the rendezvous point—Maryam, me, and whoever tags along. The Hornets will take out the missiles. And our job is to stay in touch with Byrne at the NYPD and try to terminate the bomb at its source."

"I have one other job."

"What's that?

"To come home."

"Which is why you've got the job you do. Look, no one can fly a chopper like you and I know your men are your equal in skill."

"Better. Younger."

"So you're going to succeed where those poor bastards of Operation Eagle Claw failed. They failed because shit happened and the command lost its nerve and Carter pulled the plug. They failed because we weren't ready for desert warfare back then. We didn't know we'd be fighting these same damn people for the next thirty years and more. Which is why, this time—"

"This time, we're going to get it right."

"Damn right we are. Jesus, it's hot."

"Not as hot as it's going to be."

They got out of the sun and headed for the base canteen. A cold beer would taste great right about now, and the nice thing about the Emirates and the other playpens nearby was that you could actually get one. A wise man once said that living in the old Soviet Union was like living with your parents for the rest of your life, but the U.S.S.R. was like a vacation at a topless beach in St. Tropez compared to the Arab world, where sin was resolutely hidden and more often to be found in Paris or London than Doha or, God knew, Riyadh.

Devlin bought the beers. The base was pretty quiet. Whatever Tyler was planning wasn't going to come from this direction. Danny drank, wiped his mouth, pointed east.

"That's where SOAR got its start. Even Carter could figure out that to the mobile belonged the future, and that if we ever again were going in to a place like Tabas, we'd damn sure better be prepared."

"And we are."

"Think we'll come back?"

"You will, as long as you dodge the *haboob*." That would be the fine desert sand mist that had brought down Carter's choppers.

There was no further need to go over the plan. Timing was everything. As soon as Maryam was able to get a signal out, they would move. It was all in her hands now.

"Code names?" asked Danny.

"Pick yours. I've got mine."

"Black Hawk will do just fine. You?"

"*Malak al-Maut.*"

"Malak al-Maut?" repeated Danny. "What's that supposed to mean?"

"You ought to know. You've heard me say it enough times."

A big grin spread across Danny's face. "The Angel of Death."

They shook hands. "It's a dirty job," said Devlin, "but somebody's got to do it."

It was good to finally meet a friend.

"What about the name of the op?" asked Danny.

"Only name it can have: Operation Honey Badger."

"The one that never got off the ground. The second rescue operation."

"Terminated on account of a presidential election. The minute Reagan took the oath of office, the hostages were released."

"End of story."

"But not end of problem."

He felt his Android buzz. There was no bother about taking the message—it had been coded and rerouted so many times that it would be indecipherable to all but him. He looked at the display:

QOM. DANGER. HURRY.

Devlin looked at Danny: "Let's roll."

CHAPTER THIRTY-EIGHT

New York City

"Captain Byrne? I'm Hope Gardner."

Frankie looked at the woman standing in front of his desk. She'd been brought from Stewart directly to the CTU in a car with its rear windows tinted both inside and out and a partition between her and the driver. The location of the Counter-Terrorism Unit was still a secret, and Byrne wanted to keep it that way.

"Very pleased to meet you. I gather we shared some experiences on Forty-second Street during the . . . late unpleasantness. Your husband is a mighty fine man, Mrs. Gardner."

"He's not my husband . . . yet," she said, and that explained it all.

"Then I wish you both nothing but the best, when the time is right. All I can say is, your fiancé is a lucky man."

Hope looked down. "Thank you, Captain Byrne."

"So let's both make him proud. Here's the deal. I understand that the man who flew the police helicopter for me over the East River—'Martin Ferguson,' I think he called himself—is on assignment somewhere classified, and very dangerous. I further understand—nobody told me this, but I'm not as dumb as I look—that he's with the man who saved my life—"

"—and ours. He got us to the hospital after . . . after the building collapsed . . ."

"Well, whoever he is, he is one hell of a guy and I hope some day I can shake his hand. . . . So the bottom line is, right now, you are to be the secure line of communication between Mr. 'Ferguson' and my department. Which tells me something I am very unhappy to hear."

"What is that, Captain?"

"It tells me that Washington doesn't trust my department. It tells me that my department is leaking to somebody. It tells me that I have a mole in my department who is sharing information—not with the enemy, as far as I can tell, but with the FBI."

"And is that a bad thing? I thought that the whole point of learning from 9/11 was that there shouldn't be walls between . . . between, you know, all those agencies."

"This is one wall that needs to stay in place, for a lot of reasons," replied Byrne. He paused a moment to collect himself, trying to decide exactly how much to tell the attractive woman sitting across the desk from him. He decided to tell her everything; a world of deception was not something the country could afford at this moment.

"Mrs. Gardner—"

"Hope."

"Hope, we have very strong reason to believe that there is a nuclear device hidden somewhere in the Mount Sinai Medical Center uptown." He watched her carefully for a reaction. Nothing. Good. "In fact, information has just come to light that means were are certain of it. This bomb, based on the telephoned warnings we've received, is set to go off within the next twenty-four to forty-eight hours, and my detectives, members of the NYPD bomb squad, and personnel from the Atomic Energy Commission are all on the site. I will do my damnedest not to put you in any danger, but I want to be very clear with you that it can't be ruled out."

"You mean the bomb could go off. What would happen then?"

"Depending on the yield—and mind you, we're not certain the technology really exists to fashion such a device; for all we know, it may just be a dirty bomb, although a very dangerous one—it could destroy the Upper East Side and render much of the island of Manhattan uninhabitable for a hundred years. There would be a tremendous loss of life."

"I understand."

"And worse—yes, there is a 'worse'—it would completely panic the country. After 9/11 we still had some spunk although, if you want my opinion, we reacted in exactly the wrong way. Instead of cowering, and rushing to assure the Muslim world we meant it no harm, and putting a bunch of Muslim-looking bylines in the *New York Times*, we should have taken the fight right overseas—not to Afghanistan, who gives a shit about Afghanistan, but right to Saudi Arabia, where we should have deposed the royal family and taken the Saudi oil fields into protective custody, to preserve the supply of energy for all the world. Wait, I'm not finished.

"Instead of treating our own people like potential terrorists every time they get on an airplane, we should have shut down immigration from the Middle East, expelled all the 'students' from that region until they could be vetted, and cut off all travel and technology to the Islamic countries—thrown a *cordon sanitaire* around them until they learned to act like civilized human beings. And then allowed them to kill each other until they had sorted themselves out and were ready to play nice with the rest of the world again. If ever. That way, your kids could get on a plane and not be pawed by the TSA gorillas, OPEC would have been broken, and we—especially we here in New York—could resume our lives without fear."

Hope looked at him in amazement. She'd never heard anybody talk like this.

"Now you see why I'll never be elected president," said Byrne, rising. "Do you think you can handle a trip uptown, have a look around?"

"Of course, Captain."

"Great. Now, how are you going to communicate with Mr. 'Ferguson'?"

"Danny. His name is Danny. Danny Impellatieri. With this." She reached into her purse and pulled out something that looked like a stripped-down smartphone and showed it to Byrne. "They told me it was a prototype, a direct line to him, totally secure."

"And I'm sure they're right. Now put that thing away and don't let anybody see you using it. There are a couple of people at the hospital you need to meet."

They got into one of the secure blacked-out cars in the basement. "I'm sorry to have to do this, but it's for your own protection."

"I've seen New York already, Captain," said Hope.

The ride uptown was uneventful. They went in through the hospital's VIP entrance on Madison.

But it didn't matter. She was right there, as Byrne half-feared.

"Hello, Captain Byrne," said Principessa. Byrne looked around. She was alone—no team, no cameras, no sound guys. "Don't worry, I won't bite." She gave Hope the once-over. "Who's your date?"

"Knock it off, Ms. Stanley," said Byrne.

"It's the same guy, isn't it? Archibald Grant and this ghost you're chasing. The guy who saved me . . . and the guy who saved you, too . . . Am I right?"

She really was much smarter than she looked.

"I'm afraid I'm busy just now, Ms. Stanley."

"Principessa."

"Whatever. Call my office and we'll talk later."

She blocked the way. She was a big, healthy girl who had long since learned how to use that body of hers as a weapon. She got close to him, dropped her voice. "What's going on, Frankie? And who's the dame?"

"What, do you think you're in a road-company version of *His Girl Friday*? Gimme a break and let me do my job, lady."

"I'm just trying to do mine. We ought to be on the same team, Captain. The Archibald Grant team."

"Who's Archibald Grant?" asked Hope, innocently. Byrne cringed. Principessa Stanley was like a shark, and she always headed toward the blood in the water.

"He's a fake," she said. "A character, a joker, who poses as a bigdome while saving the world in his spare time. He's Batman and Superman combined and, you know . . . when you get him out from underneath that makeup and that fat suit, he's probably hell on the ladies. Except that I gather he has a girlfriend, so I guess we're both out of luck."

There had been a woman in the car. A real babe. That's what Sam Raclette had told her after he recovered from the car crash in New Orleans. She had paid Raclette to follow Grant after the RAND lecture in the Crescent City. Exactly what had happened to him when he was tailing a car with a man and a woman in it he wasn't exactly sure, except that all of a sudden his car flipped over under the Pontchartrain Expressway and that was the last thing he remembered until he woke up in Charity Hospital.

"Come on, Captain. You know who he is, don't you? You can tell me. I need something to take back to my boss, Jake Sinclair."

Byrne took Hope by the arm and started walking. "Jake Sinclair is the last man on earth I'd want to help. So why don't you run back to him like a good little girl and tell him mean old Francis Byrne won't give you a thing."

Byrne stopped and turned around. "What are you doing here, anyway?" he asked. He knew she was a good newswoman, so something must have brought her here. He said a silent prayer that it didn't have anything to do with his case, but in his heart, it knew it did.

"I got a tip," she said coyly. She took a step or two backward. Make him come to her, now that she had his attention.

He bit. "What kind of a tip?"

"That some big shot was coming up from Washington on a national-security case. I figured I'd show up and say hello."

Byrne let go of Hope and walked back to Principessa. He dropped his voice. "I ought to rip that fucking wig right off your head. You know something, tell me."

"Oooh, trying to scare the little girl," mocked Principessa. The chick had balls, he had to give her that. She'd taken just about the worst that Raymond Crankheit threw at her and had survived. She wasn't about to be intimidated by him.

Whether she was or was not, however, was immediately rendered moot as a taxi pulled up in the underground driveway. Byrne knew instantly who it was. The last person on earth he wanted to see.

A man got out of the car. Principessa sashshayed over to him—that really was the only word to describe her motion—and greeted him with a kiss as he got out. "Look who's here," she said, indicating Byrne and Hope Gardner.

He let out a short, barking laugh. "Old home week. Hello, Frankie," said Tom Byrne, deputy director of the FBI.

CHAPTER THIRTY-NINE

Baku–Tehran

If there really was such a thing as a controlled purple rage, thought Mlle. Derrida as their plane taxied along the runway, Emanuel Skorzeny was managing it. The news of Amanda Harrington's defection had not surprised her in the least. She had warned him, but he would not listen. Men were such fools around women, which is why she could never love a man.

She sat near him, in case he wanted company. The 707 was always ready to leave at a moment's notice, and everything went smoothly. All they had to do was file a flight plan and get landing permission from the Iranian authorities and they were on their way. It cost one of Skorzeny's shell companies a fortune to keep his personal plane in a constant state of readiness, but what did it matter? He could just manipulate another currency or indulge in some other arcane aspect of international high finance and the expense would be covered.

"Don't say anything," he said to her.

"I didn't."

They flew in silence for a while. Maryam's computer lay closed on the table in front of him. Mlle. Derrida wished she had a book.

"Confound your damnable silence," he said.

She took that as a cue. "Would you care for some music, sir?"

"When I want music, I shall ask for it.'

"Then what do you want?"

"I want your opinion." That almost never happened.

"May I ask in regard to what, M. Skorzeny?"

"Regarding what? Regarding what just happened? How did she do it? Why? I am both troubled and puzzled at the perfidy of women, Mlle. Derrida."

"You know what they say, sir—the only thing that men and women can agree on is that neither sex trusts women."

"In that case, I cannot understand your, how do they say these days, your 'sexual orientation.' "

Emanuelle Derrida laughed. "I make love with them," she said. "I didn't say I trusted them. . . . Do you have a plan, sir?"

" 'We,' Mlle. Derrida. Do 'we' have a plan is the question. And the answer is, yes, we do."

She wasn't sure if she liked hearing that. M. Pilier had met his untimely end the last time Skorzeny had had a plan. From what she'd heard of that event, she was quite sure she didn't want to come up against either the man or the woman when someone's life was on the line—in this case, hers.

"My arrangement with Col. Zarin was simple—Miss Harrington was to deliver the lady in Tehran. What happened to the lady after that was none of our concern. In exchange, we were to be given access to the Iranian nuclear program's first live-fire test."

"What?" asked Mlle. Derrida. This was the first she had heard of that.

"You do understand that what we have been doing with the laser projections, through our contacts in CERN in Switzerland, was simply prologue. The Iranian government needs a bit of theater, a pretext, in order to proclaim the Coming of their Mahdi, and that is what we have provided them. Conflict on a global scale, all for the nugatory price of a little technology and a piggyback ride on the comatose clods at NASA. If America wishes to abdicate its role in space, there is certainly no reason for others not to take advantage of it."

He drummed his fingers lightly on top of Maryam's computer. "Consider this. I know *he* gave it to her. I know it represents the very latest in NSA communications and analytic software. I know it is a poisoned gift, and he knows that I know it. He knows that the word for "poison" in German is *Gift*. He suspects, but cannot be sure, that I won't care, that I will somehow find a way to use his own weapon against him—that I am, in short, smarter than he. Which is, in fact, true."

"If you're so smart, sir," observed Mlle. Derrida, "then why is Maryam presumably free and Miss Harrington fled?"

He glared at her with those basilisk eyes. "That is not a question I wish to entertain at the moment, Mlle. Derrida," he said. "Now, if I may continue with my ruminations . . . what if I activate this computer?"

"It might blow us out of the sky," she said.

"Correct. But the Iranians don't know that. Should I come to Iran, filled with apologies over Miss Harrington's unconscionable treachery, and bring with me this splendid piece of NSA intellectual architecture, do you not think they would be appreciative?"

"Will you warn them, or just let them blow themselves up?"

"Appropriate, if somewhat vague, caveats will be given, of course."

"That's very kind of you, sir. So what is the plan? If I am to be there with you, I feel I have the right to—"

"You have the right not to ask questions, and to absorb any information I choose to give you. But since I require your assistance beyond your usual capacity, this is what we are going to do." He explained in as little detail as he could. Then he said:

"From there we journey to the Holy City of Qom, where we will witness a very great miracle—provided by me of course. But that miracle will come only after we herald it with another miracle, this one in New York. They are related, you see, all the signs and portents. The Last Trump shall sound, and the world will be the better for it, if less populated when all is said and done. And I shall be infinitely richer and, may I say, happier. My life's work will be fulfilled, and although I have absolutely no intention of dying anytime soon, I shall be able to die happy when the appointed hour and place comes."

"Your own appointment in Samarra."

"I will have her back. Do you understand me? I will have her back. Her place is with me. She knows that. I know that."

Mlle. Derrida decided to ignore that. "Where will we go? After . . . whatever it is that is going to happen."

"It is enough for me to know. Now, leave me, for I need to ponder all these things in my heart, as the Bible says."

"The Bible was talking about Mary, sir."

"Precisely," said Skorzeny, signaling for some music and closing his eyes.

She knew just the thing. After all, they were going to the ancient land of Zoroaster.

A minute later, the plane filled with the sounds of Richard Strauss's *Also sprach Zarathustra*.

CHAPTER FORTY

New York City

Jake Sinclair sat in his office near Times Square and admired Principessa Stanley. The woman was looking more attractive all the time, damn it. He loved the way she moved, the way she used her hands, her wide mouth, her amazing figure; except for her hair, which presumably was still growing back in, she was a work of art. Not that she would stay that way forever; no woman ever did. Women were like fruit or flowers. You had to know just when to pluck them.

That was about as original a thought as Jake Sinclair could muster at this moment as he watched the delicious Ms. Stanley deliver her report. Surreptitiously, he glanced at the clock. He was meeting Angela Hassett in her private suite at the Waldorf in less than half an hour, but it wouldn't take him that long to get across town, and beside Principessa hadn't yet—

Hold on. What had she said to him back in L.A., the first time they met? That if he ever kept her waiting again she'd kill him? And she probably would, too.

"I'm sorry, Ms. Stanley," he said, rising. "But I have a

most urgent appointment across town that I simply can't be late for."

She stopped in midsentence, switched gears. "I get it. Life or death, huh?"

She didn't know the half of it. "I wonder if we might continue this conversation later today . . ." Might as well go for it. "Say, over dinner?"

She gave him a look. No, she gave him *that* look. Then she made him wait. The bitch . . .

"That would be . . . wonderful, Mr. Sinclair."

"Jake. Shall we say seven-thirty at Los Pescadores?"

Her face fell as she consulted her smartphone. "I'm afraid I can't do seven-thirty. . . . Would eight-fifteen be okay? There's a couple of things I have to move around."

"Pick you up?"

"Meet you there."

He got up and put on his jacket. "What were you saying about this mysterious Mr. Grant?" he inquired. He hadn't really been listening at all. But she knew that.

"Tell you tonight," she said.

Jake Sinclair was feeling pretty good about his chances when he got to the Waldorf. He was five minutes early, thank God.

He took the private elevator up to the tower where Lucky Luciano once had lived. Those were the days in old New York, he thought to himself, when real men walked the streets of Manhattan, a gun on one hip and a flask on the other. Today, the city felt like a Puritan concentration camp, with sin banished and only the wide-bodied tourists to tell you that this had once been a city of giants instead of financiers. The sooner he was back in L.A., the better.

Unless, of course, he got a better offer from Ms. Stanley. Then he was sure he could find a reason to spend more time in the city and leave Jenny II to the tender mercies of her tennis instructor and the pool boy. The only thing wrong with Ms. Stanley was that her first name wasn't Jenny, but he figured that body was worth having to learn a new name. He was at the door of her suite—the suite of the next President of the United States. JFK would have been so proud.

Angela opened the door on the first ring. My, she did look rather good. "We have a problem," she said.

He stepped inside. No kiss, no hug, nothing. Fine. His date with Ms. Stanley was starting to look even better. "What's the beef?"

"Something's up. I can't tell you what it is because I don't know and anyway that's your job, finding out what's up. That's why you employ all those horrible reporters who are always bugging me about something or other when I'm just trying to get my message out. Why do you let them do that?"

"Angela, we have to pretend to play fair, at least in the news columns and on the news broadcasts. On the opinion shows and the op-ed pages, you know you have our fullest support and of course in the blogosphere there are no standards at all. In fact, we've been hammering that son of a bitch Tyler pretty relentlessly. Why, just the other day I wrote our lead editorial—you remember, the one that was headlined 'Still More Mush from the Feckless Wimp.' "

That was a lie. Sinclair couldn't write a shopping list if you spotted him the milk, butter, and eggs, but it was his idea, more or less.

"I don't care. Anyway, something's up. Tyler's acting weird—that's what my spies inside the White House are saying. He's been having secret meetings. He even left the White House the other day and went somewhere in the suburbs—he covered his tracks pretty well, so nobody's quite sure where he went."

"Maybe to see a girlfriend?" suggested Sinclair.

"That eunuch? Don't be silly. Anyway, I want you to get your best reporter on it right away. Whatever he's up to, we need to know about it. We can't let him pull one of those October Surprises. Why don't you put that big girl of yours on it, you know, the toothy one with the boobs and the funny name?"

Sinclair couldn't believe his luck. "Principessa Stanley," he said, trying to control his voice.

"That's the one." Finally, she softened a little. She was wearing a bathrobe, and now let it fall open a little to keep his eye on the ball. "You know, Jake, that really was a stroke of genius on your part, bumping her all the way up to the national broadcast after that creep scalped her in Central Park. I mean, who wouldn't want to tune in and see the chick that some pervert practically buried alive, and now here she is, shorn but sassy. Real triumph-of-the-human-spirit stuff. Your shitty movie studios ought to be turning out more pictures like that instead of those fucking cartoons and that anti-war crap. America hates a loser, Jake. Remember that."

"You know," said Sinclair, seeing an opening, "she was still in the office when I left. Why don't I go back there right now and brief her? We've got—what is it?—a few weeks before the election. Plenty of time."

Angela saw her opening as well. This idiot was beginning to bore her with his mindless, solipsistic prattle. "That's a great idea. I'm kind of tired anyway, and you know I have that big speech tomorrow in Madison Square Garden: 'A New Vision for America.' The crowd loves that shit, but I need to be sharp."

She moved forward and let her robe fall all the way open. She brought his mouth to hers and kissed him almost as if she meant it. That would keep him in line, and coming back for more.

Jake Sinclair left a happy man. He had two angles to play and time to kill. Instead of going back to the office, he thought he'd take in a movie, just like a civilian. One of the cartoons would do just fine. With what he was sure was in

store for him tonight, cartoons were just about all he could
handle.

Three hours later he was at his customary table at Los
Pescadores. He liked being recognized—not by the public,
because that was always a pain in the ass, but by waiters and,
more important, the maitre d's. And then there she was,
sweeping in, and he forgot all about being recognized.

For Principessa Stanley was instantly recognized. He'd
had no idea what a celebrity she was now in New York—
everybody in the place knew her, wanted to shake her hand,
get a pat on the head, maybe get a picture with her. He hadn't
thought of that. If he was going to make a play for Principessa Stanley tonight, suggest they get to know each other a
bit better back at his place, he was going to have to play it
plenty cool. No footsie, no hand holding. From the outside,
it had to look like all business—kind of like a secret code
between them. Too bad he didn't know a damn thing about
codes.

Dinner was miserable. He couldn't taste his food. He kept
looking at her like a love-struck calf. Other big shots could
get away with it, cheating on their wives very publicly, being
seen with beautiful women in strange cities, and no one
thought the less of them for it. A little whiff of the lothario,
in fact, was a positive benefit for certain politicians—con-
quests rumored or imagined just burnished their luster as
lovable rogues.

So he was the most surprised guy in the joint when, after
they got the check—the prices here really were outrageous,
but luckily the company was paying for it—she leaned over,
very casual-like, and suggested that they go back to her
place for a nightcap—in separate cars, of course.

Good. At least one of them knew code.

He got there about twenty minutes after she did, as she had requested. She wanted to get out of her work clothes, change into something more comfortable, get the champagne out of the fridge. All good signs. This was going to be his lucky night.

He had the driver let him off half a block away and around the corner. Nobody needed to know where he was. He didn't need any whispers about power imbalances or workplace violation—hell, he owned the damn workplace. This was a simple consenting-adult transaction. He would help his lover win the presidency, Principessa would get the story of a lifetime, everybody would get laid—no harm, no foul.

It was one of those private elevators that opened right into the flat. The apartment was spectacular—not as spectacular as his, of course, because he always prided himself on the best of everything. But it was pretty darn good just the same, two thousand square feet of living space overlooking the East River near Gracie Mansion, with a windswept terrace that made you forget the automobile noise from the FDR far below. He must be paying her too much.

She was wearing . . . well, not much. Everything he had imagined about that bod . . . well, as they said in the movie business, it was all right up there on the screen.

He took in his arms and kissed her, ran his hands over her. She responded in kind; good Lord, she was powerful. They knocked each other around the terrace, then toppled back into the living room. He had just gotten his pants down around his ankles when the flash of a cell-phone camera caught his bare ass high, wide, and handsome, and he knew he was fucked. And not in a good way.

"I'm sorry, Jake," said Principessa, pulling herself together, "but you ought to know better than to try and screw the help."

Sinclair couldn't see the man sitting in the darkness, but

he could hear him chuckle. It was a low, sinister exhalation and it frightened him. This was no ordinary wronged lover or professional gumshoe, sent by Jenny II to see where he was parking his dick when he was out of town. This guy was scary.

"Whatever she's paying you, I'll double it," he whined. "Triple it. Name your price."

"*She*'s not paying me anything," said the man. Sinclair could tell he had risen from the sofa on which he'd been sitting and was walking toward him. He wasn't at all sure that he wanted to see his face. He looked around for Principessa, but she was nowhere to be seen.

"Who are you working for? What's he paying you?"

"More like a 'they,' " said the man, still approaching. "But don't worry, even you can't afford my fee."

He had his pants back on now, and was feeling a little braver. "That's bullshit. Do you know who I am?" He realized what a stupid question that was the instant it came out of his mouth.

"Your fly is still open, so zip yourself. There's a lady present, or have you forgotten?"

"You're fired, Ms. Stanley," he said.

"Oh, I doubt that very much, Mr. Sinclair," the man said. "In fact, I would say that you're working for us now. You see, I have a job that I very much want to keep, and I need your cooperation and assistance to help me to keep it. It's worth a lot to me, so I and Principessa and several other very important people would really fucking appreciate it if you would become part of the team."

"What if I don't?"

The man held up the cell camera and illuminated the screen. Yup, that was his bare behind all right, about to slip the sausage to a woman whose face couldn't be seen. There was no way out but to play along.

"What do you want me to do?"

"Very simple. Nothing."

"Nothing?"

"Nothing, as in neutral. You stop pounding on Tyler. You tell your papers and your crappy cable channels and your shit-assed websites that, as we enter the final phase of the campaign, you have decided, as president and CEO of Sinclair Holdings and Sinclair Worldwide Media, that henceforth true patriotism demands that the media act fairly. No more taking sides. No more rooting for one team or the other. No more fabricating documents, reporting innuendo, and imagining total crap and then rushing it onto the TV or into print. Your days as a kingmaker are over. *Capisce?*"

God, he hated that expression. New Yorkers said it all the time, like they were all goombah-wannabes, auditioning for crime dramas. "Yes, I understand."

The man was standing over him now, very close, but he still couldn't see his face. "Now, you're probably thinking, 'Fuck this guy. The minute I get out of here, I'm going to unleash my whole fucking empire on this cocksucker, and make him rue the day he was born. I am going to unleash hell, sic the dogs on him, finish him in this world and in all universes, known and unknown.' That about right?"

"Maybe. Can I stand up now?"

"Sure. Let me give you a hand." A powerful arm reached out and hauled him to his feet.

"I'm sorry, Jake," said Principessa, returning dressed and decent. "Looks like they got us both by the nuts."

"That's right," said the man, stepping out of the shadows and into the dim light. "You're both working for me now— for me and the President of the United States. Do we have a deal?"

Sinclair recognized him right away. It was Thomas Byrne, deputy director of the FBI, and very much a man you didn't want to fuck with. Byrne had put in the ground more opponents, whether criminal or political, than Crazy Horse at the Little Bighorn. A major bad-ass.

"We have a deal," said Sinclair.

Principessa walked over to Tom. For a second, Sinclair wasn't sure what she was going to do. She looked like she might slap him.

Then she threw her arms around his neck and picked up with him right where she had left off with Jake. Only this time, she meant it.

"Why don't you let yourself out, pal?" said Byrne. "Ms. Stanley and I are going to be busy for a while."

Byrne must have already summoned the elevator because it was right there, waiting for him.

"I'll be in touch," shouted Byrne from the bedroom. "Remember, Jake—you can run but you can't hide. I know where Laughlin Park is, and you can bet that if I do, other folks do too. So keep your nose clean and your head down and wait until your country needs you before you say another damn thing."

Jake Sinclair could hear them going at it as he sheepishly tiptoed into the elevator. He'd be on his way back to L.A. tomorrow morning. There would be no dossier released in dribs and drabs, no October Surprise from the Sinclair media empire. Angela Hassett was on her own.

Jenny II was starting to look pretty good after all.

CHAPTER FORTY-ONE

Over Iran

The MH-6H Little Bird zipped across the desert, flying low and flying fast. It had been stripped of its Hellfire missiles and its M230 Chain Gun and carried just two passengers, one of them the pilot, the other a man dressed all in black. They had taken off from the deck of the *Eisenhower*, stopped to refuel in Iraq near Amarah, and then dipped under the Iranian air defenses and ran like hell. The MH-6M was known in the trade as the Killer Egg; it didn't look particularly fearsome, but it had a maximum speed of one hundred fifty-two knots and a range of four hundred thirty kilometers at an altitude of five thousand feet. That wasn't quite enough to get Devlin all the way to where he wanted to go, but he was a big boy. Better to get him past Borūjerd and send him on his way.

They said nothing on the flight. Everything that needed to be said had already been said. Either they would make it or they wouldn't. They had a plan, they had backup, they had the personnel, and they had each other. They'd been in combat many times before.

They were going to make it.

Danny brought the Little Bird down, to just a few feet off the high desert floor. Devlin rappelled down, hit the ground, and started running. With Devlin off-loaded, Danny didn't bother to look down or chart his progress: Inshallah, he would be all right. If not, there was an end to it.

For a Muslim state, the Iranian air defenses were fairly sophisticated, but beatable. Since the Russians had pulled the plug on selling the Islamic Republic its S-300 anti-aircraft missiles, it was largely confined to radar, rockets, and its own air force. But eternal vigilance only seemed to be the price of liberty in free countries; in the countries of the Middle East, sloth and corruption ruled the day, and there were plenty of holes in the sky to fly through if only you knew where to look.

Danny knew where to look. He'd been flying in this territory since the first Gulf War, knew the capabilities of both the systems and the men who operated them. You never wanted to underestimate your enemy, but his regard for the Muslim capacity for war was low. The culture prized and rewarded familial connections and tribal loyalty over the alien notion of the nation-state, and while Iran had a proud history stretching back thousands of years, its sense of national purpose had been destroyed by the Islamic Revolution and subordinated to the *ummah*. With its next-door enemy of Iraq neutralized, thanks to the United States, its guard was down. Which is why they wouldn't be looking for what was coming.

He checked for bogies. Nothing tracking, nothing locking on. No visible. The events of the past few days, the mysterious apparitions, had the country's undivided attention. He was, as the saying went, an ant in the afterbirth.

Good. He'd be back in Iraq in no time. And then the real fun would begin.

* * *

As he approached the first village he saw, Devlin slowed down. He had already changed out of his camouflage and into the local costume. He had been very careful about this, for there were distinct differences in dress among the towns and cities of Iran, just as there were differences among accents, and one could as easily give you away as the other. Colloquial Tehrani would do just fine.

Sir Richard Burton had always been one of his heroes. Burton, the great English explorer, translator, and linguist. Burton, the indispensable man of the Empire, who had fought and loved and traveled from India to central Africa to Brazil to the Mormon country. Burton, one of only a handful of infidels to make the *hajj* to Mecca and Medina and live to write of it. He had disguised himself as a Pashtun, which meant his speech would not be subject to the same scrutiny as that of an Arab. Still, it was always the little things that gave you away—Burton was nearly caught out when he lifted his robes to take a leak standing up instead of squatting on the ground like a native.

"O pilgrim, have you heard of the holy miracle at Qom?" asked the driver of the car, an ancient Russian Chaika that had somehow found its way here. One thing about countries in this part of the world: it was easy to hitch a ride, even if you sometimes had to share the vehicle with a dozen or so others, some of whom rode on the roof. "Seyed Khorasani has proclaimed himself, and the Occultation is nearing an end. Allah be praised."

"This is why I am on the road to Qom myself in this moment."

"Imagine—the Holy Prophet himself, may peace and blessings be upon him, has appeared in the skies about the holy city of Qom. Surely this is a sign from Allah that the Coming is near."

"Surely it is."

"And where will you be staying in Qom?"

Great. A garrulous driver. He did not want to take the conversation down this road. "I will leave that to the holy will of Allah, that I might find appropriate lodgings."

The driver shook his head and made clucking noise. "Ah, but this will never do. The town is filled up. I am told myself that there is not an empty inn for miles around. Truly, brother, Allah must smile upon you in your hour of need."

"Allah always helps those who believe in His holy word, and live by His holy book."

The driver look at him warily, as if wondering whether he could trust him. Then he looked into the backseat, in case anyone might be lurking there to overhear, even though it was his own car. "But sometimes," he said in a low voice, "Allah must be assisted in the most trifling of matters, and surely, brother, lodgings are a trifling matter when compared with the holy miracles that are sure to come."

"Surely."

Now a big smile broke across the driver's swarthy face. They were on highway 56 from Arāk to Qom, maybe an hour, maybe less, maybe two. You never knew in Iran. "In that case, fellow believer, this is your lucky day. For as sure as there is no God but Allah and that Mohammed is his Holy Prophet, just as sure is it that I have a brother-in-law dwelling within the sacred precincts of the holy city of Qom, very close to the sacred mosque at Jamkaran, and for a small sum I am certain that he will be able to accommodate you handsomely."

The driver dropped his voice and leaned toward Devlin. "Might I also add, that his wife is renowned throughout the province for the excellence of her cooking, and his daughters are acknowledged by all as the fairest maidens of virtue in all of Iran!"

"Then you have made me an offer impossible for me to

refuse," said Devlin, taking out a fistful of rials and handing them over. The driver smiled at his great good fortune.

Excellent. He was getting a ride right into the heart of the city, and he was complicit with his new best friend, the driver, in a mutually beneficial transaction that had just involved the exchange of money. By the time-honored customs of the Islamic world, he and the driver were now informal allies against the state, and he could rely on him—except under duress—to do what he said he would do.

They rode largely in silence the rest of the way. The driver, having accomplished his mission of earning some money, had nothing more to say, which was just fine with Devlin. The less he had to speak the better. The more he could concentrate on the task ahead, the better. The closer he got to her, the better.

There—up ahead. The holy city of Qom.

Faster. Please, faster. But he could not let his impatience show. In this country, everything unfolded in Allah's good time. It would be like raising your robe to pee.

"I am most grateful to you, brother, for extending the generosity of your family to me. This is a kindness of which Allah would approve, for is not hospitality among the duties of every Muslim?"

"It is indeed, brother."

"And does not every Muslim have the sacred obligation to repay such kindness in kind?"

They were in the city now. Deep in an interior pocket, he could feel the Android vibrate.

"He does, brother."

"Then so shall I repay you. I know not the hour, but assuredly that hour shall come."

"The house of my brother-in-law is not far now," said the driver.

"You have my security," said Devlin, "but now I fear I must ask you a favor that no Muslim can refuse another. I wish first to be taken to the holy mosque, that I might see the wonders with my own eyes, and offer my prayers to the Twelfth Imam."

"Of course," said the driver, turning right between Qom University and Mofid University and heading east.

There, up ahead—Jamkaran.

The specially modified Android vibrated again.

The car pulled up near the mosque. Devlin tried to control his excitement as he made his dignified and stately way from the car. "In the name of Allah, I thank you, brother."

"And I you, pilgrim," scribbling down an address. "Give this to anyone in town and they will direct you to the home of Mohammed Radan."

Devlin took the piece of paper with great dignity. "Go in peace. And now, I, too, must go."

"May peace attend you, brother," said the driver.

Start your engine. Go in peace, go with God—but go.

At last, after God's own eternity, the car swung north and disappeared.

Devlin ducked into an alley and bowed, as if he were reciting a prayer before approaching the mosque. In his crouch he was able to see his messages:

The first was from Seelye. He read the instructions and permitted himself a small moment of triumph. If he knew his man, Skorzeny, he was way ahead on that one already; the STUXNET virus he could use for backup.

He read the second message—it was from her.

HELP

CHAPTER FORTY-TWO

Tehran

"I am sorry, but Col. Zarin is in Qom. And no infidel may travel to the holy city. It is the law."

Skorzeny was not used to being refused. He looked at the customs functionary standing before him in his comic-opera uniform and said: "It is not the law."

"I am sorry, but for you, on this day, it is the law." The man turned to Mlle. Derrida. "For you too as well, missus."

"I'm nobody's missus," she replied in French.

The customs man grinned and spoke to her in rapid-fire French. There began a prolonged prattle that lasted until Skorzeny could stand it no longer. "Please," he said in English. "I have important business."

The customs official once again made a great pretense of studying their travel documents. He double-checked whether the exit visas from Azerbaijan were in order (they were) and whether the proper visas had been obtained for entry into the Islamic Republic (they were as well). He could find nothing wrong with the legal formalities.

"I am happy to tell you that your documents are completely satisfactory. Now, what is your permanent address in Tehran and on what business do you journey here?"

"For the last time," said Skorzeny, "we are here at the personal invitation of Col. Navid Zarin of the Revolutionary Guards. I understand that he is in Qom, and so it is to Qom that we must go. Therefore I would appreciate it if you stamp our papers with the appropriate stamp and let us be on our way."

The man look chagrined. Disconsolate. "I am sorry, mister, but this thing is not allowed to be done at the present time. Perhaps inshallah things will change in the coming days. But for right now, no."

"I would like to speak with your superior. Is that possible?"

"Yes, of course, sir. I will summon him in this moment." The man pressed an emergency buzzer under the customs table. "See, he comes now."

"Thank you," said Skorzeny, walking over to meet him.

The customs official looked at Mlle. Derrida. "What brings you to the Islamic Republic, missus?" he asked. "It is a very great honor for me to meet so fine a lady."

"Have you read *La Disparition* by Perec?" she asked.

"No, missus—should I?"

"You might want to consider it," she said.

Skorzeny was on his way back. "Let's go," he said, holding out his hand for their passports.

"Is everything now in order, mister?" asked the customs man.

"Indeed," said Skorzeny, taking Mlle. Derrida by the arm and leading her away. As they walked they could hear the superior shouting at the customs man, whose life was about to become very unpleasant.

"I wouldn't want to be in that little fellow's shoes," said Mlle. Derrida. "I told him he should take off and vanish like the letter *e*, but I guess he thought I was kidding."

"More likely he was entranced by your beauty, cold though it is," retorted Skorzeny. He pointed to a black limousine with its engine idling in front of the terminal. No terrorism worries here, he thought to himself—what would they be afraid of? Irish nuns? The Swedish Bikini Team?

They got into the backseat. The driver stubbed out his cigarette and the car pulled away from the curb, darting right into the traffic flow without so much as a backward glance.

"What did you say to him?" asked Mlle. Derrida.

"Nothing. I paid him."

"And he got the message?"

"Money speaks a universal language, Mlle. Derrida, especially when wedded to fear."

He pressed a button and the partition slid into place. The car would be bugged, of course, but at least they could pretend they didn't know that. To make their conversation a little more secure, Skorzeny switched to Russian, which Mlle. Derrida, being Polish on her mother's side, also spoke fluently.

"The colonel was suddenly called away to Qom. This in itself is not surprising, since Qom is, as the Americans say, where the action is going to be. Which means, judging from his behavior, that Miss Harrington is also in Qom. How, I don't know, but she always was a very resourceful woman. I admire her pluck and her savvy. Nevertheless, she must be forced to admit once more the error of her ways."

"Which means?"

"Which means that I cannot let the Iranians have their way with her. If there is any punishment to be meted out, I should do the meting. I cannot bear the thought of these animals' hands on her."

"Nor can I," said Mlle. Derrida. Was that a quizzical look from him? But desire and empathy knew no bounds.

"And, of course, we have other work to do. Important work. My life's work, in fact. How I wish to share it with her, to have her witness the moment of my greatest triumph. Then, and only then, I will kill her for the grievous harm she has done to me."

Mlle. Derrida raised an objection. "To kill her, you're going to have to convince them to let you have her. And why should they? You've already cheated them out of Maryam. It seems to me, M. Skorzeny, that your Col. Zarin is going to be very unhappy with you." A thought struck her. "What if he is using us as pawns as well? What use to him are you—alone, in his country and in his power?" She was beginning to be frightened now. "Why should he let us go? Why not hold us hostage, for ransom?" She started to sob quietly. France was never so beautiful.

Skorzeny put his arm around her, and she did not object. Ordinarily she hated it when he touched her, but things were different now.

But what if she was right? Of Zarin's loyalties he was fairly certain, because there was a very sizable bank account waiting for him in the Caymans, but in this part of the world one never knew. Zarin could double-cross him out of some misguided religious fervor. The mullahs could be holding his family hostage. There could be some residual anger over Kohanloo, although he could point out that Kohanloo's name never surfaced in the inquiry and that the Islamic Republic was in no way implicated in the attack on Times Square. Anything was possible.

That was where Devlin came in. The man had been fool enough to entrust his computer to maid Maryam, rigging it to harm Skorzeny. But he had no intention of having the accursed thing explode in his face, either literally or figuratively. He had a better plan.

He would trade it for Miss Harrington.

Let the Iranians have it. Let them deal with it. Whatever damage it was programmed to do to him and his financial empire, it would have no effect on them. They could take it

apart, reverse-engineer it, break right into the heart of the Black
Widow back in Fort Meade, worm their way into the highest
levels of NSA and CSS cryptology, and destroy the Americans from within. They could not hope to defeat them on the
field of battle, and even public opinion was finally beginning
to turn against them, as the pet media poodles—who leapt to
the defense of any "oppressed minority," no matter how un-
oppressed, vindictive, or malicious they in fact actually
were—finally began to notice that their own necks were
being sized for the chopping block.

His hand moved to the briefcase, in which he kept the
computer, as if to reassure himself that it was still there.

"It's all right," he said. "Trust me."

Only two things mattered to him now. The first was the
full realization of his great vision: the setting-off of the great
religious and cultural war that would finally destroy the
West, and all that he asked was a moment of revelation at the
end, a moment when the people of the West would look at
him and see the man who put finally them out of their misery.

The second was Miss Harrington. She must share in his
apotheosis, and then expiate her sins.

We are discovered. Save yourself. How perfectly appo-
site, how resonant. One link in the chain of doom.

There was Qom, dead ahead.

CHAPTER FORTY-THREE

New York City

The sun rose, clear and bright. The October sky had kicked away the clouds and left the heavens azure—the perfect setting for a great miracle.

She appeared over Manhattan, nearer the East River than the Hudson, but visible from Queens and Brooklyn and Jersey, too, hovering with that same ineffable look of sadness on her face. It was the same vision the children at Garabandal had seen, the Muslims and Christians and Jews and the international news media at Zeitoun had seen. The same image that the poor Nigerians had seen, before they went at each other with weapons, before the long-standing conflicts of East and West, of the *dar al-Islam* and the *dar al-Harb,* had finally come into irrevocable conflict. Before war broke out in the Philippines.

And now she was here, floating above the capital city of the infidels.

It wasn't like in the movies. Taxis did not suddenly slam on the brakes and cause multiple-car pileups. Women did not start screaming on the sidewalk. Whole office buildings did not suddenly empty and people did not rush into the streets or to the tops of tall buildings. Instead, they looked out their windows, or up at the sky, and wondered.

Many, maybe most, did not credit their senses. It had to be some kind of hoax, an optical illusion. Others blessed themselves and prayed. The city's large Hispanic community was especially devotional. Someone set up a makeshift altar in the middle of Flatbush Avenue, and thousands of devout Haitians attended Mass on the spot.

The cardinal archbishop of New York took to the Fifth Avenue steps of St. Patrick's Cathedral and urged calm. So did the mayor, from his private island in the Caribbean, where he was vacationing with his mistress. The cable channels put the vision in a box and kept it on the screen at all times. Live cams streamed the image via the blogosphere across the globe.

The image took shape high in the sky in the early morning. At first it looked like nothing, mere light among light in the sky. Gradually, however, it began to assume human form. It took a while for everyone to realize that slowly, imperceptibly, it was gradually moving toward the earth, growing larger as it came into view. The progress was very slow, but it was steady. The Virgin was descending toward the earth.

Lannie Saleh, Celina Selena, and Alonzo Schmidt saw none of this. Dr. Leopold had given them carte blanche to inspect the hospital and had assigned a few trusted people to act as point men. They had to tear the place apart without alarming anybody.

"It needs a power source," Lannie was explaining. "These things can't work without electricity, without something to act as the trigger. The good news is, it doesn't seem to be attached to one. The bad news is, it may not need to be. Some of the Russian designs have a transmitter that signals when its internal battery runs low and it's thought—remember, until today, we had no proof that such devices even existed, except for the testimony of a Russian defector—that it can somehow be powered externally—"

"It can."

Everyone turned to see the speaker. It was Tom Byrne, accompanied by Principessa Stanley.

Tom moved to the front with the ease of a natural leader. "Thanks, Lannie," he said. "I'll take it from here."

"What's she doing here?" objected Lannie.

"She's getting the story," replied Tom. "You got a problem with that?" He turned to the group. "We know that a psychopath named Raymond Crankheit left some sort of device in the hospital during the attack on New York. We also know that this same psychopath attacked Ms. Stanley here, buried her alive behind the Metropolitan Museum, and damn near scalped her. If anybody deserves to be in on the finish, it's she. So that's the last I want to hear about it."

"Who are you?" asked Celina.

"I am Thomas Byrne, deputy director of the FBI. And these are my people." Into the room came a dozen special agents, each one looking exactly (as Celina Selena admitted to herself later) the way everyone pictured an FBI special agent looking. "These men and women are trained in this, and they'll find the bomb. That's not my worry. My worry is that the bomb will find us first."

"But what about the trigger?" asked Lannie.

"Come with me, please," said Tom. Then, turning to his team: "Get started. From the rate of descent, it looks like we have five, maybe six hours."

He left Principessa behind with the bomb squad and led Lannie, Celina, and Alonzo out onto the street and pointed to the sky. Celina gasped and crossed herself. "Damn," muttered Alonzo. Lannie didn't know what to say.

"She may look like the Virgin freaking Mary," said Tom, "but she's our trigger. She's a holographic laser projection coming from the surface of the moon—no, it's not originating there, little green men aren't attacking. It's a relay from the reflector shields the Apollo astronauts left behind, back in the days when this country actually got a bang for its buck, instead of just spreading the wealth around and pissing it away. She's coming not to save humanity but to blow the shit out of the city of New York. And that's just not going to fucking happen."

"How do we stop it?" asked Lannie.

"We don't."

"What?" said Celina.

At that moment, a car pulled up in front of the hospital. A man and a woman got out. Celina recognized the man right away.

The man walked right up to the group, like he was used to being in charge.

"Hello, boss," said Lannie.

"Hello, Frankie," said Tom Byrne. "Keeping that temper of yours in check?"

"Cut the crap, Tom," said Francis Byrne. "We're only working together because we have to. Because you fucked me and turned one of my best men against me. Because you ran out on our city and took your fancy job in Washington while I've stayed here, year in and year out."

"Great job you did last year," said Tom. "How many people died again?"

And then he was on the seat of his pants on the sidewalk, his jaw smarting from the blow his younger brother had just delivered. "Say that again and I'll shoot you myself, right here, in front all these witnesses. I'll go to jail for murder, because I won't miss and you know I won't miss. And not even your boy Saleh here will try and stop me."

Frankie turned to Lannie. His eyes reflected the pain of betrayal. "I knew it was you, Lannie. What I don't know is why."

"I was just . . . just trying . . ." He looked over to Tom to help him out. "He's your brother isn't he? They're threatening my family, Frankie."

"We're your family, too, Lannie," said Frankie. "That's what I've been trying to make you understand. That's why I took your ass off the streets of Brooklyn and made a detective out of you. I saw me in you, kid—this is New York, and we all need a rabbi. We're all tribes here in New York, but the thing that made this city great is that the tribes learned to work with each other, learned to embrace each other—they realized that tribes are just like individuals, and that while you can't choose your tribe, you can choose to make a new family. That's what we all did, the Irish, the Jews, the Italians. It's why Sy Sheinberg was a father to me, after my father—our father, Tommy—was shot down from behind in cold blood and they never found the killers. I've been looking for those fucking dirtbags all my life and you know what? I'm never going to find them, but I'm going to die trying. I thought I was a father to you, Lannie, just the way Sy Sheinberg was my father. Ethnicity doesn't mean shit. Somebody's threatening you or your family, then they're threatening my family, too, and in New York that means I have a license to fuck them up two times—once because they've got it coming and twice just for laughs. Because this is my town, and I'm still the sheriff."

He looked at Hope. "We're going to get them. All of them. Isn't that right, Mrs. Gardner?"

Everyone turned to look at the woman who had arrived with Byrne. Behind her, still high in the sky, floated the Virgin Mary, slowly coming down to earth.

"Right now," she said, "my . . . husband . . . and another man are in the Middle East. What they're doing is very dangerous. We don't know if they'll come back alive. But they're there to get to the source of all this, and to put an end to it—once and for all. And we have to help them. So please don't fight. Please, everybody, let's work together."

Frankie held out his hand to Tom and helped him to his feet. "Peace?" he asked.

Tom dusted himself off. "No peace," he said. "Truce."

"Good enough," said Frankie. He took a reading of the apparition's location in the sky and turned to Hope. "Relay these coordinates to your . . . husband. Even if we find the bomb, we might not be able to disarm it in time, so this is the mission timer. If they don't get the job done . . . then my city dies."

"I won't let you down," said Hope.

Byrne put a hand on her shoulder. "Let's get to work, people."

CHAPTER FORTY-FOUR

Qom

"Why are you alone, sister?"

These were not words Maryam wished to hear, especially from a member of the morality police. The Iranian vice cops—"vice" in this case applying to the very existence of women—were not as notorious as the *mutaween* of Saudi Arabia, or the Taliban of Afghanistan, but they were plenty dangerous.

She tensed as she answered. "But I am modestly dressed, worshipping at the sacred mosque."

They moved closer to her, boxing her in, forcing her into an alley. Maryam glanced around and saw there was nobody else in sight. Whatever was going to happen was going to have to happen fast.

"Where is your husband, sister?"

"I have . . . he is away, on state business. But he will be here soon, that I can assure you."

"Then where is your father?"

"My father, may Allah bless him, is dead."

"Your brother?"

"Alas, I have no brothers."

The two police looked at each other. In Iran, with one of the highest proportions of young people in the world, everybody had brothers and sisters. She was obviously lying.

"Sister," said the first cop, "I am afraid we are compelled by force of holy law to request that you accompany us."

Maryam kept edging backward, into the alley, away from the crowds. She knew the religious police were lightly armed, with knives for protection and sticks with which to beat helpless women. This is what came of a country that had reduced some of the proudest, most glamorous women in the world into servile, cringing slaves. The men had no fear.

They were about to learn different. They were about to take a very fast trip from the seventh century to the twenty-first. And they weren't going to like it very much.

"Perhaps," she said, "we can discuss this in a more private place."

One of the dirty little secrets of Iran was that whores flourished everywhere. Probably not since Dickensian London had the world's oldest profession commanded such a large part of a nation's economy, or its attention, or its fantasy life. She need not say anything, merely hint. They would get the message. They would take the bait.

The men grinned at each other. Fringe benefits were part of the job. A doorway would be good enough.

Maryam took a deep breath and said a silent prayer. This would have to be fast and lethal.

She moved back into a doorway, letting them come to her, feeling their hands on her body. She needed them to do just that, to drop their guard, to reach for her with a repressed passion that would dull their other senses until it was too late.

Closer . . . closer . . .

She raised her veil as one of them moved in to kiss her, and her hand strayed to the privates of the second cop. She could feel the first man's mouth on hers, his tongue seeking hers, feel the tumescent excitement of the second man. . . .

Now.

She bit the tongue off and wrenched the other man down, hard. They both screamed, but their screams were immediately cut off as she drew the knife from the scabbard of the first cop and slashed his throat. Gurgling, he fell into the second man, who was still in agony. As he put up his hands to fend off the falling body, she plunged the knife into his heart. As he died, she saw the look of disbelief in his eyes, that a woman had done this to him, and then a look of bliss, as if all his suspicions of the evil sex were, by his death, finally justified.

"Fuck you," she said in English.

She pulled both the bodies into the doorway as best she could. They'd be found almost immediately, that she knew. She wiped the knife clean of fingerprints and placed it back in its sheath.

She was wet with blood, but the blood would not show against the black of the chador, and in this heat it would dry quickly. She just had to stay away from people for a while. And wait . . . wait for him.

And then, in the greatest miracle of her life, for which she would forever give thanks and praise to Allah, there he was. She knew him immediately, saw right through his disguise, knew by the cock of his head and the way he walked, the way he moved, that it could be no other. That at last he was come, and that she was whole again, and that no matter what now happened she knew the truth.

He moved toward her quickly but without haste. Still nobody around.

"Hello, Frank," she said quietly.

"My name's not Frank," he said.

"I know it isn't," she said. "Everything you've told me since the day we met was a lie."

"Would you have had it any other way?"

"How did you find me?

In answer, he reached inside her chador, until he found what he was looking for. The smartphone with which she'd signaled him. "Thank Allah for GPS," he said.

"You're late."

"And they're dead," he said, looking at the corpses. "So let's ankle."

"Home?"

He gave that look of his that she loved so well. The one that said, *Are you kidding?* "You are home, remember? And he's here." She didn't have to ask who "he" was.

"He's looking for her," she replied. He didn't have to ask who "she" was.

"Then I guess we both have jobs to do."

"I'm not going to leave her."

"That's what I just said."

"There's more to it, right?"

"Would I be here if there wasn't?" That was the answer she expected, but didn't want. "We haven't got much time and we have a lot to do, including not getting ourselves killed and saving the world, not necessarily in that order, so let's get a move on."

"Where?"

He brought his face close to hers. "As long as we're to-gether," he said, "Qom is as good a place as any."

"You double-crossed me, you infidel bastard," said Col. Zarin.

"I am an infidel in many faiths," replied Skorzeny coolly, "so please do not think that your cheap superstitious impre-cations can frighten me."

They were in the heart of the nuclear complex on the out-skirts of Qom, deep inside a mountain, where the uranium-enrichment process had been taking place right under the noses of the U.N. inspectors, who preferred to look in the direction of the known facility at Natanz, rather than anywhere else, just in case they might find something. Emanuel Skorzeny had no illusions that he was allowed admittance because he was a welcome guest of the Islamic Republic. He was here because they were business partners, and the minute they ceased being business partners, his privileges would be revoked with extreme prejudice.

And he had a business deal with Col. Zarin.

"I have another proposition for you," he said.

"I am not interested in another proposition," replied the colonel. "You have used me, and jeopardized my future and the future of my family. They have my voice on tape, threatening this Detective Saleh, may Allah curse him and his seed. I should kill you for what you have done."

"Not for what *I* have done, Col. Zarin. For what *he* has done. And I am about to deliver him—and her—to you."

"Why should I believe you?" Col. Zarin looked at the clock on the wall. That, thought Skorzeny, was a measure of just how backward this country was—not only that one would look at a clock on the wall to see what time it was, but that there even were clocks on the wall.

Skorzeny ignored the question. "I propose a trade. One that will enrich us both."

Col. Zarin's glance fell upon Mlle. Derrida. "Why do you bring your whore to a meeting of men?" he snarled.

"Because she's not my whore," Skorzeny answered levelly. "And I'll thank you not to talk about her in such a disrespectful manner. You savages are simply going to have to learn that not all the world subscribes to your Dark Ages notion of male and female. Your entire civilization is not worth a Mass, although Paris was."

"Then why are you giving us Paris?" laughed Col. Zarin.

"Because Paris is no longer worth a Mass, either. But do

not think you have triumphed. It is I, Emanuel Skorzeny, who has triumphed, and you are a mere instrument of my will. I am greater than any God, greater than your Allah, and I shall have my revenge."

Col. Zarin's hand stole toward his sidearm. "This is blasphemy. I should kill you for it."

"You wouldn't dare," replied Skorzeny coolly. "Because my death makes you a dead man. It makes your wife a widow and your children orphans. It brings down the full wrath of the West upon your pitiful head. For there will come a time, and soon, when your breast-beating and braggadocio will be as nothing. I am all that is standing in the way of the West's vengeance upon you. So listen."

He opened his briefcase, and took out the computer. "This is the very latest example of NSA/CSS technology. It was designed by their top operative, a man with whom I have come into contact, both personally and professionally, on several occasions, each of them unpleasant in the extreme. I am prepared to make you a present of it, in exchange for Miss Harrington, who can be of absolutely no use to you at this point."

"Do you love her that much?"

"Yes," said Skorzeny. It was the simplest answer he had ever given to any question in his life.

"And what does love mean?"

For the first time in his life, he felt old, tired, nearing the end. No, it could not be possible. All his life had been devoted to one thing, to one purpose—himself—and suddenly came this realization. That there was something beyond him. Not the ritualistic rote of some alien liturgy, but something more elemental, something more primitive than even religious superstition.

Her.

"I don't know," he replied.

Mlle. Derrida could sit silent no longer. She had no use

for these Iranians and their imported desert faith. She was a Frenchwoman, the heiress of Voltaire and Descartes, Rousseau, and Rimbaud and Sartre and her namesake, Derrida. She believed in rational thought. *Cogito ergo sum.* That was her faith, and that was why she had faith in him. "Of course you do," she said.

"Love is what is left when thought has fled—not religion, not faith, but love. Love is what drives us. If there is a God, and like you I do not believe that for a moment . . . but if there is, then love is what brings us closer to him. Not hate. Not vengeance. Neither orders, nor rituals. Nothing from above, or below. Just us, humanity—what we French fought and lost our Revolution for. We sacrificed our ideals on the altar of the guillotine, and we learned never to do that again. And now here we are."

She turned to Skorzeny. "Get her back, sir," she said, "and then let's go home. I want to go home. Take me home."

Skorzeny indicated the laptop. "Very simple," he said. "The computer for the girl. You get—if you can reverse-engineer it, and get past its built-in defenses—a glide path into the heart of the Great Satan. With this, you can destroy them. No need for bombs, nukes, Shahab missiles. No need for the permanent war against the West. You can end it all now, right here, right now. Break their Black Widow, corrupt her, seduce her, turn her into the whore you've always known she was. I don't care. In fact, I endorse it."

He pushed the laptop across the table at Col. Zarin. "But give my own Black Widow back to me. Give me Miss Harrington."

Col. Zarin looked at the laptop. He looked at Skorzeny. He looked at Mlle. Derrida.

Skorzeny looked at him. Neither of them blinked.

On the wall, the clock kept ticking. At last—

"I will take you to her," Col. Zarin said.

CHAPTER FORTY-FIVE

Qom

Devlin and Maryam moved through the crowd, deliberately but quickly.

"He's here," said Devlin in Farsi.

"How do you know?"

"Because he can't resist."

They were past the mosque now, heading for the home of Mohammed Radan, Devlin's taxi driver's brother-in-law. They needed a place to get out of sight, even if only for a few hours. The house of Mohammed Radan would have to do.

"Emanuel Skorzeny," said Devlin softly, "always must have the last word. Always must see the other fellow submit. He will not be able to abide her betrayal, nor will he be able to credit it. For him to have misjudged her so badly reflects poorly on him. And hearing her say it will set his world right again."

"We have to rescue her," said Maryam. "She saved my life."

"She may have saved more than that."

The address they were seeking was close now. "He's got your computer, you know."

"I was counting on it. Why do you think I gave it to you?"

He felt her stiffen. "You wanted him to get it?"

"Ideally, no. I wanted you to find him. But he found you first. He didn't get to where he is today by being unaware of danger. But he has a weakness, just as we all do. And his weakness is his vanity."

"What's your weakness?" she asked.

"You," he said simply.

Mr. Radan was delighted to meet the traveler of whom his esteemed brother-in-law had spoken so highly, and rejoiced in the mercy of Allah that his honored guest was now joyously reunited with his wife. Mrs. Radan was immediately dispatched to the kitchen to prepare a repast for their guests, and the fair Radan daughters were paraded in front of the new arrivals, each to offer a greeting in turn. Then Mr. Radan showed them to a back bedroom in his modest but comfortable house and immediately ordered the eldest daughter to bring them black tea and sweet drinks. Then he left them alone.

"You can take that off now," said Devlin. "I think we are *batin*." In Persian society, there were two modes—the public, *zahir*, in which all the sharia-based social norms were punctiliously observed, and the private, or *batin*, in which the chadors came off, and the hair went down.

Maryam took off the chador. She opened the bag Amanda had given her, took out a change of clothes, and went to wash up.

Devlin found the secure uplink NSA had provided and downloaded what he needed. There was a relay from Hope via Danny—the clock was ticking on the bomb in New York, and the trigger was the laser. They had calculated the rate of descent, which was holding steady. There wasn't much time.

Devlin let his mind travel back. The dead cattle along Highway 5. That had been a warm-up, the miracles a distraction. They were testing, and soon they would be ready to strike.

Involuntarily, he found himself admiring the length of time it had taken to plan all this, and how careful they had been. *Schritt vor schritt*, as the Germans liked to say: step by step, one thing after another, letting it unfold gradually but inevitably. He could see and admire the hand of the master, whose entire life had been dedicated to the proposition that there was nothing you could not accomplish if only you set your mind to it and went about it to the exclusion of nearly everything else.

That was Emanuel Skorzeny's life, and he had only ever let one thing intrude. And now, *inshallah*, it was about to cost him that life.

For Skorzeny was here, in Qom. He could feel his malevolent presence, just as he was sure Skorzeny could feel his. They would find each other. And then settle this thing.

He didn't want to stay online very long—no matter how secure and how shielded, a capable counter-intelligence system eventually would eventually detect him. But he'd gotten when he needed, from Seelye, from Danny. Just one more thing.

Time to bait the last trap.

The laptop, which operated at the highest level of NSA security, had a feature he hadn't told Maryam about. Even if it was shut down, it could be activated remotely—and by activated, he meant activated. It would automatically switch on in order to receive any critical communication from the Building in Fort Meade.

He could access the Building from his Android.

He accessed the Building.

He activated the signal.

The signal went out.

He switched off the Android and lay back on the bed for a moment, imagining Skorzeny's reaction. Would be it be shock or delight? Terror or triumph? Who else was with him? It didn't matter. The machine was now doing the job for which he had designed it.

Upon receiving the activation signal, the laptop would display the origin of the incoming. That would be the moment of maximum danger, since it would blow their location, but that was exactly what he needed to do. They had to seem exposed and vulnerable, otherwise an army would show up and there was no way that the two of them could fight their way through an army. He had to let Skorzeny think he alone had gotten the drop on him.

One more chess move. One more, and then it would all be over, one way or the other.

She was there, in the desert, waiting for them. Dressed beautifully in the Western style, looking as lovely as the day he'd first seen her in the City, the director of Islay Partnership Ltd., ordering some financial transaction or another, a figure of poise, beauty, and authority. She was surrounded by admirers, who stood looking up at her like some impossible vision of loveliness that they would never again see in their lifetimes. Her head was bowed as she received their adulation with the utmost humility.

They had tied a rope around her waist, which held her tight against the Shahab-3 rocket. Skorzeny could see at a glance that it was carrying a heavier payload than normal. This, too, was part of the plan. For this was one of the rockets that were about to destroy the Little Satan, the Zionist entity. These were the rockets that would set off the final cataclysm in a world already at war with itself.

These were the rockets that would trigger massive retaliation by Israel, all across the *ummah*. The Israelis would not stop to ask their provenance. They would exercise the Samson Option, and like the blind strongman, eyeless in Gaza, they would lash out at their tormentors.

Amanda Harrington would be the first to be sacrificed.

"We have a deal, Navid," said Skorzeny coldly. "Release the woman."

They were in a jeep, the three of them plus the driver. "She looks lovely, does she not?" said Zarin.

"I said, release her," repeated Skorzeny. "The computer . . ."

". . . is a trap," said Zarin. "Do you think I am stupid? Do you think I do not know that you make me this offer only to insult me?"

"The computer is perfectly safe," said Skorzeny levelly. "It was entrusted to the woman called Maryam—the woman who slipped away from you at Bandar Anzali, through your own carelessness—by one of the top operatives of the Central Security Service. The thing is worth a fortune. The woman is worth nothing to you. So honor your word."

"First, show me I have nothing to fear." He took the laptop out of his briefcase and handed it to Skorzeny. "Aside from the miracles of Allah, I do not believe in—"

And the laptop burst to life.

It was running an NSA-hardened version of Red Hat Enterprise Linux 5, which came as no surprise to Skorzeny. Many of the U.S. government's most sensitive computers used that as a baseline operating system, having abandoned most versions of Windows in favor of it and the Mac Snow Leopard.

But there did not seem to be anything unusual about it. It did not blow up in his face. No doubt there would be security protocols, but the Iranian computer scientists were a smart lot and they could handle it.

As Skorzeny watched, the machine made a connection back to Fort Meade and automatically began downloading reams of material.

"What is going on?" asked Col. Zarin.

"It's obviously been set up to communicate at regular intervals with Fort Meade and the Black Widow," he said. "If your men get right on this, you'll be able to tunnel right into NSA headquarters before they even know it. This is a golden opportunity, Col. Zarin, a miracle from Allah. It might have taken you weeks to activate the machine, and even then it might have destroyed itself. Here it is—take it."

Zarin reached for the machine.

"But first, give me the woman."

Zarin watched the data dance on the screen. Allah alone knew how long this communications session would last. The control facility was just a short drive away.

He stood up in the Jeep and signaled for the Guard to cut Amanda loose, then told the driver to get going. Skorzeny's hand shot out and grabbed him by the wrist. "Not until she is in this car," he said.

They cut her loose. Amanda said nothing as she squeezed into the backseat. The Jeep roared off.

So it had come to this, thought Amanda as they raced across the desert floor. No matter how she tried to escape him, he always found her. She would never be rid of him. How she wished Milverton had taken him out when they had the chance. But they thought they had a plenty of time. Everybody thinks she has plenty of time until time runs out.

"How are you, my dear?"

She had nothing to say. Her storehouse of comebacks, quips, observations, and pious sentimentalities was exhausted. There was almost nothing left of the old Amanda Harrington, queen of the City. He, who had given her so much, had taken it all away; she had made herself mistress to him, but at a price she could not pay. Here, in the desert, is where it would finally end.

When they arrived at the control facility Col. Zarin rushed the computer inside. Technicians and intelligence analysts immediately fell upon it, and began to chatter excitedly. Skorzeny could not follow what they were saying, but it was clear that this was a very great gift. Col. Zarin seemed extraordinarily pleased.

"I am sorry to have doubted you, my friend." He consulted his Patek Philippe. Watches were still a status symbol in Iran. "Only a few hours now. And so we wait."

Col. Zarin led Skorzeny, Mlle. Derrida, and Amanda into a private room. For a military base, this room was rather luxurious, handsomely carpeted and well appointed. "What can I get you to drink?"

"Please, no more of that awful fruit juice," said Mlle. Derrida. Her romance with the third world, which she had cultivated so assiduously as a student at the Sorbonne and at the London School of Economics, was fast coming to an end. She could see the upside of Western civilization more clearly now, especially its personal freedom; living in Iran must be like living in a cage, on more or less full-time display, with only rare moments of privacy in the dark of night.

"It is against the tenets of our holy faith to take stimulants," said the colonel. "But you are guests as well as Unbelievers, and so we are able to extend to you the courtesy you require. What may I get you?"

"Vodka," said Mlle. Derrida. Skorzeny ordered a shaken gin martini for Amanda and a small scotch, neat, for himself. He needed to keep a clear head, but one drink to steady his nerves could not hurt.

The phone rang and Col. Zarin answered it, then lay down the receiver with a big smile. "I must hand it to you, Mr. Skorzeny," he said. "What you have brought us is turning out to be invaluable. The codes alone . . ."

"I am very glad to be of service to the Islamic Republic in pursuit of our mutual goals," he replied. "Now, if you would be so kind, we would appreciate an escort back to Tehran so that I might take Miss Harrington home and see that she gets the kind of medical attention she deserves."

Col. Zarin laughed. "I could not hear of such a thing," he protested. "You are my guests, and you know how important the cause of hospitality is to one of my faith. After all we have done together, Mr. Skorzeny, I cannot believe that you would wish to absent yourself from the Coming, from the great manifestation of the holiest of holy mysteries. For you to leave now would be . . . unthinkable."

So there it was. They were prisoners.

"Tell me," said Col. Zarin, sitting down next to Mlle. Derrida. She was a damn fine good-looking woman, as the women around Skorzeny always were. It would be a shame not to get to know her a little better. "Who was that policeman in New York you had me call? For an Arab he seemed to speak very good Farsi."

"A weak link," replied Skorzeny. His mind was racing to figure out how to get out of here before the immanence. Now that he was reunited with Miss. Harrington, he did not wish to keep her in jeopardy a moment longer. Although his sources in Washington were not what they once were, not after the unfortunate suicide of Tyler's best friend, Senator Robert Hartley, they were still plenty good. Many members of Congress were on his payroll, one way or the other, and all it took was a little kindness, or a little indiscretion, from a junior staffer on the Senate intelligence committee and the personnel list had come into his hands. Frankly, he had forgotten all about the fellow—he had just needed to keep the Counter-Terrorism Unit puzzled and alarmed and he had needed a little bit of insurance to use against Col. Zarin should the need arise.

Which it just had.

"A minor member of the CTU, who even now along with his fellows is watching helplessly as our plan moves forward. Of course, should anything go wrong, it is entirely possible—more than likely I would say—that the various intelligence services of the United States, starting but not ending with the New York City Police Department, have your voice on record now, and it would only be a matter of time before Langley or DIA or NSA identifies the speaker. Amazing what they can do these days, really."

Col. Zarin obviously had not thought of that. "You mean to say they record all calls, even to hospitals?"

Now it was Skorzeny's turn to laugh. "My dear Col. Zarin, of course they do. The Americans are great fools, but in order to satisfy the primitive fears of the majority of their people, they must at least pretend to take some precautions. Fortunately for us, their enlightened classes are highly solicitous about the rights of those who would kill them. They would rather be legally in the clear and in the good odor of the *New York Times* editorial board than alive, if it came to that. They have made what would otherwise be a formidable task into something a very bright child with a Lego kit might manage in an afternoon. They offer their throats to the knife, and make sure we profit from it."

"Profit?" asked Col. Zarin. He went to the bar and poured himself a whisky. *Batin*.

That was a good sign. It meant he now trusted Skorzeny. Either that or . . . it meant that Skorzeny was never going to leave this place alive. Well, he would soon find out.

"Why, of course," said Skorzeny. "In my heart, I am devoted to the cause of my fellow man, the poor, the hungry, the tired, the oppressed. I have spent literally billions of dollars on charitable causes, especially in Africa and Latin America to see that the victims of capitalist exploitation receive some small recompense for their suffering. But philanthropy costs a great deal of money, does it not, Miss Harrington?"

Amanda nodded.

"Therefore, I have always found ways to do well by doing

good, and our joint plan today will handsomely reward me. You, too, can be a part of it if you play your cards right."

"I am listening," said Zarin.

Mlle. Derrida could feel the colonel inching ever closer to her. From time to time, as he laughed or responded to something Skorzeny was saying, he would reach out and gently touch her leg. Her leg was of course clothed, but it seemed to give him a thrill nonetheless.

"Are you acquainted with the concept of economic terrorism?" asked Skorzeny. He kept waiting for shouting from the next room, for soldiers to rush in with guns drawn, for something to have gone hideously wrong with the NSA computer, leaving them to pay the price . . . but nothing. He could not believe Devlin would be that stupid, would not have guarded himself against the thing's loss, would not have taken every precaution lest it fall into the wrong hands. And yet . . .

"For the past several years, I have been administering a serious of shocks to the American economic system. I and my surrogates and partners around the world have done our best to undermine the value of the dollar—and may I modestly say we have done a splendid job in that regard, to the point at which it will soon no longer be the international currency and medium of exchange. When that day comes, of course, America is finished as an economic superpower.

"As the dollar collapses, the country's ability to service its debt will only increase. At first, with inflation, it will seem like the balance of payments is improving, as evermore worthless dollars are applied to international ledger books. But after a time, and very soon, creditor nations will no longer wish to accept dollars that come directly from the Federal Reserve's printing presses. They will want real value, tangible assets, gold. Is there any gold left in Fort Knox? Or was the Treasury emptied out long ago? The greatest nation in the history of the world has beggared itself—and for what? A pat on the head from the *bien-pensant*?

"When the missiles fly, the flight to value will be complete. We need not try and destroy America with bombs or planes or raids upon their children in the schools. I know. I tried. No, all we need to do is make her fall victim to her own profligacy, and her own fear."

Skorzeny rose and walked over to where Col. Zarin was sitting and extended his hand. "Two percent is your share. I will not put it in writing. Miss Harrington and Mlle. Derrida can both attest that I am a man of my word. Two percent of what I make off this operation. That may not sound like much, but let me assure you, my dear Col. Zarin, that it will allow you to retire extremely comfortably for the rest of your life anyplace you choose."

The colonel thought for a moment. "But I shall be witness to the Coming," he objected. "What will it profit me to make a great deal of money if these are the end times?"

Skorzeny's hand was still extended, but he made no attempt to lower it. "Col. Zarin," he said, "I care not one whit for the End Times. As you know, I am an unbeliever, a *kufr*. Worse, in your eyes, I am an atheist. All this babble about God and Allah and Jesus and Issa and the Virgin Mary interests me not in the least. I have already been to hell and back. I lived in hell and felt its fires on my face. I saw death unimaginable, at an age when boys should still be playing with hobbyhorses and starting to think about girls. I have witnessed incinerative destruction from the skies, a rain of fire that brought down the Virgin's own cathedral, six hundred and fifty thousand incendiary bombs that turned oxygen into flames and bodies into charred carbon husks. Do you think I fear the end times?"

A knock at the door. Col. Zarin handed his drink to Mlle. Derrida. "Come in," he shouted.

The soldier saluted. "Everything is in readiness,

Colonel," he said. He glanced over at Skorzeny, who still had his hand in the air. Strange people, these Westerners.

"Thank you. You may go."

The soldier left. The door closed. Col. Zarin took Skorzeny's hand and shook it. "You are right. It would not be holy for you to witness the miracle of the Coming. Right after the first launch, I will send you back in a fast car to Tehran. Your plane will be given all clearances. You have my word on it."

They shook hands.

They passed the room in which the technicians were working on Devlin's computer. There were smiles all around. Everything seemed to be going very smoothly. That in itself was enough to make Emanuel Skorzeny want to get very far away as quickly as possible. He had a deal with Col. Zarin, true, and he intended to honor that deal in the unlikely event the colonel survived whatever was to come.

For that something was coming, he had no doubt. The devil drives.

Outside, the missiles were on their launchpads. Amanda shuddered as she saw what had been in store for her. God, how she wished this was all over. How she longed to be back in London, to open the door of Number Four Kensington Park Gardens once more, to play her piano and walk naked in her solarium at night, invisible but surrounded by the lights of London, listening to the English rain, and the voice of her absent daughter.

There would be no child waiting for her, that she knew, that she accepted. But that did not mean there could never be a child. She could think clearly now—she had Skorzeny to thank for that, the bastard. She could see a way.

All she had to do was get out of here.

CHAPTER FORTY-SIX

Qom

A couple of hours earlier, Danny had relayed topographic maps of the area, clearly marking the location of the Iranian missiles. They were going to regret that little show-off stunt the other day, which telegraphed their position. Not that Targeting didn't already know that, but for this operation, speed was everything, and if it saved even five minutes, that was a plus.

The Super Hornets from Diego Garcia were in the air. The MH-60Ks, with him at one helm, were about to launch; they had been painted with the colors of the Iranian Army. Hope was keeping him apprised of the countdown in New York. Stealth was the order of the day.

He had not yet heard from "Bert Harris," but that didn't mean anything. After this was over, it was possible, even likely, that they would never see each other again. "Harris" would disappear back into whichever shadowy recess of the IC he had come from, perhaps to vanish altogether. How he withstood the psychic strain was beyond him. Danny just

wanted to go home and enjoy the company of his family—
his old family and his new family.

"Sir?" One of the men on board ship.

"Yes?"

"You're good to go, sir."

"Thank you, son."

"You were never here, right, sir?"

"Right. You're looking at a ghost."

The kid looked around at the six Black Hawks. "Whole
bunch of ghosts," he said. "Ain't nobody gonna wanna see
these spooks show up in their backyard."

"We'll do some damage if we have to."

"Some of the guys mutterin' something about payback
time."

"You know mutterers. Always muttering about something."

"Is it true?"

Danny looked at the young sailor. There were times when
he despaired of the future of his country, and then there were
times like this. "Where you from, son?" he asked.

"Altoona, Pennsylvania," he said.

"Good state," he said. "Lot of great Navy men came from
Pennsylvania."

"Some still do, sir." The boy stepped back and saluted
him, then turned and saluted the whole crew. Not military
men anymore, but Xe types, private military companies—
the men who weren't there, the men who did their jobs in
anonymity, and the ones who always got blamed by *The New
York Times* if something went wrong.

"Go with God, sir," said the kid.

"Roger that," said Danny. He looked down as his communications device: the message he had been waiting for was
coming through. Showtime.

This wasn't going to be any two-day kluge of an operation like Eagle Claw. That one had been at once overplanned and underplanned, too nervy and not nervy enough. Looking back on it, the whole notion of hiding the choppers in the desert, flying into Tehran, liberating the hostages from the embassy, taking them to a sports stadium, and then helicoptering them out was nuts; no wonder it had failed. Technology had come a long way since then. This was going to be quick, surgical, and brutal.

He gave the signal to the men. The rotors started turning. In a few minutes, they'd be in the air and on their way to Iran.

There was no turning back now.

Attired in full Islamic dress, Devlin and Maryam left the house of Mohammed Radan with profuse thanks for his kind hospitality and effusive promises to return again one day. Mr. Radan prayed to Allah for their safe journey, and should they ever return to the holy city, well, they knew where to find him. No, he would not accept any money. No, no, no, a thousand times no. It would be an insult to him and his family. Finally, after much argumentation, he gratefully accepted the rials that Devlin practically had to force upon him. *Taarof* must always be maintained.

Midday prayers had just ended and people were going about their daily business once more. The signal from the computer had not only alerted Devlin to its opening, but it had also transmitted the exact GPS coordinates of its location. Devlin didn't need a map to know where their target was—right in the middle of a mountain on the outskirts of the city. That was where the uranium-enrichment facility was. That was where the computer was. And that, unless he was very much mistaken—in which case his end of the operation was doomed—was where Emanuel Skorzeny and Amanda Harrington would be.

He was just starting to think about stealing a car when one pulled up alongside him. It was his old friend, the driver from Arāk. "May Allah be praised!" the man exclaimed. "It is you, my traveling friend. I trust you found hospitality at the home of my esteemed brother-in-law, Mohammed Radan."

They continued walking as the man drove along beside them. Suddenly, the driver slammed on the brakes and jumped from the car—

"Where are my manners? Where? This is something I ask myself every day, and I pray to Allah for his holy forgiveness. I have not yet introduced myself. I am Sadegh Mossaddegh, at your service. Which of the many glorious sights of Qom would you like to see? Sadegh Mossaddegh stands ready to attend you."

It was not unusual for a man to augment his income by informally hacking; if this was a sign from Allah then, for this moment, Devlin was a believer. "And we are grateful for your great kindness," he said.

They got into the car. There was no air-conditioning in the ancient Russian Chaika, which was essentially a knock-off of a Chevy from the late 1950s, but it was clean and comfortable, if well-sprung.

With Maryam gently guiding Sadegh, they drove toward the north, away from the city. When they had reached the city limits, Mr. Mossaddegh was about to turn around, when Devlin told him to keep driving. When he objected, Maryam, who was riding in the back, put the knife she had taken from the religious police to the back of his neck. "I am sorry, my friend," said Devlin, "but we have need of your vehicle."

To his credit, Mr. Mossaddegh hardly flinched. Thieves were plentiful in this part of Iran. It was a shame, a disgrace—a measure of how badly the people had failed the Islamic Revolution. "Willingly do I surrender it to you," he said.

"We also have need for your services," continued Devlin. "Do not worry, you shall not be harmed. A great adventure are you embarking upon, one that you will be able to relate to your children and grandchildren and to the fair daughters of your brother-in-law, Mohammed Radan. Truly, this shall be a glorious day for you, brother."

"But to be threatened by a woman," wailed Mossaddegh. "The shame—how shall I ever relate this sad fact to my family?"

"Don't worry," said Maryam from behind him. "We are not criminals. And no one ever need know. This day shall you be a hero of the Republic, honored among the multitudes."

"What must I do?" asked Mossaddegh, feeling only a little relieved.

"Drive," said Devlin.

They drove in silence for a while along the Persian Gulf Highway. There were, Mossaddegh knew, restricted areas along both sides of the road, near the airport and the Hoz-e-Soltan lake. He prayed neither was their destination.

He was not frightened of these people. After all, had he not spent a couple of hours in the car with the man? True, the man had never offered his name, but then again neither had he. They had both forgotten their manners. If the man had wanted to kill him, could he not have killed him then? Ah, but then he would never have been reunited with his wife, so there was that.

Finally, he ventured a question: "What's in it for me?"

"What do you want?" asked the man. "Money is not a problem."

He almost bit his tongue as the words crossed it: "What about relocation?"

"Anywhere in Iran you wish," said the woman. She had a soft and sexy voice and he was quite sure that she was a great beauty.

"Elsewhere?" he said.

Devlin knew what was coming. "Where?"

Mossaddegh took a deep breath. "Well, I have cousins in Los Angeles . . . and . . ."

CHAPTER FORTY-SEVEN

Qom

Col. Zarin looked out at the Shahab-3 missiles and felt proud. No longer would the infidels of the West impose their will on the sacred lands of Islam by force. No longer would the *dar al-Islam* have to suffer the Crusaders' indignities, their petty slights and their overt contempt. They had taken the technology of the West, purchased with the money derived from the same oil resources the West had discovered and developed, and turned it back against them. Allah be praised.

For a thousand years, they had waited in fear and darkness for the Coming, but were unable to effect it. Now there would be no stopping them. The missiles would slam into Israel and destroy the country, from Haifa to Be-er Sheva. Was not the Grand Ayatollah himself the incarnation of Seyed Khorasani, the great imam who would, according to holy prophecy, restore Jerusalem to Imam Mahdi? He was.

"What, may I ask, is your timing plan?" said Skorzeny. "Will you destroy Israel first and simultaneously set off the bomb in New York, or will the experience be more . . . theatrical?"

"You will see," said the colonel.

"But Col. Zarin, I need to know. The New York part of this operation was mine, and—"

"You will see."

"What about retaliation? You know the Israelis won't go quietly. Your cities will be destroyed. Other cities in the *ummah* will burn. When the Americans are hit, they too will lash out. Many millions of Muslims will die."

"Their deaths are necessary, to bring Imam Mahdi to us."

"But they are innocent." How it pained him to say that; in Emanuel Skorzeny's world, no one was innocent, and all deserved to suffer and perish.

"They will die for the faith, as holy martyrs, and be welcomed into Paradise."

Col. Zarin signaled for the countdown to begin. "And now, if you will excuse me, I must make sure that all is in readiness. Don't worry. You will be quite safe here." And then he got into a staff car and drove off, leaving the three of them quite alone.

"He's not coming back for us, is he?" asked Mlle. Derrida. Skorzeny looked at her. It was easy to forget that for all her haughty Gallic exterior, she was still little more than a girl.

"No," said Amanda. "They mean for us to die out here in the desert. If these missiles launch, this will be one of the first places hit, you can count on that. We will be destroyed by our own friendly fire."

"Some friends," said Mlle. Derrida.

Amanda looked at Skorzeny. This time, she knew, there would be no rescue. So, at least, she was getting her wish. This would be the day that she saw him die. And if it came at the price of her own life, very well then. She had become exactly like him, a human being with nothing left to live for. But she had had something to live for, once, and that was a claim he would never be able to make. She hoped he would realize that as the flesh melted from his body in the intense heat of the strike that was sure to come. She hoped she lived long enough to see him die.

In the distance came the sound of something very much like gunfire. "What is it?" she asked.

Skorzeny had barely noticed. "This is a military base, Miss Harrington," he said. "Men are armed on military bases. Sometimes shots are fired."

Mlle. Derrida, who had been growing more and more agitated, now completely lost it. "I have had it," she exclaimed, wheeling on Skorzeny and blistering his ears in French. "When you asked me to join you, I had no idea this is what you would lead me into. You promised me a life of glamour and wealth and instead I am a fugitive. You promised me travel and look where I am. In the middle of a desert, thousands of miles from home. You promised me that I would be witness to greatness and what do I see? A bitter, dirty old man. For shame, M. Skorzeny, for shame."

And then she walked over to him and slapped his face.

Devlin and Maryam made their way on foot through the harsh terrain. The Iranians had successfully hidden the enrichment site at Qom for years, counting on a compliant IAEA to provide them cover. When its location was finally discovered by American intelligence, the Iranians immediately declared it, in order to defuse international criticism. Besides, they said, it was not fully operational at the time of its discovery, and under International Atomic Energy Agency rules, they needed only declare a new facility six months before it came online.

The intel maps Danny had provided led them through the

base's lax defenses. Any attack would surely come from the skies, not from the land, and the Iranian guards were indolent. Even today, on this day, half of them were in the barracks, playing cards, until such time as an officer came by, and then they pretended to be hard at work, doing something or other.

The first thing they needed was weapons. He had brought none with him, figuring it would be safer that way; and besides, the one thing that was plentiful in the Arab and Muslim world was guns. Everybody had one.

The Revolutionary Guards were still armed mostly with Chinese versions of the venerable Russian AK-47. It was easy to see why. The Kalashnikov, or "Kalash," the Russians called it, was practically indestructible and absolutely Third World–proof. It did not require the loving care that the high-end American-made automatic weapons required. You could run a tank over it, sink it in water, bury it in mud, and the odds were better than even money that the damn thing would come up firing the first time you pulled the trigger.

They were in desert camo now, which Devlin had brought with him in his kit. There was no sign that anyone was looking for them, so when they encountered their first guards, surprise was on their side. Maryam took the first man down with her knife, while Devlin broke the neck of the second man before he had even to look behind him, and killed the third and last man with a blow that drove the nasal bone into the man's brain.

Neither of them said a thing. This was how they had met, back in Paris when Devlin was trailing Milverton. Some first date: Maryam was wounded in the firefight and Devlin had saved her life—not knowing who she was, or why she was tailing him and Milverton, but in awe of her skill and already in love with her. Maybe someday they could tell their kids about it, if they lived to have kids.

If she'd have kids with him.

The thought made him smile inwardly. He could hardly imagine a time when he'd be too old for this line of work, when he'd be chasing rug rats around the floor in Falls Church or Echo Park or in Paris or in South America or wherever the two of them decided was safe enough for them to settle, to cash out their bank accounts that the government was maintaining secretly for them and take the money and run.

But that day was coming and, if he wanted to see it, he'd better do his job.

"What have we got?"

She was going from body to body, taking the sidearms. "1911s. Beretta M9s."

Good. The Colt M1911 had served the U.S. military well from its first issuance in 1911 to 1985, and there were still damn few soldiers who would want to be without one. It was almost as reliable as the AK-47, had major stopping power, and never let you down. "Take them all. The Berettas too."

"Got 'em. Cartridges too."

"Rifles?"

She forced open a cabinet. "AK's, M16's—oh, look, a Viper."

"We'll take it. And the magazines."

She handed it to him. It was fairly new—must have come from the black market in Iraq, where the Shias were engaged in a lively weapons trade on both sides of the porous border. "I love a one-stop shop. Now let's get going."

They both switched on their secure communicators. He could see Danny's progress across the desert. That was the thing about those new Black Hawks: they were fast, they were radar-deflective, and if anybody saw them, they could pass for local. For those reasons, they would not be flying in formation; no one knew exactly how many of the Iranian army's helicopters were still operational, since the quality of maintenance had fallen off precipitously since the Revolution, so it was best not to have more than one or two together. Nevertheless, they would all be converging exactly at the rendezvous point at the appointed time.

All except one—Danny's, which would be flying into the teeth of the shitstorm to get them out and bring them all safely home. Him, Maryam, Danny, Amanda Harrington, and Mlle. Derrida, if possible. Emanuel Skorzeny was the only one without a ticket on this particular flight. He would be getting his ticket punched elsewhere, and Devlin would do the punching.

And now for the pièce de résistance.

ARE YOU READY?

This to Seelye, back in Maryland.

NICE OF YOU TO CHECK IN. HAVING FUN YET?
WISH YOU WERE HERE
RETARGETING COMMENCING NOW
YOU'RE SURE YOU'VE GOT IT?
BELGHAZI SINGS LIKE AN ANGEL. THE LASERS ARE OURS
AND THEY WON'T KNOW?
NOT UNTIL IT'S TOO LATE. GONNA BE A LOT OF RED
FACES IN THE SOUTH OF FRANCE TOMORROW
CERN?
NEED TO KNOW AND THEY DON'T NEED TO KNOW FOR
NOW
WE'RE GOOD TO GO THEN. WISH ME LUCK
YOU DON'T NEED IT
HOW DO YOU KNOW?
BECAUSE I RAISED YOU RIGHT. LUCK HAS NOTHING TO
DO WITH IT.
SOMETIMES LUCK HAS EVERYTHING TO DO WITH IT. ASK
MY PARENTS

YOU WANT PAYBACK, THIS IS YOUR BIG CHANCE, SON.
TAKE IT. AND THAT'S AN ORDER

Devlin didn't know how to respond to that. So he didn't:

OVER AND OUT

"We're good to go," he said. "Do we have a fix?"

She looked up from her handheld. "I've just pinged her locator. Coordinates coming through now . . . 34.94373 N and 50.76056 E."

"Last thing." This was something he was really looking forward to.

His computer was on and it was telling him everything it was telling the Iranians. It was also sending back a steady stream of audiovisual information to Fort Meade, to feed the Black Widow's insatiable maw. And it was doing something else. . . .

Not just injecting the STUXNET virus. He had anticipated that and loaded it before he gave the machine to Maryam. Not simply taking out the entire command and control electronic systems that would allow Iran to launch its missiles against Israel or anywhere else. His laptop was also issuing abort and destruct orders for every single missile in the Iranian arsenal. And that included missiles with armed nuclear warheads.

Which was why Danny had to be right on the money. This whole area was going to be radioactive for a century if the Iranians were foolish enough to arm their warheads anywhere near Iranian airspace. And yet, he couldn't have them arming over Iraq or, worse, over Israel. They were going to have to blow them in Iran, before they armed. Qom was not his holy city, but it was a holy place to a billion people, and it was not his brief to destroy it.

It would be enough, for now, to show the Shias that the end times were not near, that Imam Mahdi was not coming out of his well—and that the men leading their nation to ruin had been lying to them all along. The Green Revolution had almost succeeded the last time; it would be hard to imagine it would not succeed this time.

Maryam was going to get her country back.

He sent the final set of instructions to the computer, which acknowledged and began issuing them. Like a swift-moving virus, the new codes were already in the central bloodstream. The Iranian nuclear program was about to suffer a setback from which, he hoped, it would never recover.

"Okay," he said, grabbing the Viper. "Let's do this."

CHAPTER FORTY-EIGHT

New York City

The Virgin was still sinking in the sky. They didn't have much time left.

Wherever that son of a bitch Crankheit had put the suitcase nuke, they couldn't find it. They had torn the hospital apart, disrupted the routine, probably cost a couple of terminal patients their lives. Byrne certainly hoped not, but there was no way to tell.

There was a chapel in the hospital, one of those spare, nondenominational places where you could "worship" in some peace and quiet. He would have preferred a church—St. Malachy, in the Times Square area, would have been his choice, or St. Mike's over on Thirty-fourth Street, once Irish gangland's church of choice for first-class send-offs. Because, unless Washington did its job, or they did theirs, a grand send-off was what they were about to get.

Think, you dumb paddy bastard. Think . . . No, the chapel was too antiseptic. He decided to face the music outside.

Slowly, he became aware that there was somebody standing beside him, and that somebody was his brother. "Hello, Tom," he said. "Getting any lately?"

"Nothin' you don't know about."

"Yeah, well, for a reporter she's not bad."

"It's just business, Frankie. You know how it is with me. Always just business."

He couldn't help himself. "Was it business with Mary Claire, too?" Mary Claire Byrne had been Frankie's wife, until the pressures and misery of being a cop's wife had finally gotten to her and driven her right into Tom's arms. But that was a long time ago.

"Let's forget about that, Frankie."

"Easy for you to say."

"What would Pop have thought about all this? You know. I mean 9/11 and the way the city's changed and now . . ." Tom looked up at the sky, ". . . this fucking thing."

Frankie shook his head. "I don't think Pop would have been surprised by much."

"Just that dirtbag who snuck up behind him and his partner and killed them. What was the name of his partner back in sixty-eight . . . ?"

"Rodriguez. Alfonso Rodriguez. New York was already changing back then, but what did we know? We were still just kids."

Tom took out a pack of cigarettes, lit one, and offered one to his brother. Frankie started to shake his head, then accepted. What did it matter now? "Does it still bother you that we never got him? The bad guy, I mean."

"What chance did we have? He was probably some junkie, got picked up a few days later on some bullshit B and E beef and got shivved in prison and we never heard about it."

"Mom took it hard."

"Let's not talk about Mom."

"How is she?"

"Still alive. Rufus still checks in on her every day. She's old now, Tommy. Real old." There was nothing more to say on that subject. "The kid who did this . . ."

"Who planted the bomb, you mean?" said Tom.

"Yeah. He was a born tunnel rat. In another life, he could have been a sandhog, done something useful. Got himself killed but good under the Central Park Reservoir. Buried your girlfriend up to her neck behind the Met. So I keep thinking . . . underground. That's where he felt comfortable. That's where he felt safe."

Byrne turned to look back at the building. They were looking at the oldest part, the Metzger Pavilion, which had been built back in 1904, long after the hospital had changed its name from the Jews' Hospital in the City of New York and moved uptown from Chelsea. But Brunner's original building had long since been augmented by other wings and had even leaped Madison Avenue to connect up with the Icahn Medical Institute. Connected by . . .

"A tunnel," said Frankie, tossing the cigarette away. "That's it—the tunnel under Madison." He was moving now, almost running. Tom jumped up and followed him. "It's in the fucking tunnel, Tommy. That's where he took it. That's where he set it up. We thought he'd put it among the other radioactive devices, but he didn't care about that—the whole damn place shows up radioactive in overflights and nobody was going to be poking around down here with sensors. The bomb didn't need a power source because now we know what the power source is." He stopped and looked up to the sky. The sight of the BVM looming over the Upper East Side was so remarkable that he didn't even have time to think about it. Later, perhaps; later.

The plans for the tunnel were already waiting for them when they hit the reception desk, running. A receptionist ripped them out of the printer and handed them both copies as they charged toward the Madison Avenue side of the complex.

"Here," said Tom, pointing as he ran. "There's a couple of service bays, an electrical closet . . . a water main . . ."

"That's it. That's how he knew about the Central Park Reservoir, how to get into it. I wondered about that. Here was some fucking bumpkin from flyover land and he knows his way around the bowels of New York like a born sandhog. Well, this is where he started his exploration."

They were in the tunnel now, running, two crazy Irish brothers, trying to save the whole damn city.

They found the entrance to the old main. The Reservoir had been the lifeline of Manhattan for decades, its water running down below the park and Fifth Avenue, all the way to Forty-second Street, where the Public Library now stood, but which in the nineteenth century had also been a reservoir, a great watershed enclosed by something that looked like it had time-traveled from the Egypt of the pharaohs.

That was New York for you. Even the dead past kept on affecting the living, the city that never slept and the city that never died.

"Not on my watch," said Frankie Byrne as they burst through the door.

"Son of a bitch," said Tom.

There it was. Just sitting there, unmolested, undiscovered. The nasty bastard had brought it here, in something that looked like a large duffel bag, unnoticed by anybody. Just another anonymous kid in a deliveryman's outfit, going about his business.

"Careful," said Tom to his brother as Frankie picked the accursed thing up. Frankie could not remember the last time his brother had looked out for him.

"Little help here," he said.

"Right." Tom was on the phone to the bomb squad two seconds later.

"Where are you going to take it?" ask Frankie. He had slung it over his shoulder and together they were making their way up into the lobby of the Icahn building. The squad would be coming down Madison any second now.

He was puffing hard as they made the street. Was it his imagination or was the rate of descent speeding up? How much time did they have? Would it be enough? It would have to be.

And there, right on Madison Avenue, Captain Francis Byrne fell to his knees, blessed himself, and said a prayer to the Virgin—the real Virgin, not this apparition—to spare his city, spare his people, the good and the bad, the saints and the sinners, all the people of New York. That was his sworn duty as a police officer to protect them, but now he was asking a higher power. It didn't even matter whether there even was such a higher power, whether the Lady was as much a fantasy as any other religion's icons.

None of that mattered now. Because, at a moment like this, all he had was his faith, and it was his faith that was going to have to get him through.

The bomb truck was there. The bomb went inside it.

And then it was gone.

"Captain Byrne!"

Byrne unfolded his hands and looked across the street to see Principessa and a camera crew filming him. Ignoring the traffic, she dashed across Madison. "That was great," she said. "The perfect image. 'The Praying Detective.' In two hours, you'll be famous."

Byrne took her by the arm. "Listen, Ms. Stanley, I don't want to be famous. I don't even want to be rich. I just want to be Captain Francis Byrne, the kid from Queens who does his job."

"But—"

"But nothing. Kill it. You want the same shot, shoot your

boyfriend over there. Nobody who knows him will ever believe it, but go ahead. He's already famous. He's the great Tom Byrne of the FBI and you know what publicity hounds those clowns are."

"But—"

"But nothing. You want me to help you find this Archibald Grant, you'll do it. If not, no dice."

Principessa thought for a moment, but only a moment. "Deal," she said.

"You really got a jones for this Grant guy, don't you?" said Byrne. "Why?"

She had her answers all set and ready. "Because he's a fraud and the public has a right to know about it. Because he's arrogant, cold, aloof, and superior. Because he put me in my place in an off-the-record RAND lecture and made me look ridiculous."

Byrne got it. "In other words," he said, "you're crazy about him."

She hadn't expected that. She pulled back a little. "Promise you won't tell your brother?" she said.

"Believe me, sweetheart, he already knows. And you know what—he doesn't care."

"A real bastard, huh?"

"You don't know the half of it."

"I know the whole of it. But I don't care."

"That's what they all say—at first."

He started to walk away. Whatever happened now, it was out of his hands. Either the government would stop the laser or it wouldn't. Either the bomb squad would defuse a nuclear bomb or it wouldn't. Either the sun would come out tomorrow, or it wouldn't.

She was following him down Madison now. "Will you call me?"

"No."

"Why not? Don't you like me?"

What a chance this would be. Payback time for Mary Claire and everything else. "No."

She had caught up to him now, as they were crossing Ninety-eighth Street. "Why not? Don't you find me attractive?"

"I'd have to be blind not to. And I'm not blind."

"Then why not?"

"I try not to share with my brother."

She stopped. So he had to. "Strictly business, then?"

Byrne stepped back so he could get a good eyeful of her. He'd seen her on television many times, especially now that she'd become a big star. Just about every guy he knew desired her. She was single and so was he. The department generally frowned on cops boinking the media, but he knew Matt would turn a blind eye to it. That was their deal, locked into it for life: a blind eye to everything except what absolutely, positively, could not be ignored or swept under the rug.

They'd been sweeping stuff under the rug ever since Matt put two .38 slugs in Enrique Marcon's head and then gave him four more in the body just for good measure. Just to make sure he was dead. Just to make him feel the pain that Rosa Montez had felt when Marcon ice-picked her to death. It had been frontier justice in Park Slope, and it had been real justice.

"Strictly business," said Frankie. They shook hands.

Then Principessa leaned over and kissed him tenderly on the cheek.

In the sky, the image of the Virgin had stopped descending and was now fading rapidly. In a few moments, she would be gone forever.

And then Principessa's news van pulled up and she was gone and Francis Byrne was left to find his own way back downtown.

Story of his life.

CHAPTER FORTY-NINE

Outside Qom

"There they are." In the desert, near the launchpads.

The Viper could be used as a sniper rifle, and while Devlin didn't have a sniper scope on this one, what he did have was powerful enough to let him draw a clear bead on the three figures in the distance.

He could put a bullet through Skorzeny's head right now, and none the wiser.

At first Maryam wasn't sure whether he was talking about the Shahabs or the hostages. Three people standing alone in the desert. Even from this distance, she recognized Amanda's tall form, Mlle. Derrida, short and chic, and Skorzeny. She shuddered inwardly, and hoped it didn't show.

"I should kill them all now, save us time and trouble," Devlin said.

"Don't you trust your friend?" She wasn't sure which name he was going by for this operation and could not ask.

"Don Barker. That's his name. Don Barker."

"Just like yours is Frank Ross."

"It is to you—little Miss No Last Name."

"Do you think we'll ever trust each other?"

Devlin resighted. Pumpkin time: one, two, three . . . "Probably not."

"Does it matter?"

"Probably not." And then he heard it. *Thwack thwack thwack* . . . It was like the beating of wings.

Danny.

"I used to think that sound was angels," she said.

"It is," he said, up and sprinting now. "Black Angels."

The sound was bringing out the soldiers, but that didn't matter. Danny was here, right on schedule. The poison in the system of the Iranian nuclear program was working. The lasers were being retargeted. In a few minutes, if his aim held true and his nerve was steady and his luck held, they would all be on the chopper, heading for the rendezvous point at Desert One while the Super Hornets came in and bombed every single one of the Iranian nuclear-enrichment facilities. The Iranian air force would be no match for them, and with chaos breaking out all over the country as the miracle failed to appear, their pilots would be distracted. The mullahs would be the bride stripped bare by her bachelors, helpless against the rage of their people.

At last, the West was using the East's most potent weapon against it—superstition.

Payback time.

The time of the Black Angels and the guardian angels. He had his and she had hers. For the first time, they were in together, going into action the way Branch 4 teammates should, going into battle with another of their own.

And they were all going home. Life would triumph over death. The end times, with all their apocalyptic carnage, would have to wait for another day, another year, another millennium, another eon. Back to the eternally receding future with you, O Legend. There was no need for ghosts here. Not among the living.

He started firing. The Viper was a fine piece of equipment and the soldiers fell one after another, toy soldiers dying for a cause they didn't understand and couldn't understand. *Pop pop pop pop pop . . .* he was firing on semiautomatic, setting them up and knocking them down. There was no use in putting it on full assault-rifle auto and wasting ammunition. In his experience, when you got to the full-auto part of the program you were already in big trouble, and big trouble was a place he did his damnedest to stay away from. Full-auto was Last Stand time. Full-auto was a marksman's pathway to hell.

He was not ready for hell yet.

He kept firing and the men kept dropping. Two of the three figures in the desert had dropped to the ground, the women sheltering each other, Skorzeny trying to make a run for it.

Shoot him . . . shoot him now.

He took aim.

Thwack thwack thwack . . .

And then he saw—the first missile was starting to launch.

"Come on!" he shouted to Maryam.

The big Black Hawk was directly overhead now. Would Danny lower the ropes or would he try to land?

No time to ask. No time to worry. Danny would do what he had to do. And now he had to do what he had to do.

He charged, firing as he ran.

In the distance, he could see a phalanx of Jeeps, tearing out of the mountainside and streaming across the salt desert.

Twin M240 machine guns spat hot death. Nobody could shoot and fly like Danny. Two of the Jeeps flipped and burst into flames.

"Rockets, damn it, rockets!" he shouted.

On the launchpad, the first of the Israel-bound Shahabs was shuddering on the launch pad. No time . . . no time . . .

And Hellfire roared.

AGM-114s. The specially equipped Black Hawk had two of them. It needed both.

The missile was starting to lift off.

Covering fire was raking the Black Hawk, but Danny wasn't going anywhere. He kept the bird steady, trying to get the second Hellfire into position for a kill shot on the Shahab. Kill it on the ground, strangle it in its cradle, before the demon bird could take flight and visit destruction a thousand miles away.

"Come on!"

One of the Jeeps had a .50-caliber gun and it was firing as it raced toward the launchpad. Danny couldn't fight back—his attention was on the missile. He was going to stop the missile or die trying.

No need—the virus was already killing it. But he didn't know that.

Devlin had to stop the Jeeps.

He was closer now, with a good bead on the Jeep. His first shot was a kill shot, right through the head of the gunner. The .50-caliber spun wildly, firing with a dead man's hand on the trigger.

Devlin's second shot took the man's hand off, and the firing stopped.

His third shot penetrated the engine block and the fourth shot penetrated the driver's skull. The Jeep careened, spun and flipped over.

Just as—

—the Shahab began to lift off and—

—the Black Hawk fired its second Hellfire.

Wobbling, the Shahab lifted into the air . . . and then started to gyrate wildly, spinning out of control. It was no longer going straight up but toppling . . . heading into the desert.

A burst of gunfire to his right. Maryam had the Kalashnikov and was peppering the other Jeeps, taking out the front tires of one and sending it head over heels.

Amanda was down, motionless, and Mlle. Derrida was screaming for the noise to stop as he passed the women. Skorzeny was up ahead, running into the missile field.

He followed him. This time, he would not get away. There was no bolt-hole for the bastard. At long last Emanuel Skorzeny was his.

Devlin closed the gap easily. Maryam and Danny could cover him.

Closer . . . closer . . .

And then the other missiles died.

Inside each lethal weapon, the guidance systems melted down, obeying the instructions of the poisoned NSA computer. His instructions. Delivered by none other than Emanuel Skorzeny.

Checkmate.

He tackled him on the fly.

He had his hands around his throat.

He was choking him to death.

"Die, you bastard," he hissed. "Die. Die for everything you've done to me. Die for everything you've done to humanity. I don't care what you die for, but die."

Skorzeny was gurgling, turning purple. There was no sport in choking to death an old man, but he didn't care. His blood was up, he was doing the thing he had been trained to do all his life, all his life since his mother had died in his arms in Rome, since his father caught the terrorists' bullets to save him, since his parents had died because of this man, this Skorzeny, this beast, this animal, this monster.

"Stop!" cried Skorzeny. "You can't kill me. I can't die like this!"

"Why not?" In the distance, beyond his bloodlust, he could hear Maryam still firing. Something was wrong. Danny should have her by now. The fight should be over.

"Because it is not for you to kill me. You have not earned that right."

"Try me."

Something distracted him for just an instant, but an instant was all it ever took when you were parsing the line between life and death.

Somehow Skorzeny managed to squirm from his grasp. It was amazing what feats of strength a man was capable of, even an old man, when his life was on the line. That was the thing that always gave the lie to the nihilists and the atheists—that, when the chips were down and death was at the other end of the wire, every living creature struggled, nothing wanted to go gently into that doubleplusungood night, all fought for life, all pleaded, all begged.

A falling missile nearly brained him. Devlin rolled away as it came down, but in that same motion Skorzeny also rolled away, the two of them scrabbling for a foothold on a desert landscape that was suddenly undergoing something very much like a man-made earthquake. *His* earthquake.

The bastard was getting away.

Another missile toppled over. Whatever satisfaction he could take in their destruction was lessened by his chagrin at seeing his nemesis escape.

It was not going to happen.

A huge burst of fire from the Black Hawk. He looked up to see the rope ladder hovering just above his head. Maryam was firing from inside the chopper.

"Come on!" shouted Danny.

Devlin saw the others were already aboard. He could not hold up the mission. He had done his job. Almost.

Decide.

He decided.

He tugged twice on the ladder. "Go!" he shouted. "I'll meet you at Desert One."

Danny wouldn't have to be told twice. He would take or-

ders from the mission commander. He would leave him behind, to die if necessary. It was the chain of command, the
only way a military operation could work. No time for feelings.

His last view was of her, looking down at him, the AK
still in her hands, still firing at the new waves of Jeeps racing
toward him.

Then the Black Hawk banked and climbed and was gone,
disappearing into the night sky.

And then the Jeeps were upon him and he was alone, out
there in the Iranian desert, with only his 1911 to keep him
company.

He liked his odds.

CHAPTER FIFTY

Qom

On Iranian state television, the Grand Ayatollah Ali Ahmed Hussein Mustafa Mohammed Fadlallah al-Sadiq was addressing the faithful:

"O Muslims," he said, holding up his right hand so that all might see the mark upon it, that they might know that he was the Seyed Khorasani of sacred prophecy, "today I bring you great tiding. A mighty miracle shall you witness, born today in the holy city of Qom."

The cameras cut to the holy city, and the mosque at Jamkaran, outside which an expectant crowd had gathered, then back to the Ayatollah in Tehran, to which he had returned for the great national moment. He was flanked by various mullahs and civilian members of the government, including the fractious president.

"O Muslims," he continued, "rejoice, for today marks the day of the Coming. A great awakening shall spread across the lands of Islam and even unto the *dar al-Harb*, the land of conflict and war wherein the final battle shall be fought. For

has not Evil come into the land, everywhere assailing the
forces of Good? In the words of the sacred *sura* 50: 41-45,
'And listen for the Day when the Caller will call out from a
place quite near. The Day when they will hear a mighty Blast
in Truth: that will be the Day of Resurrection.' So it is written and today, so shall it be done."

The screen split now, half the imam and half the sacred
mosque. The Faithful knelt in prayer.

"O Muslims, hear the words of the Prophet, and believe."

Off-camera, the Grand Ayatollah looked at the president
of the Islamic Republic, who nodded confidently. The missiles were about to fly. The death of the Little Satan would
quickly follow, and the great cataclysm to come would
surely call forth the Imam Mahdi. He could therefore speak
with confidence when he said—

A cry went up from the crowd in Qom. The Grand Ayatollah looked at the monitor. Something was happening. Had
it begun?

"We can't leave him there," said Amanda, lying cradled in
Maryam's arms as the Black Hawk ascended. "They'll kill
him."

"He knows the risks," shouted Danny, "and I follow orders."

Amanda had been hit by small-arms fire, but was still
conscious, although bleeding profusely from a wound in her
side.

"I have to get you medical attention," said Danny. "If I
don't, you're not going to make it." There it was: blunt. But
this was no time to be coy.

Maryam was working on her with the first aid kit, trying
to stanch the flow of blood. It was a losing effort.

"Go back!" shouted Amanda. "Don't leave him there."

The exertion was too much for her. She sank back and whispered to Maryam, "Don't let them kill him. We need him. You need him. Make him go back."

Maryam looked down, but she was rapidly losing sight of the battlefield. The toppling missiles had kicked up a mini-sandstorm; even if they'd wanted to go back for him, there would be no way a responsible pilot would make the attempt.

"He knew the rules, Amanda," said Maryam.

Amanda gathered all her strength and struggled to a half-sitting position. Her eyes alighted on the pilot's area, and on a photograph prominently displayed there. It was a picture of Hope, Rory, and a girl she didn't recognize and one whom she very much did: Emma. Her Emma, the daughter she'd had for such a brief time in London. It was wrong what they had, she knew that now. She could think clearly now, more clearly than at any time in her life. She knew what to do, what to say.

"To hell with the rules," she said. "Save the man you love."

Maryam rose. From the day they had met, "Frank Ross" and she had been each other's guardian angels. He would go back for her, she knew he would. He had crossed half the earth for her. Her obligation was clear—it was the mission, certainly. But he *was* the mission.

"Go back," she said to Danny.

"No way, sister," he shouted. "The zone is too hot."

She put the Colt 1911 to his head. "Go back."

"We go back, we all die."

"No, we won't."

Danny turned his head. The safety was off and he knew there was a round in the chamber.

Would she shoot him? A sane woman would not. Shooting him meant they would all die. But who said she was a sane woman?

The gun nuzzled his ear. "Now," she said, "before it's too late."

She certainly had a way with words.

Danny banked the chopper and looked down. The place he had last seen "Bert Harris" was in a choking cloud of dust and debris. And there was one other complication—the Super Hornets would be there any minute. Even now, they were streaking across the Iranian sky. He'd been through some shit in his time, but this would be right up there.

What the hell. He was in the shit business, wasn't he? What was a little more shit among friends?

He swung hard and headed down. "You got it, sister," he said. "Now take care of Amanda—and get ready to fight when I say fight."

He felt the gun move away from the side of his head, then felt her face next to his. She kissed him lightly on the cheek, and then she was gone.

Behind the mosque, a huge cloud of dust was rising. Surely, this was a sign. The crowd before the mosque began to chant: "*Allahu akbar! Allahu akbar! Allahu akbar!*"

In the studio in Tehran, a phone rang in the distance, but the Grand Ayatollah was only dimly aware of it. His attention was riveted on what was going on in Qom. At any moment now, the Shahabs should be leaping into the air, on their way to their appointment with destiny in Israel. The order had been given, and it was just a matter of time now. . . .

"What? What?" He could hear shouting. But the cameras would be back on him very soon, so he could not react.

There! There was that damned red light again. This demon of Western technology would wait for nothing.

"O Muslims," he began again, and then stopped. Something was moving in the sky about the holy city.

Allah be praised, it was a miracle. . . .

Since the disaster at Desert One, helicopters had come a long way in desert warfare. A decade and more of fighting in Iraq and Afghanistan had taught the manufacturers exactly what sort of conditions their products would be used under, and they had built in all sorts of protective devices. The new generation of special-ops MH-60Ks were all-weather capable and boasted terrain-hugging radar that let the pilot fly practically blind. In any case, a KG-10 real-time map display told the pilot where he was at all times and on-board radar would alert him immediately to any laser targeting. With the two external extended-range fuel tanks, he could still make the rendezvous point and get out of Dodge when the time came.

This was about as good a horse as a cowboy was going to get. Danny took a deep breath and dove.

On the ground, it was an inferno and about to get worse. Rocket fuel was flowing from the damaged Shahabs and the whole place would go up any minute. Using the cloud as cover, Devlin was moving away from the field as fast as he could, heading for the small shelter of some hills to the east.

Through the dust, Devlin could see the troops streaming across the desert, firing. He wasn't afraid. A lucky bullet might catch him, but then a lucky bullet might catch anybody. He had his 1911 and a couple of magazines.

This was the way he'd always wanted to go. Last stands were not for cowards.

He began firing as soon as they came in range. They might not be able to see him, but he could certainly see them. He went for the drivers first, and got two of them immediately. The Jeeps spun out, collided, rolled over, and crashed into the rocket debris.

His fire attracted the attention of the others, and they

turned, heading for him. He was fast but he couldn't outrun them, and it was still another fifty meters or so before he made the hillocks.

He ran, firing as he went.

Bullets kicked up all around him.

He dropped to the ground as a .50-caliber opened up on him, rolled, then popped back up to his feet and shot the gunner. Then he turned and ran again.

Almost to the hills now . . . almost . . .

The .50-caliber opened back up. Someone must have jumped into the dead man's shoes. No time for tricks. He had to make safety. He cast a glance backward. . . .

The man had a bead on him. He wasn't going to make it.

The man opened fire. Bullets tattooed the desert floor, heading right at him.

No time, no time . . .

And then a miracle happened—

It was a miracle, just not the kind of miracle the Grand Ayatollah was half expecting.

It was a helicopter. An American Black Hawk, painted to look like part of the Iranian Army. But the Grand Ayatollah knew that the army had no such Black Hawks like this one. In a blatant violation of international law, the Americans were attacking Iran!

He could sense the consternation behind him. He could hear shouts—something was destroying all the Islamic Republic's missiles right on their launchpads, all across the country.

This was no miracle. This was treachery. And he knew just whom to blame:

Emanuel Skorzeny.

This was the second time the man had betrayed them. He had lied to them about the event in New York, and that had

cost the mullahs one of their best go-betweens in Arash Kohanloo. The only real miracle there was that Tyler hadn't
come after them with everything he had. But such was the
beauty of asymmetrical warfare: that without a smoking gun
to prove guilt beyond a reasonable doubt in a court of law,
the great powers could no longer act. They were not led by
men, but by lawyers, many of them women.

And now this. He had partnered with them, told them that
the bomb they had purchased at great expense from a rogue
Russian agent would explode in the Jews' hospital, the one
they named after the place where their prophet Moses was
said to have received the Ten Commandments. Instead, the
only thing exploding were the Islamic Republic's missiles.

Right there, on the spot, on national television, the Grand
Ayatollah issued a fatwa against Emanuel Skorzeny.

The Black Hawk appeared out of the smoke and dust,
guns blazing. The soldiers had never seen anything like the
concentrated firepower of a special-ops Black Hawk, and
many of them fled its terrible wrath. But not Col. Zarin.

He leaped atop one of the disabled Jeeps with a functioning machine gun and began to train his fire on the Black
Hawk. These infernal machines were not supernatural; primitive Somalis in Mogadishu had taken one down and made a
terrible example of its crew to all the Unbelievers. Could he
do any less?

"Incoming," shouted Danny, flying low, still firing. One
of the Iranian officers was peppering them with .50-caliber
fire.

Maryam grabbed the AK-47. "I've got him." She leaned
out the side and began firing down.

The side of the Black Hawk was getting pockmarked. "Lower," she shouted. "I need him a little closer."

Danny dropped the chopper down, knowing the risk. They had to take out the gunner, and fast, or they'd never find "Bert Harris." Out of the corner of his eye, he could see a fire starting. In moments it would hit the rocket fuel, and then . . . "Hang on!" he shouted.

Mlle. Derrida grabbed Amanda, who was lying on the floor. Maryam wrapped herself into a halter, braced, and aimed—

He dropped the Black Hawk in a straight vertical fall, then pulled out at the last instant.

The Black Hawk came within fifty feet of Col. Zarin, who was astonished to see the big bird maneuver like that. "Why can't our pilots fly like this?" he was wondering to himself as he brought the gun around.

Now he could see the whore who was firing at him. She was slamming another magazine into her rifle.

He would have her in his sights in just moments. . . .

"Boro gomsho pedear soukteh, jakesh!" she was screaming at him. Even over the noise of the chopper, he could hear her, and he could not believe what he was hearing. That such filth should come out of the mouth of—

Three bullets hit him in the chest, in a perfect shot group. He might have appreciated the marksmanship were he not already dead when he toppled from the Jeep.

"Goh bokhor!" she shouted, and spat at him.

"'Zat mean let's get the hell out of here?" yelled Danny.

"You're damn right it does," Maryam yelled back. There—

A man, running into the low hills. Him.

"There he is!"

But Danny was already swinging the bird around, flying low, gunning the sucker and hoping like hell they could snatch "Bert" before the whole place blew. . . .

* * *

In front of the mosque, the large crowd looked on in wonder as the events in the distance unfolded. No one was quite
sure what was going on. Some said it was the Coming. Others said it was the forces of the Great Satan, attacking the
holy lands of Islam. The Grand Ayatollah's image had disappeared from the screens.

And then they heard a terrible screaming, like the voices
of a million birds in their death agonies. This was a screaming such as they had never heard before, and it grew louder
and louder until it was almost unbearable.

Surely, this was the sign they had been waiting for, said
one imam.

All eyes turned to the mosque. But the Hidden Imam sal-
lied forth not from the sacred well.

"Have we been deceived?" shouted one man. "We were
told that the Coming was upon us? What manner of blasphemy is this?"

The noise grew louder. Now they could no longer hear
themselves. Women and children pressed their hands tight
against their ears, so as not to hear the voice of the devil,
who the people were now sure was coming for them.

And then, in the sky, a vision. A terrible vision . . .

The Hornets, coming in low, firing as they went. In an instant, all opposition on the ground ceased. And then the
F-18s really went to work.

The Hornets came in waves, each one prepping the battlefield for the next. Mavericks and SLAM-ERs punched holes
into the mountainside. These were followed by the JDAMs,
the Joint Direct Attack Munitions, the smart bombs that
would shoot down the rabbit hole and blow the living shit
out of anything down there. The enrichment facility might
not be completely destroyed, but it would be buried under

tons of mountain rubble for a very long time. And then all the other sites would follow.

But Danny wasn't concerned about that now. Those boys could do their job without him. The fire was raging fiercely now, and it was just a matter of time before—

The first explosion rocked the Black Hawk, sending it spinning just as Maryam was dropping the rope ladder. Danny fought hard for control of the chopper, but the force of the blast knocked him off course. He was going to have to come around again.

Another blast, then another. The field was an inferno.

The Hornets made their last run. Half the mountainside crumbled. The remains of the Shahabs were burning fiercely and the heat was nearly unbearable. Only one last chance . . .

He looked back into the interior. Her eyes wide with fear, Mlle. Derrida was clutching Amanda tightly. Maryam had fastened herself down and was able to lean out as far as possible as the chopper dropped down. Showtime . . .

On the ground, Devlin had dived behind a rock as the explosions began. He was out of ammunition, but still ready to sell his life dearly when he saw the Black Hawk buffeted by the exploding Shahabs.

There—the rope ladder . . .

Once chance.

He sprinted for it. Another explosion, this one the biggest of them all, nearly knocked him off his feet. But Danny had been ready for it, and rode the shock wave like a bucking bronco.

The ladder was just within reach.

So reach . . .

Jump . . .

He looked up, and there she was.

He reached and jumped . . . caught the edge of the ladder.

No time to wait. Danny gunned the Black Hawk, up high and hard, picking up speed to get away from the final explosion he knew was coming.

Devlin fought to hang on . . . not just to hang on but to *climb*. He had to get inside the chopper, fast, before—

A rumbling from the depths of the mountain.

Up the steps, hand over hand, feet grabbing a purchase now, a kick—

Higher now, she was reaching out to him—

Swinging wildly through the air . . . almost losing his grip . . .

Another kick. He was taking the steps two at a time.

Not climbing, flying . . .

Her hand, reaching for him—

And *in*.

Maryam pulled up the rope ladder. In the distance the Super Hornets were disappearing into the blue, on their way to the next targets. If the Iranians were smart, they wouldn't interfere with them.

"We have to go back!" he shouted at Danny. Skorzeny was still down there. Nothing human could have survived the holocaust below, but Skorzeny could.

He was still alive. Devlin knew: *He was still alive.*

"No chance," Danny shouted back, indicating Amanda.

He looked at Amanda. Her eyes were closed and she was breathing heavily. Mlle. Derrida was doing her best with the first aid kit, but the bandage on her side was rich with red blood.

She was dying.

He had a choice. He was the commander of the mission. He could order Danny to go back, to search for Skorzeny, to operate on a hunch. Or . . . he could repay the woman who had done so much for all of them.

It was no choice at all. "Let's get her some medical attention, *now*," he ordered.

"Way ahead of you, partner," shouted Danny, who was already heading to the northeast, and the rendezvous point—the old Desert One site where so many of America's misfortunes had begun. The other choppers would be there, with medics, and they could attend to Amanda, stabilize her, and get her the hell out of there, to the hospital on board the *Eisenhower*. The nightmare was almost over. He reached for Maryam.

"Who are you?" she said, clutching him tightly as the Black Hawk gathered speed.

"I was going to ask you the same question."

"You know who I am," she said. "I'm your guardian angel."

CHAPTER FIFTY-ONE

Qom

After Dresden, the fires held no terrors for him. He was the Erlking now, not the boy; the chaser, the pursuer. This whelp, this bastard had bested him, and he could not, would not, rest until he put him in the ground.

As they drove out to the launch site, Skorzeny had seen the Shahed 285s and knew now that scrambling on board one of them was the only way out. And when he saw the Black Hawk, he knew where he must go.

The bastard had *her*, and he must follow.

The explosions were just starting as he reached the first helicopter. A terrified pilot was already firing it up and making ready to escape.

"You are under my command now," he intoned. Good. The man recognized him. "You will fly where I tell you. Is that understood?"

Skorzeny spoke with authority. He was a friend of the Islamic Republic. He was a man of parts and property. He also had a gun.

He pointed at the Black Hawk, now soaring away toward the east. "Do you want to be a hero?" he asked the pilot in both French and English. Any educated Iranian spoke one of those Western languages.

The man nodded. "Yes," he said in English, with a look of understanding in his eyes. Skorzeny might have expected greater resistance, perhaps even greater fear, but this man was docile and cooperative. They were going to get along just fine.

"Get on the radio. I want a fleet. We must chase the Americans and kill them for the insult they have dealt to a holy place. But you must hurry—we must follow."

The man spoke rapidly into a transmitter as the Shahed rose into the air. It would be no match for the Black Hawk, that he knew, but in numbers there might be strength.

The pilot gave him a thumbs-up and then they were in the air and following the Black Hawk. Skorzeny turned around to see half a dozen more Shaheds following them. As he was now following Devlin. He would follow him to the gates of Hell and beyond if necessary.

Below, fireballs were erupting. And then he saw the Super Hornets, bombing and strafing everything, burying the plant inside the earth forever.

"We've got a tail," said Danny. "Multiple bogies." He'd picked them up on the radar.

"How long to Desert One?" asked Devlin. He was sitting beside his friend. "We don't have much time." Behind them, Maryam and Mlle. Derrida were doing their best to make Amanda Harrington comfortable, but it was a losing battle.

"Half an hour. She's probably not going to make it," said Danny.

"We'll see about that. What about the bogies?"

"Let them tail us. They can't outrun us. I've radioed ahead and alerted the strike force. If these boys want to mix it up, they're going to be several kinds of sorry."

Devlin extracted his Android and checked it. The thing had taken a tremendous beating down on the ground, but the son of a bitch still worked. One message:

```
LASER RETARGETING COMPLETE
BRING IT ON
YOU'RE SURE? ON YOUR POSITION?
LAST PLACE THEY'LL LOOK. AND THEY'RE ON OUR ASS
NOW
STILL WANT THE FULL SHOW?
GODDAMN RIGHT. THEY WANTED A MIRACLE, THEY'RE
GETTING A MIRACLE
ROGER THAT
ALERT EISENHOWER THAT WE HAVE A SEVERELY
WOUNDED HIGH-PRIORITY PATIENT COMING IN
DONE
WHAT ABOUT THE MISSILE PROGRAM?
TERMINATED. WILL TAKE THEM YEARS TO RESTART,
EVEN WITH HELP FROM THE PAKS AND THE NORKS
AND?
REPORTS OF MASSIVE CIVIL UNREST IN TEHRAN AND
OTHER MAJOR CITIES. YOUNG PEOPLE IN THE STREETS.
MULLAHS SEEM FLUSTERED
THAT WAS THE WHOLE IDEA
ONE OTHER THING—THE AYATOLLAH FADLALLAH JUST
ISSUED A FATWA ON YOUR PLAYMATE. HE'S FUCKED
```

Devlin thought about his answer for moment, then typed:

```
THEN I GUESS I'D BETTER HURRY. OVER AND OUT
```

"Keep them within sight," he said to Danny. "I don't want to lose them."

"You know we're leading them right to Desert One."

"That's the whole idea. First time farce, second time tragedy, as Marx said."

"Marx didn't say that."

"He would now."

They were on the Black Hawk's tail, Skorzeny and his fleet of Shaheds. The pilot was growing increasingly agitated, as reports came in over his radio. Skorzeny had no idea what those reports were, but something was clearly amiss. From time to time the pilot cast a look in his direction, as if they were talking about him, but he saw nothing sinister in the glance. On the other hand, these people did tend to smile just before they cut your throat.

But none of that mattered right now. What mattered was getting her back, and killing him. And if they all died making the attempt, well, it would be a glorious death. A glorious death was something that had never occupied his thoughts much before.

The Black Hawk began to drop down, back into the desert. Skorzeny could tell this was no random location. He was heading somewhere.

The pilot started to jabber in Persian. He seemed very excited about something. He pointed down.

"What is it, man?" shouted Skorzeny.

"Desert One!" he exclaimed. "Desert One!"

So that was it. That would be just like the boy. Symbolism was something Islamic cultures understood; locations and anniversaries were very important to them. Here, at the site of one of America's most humiliating failures, they were going to make a stand.

"Attack," shouted Skorzeny. "Attack!" At the first shooting, they would release the passengers and send them scattering into the desert. She could not get far. And he would die.

The pilot squawked away. The other Shaheds, five or six of them, came up and assumed attack formation.

The Black Hawk was on the ground now, a sitting duck.

"Fire," commanded Skorzeny.

The Shaheds swooped—and then, from out of nowhere, they were riddled with gunfire.

Behind them, five Black Hawks had suddenly appeared. The Shaheds were no match for the Hawks. One went down in flames immediately. Another turned tail and tried to escape, but the Black Hawks cut it off and blew it out of the sky. Another Shahed crashed when its pilot panicked and flew it straight into the ground. Two more were forced down, choosing disgrace over death. Only the chopper with Skorzeny aboard was left in the air.

Two of the Black Hawks flanked Skorzeny's helicopter and motioned for it to land as well. "Do as they say," he told the pilot.

"I must not," said the man. "I have orders never to surrender my helicopter."

"You don't have any choice," Skorzeny informed him. "If you don't take us down, they will annihilate us."

"Ah, but I do, infidel," said the man, who suddenly holding a pistol on him. "The Grand Ayatollah himself has pronounced fatwa on you, and it is my sacred duty to kill you."

"Don't be silly," said Skorzeny with a tone of contempt.

The man fired.

By some holy miracle, he missed. Even though Skorzeny was sitting right beside him, he missed. The shifting wind currents no doubt were to blame, the buffeting the Shahed was receiving from the two Black Hawks near it.

Emanuel Skorzeny had not lived this long without knowing how to take care of himself. Before the man could fire a second shot, he grabbed the gun and wrested it from his hand. He trained the gun on the pilot. "Down," he said.

Down they went. The Black Hawks saw they were obeying orders and peeled off.

Devlin was waiting for them as they landed. He was alone. Near a piece of charred, rusted, twisted metal, perhaps a piece of the Sea Stallion chopper that had collided with the Hercules transport plane—a memento mori of the debacle. A fine sand mist, kicked up by the helicopters, was starting to fill the air.

Skorzeny didn't wait. As soon as he hit the ground he raised his weapon and fired at Devlin as the sand enveloped him. He fired again and again, shooting at the ghost he knew must be there.

A blow to the head felled him. The gun flew from his grasp. He felt himself being dragged across the desert, then lashed to something.

"She's dying," came the voice. "You've killed her. I'm doing my best to save her, but thanks to you it's probably too late. Live with that, for as long as you live."

As quickly as it had come up, the sand mist cleared. There was the face he had loathed for so long, mocking him.

"Show me. I must see her."

"No."

"I must see her." He was, he realized, bound to the wreckage and immobilized.

"No," repeated Devlin.

"Yes," came a voice behind him.

Held up by Maryam, Emanuelle Derrida, and Danny, Amanda Harrington was making her way toward them. "Look," she said, pointing up at the sky.

Two images, the Virgin and the Prophet, rapidly descending as night fell.

"You recognize them, don't you?" said Devlin. "You

wanted to change the world with them, to set Muslim against Christian, to set nation against nation. And for what? How much money do you need?"

"It was not for money," gasped Skorzeny. "Never for money."

"Then what was it for?" asked Amanda. They lay her down next to Skorzeny, and Emanuelle kissed her gently as she released her.

"It was to end it all," whispered Skorzeny. "To finally quiet the ghosts."

"I hear them too," said Devlin. "Every day. Every night. But I've learned that you can never silence them. They go on with us, 'til the end of the time. Until the Last Days."

"These are the Last Days," said Skorzeny.

"And I," said Devlin, "am Malak al-Maut."

Mary and Mohammed were drawing closer, losing their material shape and turning into pillars of light in the desert, merging, combining into a single beam—

"No!" screamed Skorzeny, understanding. "You can't."

"It is finished," said Devlin. "Amanda, you don't have to do this. Come with us. You'll make it."

"No," she said, "I won't. I can't. Besides, my place is here with him. In expiation for all my sins. And for his."

They could feel the heat of the approaching lasers—now under American control—dissipating the chill of the desert. Amanda gestured to Danny, who ran over to her. She drew him close:

"Kiss them all for me. Kiss her for me. Tell them I'm sorry. Tell them . . . tell them I'll pray for them."

Danny handed her the picture. "Take this with you," he said.

Devlin lookd at Skorzeny and Amanda. The man was a liar to the end. He was not dying to end it all. In his own twisted way, he was dying for love. He was just too consumed with bitterness to realize it.

"Let's go," said Devlin.

The Black Hawks rose and circled as the lasers met, fused. The Shaheds on the ground exploded as the lasers grazed them. Even at this altitude, Devlin could feel the heat rising. In a vision of heaven, he had unleashed hell.

Maryam clung to Devlin as they watched the awful, inevitable progression. . . .

On the ground, Amanda gazed for the last time at the picture, which was gradually curling in her hands. It burst into flames. But she did not feel the heat. Pain could not harm her anymore. Her last vision was not of hellfire, but of redemption. By the time her skin started to char, she was already dead.

Skorzeny screamed as his clothes caught on fire. His hair burned off and then his skin melted away in the terrible heat. And still he screamed, howling curses at the heavens, unrepentant to the last. The only thing left of him was rage.

He was still screaming when Devlin fired a single round from the Viper into his head. "I am the Angel of Death," he whispered as he pulled the trigger.

"O Mother," he shouted, "O Father. You are avenged."

The Black Hawk wafted upward, as if borne aloft on heavenly hands. Then it turned toward the southeast, the *Eisenhower*, and home, and disappeared into the night.

TWO WEEKS LATER

EPILOGUE

Los Angeles—the La Brea Tar Pits

He was back where he had started, only this time she was with him, which made the whole thing seem even more like a dream.

They had already walked through the Page Museum devoted to celebrating the bones of the early mammals caught up in the vast oil field that sat, like a black lake, beneath Wilshire Boulevard. Now they were out front, confronting the woolly mammoth, still struggling against his fate and still losing.

"Did it really happen?"

"What?" she said. "Iran? Of course it did. It's only a matter of time for the mullahs now. Their miracle fizzled and the people are on the march everywhere. Soon it will be my country again."

"And then you'll leave me," he laughed. "Go back to Tehran and turn into a little Persian butterball with a husband and six screaming children."

She punched him. "Watch it, buster, or I'll toss you in there."

"You might be doing us both a favor." He thought for a moment. "I mean the priest, the cathedral, the cars tailing me . . . Was any of it real? Or did I—" He looked at her. "Can you ever forgive me?"

"You did what you had to do. I would have done the same thing."

"Would you?"

His eyes scanned the other visitors, tourists mostly, looking for Jacinta. He wondered if he'd recognize her. "You know what they call this part of town, don't you?" he said.

"Um . . . I give up."

"Miracle Mile. Do you believe in miracles, Maryam?

"I wrote a prayer to Imam Mahdi at the holy well. So maybe I do." She reached into her bag and handed him something. Flowers.

Hyacinths.

"What do you pray for?" he asked.

"I'll never tell."

"Did you get it?"

"We'll see, won't we?"

"I got you something, too," he said. "They're in the car."

"Give them to me when we get home. Right after you make love to me."

"We're meeting the newlyweds for dinner tonight at their house in Los Feliz, remember?"

"So?"

"Good point."

They sat in silence for a moment. Even the late-fall heat of Los Angeles felt good.

"It will be great to have him on the team," she said. "For real, I mean."

"I'll say. Now I can call him Danny." He paused, trying to figure out how to say what he was trying to say without sounding crazy. "I was talking about what happened before I left for Iran. About the cattle slaughter, the image on the wall that Danny saw . . . what I saw, in the California desert."

"And what was that?"

Something, someone, caught his eye across the grounds, on the other side of the tar pits. It couldn't be . . . a man, walking along, reading a book, probably a breviary. No dog collar, but that didn't mean anything these days. Padre Gonsalves. To whom he still owed a report. And who owed him ten thousand dollars. Good luck with that. Maybe they should just call it even.

"A doorway in the sky. *Her*."

She put an arm around him. "After what we just saw? And you still believe?"

"I don't know what I believe anymore. Except that I love you. And I don't believe that—I know it."

Maryam smiled. "Then I guess I'll stick around for a while."

He started to say something, but then noticed that the man was looking at him. And that he had been joined by a woman.

Skin: light brown. Age: somewhere between thirty and ninety. Height: five feet in heels on a footstool. Weight: don't ask, don't tell. Ethnicity . . .

Human being.

"Is it too early for a drink?"

She shook her head. "You're incorrigible, Frank."

"My name's not Frank."

"So what?"

"Good point," he said.

They walked to the car, which was parked over on Curson. He didn't get a ticket. A sign from heaven.

He opened the trunk and handed her the gift. A dozen long-stemmed roses, freshly cut and still glistening with the hint of raindrops.

"They're beautiful," she exclaimed. "They're so fresh—where did you get them?"

He looked back at the Tar Pits, but the man and woman had vanished. Priest and petitioner? Or two ghosts from a past he had not yet met?

"I'll never tell," he said.

They got in the car, Maryam holding the roses on her lap. She had never looked more beautiful.

"What day is it?" he said as he turned east onto Sixth Street.

"Election Day," she said.

And then they were gone, into the anonymity of the city, to join the millions of other ghosts, born and unborn, all of them waiting their moment, however brief, in the sun.